THE EDUCATION OF RYAN GREGORI

A NOVEL

By
Gregory Josephs

Stale Orange Press
1283 Massachusetts Ave #2
Arlington, MA 02476
www.gregoryjosephs.com

Publisher's Note: This is a work of fiction. Names, characters, places, and incidents are a product of the author's imagination. Locales and public names are sometimes used for atmospheric purposes. Any resemblance to actual people, living or dead, or to businesses, companies, events, institutions, or locales is completely coincidental.

Book Layout ©2017 BookDesignTemplates.com

Ordering Information:
Quantity sales. Special discounts are available on quantity purchases by corporations, associations, and others. For details, contact the "Special Sales Department" at the address above.

The Education of Ryan Gregori/ Gregory Josephs -- 1st ed.
ISBN 978-0-9992636-0-0

Library of Congress Control Number: 2017914257

For Brian,

*Because with you
all things are possible.*

"In the depth of winter,
I finally learned that within me there lay
an invincible summer."

-Albert Camus

Contents

PART ONE:

LOSS

CHAPTER 1

Between the heat blasting from the dash and Darren's silence, Ryan found it difficult to breathe. He turned the crank to lower the driver's side window and exhaled with relief as cold air caressed his face. "Have you thought about what I said?" he asked.

"It's the tenth of January and you've got the windows open," Darren replied.

Avoidance, again. As they approached a red light, Ryan shook his head, gently applied the brakes, and shifted back down to first gear. The old red pickup groaned and sputtered to a halt, and he exhaled. He knew he shouldn't have brought it up again tonight, but it was getting harder to ignore the reality. The regular evenings they spent together were dwindling. The unanswered phone calls were mounting. Perhaps it was the stress of the holidays, but Ryan didn't think so. Darren was slipping away.

"Hey, creeper," Darren said. "The light is green. Stop staring off into space."

"Oh!" Ryan eased off the clutch, stepped on the gas, and the truck started rolling forward again. "Sorry, I was just—"

"It's alright. And about what you said—you know I heard you the first time."

"I know, but that was months ago and—"

"And nothing is different. I said we'd figure it out, and we will." Darren reached over and placed a hand on Ryan's knee. "You're my

13

best friend, Ryan, and you always will be. I love you too—in my own messed up way."

"What's messed up about it?"

Darren laughed. "Look, we haven't seen each other since before Christmas. Let's just get through this party tonight, alright?" Removing his hand from Ryan's knee, he pulled a bottle of vanilla vodka halfway out of the paper bag at his feet. "This was a good choice, don't you think?"

"I guess so." Ryan sighed, reluctantly conceding the change of subject. "I wish you would've just picked it up on your way over, rather than have me wait in the truck a half a block from the liquor store."

"Aw, get over it!" Darren shoved him lightly. "You'll be twenty-one soon enough."

"Yeah! Like, a year and a half! It feels really sketchy is all."

"Ha! It *is* sketchy!"

Ryan laughed, and flicked on the right turn signal. The truck slowed, and he rounded the corner, turning away from the bright lights of the main road onto Elizabeth Street. The dark of the surrounding neighborhood was cut only by the soft yellow beams of his headlights and the warm amber glow from the front porches and curtained windows that lined the cozy street. He accelerated slightly again and smiled.

"Alright," he said. "Almost home."

"Yep. Then we'll get ourselves turned around and go." Darren was quiet for a moment. "Ryan?"

"Yeah?"

"We're going to have a great night."

As the truck rolled into the next intersection, Ryan turned his head toward Darren and smiled again. Maybe this love he felt was still unrequited, but someday that would change. Sooner or later Darren was going to realize—

Through the passenger window, he glimpsed a flash of white in the dim street lights, and his eyes widened in slow realization. In the brief moment before instinct took hold, he focused on Darren again and felt the sudden, crushing pain of imminent loss. Adrenaline shot through him like lightning, and he stomped on the gas.

"Ryan?" Darren said quietly. "What—"

The impact was swift and deafening, just behind the cab. He clutched the wheel and pushed the brake all the way to the floor as the back end of the truck first lifted, then spun to the left. Darren was screaming. Time slowed down as the truck continued its spin. Ryan pressed his eyes firmly closed and caught his breath as the seatbelt cut into his neck. *This is it*, he thought. *This is the end, and we never had our chance.*

Time accelerated again as the truck slowed and finally came to a stop.

Beside him, slowly, the sound of Darren's heavy breathing filled his ears. When he opened his eyes, they filled instantly with tears. "D—Darren? Are you alright?" He choked.

Darren looked straight ahead, wide-eyed and clutching the side of the door with white knuckles. "Fuck! Yeah, I think I'm fine, but if you hadn't stepped on it—I'd have been crushed! Are you alright?"

"Yeah," he said as he wiped his eyes. "Oh God, I thought for a minute there I was going to lose you. I thought—"

"Fuck. Well, I'm still here. We're both still here."

In the impact the truck had turned just over a hundred eighty degrees, and through the windshield Ryan could see a crumpled white sedan steaming into the night. He fumbled to release the seatbelt, shoved the door open and stumbled out into the street.

A lanky young man climbed out of the sedan, dusted in white powder from an airbag. He placed a hand on his forehead and pulled at his short brown hair. "Oh, shit," he mumbled, then looked toward Ryan. "You alright?"

Darren was beside him now, and before Ryan could speak, he said "Yeah, we're fine. What the hell?" He looked toward the intersection. "You could've killed us! Not only did you clearly run a stop sign, but you didn't have your fucking headlights on! What the—"

Ryan grabbed his arm and whispered harshly "Let it go." He exhaled, then turned to the other driver. "I'm just glad everyone is okay. Darren, can you call the police?"

"On it." Darren scowled as he pulled his cellphone from his jacket pocket and walked a few steps away.

"Oh, man," the other driver moaned. "I'm sorry I'm—oh, man."

"It's alright," Ryan said. He looked back at the mangled remains of his pickup and sighed. *We're going to have a great night*, he thought.

Darren was beside him again. "They're on their way. Do you want to call someone to pick us up? Steven, or maybe your mom?" He shivered, pulling the collar of his jacket tighter around his neck. "Fuck it's cold."

Ryan considered mentioning that he could keep both of them warm, but held back, thinking that Darren didn't want to hear that right now. Instead he took the phone and said, "Yeah, no reason to bother Steven. I'll call my mom."

~*~

An hour later, after the police finished taking their statements and photographs and measurements, and the tow truck had loaded up the old red pickup, Ryan's mother parked in the alley behind the little bungalow on Elizabeth Street. She turned off the engine and sighed.

From the back seat, Darren leaned forward. "Ryan," he asked, "Can I have the keys? I need to run to the bathroom."

"Oh," Ryan replied, pulling the keys from his pocket. "Sure. I'll be right behind you." He handed them over and watched as Darren climbed out of the car, vanilla vodka in hand, and scurried across the lawn, down the dark side yard to the front door.

His mother turned in her seat and kissed him lightly on the cheek. "It's a scary thing for a nineteen-year-old. It's a scary thing for anybody."

"Yeah," he said. "Terrifying. I'm still a little shaky I think."

"Your Uncle Charlie is going to be really sad. That truck was around a long time between him, your Dad and—and you."

"Seriously, Mom? You know it wasn't my fault. You know—"

She laughed. "No no! I'm not accusing you. I know it wasn't your fault." She was quiet for a moment. "Do you—want me to come in?"

"No, I'll be alright. We were supposed to go to this thing tonight, but I'm hoping Darren isn't in the mood anymore. I'd better go find out."

"Alright. I love you." She kissed him on the cheek again.

"Love you too. And thanks for coming, Mom." He opened the door, climbed out into the alley and headed toward the house.

The front door of the little bungalow was slightly ajar, and as Ryan pushed it open the rest of the way, he smiled. Just inside, Darren was sprawled out on the couch with the television remote in his hand and a glass of water. If Darren could only see himself, he thought—so comfortable and natural in this home they ought to be sharing—then he'd understand what Ryan felt. He let his mind drift, imagining the inevitable moment when all the concerns about ruined friendships and the uncertainties about *crossing that line* would go up in smoke and blow away like ashes in the—

"Earth to Ryan," Darren began. "You're doing that thing again, where you stare off into deep space." He laughed.

"Oh, sorry!" He blinked his eyes rapidly. "I think maybe I'm still a little shook up."

"Understandably so." Darren stood. There was an envelope in his hand that Ryan hadn't seen before. He extended it, gingerly. "This was taped to the front door with your name on it."

Ryan retrieved the envelope and regarded it suspiciously. The outside bore only his name, hastily scrawled. Exhaling, he tore it open and removed the letter inside:

10th January 2004

Dear Ryan,

Thanks for getting the rent in the mail on time, and signing the lease. Unfortunately, on second thought I have some reservations I just can't get over. I'm mailing the original back to you, unsigned. I know you've been there since November, but Cara should have told me more about you before she gave you the place when her lease was up. I'm sure you're a great kid, but I've had some serious problems with tenants your age in the past, so now I have a pretty strict vetting process, and college-aged kids aren't a part of it. Please don't take it personally; I just need to stick to my own rules and protect my investment.

Colorado law requires I give you sixty days' notice, so you can stay through the second week of March if you need to. Of course, if you find something sooner just let me know.

Sorry for the bad news, and best of luck.

John Carpenter

Silently, Ryan handed the letter back to Darren. As he looked around the warm, close living room, he fought to hold back the dampness forming in the corners of his eyes. In the autumn, when Cara told him she was moving out, and the place would be available, he'd been overjoyed. He gave his notice at sterile, cookie-cutter Asbury Drive and moved into the spare room at the beginning of November. It took no time at all to feel completely at home. He loved the large, square kitchen with the wide windows, the tiny but comfortable bathroom, and the skylights in the living room and bedrooms. Every day since, returning home actually felt like *returning home* in a way he hadn't experienced since leaving his parents' house a year ago. This was the neighborhood he'd grown up in, and the little house was full of the early twentieth-century charm he loved.

He'd dreamed of Darren taking the other bedroom—of the little house on Elizabeth Street becoming their home. He'd dreamed of the day they wouldn't need the other bedroom anymore.

A few short sentences inside a white envelope changed all of that. He almost laughed. This was the second time tonight he'd been blindsided.

"What am I going to do?" he asked.

Darren frowned. "Die homeless on the streets?" When Ryan didn't laugh, he continued. "It'll be fine. There are so many apartments around here. You can find another one. I mean, it's not like you're actually going to be homeless."

"I might be." He scowled. "Isn't this illegal? I don't want to live here anyways if my landlord is going to be some ageist—"

Darren laughed. "Calm down. You could always move home for a little while if you had to."

"That's *not* an option. That would be absolute failure."

Darren shrugged. "You know what you need?"

"No—"

"A drink!"

"Ugh, alright. I think I have soda in the fridge to mix with."

"No. Not here. The party tonight, or have you forgotten already?"

"Really?" Ryan groaned. "After everything that just happened you still want to go? It's all the way in Greeley. How do you even know these people again?"

"An old high school friend is going to school there. I told her we're going, so—we're going!" Darren said. "Now get changed!"

His shoulders slumped, defeated. He wanted to curl up on the couch the way they'd done so many nights over the last year, not go to a random party in a town a half hour away.

"Are you sure you don't want to just find an old movie?" He asked. The stern look Darren gave in return was answer enough, so Ryan walked into his room to get changed.

When the bedroom door was closed, he looked around and breathed a sigh of forlorn contentment. He'd painted the walls a deep red, and in the small, cozy room, the color pressed in around him. The rich hue felt safe and warm, and its days were numbered now that he had to move.

He opened his closet and chose a pair of light blue jeans that Darren had persuaded him to buy—boot cut with pre-worn distress patches on the legs—and then rifled through a collection of shirts on hangers. After mulling over the options, he pulled out a plain green T-shirt and got dressed.

He examined his reflection in the full-length mirror that hung on the outside of the closet door. The outfit was relaxed but nice. The green shirt set off the blue of his eyes, and the jeans fit just right. Through the mayhem of the previous hour, he was surprised to see how nicely his hair fell—long and curling over his forehead and around his ears. He wasn't always content with his appearance—his chest was a bit too large, and he thought his face was too round—but tonight he liked what he saw.

From the living room, Darren called to see if he was ready yet. He ran a hand lightly through his hair as an extra measure and headed out of the bedroom.

~*~

A half hour later they were in Darren's car, driving east across the dark, vast openness of Weld County. Keeping one hand on the steering wheel, Darren rifled through the plastic sleeves of a compact disc binder with his other. Finally finding the disc he liked, he said "This one. Can you put it in?"

Ryan took the binder and smiled. "Mercury Falling, by Sting?" He slid the album into the after-market CD player in the dash, and the music began to play.

"I can't believe I only just discovered this album," Darren said. "It's been out forever. I think literally every song is amazing."

Ryan half-listened, amused by Darren's excitement, and turned his focus to the sky ahead. In the distance, the glow of Greeley's street lights reflected an ominous stale orange against the low hanging clouds—a color Ryan knew to mean snow.

As the last notes of 'The Hounds of Winter' came to a close, he forced his mind from musings of snow to the present moment. He realized he was treading in a vast ocean of uncertainty with just a twinge of—he couldn't place it. In only a few short hours, everything had gone belly up. It wasn't a nice way to start the new year.

And yet, he realized, he was still breathing. He thought he should feel more than uncertainty—where was the anger or fear? There was that *something* again, right on the edge of his mind.

"I love how dark it is out here," Darren said.

Ryan looked at him, and his thoughts fell into place.

Safe.

In spite of the uncertainty, and the trauma of the day—the danger for the future—at the edges of things he felt safe. It came down to Darren. As long as he had Darren, the rest didn't matter. It was just details. He'd mourn the loss of the truck. He'd mourn the loss of Elizabeth Street and all it could have been even more. And yet, though he was losing his home, he wasn't losing the sense of it he'd yearned for. *Darren* was home.

"Why are you smiling like that?" Darren asked, looking quickly from Ryan to the road ahead, and back again. "What is going on with you today? Maybe you were right, and we shouldn't have come all the way—"

"It's nice," Ryan interjected.

"What's nice?"

"The dark. It's nice."

~*~

Ryan didn't work the next day, so he spent the morning cleaning the house and letting the weight of John Carpenter's letter sink in. Part of him—a very big part—wanted to stay in the little house as long as he could, savoring every moment. But the reality of the situation was clear; he needed to find a new place as soon as possible. He tried to convince himself it was just as well—all of the furniture in the apartment belonged to Cara, and once she finished the renovation on the condo she'd just bought, she was going to need it back. Because any new apartment he found was likely to come with roommates, he wouldn't need to worry about furnishing a whole house.

After lunch, there were no more chores to be done, so he indulged himself with an hour of television. One hour turned into three, and then the sun was nearly down. He called Darren, hoping to make plans for the evening, and left a message when he didn't reach him.

By eight o'clock he was fairly certain Darren wasn't going to return his call. It was just another reminder of the emerging trend. For the last year, they'd been inseparable. Darren always answered his phone when Ryan called—usually on the second or third ring—but something was different these last few weeks. The consistency was gone.

It was getting to be too late to call anyone else for company. After the events of the previous day he still felt vulnerable, so he didn't mind the isolation.

It was an excellent opportunity to write, and tonight he ached for it. At first, choosing to take a year off after high school and focus on his music seemed like a great idea. But now one year away from school had bled into two, and he hadn't written in months. Tonight, with everything he was feeling, it was time to start again.

Laying on his bed, he stared up at the ceiling. His favorite part of the little red bedroom was the skylight, and it was here that he focused his eyes. He squinted and strained, searching for stars overhead, but even the dull light of his bedside lamp defeated the endeavor, drowning out any starlight that tried to show through. He breathed deeply, wishing Darren would call.

He began to hum, then to hear the words. He sat up, grabbed the little journal he used to keep lyrics, and started to write—

Red room, red night,
Red eyes looking through the skylight
Looks like another night alone—

He smiled to himself. It was going to be a sad song, but that was the point. Emotion poured into music could be bottled. Any pain, anger, or poison he felt could be removed through melody and lyrics, and put on a shelf. He continued—

If you could hear

This song, my song,
You'd see how wonderful this could be
If you'd just dial the telephone—

He hummed the words again and wrote down a chord progression, then moved to the little Yamaha keyboard he kept against the wall to test it. The process went on and on—lyrics, chords, playing it back—until it was nearly midnight. He played the bits of the song he'd completed and felt much better.

As he lay down to sleep, his heart felt lighter.

~*~

Ryan worked at ten the next morning. The weather was warm for January—a good thing since his bicycle was now his only mode of transportation. As he pedaled through the brisk but sunny streets, he took his mind off car accidents and John Carpenter and moving, and focused on work. Nine years of competitive swimming had transitioned naturally into a part time job for the City, teaching swimming lessons. Then, when he'd chosen not to go straight to college, the City offered him a position as a full-time Aquatics Manager. On a typical day, he spent about half his shift in a guard chair, but when he wasn't lifeguarding, he got to do the things he really loved—teaching swimming, running the lessons program, or working short stints at the front desk. Some days he thought if songwriting didn't work out, he could do this for the rest of his life.

After arriving at the pool, he went immediately to Cara's office. She was seated behind her desk going through a stack of papers, but looked up in time to see him flop dramatically into a chair across from her.

"Hey, Ryan!" she said. "How's the old homestead?"

He let out an exasperated sigh. "Not so good."

Cara looked worried. "Uh-oh. What's wrong?" He fished John Carpenter's letter out of his black messenger bag and handed it over. She read it quietly. "This isn't okay."

"You're telling me!"

"Do you want me to call him? What are you going to do? I spent six years in that house. I can't believe he wouldn't trust my judgment."

"No, it's not worth it."

"What a jerk. How soon are you going to move out?"

"February if I can find a place."

After a quiet moment, Cara said, "You know, I think Jay needs a new roommate."

"Jay? The lifeguard?" Ryan asked.

"Yeah. He's on deck right now. You should talk to him." She changed the subject. "How was your day off otherwise?"

"Don't even get me started."

As the morning stretched on, Ryan weighed whether or not to approach Jay about the available room. The move seemed desperate. The little he knew about Jay he didn't like—the chain-smoking and the weed and the constant bragging about female conquests. Jay was the stereotypical frat guy—the bro—and Ryan wasn't sure he could handle that in a living situation. Still, something had to give; he only had two months to find a new apartment in the dead of winter. He rolled the idea around in his head. A conversation about the room wasn't necessarily a commitment. It couldn't hurt to ask, he reasoned.

At noon, Jay's shift for the day was over, and he'd changed into street clothes. Ryan watched as he haphazardly shoved his lifeguarding uniform into his backpack. It was now or never—he'd already checked, and Jay wasn't working again until the weekend.

"Hey, Jay?" he said.

The other boy looked up and smiled. "Hey, man, what's up?"

"Cara told me you—have a room available?"

Jay's eyebrows rose. "Oh, yeah! You need a new place?"

"Unfortunately, yes."

"Oh, man, you've got to come see this apartment. It's me and my friend Mark. Our third roommate dropped out of school, and we haven't found anyone to take his place yet. The room is sweet, too— it has its own bathroom."

"Oh yeah?" Ryan smiled in spite of himself.

"Yeah, and the place is huge."

"How much?"

"The rent? Totally easy. $317 a month per person."

"Wow!" Ryan coughed in surprise. "I can't believe you haven't filled the room at that price. That's great!"

"Yeah, man. You're telling me. Do you want to come by and see it?"

He hesitated a moment, thinking it was too good to be true. Jay waited expectantly with eyebrows raised. Finally, he smiled. It hadn't hurt to ask, and now it couldn't hurt to look.

"Alright," he said. "I'll see it."

CHAPTER 2

Ryan watched as Steven greedily inhaled the freezing February air. Each breath seemed to fortify him against the terror that had just consumed his nose and lungs. After twenty seconds, he bravely pulled his head back inside the window and said, "Ryan, you can't live here."

Ryan swallowed hard. He wasn't sure he could live here either, but the price was right, and Elizabeth Street was no longer an option. He could make this work, or he could move home. Forcing a smile, he replied, "Oh come on, it's not that bad."

"Ryan! There is a forty-ounce bottle of urine in the refrigerator."

He grimaced. "Yeah, disposing of that is on the top of my list, I think."

"Why would anyone do that?"

"It's just a prank—" he held back a further grimace, "—you know, to see if one of their friends will think it's beer, or something." He shuddered in spite of himself and looked around again trying his best to swallow his horror for Steven's sake.

The apartment filled the entire second story of The Garden, a popular new age restaurant. Specializing in vegetarian and vegan cuisine, the clean, your-body-is-a-temple healthful atmosphere of the restaurant below couldn't have been in greater contrast with the sordid, dilapidated apartment above. The tiny kitchen where they stood looked out across an open floor plan, separated from the rest of the living space by a narrow peninsula only large enough to hold a short counter and a glass-top range. Above, plaster ceiling tiles were stained with water marks and cigarette smoke, and the glossy white walls were dulled by a film of grease and dirty handprints. Everywhere Ryan looked, half-crushed cans of Miller Light lay strewn about on their sides, leaking stale beer onto the once cream-colored carpet.

Ryan sighed. A sudden gust through the open window whipped through the kitchen and sent ashes from an overflowing ashtray dancing across the counter and onto the floor. "They had a party last night. It just needs a little cleaning," he said, as brightly as he could manage.

"I can't handle this," Steven said, moving around the peninsula into a wide-open dead space that served as a dining area. He looked down the length of the apartment. A few feet further into the long room, a short wall jutted outward, narrowing the open space, and then receded again, creating a separation between living and dining areas. He moved to the outer wall to his right, where a long line of paned windows stretched across the entire apartment, and swung these open and outward one by one, navigating around heaps of trash and ancient, soiled furniture. "I hope you don't pay for heat," he said, "because these windows need to stay open for about the next month. Where did you find these guys?"

"I work with one of them," Ryan replied, following Steven deeper into the apartment. A shock of cold air blew in from an open window, and Ryan sighed with relief as it caressed his face.

"And this was really a better alternative than moving home for a few months?" Steven looked around, perplexed. "Is this place falling over?"

Ryan laughed. There was a definite slope from the outer wall to the center of the room. "Only slightly. Come on, Steven. I can't move home."

Steven looked at him sternly, "Why not? It's not like it would be permanent. You could take your time looking for a new place."

He considered the question. "I can't handle the pressure. My parents would constantly be asking when I was going back to school and wondering why I was wasting my life with this—music thing."

It wasn't true: his parents supported his choices and would have loved to have him back at home. Secretly it's exactly what he wanted. Nearly a month had passed since the accident and the letter from John Carpenter, but the experience still felt raw. Then there was the continuing disconnect from Darren, who was supposed to be here right now, but wasn't.

He turned his lips up into a smile and continued. "Anyways, this place has amazing potential, and my roommates told me they're leaving in the fall. All of this will be mine, and I can fill it with people who aren't—"

"Aren't disgusting pigs?" Steven coughed.

Ryan stifled a chuckle. "At least my room is kind of clean. Let me show you."

Steven frowned, but followed him to a door across from the dining area. It opened onto a spacious room with three more windows. A door on the left led into a small private bathroom, and in the back right there was a walk-in closet. The walls were still dirty, but the ceiling tiles above were slightly cleaner, and overall the bedroom showed some of the potential Ryan felt certain The Garden promised.

Steven leaned against the wall, scowling. Beneath his thick brows, his brooding eyes darted around the room with obvious disapproval. He pushed his straight, dark hair away from his forehead and succeeded in looking *very* serious. "I still think you should just cut your losses and go home," he said.

"You'll love this place. Just give it some time. Should we start bringing things up?"

"Yeah, we've got a ton of trips ahead of us, and you still need to paint at Elizabeth Street." He paused. "By the way, where the hell is Darren? This would go a lot faster with another set of hands."

"I don't know." Ryan was quiet for a moment. "He said he'd be here—I talked to him twice yesterday."

"He's been acting odd lately." Steven shook his head. "Come on, do you want to call him from the car once we get everything up? You can use my phone."

~*~

After everything from the current trip had been hauled upstairs, Steven drove Ryan back to Elizabeth Street to put another coat of primer on his bedroom walls. He dropped Ryan at the curb and said he'd be back shortly—he had to pick up some cleaning supplies and run an errand or two. Ryan said goodbye, walked into the nearly empty house, and headed straight for his bedroom.

He touched the wall and frowned as he pulled his hand back again. The room was cold, and the first coat of bargain white primer was still sticky to the touch. Shivering, he closed the windows he'd left open earlier that morning. He thought circulating air might help the primer dry more quickly in spite of the near freezing temperature outdoors, but now he doubted his logic.

He stepped into the hallway and turned the dial on the thermostat from sixty-five degrees to eighty, then sighed and let his shoulders sag. Farther along, the hallway opened into the living room, and a subtle patch of light on the barren floor caught his eye. It drew him forward, almost entranced, until he stepped into the empty space.

His footsteps echoed around him, resonating between the walls a loneliness that only a vacant room could sound. Gone now were Cara's plush, over-sized sofas, the television hutch and DVD racks, and the enormous mirror on the long wall which had given the otherwise modest room such incredible depth. Removed were the rubber tree in the corner, and the pothos hanging in front of the wood blinds. Cara's paintings had been packed and moved, leaving only faint halos of dust on the walls to mark where their frames had once been. This place, formerly Ryan's ideal manifestation of home—at least in a physical sense—was now desolate and cruel, and it was all he could do to keep from crying for its loss.

The source of the light that had drawn him away from his bedroom in the first place was a watery patch of sun falling through the skylight above. Here—Ryan thought—was the symbolic distillation of it all. He had truly believed what he said to Steven earlier about The Garden's potential, but as he stared down at the rectangle of light on the polished hardwood floor, it was hard to stay faithful to that belief. Though the February sun was weak, in the places it touched, the pine floorboards turned to fire. The rest of the floor—indeed his life—seemed to retreat, lackluster and sullen.

Sighing, he moved into the kitchen. This room—formerly his favorite—was now just as empty as all the others. Aside from a single cardboard box and a collection of plastic shopping bags filled with odds and ends, the only item left in the kitchen was a black cordless telephone with answering machine mounted to the wall. He considered this for a moment before pulling the phone away from the base and pushing the 'Talk' button to initiate the dial-tone. *Oh, Darren*—he pleaded—*please answer*. He dialed the number and moved the receiver to his ear.

Nothing.

The phone was dead. He remembered asking to have his service moved today, but it was Sunday, and the earliest installation appointment for The Garden wasn't until tomorrow. The phone company must have made a mistake and cut his service at Elizabeth Street already. With annoyance, he replaced the phone and sighed again. Thinking he'd better get started on the second coat in the bedroom—Steven would be back soon with more cleaning supplies—Ryan refocused his mind on the task at hand. Knowing he'd indulged his self-pity long enough, he turned and headed back to the bedroom.

His resolution faltered as he stared mournfully at the few patches of crimson that tried to shine through the oil primer. The rich, deep, candy red he'd painted the walls was now obscured, suffocating beneath the pressure of an oppressive institutional white. He opened up a can of primer and poured it into his paint tray. The fumes were sickening, and he wished now more than ever that he could have the windows open. Before loading up his roller, he leaned toward the center of the room and pushed 'Play' on his aging CD boom-box. Dido's deliciously cold, crystal voice started into the first verse of 'Here With Me,' and Ryan began.

The roller glided up and down, slurping, smacking and hissing softly as it pulled against the not-quite-dry first coat. Even though he hated the present task, he had to admit there was something therapeutic about painting. Here was his closure—an end to this too-short chapter in his life and the beginning of another—and he took to it as if in a trance. The fumes from the primer were making him feel dizzy. As though no time had passed, first one wall was finished, and then the next. He was overzealous around a window frame and clumsily reached for a cloth to wipe the woodwork clean before it was ruined. Dido whispered through what must have been the eleventh verse of 'Honestly Okay,' and Ryan laughed because he didn't remember this song being so long.

Suddenly he didn't feel very well, but he didn't feel badly either. He'd made it to the last wall now. There was an intoxicating rhythm to his movements—roll, dip, roll, dip, roll, pour. His feet were unsteady, and he stumbled, throwing a few large drops of paint onto the floor. Laughing, he reached for his cloth and wiped at them ineffectually. He painted around the trim of the closet sloppily, trying to steady his hand, then reached for the cloth again and made things worse. As quickly as he'd begun, the job was done, and he laughed uproariously as he nearly started over on the first wall. Dido continued singing. Was this still 'Honestly Okay?' Then there was a voice—

"Ryan!" Steven pushed the pause button on the boom-box, and the music died. "Why aren't any of these windows open?"

He blinked at him and swayed slightly on his feet. Smiling broadly, he replied, "Steven! Why are you back already?"

"Ryan, if I didn't know any better—are you high?" He laughed. "Ryan Gregori, the kid who'll barely touch alcohol, is high on paint fumes!"

Ryan twisted his face in confusion. "I—" he began, but no other words came to him. A panic was welling up inside. He couldn't be high. He'd never *been* high. Drugs were vile, and he couldn't understand why anyone would seek to chemically alter their—

"Ryan, it's okay." Steven smiled with genuine compassion. "This'll pass."

"But—why are you back already?"

"It's been over an hour."

He shook his head vigorously, "No, Steven. You just left. I still have to paint—"

Steven gripped his shoulder's firmly. "Ryan. Look around you! You've already done it. Come on; we need to get you out of this room. Fresh air!" Steven took his hand and led him forcefully down the hallway, through the barren living room, and out the front door.

He sat on the short step directly outside, closed his eyes and tried to orient himself. With the lucid part of his mind, he attempted to focus on the act of painting itself—to remember the pouring, the rolling, and moving from one wall to another. He tried to remember Dido, moving from track to track but his mind kept coming back to 'Honestly Okay.'

He didn't like it very much.

Steven sat down beside him and said, "It's alright. Are you feeling any better?"

Ryan opened his eyes and emitted a sound somewhere between a laugh and a whimper. "Not really."

"A lot of people do this on purpose, you know. Doesn't your body feel different? Or don't things seem—funnier?"

"I've never been high—" Ryan groaned, "On anything! I never wanted to—" He looked at Steven, pleading. "Can I use your phone? I need to call Darren."

"Yeah, you do. I can't believe he still hasn't shown up." He stood briskly. "I'm going to grab a few things inside, and then I think we should head back to The Garden and get your bed set up, at least. You can call him from the car."

~*~

A few hours and two trips later, Ryan and Steven carried the last of the things from Elizabeth Street into the apartment above The Garden. All the windows were closed again, and the place still reeked. With a lit cigarette in one hand and a Miller Light in the other, Jay greeted them in the kitchen. "Are you sure you guys won't have a beer?" He raised his can with one hand and flicked his ashes into the sink with the other.

Steven grimaced while Ryan smiled weakly and said, "No, thank you. Probably next time. I think I just need a quiet night after moving, you know?"

Further into the apartment, Mark's girlfriend Cassie was busy duct-taping a forty-ounce beer to each of his hands. The boys watched, and Ryan hoped his thinly veiled horror didn't show too clearly on his face. Jay laughed gutturally and took another drag off his cigarette.

Mark scowled. "Dude, I've got a couple of forties strapped to my hands. I can't even piss until I get these things off. You guys can have *one* beer."

"Yeah!" Jay chimed in, excitedly. "And I won't let her—" he indicated Cassie, "—take them off him until he's finished both."

"Heh," Ryan laughed. "Sorry, guys, really."

Mark shrugged and lifted the bottle taped to his right hand toward his mouth. "Suit yourself!"

Later, Ryan lay on his bed, breathing deeply. Ignoring the noise from the impromptu party his new roommates were holding on the other side of the wall, he focused on the music playing through the speakers of his boom-box. Céline Dion was singing in French; a sad song about the prospect of life after love.

Sounds of revelry rose and fell like great ocean swells beyond the bedroom door, but Ryan didn't feel like celebrating just now. Though he'd been invited over and over again, he still hadn't reached Darren, and now he was in a foul mood. Mark and Jay were nice enough, and he didn't fault them for trying. He actually thought he might grow to like them, but they'd started the night early and by the sound of things they weren't winding down anytime soon. He was more grateful than ever he hadn't gotten involved.

As the saxophone solo started on the Céline Dion track, there was a knock on Ryan's door. He rose groggily and with some annoyance, ready to launch into a speech about how he was sorry he wasn't hanging out and had fallen asleep hours ago. He turned the knob and pulled the door open.

Darren stood on the other side with shoulders slumped. "Hey. Mind if I come in?"

Ryan shook his head with surprise and ushered Darren into the room. "What are you doing here?" he asked.

"You know," Darren said, surveying the room, "She sounds way better in French."

Ryan blushed and quickly paused the boom-box. "Did Jay or Mark let you in?"

"Actually, I don't think I've met them yet. There were a ton of people on your porch, so I just walked in." Darren sat down on the bed with his back against the headboard.

"I'm really pissed at you right now, you know?" Ryan said as he climbed onto the bed next to him.

Darren grinned sheepishly and began to roll the thumb ring he wore on his right hand between his thumb and index finger, nervously. "Yeah, I figured."

"Why didn't you come help us? You said you were going to come by—I was really counting on you."

"I'm sorry, Ryan. It's just that some things came up." He gripped the thumb ring with his other hand and began to turn it back and forth in a nearly frantic rhythm.

"Yeah? Like what things?"

"Don't worry about it." As if to release the tension of the moment, he wrapped an arm around Ryan's shoulders and shook him forcefully. "Were you really high when you left me that message from Steven's phone?"

"Yeah, I really was. And I was really upset. I needed your help to calm down."

Darren laughed, his temporary nervousness gone. "I doubt it. You look like you're fine. I'm just upset that I missed it! I'll bet you were hilarious!"

"I mean—" Ryan felt tears starting to build up behind his eyes.

"Ryan. Don't."

He was starting to get angry now. "You *always* answer your phone. What could have been so important that you couldn't help me move, and you couldn't be there for me when I was freaking out?"

"I said don't worry about it." Darren's voice was quiet. He began to roll the ring again.

Ryan threw his hands in the air. "I just—Darren!" He took a deep breath. "I'm sorry I get crazy like this. I just—"

"Really, Ryan. Don't. Not tonight, okay—"

"I *love you*, Darren. Not tonight isn't okay. We need to talk about this. Every time I bring it up you say we'll figure something out—a way to deal with it. Well, we haven't yet, have we? Instead, you're just—there is a distance between us and I don't understand it."

Darren closed his eyes, tilted his head back, and pulled at his hair. "I don't know what you want, Ryan. I don't want to flat-out say it's not going to happen because I don't even know how I feel about it. I don't want to slam that door, but that's not a place I'm in right now. You're my best friend, and I wish that you could let things be. Isn't it good, what we've got going right now? I see you almost every day. We do everything together." He paused, "And I can't take a chance at messing that up."

The same old excuse. Ryan thought for a moment, then said quietly "I really needed you today. You weren't there."

Darren laid his head on Ryan's shoulder. "This is *my* problem, you know? This is all still so new to me. You've been out since you were seventeen. I only came out last year, and I'm two years older than you. I'm not good at this yet."

Ryan began "Yeah, but, Darren—"

"But nothing. And as far as me not being there for you—I'm really sorry. I'll always try to be." After a few moments of silence, Darren continued. "That actually bothers me a lot, you know?"

"What does?"

Darren lifted his head up again and turned to look directly at Ryan. "How much people need me sometimes. It's like—somebody always expects me to be doing something, or taking care of this, or that. And I've always had these—empathic tendencies that make it really hard."

"What do you mean?"

"Well, you know—empathy. My mother is the same way—she's the only one who really gets it. But it's like—if you cut yourself, I could feel it."

Ryan laughed. "That's not possible."

"How do you know?" Darren replied. "How can you know what I do or don't feel?" Like a spring, compressed and twisted too tightly, he sprung up off the bed. Pacing manically to and fro, he continued. "See, that's the problem. And it's not just physical pain. I know when people around me are upset because I don't just sense it—I feel it, the same way they do. It's really exhausting. It makes me wonder what would happen if I weren't around to, you know, carry that burden."

"I don't understand." Ryan frowned.

"Like—if I moved somewhere totally isolated from everybody and didn't tell a soul. I've thought about it. Or if I died."

"That's ridiculous."

"No, it's not. I could've been crushed that night in the truck. Hell, I could get hit by a bus tomorrow! Really. If I died, what would happen to all the people that cared about and depended on me?"

Ryan was silent for several seconds. He considered the question, allowing its weight to settle on his exhausted mind. For a moment, he let the idea become truth, then pushed it away as a feeling of inky blackness overtook him. A world without Darren wouldn't be a world. It would be a void—a vacuum. He knew suddenly there could be no love like the one he harbored for Darren, and so to consider even briefly how he might live without Darren was ludicrous.

"Well, we'd mourn," he said, his tone flat.

"You'd *mourn*? Why? It's not like it would bring me back! Gone is gone and you'd all still be breathing. Feelings of loss are wasted."

"Wasted?"

"Yes!" Darren continued. "Wasted! I just told you I can *feel* what happens to other people—real living ones. Why should I dwell on death? Sure, it's sad for a minute to think that I might never again be able to see or talk to—"

"Or touch—" Ryan interjected.

"—Or *feel* with someone who has passed, but what is the point of wasting my life *in the now* thinking about those who have gone? They're gone. It's the people around me—in the moment—that matter."

"So, if your mother died tomorrow, you're saying you wouldn't let it affect you?"

"That's exactly what I'm saying." Darren crossed his arms defiantly.

Ryan didn't believe him. "Darren. Everyone loves you, and it's always been that way. It always *will* be that way. You're like the Phineas to my Gene—"

"The what?"

"Never mind, it's not important. What I'm trying to say is that a lot of people really care about you. And you have this talent—this special ability—to make each of us feel like we are loved and cared about also. So, if purely hypothetically you were to be gone, you'd leave a void. When people see you—when they're *with* you—they feel better about themselves. If you weren't here, *that* is what we'd mourn."

Darren nodded his head, slowly. "Okay. Go on, please."

"Well, I don't know what else to say, really. It's like—a flow of emotions. Maybe each of us has a certain capacity for inflow and output. Like—what if each of us served as a reservoir of emotion? The love people feel for me fills me up, and the love I output back to them and to others maintains the flow and helps to fill them instead." Excitedly, Ryan got off the bed. "You can imagine this flow as moving through a series of pipes, right? From one reservoir to the next, to the next, indefinitely. And if, all of a sudden, one of those reservoirs was gone, but all the pipes—the connections—were still in place, it would be mayhem! All of that emotion would spill out to where the reservoir should be but find itself not connecting."

"And so that's how you'd explain mourning? The water of love spilling into the ether?" Darren laughed a little.

"Just hear me out! It's painful when the flow is disrupted." Ryan thought for a moment. He continued, quieter. "But slowly and surely as time goes on we'd start replacing those old pipes with new connections—solid ones that lead somewhere. And I think that's where your logic comes in, ever so slightly. Let's assume this flow of emotions must be constant. If it's always moving, then no-one—not even the most stubborn person on earth—could stand to let their emotions spill into a vacuum forever." He swallowed hard, hating the thought he was about to express. "We'd replace you, slowly and surely. For some, it might be days, and for others, I guess it would take years, but someday the mourning would be done."

"You seem to know a lot about this."

Ryan laughed. "No. Nothing. It just—makes sense to me some-how."

"And let's hope you don't have to worry about any of this for a long time." Darren looked around. "This place is pretty nasty, but I kind of love it."

Ryan perked up. "You do?"

"Well, yeah. Imagine the stuff you can do here. The restaurant on-ly serves breakfast and lunch, so you can be as loud as you want at night, and the rent is a steal, right?"

"Right." He was quiet, considering. "Well, I guess now is as good a time as any. I mean, you'll probably want to think about it in light of everything else we talked about tonight but—"

"But—" Darren raised his eyebrows, expectantly.

"But my roommates are moving out in the fall. And I was thinking that maybe you'd like to live here too."

Darren was silent for too long. Ryan looked at his hands and fo-cused on breathing. Finally, Darren spoke. "Do you think that would be a good idea given how you feel?"

Ryan sighed. "That can all be worked out. And maybe in the pro-cess you can—"

"I'll think about it," Darren said. It was the end of the discussion.

The conversation lightened as the hour grew later. Sleepily—as he had done on so many occasions at Elizabeth Street—Ryan lay on his back on the bed while Darren sat at the computer in the corner of the room. 'Echoes,' with host John Diliberto, streamed through the tuner of the trusty boom-box. Between colorful declarations that Ryan needed a new radio and bouts of frustration that Ryan's computer was so much faster than Darren's, Ryan smiled inwardly. This was the realization he'd come to on the way to Greeley. Today, Darren had missed the details. But he got the point. And maybe he was right—what they had right now was incredible, and Ryan shouldn't be in such a rush to ruin it.

And he didn't say no.

Darren was still sitting at the computer—transfixed—as Ryan felt sleep begin to take him. This is how it had been most nights during the last year, and Ryan reveled in it. Knowing that he'd be snoring soon, he promised himself he'd do better regarding Darren tomorrow. He lifted his head and gazed across the room at his beloved one final time before the weight of his eyelids sent him crashing into the pillows below. Soon, he knew, Darren would hear him sleeping, and let himself out. A final thought—light and imperceptible as a butterfly at twilight—drifted across Ryan's mind before unconsciousness took him.

One day, perhaps, he'd stay.

CHAPTER 3

Darren frowned. "That's what you're wearing tonight?"

"I mean, I was planning on it," Ryan replied. "Is there something wrong with this? I think it's nice for Valentine's Day." He smiled at himself in the full-length mirror on the door of his small private bathroom. Turning back and forth he examined the outfit—a pair of nicely shaped cream-colored slacks and a thin, red, long-sleeved turtle-neck. Tonight, he and Darren were headed to Steven's for an anti-Valentine's party.

"You just look so—"

"So—what?"

"So damned eccentric!"

"I'd like to know what's gotten into you tonight. You're in a terrible mood again." It was true—for the last couple weeks, Darren seemed to be perpetually fatigued and irritable. It was worrisome, but the attitude wasn't the only problem. Though he'd never say it aloud, he thought Darren looked awful tonight. His eyes were recessed, and his skin was gaunt and stretched. His inner light—the warmth and joy that made him so attractive—was obscured.

He was slowly changing into someone Ryan barely recognized.

"I'm fine. It's just winter, you know?"

Ryan turned from the mirror and looked at him. "Yeah, it can be rough." He bit his lower lip softly as he considered. "Are you sure that's everything?"

"Last I checked." Darren was silent for a few moments as he rolled his thumb ring manically across his index finger. "I'm sorry. Honestly, I just don't want to go to this party tonight."

Ryan sighed with a mixture of relief and exasperation. "Why not? I don't think you've ever wanted to miss a party. You're usually the one dragging me—"

Darren waved his hand vehemently for Ryan to stop. "Yeah, yeah. I know. But come on, do you really want to go hang out with Steven tonight? You know the whole party is going to be filled with Steven's *almost lovers*! I mean, what kind of masochist surrounds himself with all of that rejection and failure on Valentine's Day?"

"The kind that knows how to turn the wrong idea into a great friend. Let's not forget he was interested in both of us at one point. And it was Steven that brought us together."

Darren tried to scowl but Ryan looked at him sternly, and he smiled instead. "Fair enough."

"Anyways, that's how it is anytime we hang out with Steven. I don't think he has any friends he hasn't tried to date. So that can't be it. Try again."

Darren chewed his thoughts through a long, uncomfortable silence. "Alright, there is something else."

"Go on."

"I ran into Brandon today. You've met a few times I think." Ryan nodded that they had. "I think he—" Darren turned to look at the alarm clock beside the bed. It was just after nine-thirty. "Is it really that late? Come on; we'd better go."

"What were you going to say?"

"I'll tell you in the car."

Darren walked briskly through the bedroom door, down the short hallway from the kitchen and out the entrance to the apartment. Ryan followed, not quite catching up to him on the wide porch out-

side. Darren continued down to the parking lot of the restaurant below, almost gliding down the flight of wooden steps between the
porch and the ground. Following as closely as he could, Ryan realized
he'd forgotten a coat and considered turning back. It didn't matter,
he supposed; he was only going to be outside a short time. Darren
was already unlocking the doors to his old grey Subaru, so he sped
forward, hoping the car would heat up quickly.

He climbed into the passenger seat, winded. "What the hell was
all that about?"

Darren started the engine and headed out of the parking lot, down
the dark alley and into the street before he replied. "I think that
Brandon really likes me. He saw me today—cornered me actually. He
asked if I was going to Steven's tonight because he wasn't sure if he
was going to. I couldn't lie to him, but he's just so—"

"Just so what?" Ryan demanded. His mind raced, terrified of the
answer. Darren hadn't mentioned Brandon before.

"I don't know? Overbearing?"

"Overbearing?"

"Yeah. He makes me uncomfortable. Whenever he's around it's—
intense. I can *feel* his eyes."

Ryan didn't like this at all. "So, you don't like him? You're not—"

Darren shook his head dismissively, and Ryan relaxed. "He told
me he'd probably be there around eleven, so I wanted a chance to get
a couple drinks in before he shows up." When Ryan didn't immediately respond, Darren pressed the power button on the after-market
CD Player in the dashboard. "I just found this, and I think it's awesome. The band's name is Kosheen."

Music flooded the car—cold and wonderful, with deep electronic
pulses. Ryan wanted to talk more about Brandon, but instead, he
closed his eyes for a moment to breathe in the sound. A woman
started singing, and her coffee-rich, dark tones enveloped him like an

avalanche. After about a minute the car glided to a stop and Ryan opened his eyes again.

He looked out the windows. With almost supernatural precision, the music fit the setting—the snowbanks reflecting the red of the traffic light above, and the silhouettes of tree branches against yet another stale orange winter sky. The music was cold and deep—it was winter, and it was night. It was everything he could see and feel and all of it fused together into a single, flawless moment.

"I love this," Ryan said. "I don't think I've ever heard something like this before."

As the light turned to green, Darren smiled. "This is my favorite part. She doubles up kind of. It's like—everything stays the same up to this climactic moment where her words come twice as fast."

Ryan smiled and closed his eyes again to listen. This moment was idyllic. "I hope you feel better," he said, "since we're almost there."

"I'm working on it." Darren's voice was strained, and Ryan wondered if he was rolling the thumb ring again.

Minutes passed without exchanging words as they consulted their own thoughts. Finally, Darren pulled into the parking lot of Steven's apartment complex, they exited the vehicle and walked up a flight of steps to Steven's front door.

Darren pressed the bell and waited patiently. After several seconds the door swung open, and the tall, lean figure of their friend Max stood silhouetted in the doorway. Ryan let his eyes adjust. He was dressed in a suggestively tight pair of low-rise, boot-cut jeans, and a thin, blue-striped cotton button-up. Even obscured by the backlighting of the apartment within, his icy blue eyes cut through his square glasses and sat in stark opposition to the boxed-dye, candy-apple red of his spiky hair.

They locked eyes, and Ryan found himself momentarily unable to turn away. An unexpected warmth blossomed around his neck as his lips parted and turned up into a slanted smile. Max held his gaze with an unfamiliar intensity, and he felt a sudden, intense desire to lean forward and taste—

Then, as suddenly as it had begun, his initial feeling of excitement was canceled by a jolt of shame that coursed through his veins like ice water. He quickly diverted his gaze to Darren—he was the one Ryan really wanted—then swallowed hard and pushed the unsolicited thoughts about Max out of his mind.

"Welcome, guys!" Max said, brightly. "I was wondering when you were going to make it." He opened his arms as if to embrace them both.

"We made it!" Darren replied before stepping determinedly into the apartment.

Max gave Ryan a wide-eyed shrug as if to ask what Darren's problem was. "He's a bit chipper tonight, no?" Letting his arms fall to his side, he looked Ryan up and down before he continued. "Well, you look—great! Wow!"

"Thanks." Ryan blushed in spite of himself. He wanted desperately to return the compliment. Instead, he tilted his head to look down the hall into Steven's apartment. He needed to see where Darren had gone so quickly—to see if Brandon had arrived early. Darren was just taking off his coat, so he refocused his attention. "Yeah, sorry about Darren. Are you guys having fun so far?"

Max smiled brightly. "Yes indeedy!"

"Indeedy?" Ryan laughed. Max never failed to be simultaneously fun and ridiculous with his language.

"Yes. Indeedy!" He raised his arms again and this time pulled Ryan into a tight embrace. Letting go a few moments later, he said, "It's always great to see you, Mister. Are you coming in? It's the middle of February for God's sake, and you're not going to last long out there dressed like that!"

Awkwardly, Ryan stepped into the house and allowed Max to close the door behind him. In the living room beyond, a handful of guests laughed and drank from red solo cups while sprawling out across a futon, a love seat, and several bean bags scattered around the floor. Steven's 40-inch television—whose massive cathode-ray tube made it the biggest piece of furniture in the living room—was set to a moderate volume, playing music videos on VH1. To the right, lined with at least twenty bottles of liquor, a long dining bar separated the living room and kitchen.

Brandon hadn't arrived yet.

Steven leapt up from the futon and swaggered forward. "Ryan! How's it going?" He smelled strongly of rum.

Ryan laughed. "Good!" He gave Steven a quick hug, then held him at arm's length, smiling at the slight squint in his friend's eyes. "It looks like you're having a marvelous time!" Then, more quietly. "Are you doing alright? I know today isn't your favorite day."

"Well, no. Not my favorite day. I'm okay though; Captain Morgan is my date for the evening. He brought me a bottle of something really nice. You'd better catch up!"

Suddenly Darren's hand was on his arm pulling him away. "We're never going to catch up if we don't get started. I asked you twice already what you want to drink and you're off in outer space again!"

Ryan scowled and excused himself. "I have no idea! Make me whatever. What are the options?"

Darren started to rattle off the various liquors displayed on the bar. Most of the names meant nothing to Ryan. He'd only had his first drink a few months ago when Darren brought a bottle of vanilla vodka and a two-liter of Sprite to Asbury Drive. Despite his initial resistance he quickly grew to like the concoction, and by the end of the night, he was happily drunk. Since then he'd tried a few wines and a couple more vodkas—always with Darren—but otherwise, he was utterly clueless.

"Gin and tonic?" came a voice from behind him. Ryan turned and found Max—grinning as brightly as before—holding a plastic cup of clear liquid in the air. He continued, accenting his words clumsily but with great effect. "I'm pretending to be British tonight, and I'm thinking a bloke like you could use a good ol' G-and-T. Yeah?"

Ryan laughed and accepted the cup Max extended to him. He sipped it and winced; the concoction was bitingly herbal and bitter. His face must've shown his disdain because Max chuckled softly. Was this a challenge?

"Darren!" he called. "Can you make me a gin and tonic?" He handed the cup back to Max, whose smile grew even larger. A challenge indeed.

A moment passed, and then Darren replied. "Sure can!" There was a hollow sound of ice hitting the inside of a plastic cup, a glug and a fizz, and then he handed Ryan the drink before stepping back into the living room and sitting heavily on the futon. Ryan raised his eyebrows at Darren's theatrics, sipped the unfamiliar concoction and folded gracefully into a beanbag. Max followed suit and occupied one next to Ryan.

Conversation within the room moved easily, alternating between talk of school projects, bad professors and ridiculous commentary about the music videos playing on-screen. The former turns in conversation left Ryan feeling out of place since he was not presently a student, but the latter he rejoiced in.

As the minutes passed, the bitter tonic water in his drink went down more smoothly. Max directed his attention toward the television, and they laughed as Gwen Stefani methodically killed the other members of No Doubt in their 'It's My Life' video. By the second verse, everyone in the room sang along, and Ryan relaxed, allowing himself to sink deeper into the bean bag. He closed his eyes momentarily and rolled his neck back and forth, feeling luxuriously at ease. When the song ended, he lifted the cup to his mouth and tilted it backward, only to find it empty.

He rose gingerly and smiled at Max. "I'm empty. I think I'll try my hand at making one myself." He looked at Max's cup. "You're almost out. Can I make you one too?"

Max sighed. "I wish! I could drink these all night, but I'm pacing myself. I have to drive home later. I might have one more in a while, but thanks."

"How very responsible of you!" He nodded curtly. "I'll be right back. Wish me luck!"

After fumbling in the freezer, Ryan filled his cup halfway with ice and pulled the bottle of Bombay Sapphire from the counter. He poured, slowly and carefully, a perfect quarter of the way up the side. Replacing the gin, he opened the refrigerator, pulled out the bottle of tonic water and unscrewed the cap. As he prepared to fill his glass the rest of the way, he examined the bottle more closely.

'Contains Quinine' the label displayed, proudly. As he poured, he considered—of all things—how one was to pronounce the word 'Quinine.' Would it be 'kwi-nin'? He screwed the cap back on, liking how the pronunciation sounded, but fearing it was more like 'kwigh-nine.' He placed the bottle back in the refrigerator, and turned around to pick up his drink.

Darren was standing inches in front of him.

"Hey!" Darren laughed, cruelly. "Off in your own little world again?"

Ryan blushed. "No, I was just trying to think of how to properly say the name of the stuff they put in tonic water—you know, the actual—"

Before he could continue, Darren's face grew serious. "I didn't make your drink *that* strong. The doorbell just rang, and I said I'd get it." He thrust an empty plastic cup into Ryan's hand. Can you make a Malibu and Sprite? But don't make it as weak as you usually do—like you make yours. Lighten up a little and let it flow." Darren narrowed his eyes and pressed his lips into a scowl, then laughed and patted Ryan on the shoulder as he turned and headed to the door.

Ryan knew even before he saw him that the latecomer must be Brandon. Jovial voices rang out in welcome, and he felt a knot begin to turn in his stomach. He reasoned with himself for a moment. He barely knew Brandon—they'd met two or three times at most—so there was no reason for him to harbor such instant feelings of dislike. He certainly wasn't the first person to express an interest in Darren, nor would he be the last. They were hardly in competition with one another; Darren said he had absolutely no interest in Brandon's affections. Still, as they walked together into the kitchen, Ryan felt a cold sweat beneath his arms and a slight flush around his cheeks.

Brandon held out his hand. "Ryan," he said, "Nice to see you again."

Ryan shook it weakly. "You too." He smiled a bit too widely as he examined Brandon from head to toe and back again.

There was reason to worry. Brandon was Darren's height—shorter than Ryan with a more compact and defined physique. Though he tried to assure himself that Brandon's apparent musculature was simply a product of his stature, he knew that by conventional standards Brandon was extraordinarily attractive. Despite the slightly amorphous cover of his fitted but roomy white button-up shirt, and light-colored, relaxed-fit jeans, it was impossible to mistake the Michelangelo's David-like quality of Brandon's form for anything but living art. To make things worse, Brandon's ears were pierced with a pair of thick gauged steel horseshoes that gave him an alluring aura of bad-boy sexuality. The overall presentation was stunningly heartbreaking.

There was—Ryan perceived—an awkward moment of silence. Then Brandon said, "Hey, what are you mixing?"

"Uh—" Ryan, too caught-up in his assessment of the other seemed to forget his words. "Malibu and Sprite." He coughed.

Brandon raised his eyebrows slightly. "Would you mind pouring one for me too?"

"Sure."

Ryan turned toward the refrigerator and scowled, trying not to let his emotions get the better of him. Inhaling deeply, he raised his chin—brave face now—and set about mixing a pair of Malibu and Sprites, making sure to *let it flow*. By the time he finished, he was certain he could handle Brandon. Smiling with genuine optimism, he turned toward the living room.

His heart sank. Darren had moved to the love seat, and Brandon was sitting dangerously close on the cushion next to him. A wave of chemical heat rushed through Ryan's veins as he fought to keep his smile. They were talking animatedly, and he worried he was going to have to give in to his jealousy or his rage—he wasn't sure he could swallow both. In a decision he almost immediately regretted, he walked boldly forward, drinks in hand, and planted his feet firmly in front of them.

Silently, he awaited acknowledgment.

Darren, who had been laughing, stopped abruptly. Stone-faced, he looked up at Ryan, extended his hands toward the cups and said "Thanks." He gripped the drinks and pulled his hands away slowly.

Brandon said nothing.

Ryan, still standing awkwardly, felt a gentle hand on his shoulder. Broken from the spell of his tumultuous thoughts, he turned to find Max standing behind him. The other boy gave an almost imperceptible smile before placing Ryan's own forgotten gin and tonic into his hand. "Sit back down, Mister."

After following Max's cue, he tried to force himself to watch the music videos—a futile endeavor as his thoughts began to spin around the present situation, circling a drain of despair. He could not understand why Darren was acting this way. Somewhere through the toxic fog of pain and betrayal that muffled his ears and clouded his eyes, he could hear Darren still laughing. He could see Brandon touching—a hand to Darren's knee, or shoulder, or a tousle of his straw-colored hair. He might have forgiven an act of politeness on Darren's part— five minutes of pleasantries ahead of an expertly timed excuse to talk to anyone else—but this was something different. Either Darren lied to him about his lack of interest in Brandon, or he was simply being cruel. In the end, Ryan supposed it didn't matter, as both scenarios hinted at an idea so often glimpsed, but never truly grasped.

Darren didn't care about—

"Mister!" Ryan shook himself out of his daze, glad that Max had interrupted the thought.

"What?"

"Snap out of it!" Max laughed. "Do you need another G and T?"

Ryan chuckled despite his mood. He looked down to find his cup not only empty, but half crushed. Guiltily, he replied, "Yeah, I think I need one—" he paused, "Don't you—think I need one, that is?"

Max's shoulders sagged almost imperceptibly. In a harsh whisper, he said, "I think you could do better."

"He could absolutely do better."

Max shook his head. "I said, I think that *you* could do better." After a long pause, he rose from his beanbag, took Ryan's cup and headed to the kitchen. When he returned, he also had one for himself. "Let's talk about something else, yeah?" He took his seat and handed Ryan his cup. "Have you written any more music lately?"

The tactic worked. "Yeah, I have a couple things going. I don't know; they're alright."

"Why just alright?" Max frowned. "More importantly, when do we get to hear some?"

Ryan thought for a moment, trying to decide the best way to answer. "That's a great question. I've got so many songs, but I feel like once I finish writing them, that's sort of it. You know? I record them sometimes but I'm not the greatest singer, and the background is just MIDI from my notation program—"

Max rested his hand on Ryan's forearm and turned his mouth into a knowing smirk. "Sounds like a lot of excuses. You should pick your favorite song and just put it out there. Go to an open mic or something."

Ryan choked and took another sip of his gin and tonic to clear his throat. "I don't think I'm ready for all that. But I'll tell you what. You can come over sometime and I'll play a few pieces for you."

"I'd be honored. But Ryan, I don't think you'll make it as a songwriter if you only play private listening-parties-for-one in your living room."

"I know, I know." He didn't really want to talk about this anymore. Off to his right, he heard Darren chuckle. There was a levity to his voice Ryan hadn't heard in weeks. His mind began to wander down a trail of thoughts he didn't like, so he turned his attention back to Max. "I'm kind of a perfectionist, and the problem is that I'm not a perfect musician. I know I should get over it, but I feel like I can't share anything with the world until it's, I don't know—"

"Perfect? No such thing."

"And I need to get better with the piano. I can write beautifully, but some of it I can't play."

Max nodded. "Did you know I've been playing since I was eight?"

"No!"

"Great instrument, but after all these years I still hit a few wrong notes. Just stick with it."

As they continued to talk, Ryan did his best to keep his focus squarely on Max. Still, he couldn't shut off his awareness of the injustice being done a few feet away. He feared that if Max stopped talking everything would bubble up to the surface and envelope him again, so as each topic of conversation began to draw to a close, he made sure to change the subject. He started to list them in his mind—line them up one after another to be recalled at a moment's notice.

Through the cloud of conversation—the volume was ratcheting steadily higher as the partygoers reached a further point of intoxication—Ryan heard sweeping strings. He turned his face swiftly from his conversation with Max toward the television.

"Max!" He practically shouted—he was no less immune to the alcohol than anyone else present. "I just *love* her."

Max turned and looked. "Dido?"

"Dido makes everything better." He watched, transfixed as the songstress started into the first verse of 'White Flag.' Max smiled at Ryan's apparent delight and settled in to watch the video.

His mind swam, captivated by the crystalline vocals and soaring melodies. But mostly he focused on the lyrics—the themes of resilience and defiance in the face of love lost. Tonight, the song spoke to him, fortifying his resolve. In a single moment, all of Max's well-intentioned distraction fell away, and Ryan realized he couldn't stand the idea of languishing, stoically holding on to unrequited love.

Perhaps Dido was content to keep her mouth closed and stubbornly suffer her feelings for David Boreanaz in the video, but he refused to do the same for Darren. He knew what he had to do. The instant the song ended he rose swiftly in an effort to keep the moment—the motivation—from passing.

"Ryan!" Max said. "Where are you going?"

"Bathroom." He replied, and moved quickly out of the living room. Once behind the closed bathroom door, he looked in the mirror. His face was whiter than usual, and glossy from the drinks. Running the hot water a little too warm, he scrubbed his face with his hands and breathed the hot, damp air that lifted upward out of the basin. Once and for all, publicly, Darren was going to hear how Ryan felt about him. It had to be done here, because too often when the subject was raised in private, Darren found a way not to acknowledge it. And Brandon, whom Ryan had so pathetically feared at the beginning of the evening, was nothing now.

Determined and confident, he swung open the bathroom door and stepped into the hallway. He saw Max's face first, full of fear. Steven and the other guests tried ineffectually to blend in with their seats. Ryan heard laughter, and clutched his neck in an attempt to choke back a sob.

On the love seat, Darren chuckled and laughed, his head turned to the side with eyes closed. Brandon lay on top of him, kissing his neck and moving a hand deep beneath them between Darren's legs. Brandon pressed hard against him, and Darren squirmed with apparent delight. At some point he'd removed his shoes, and his legs hung over the side of the small sofa. Ryan watched in terror as his toes curled. Realizing he'd been holding his breath, he moved his hand from his throat and gasped. Perhaps hearing this in the now, nearly silent room, Brandon lifted his face from Darren's neck and looked directly toward Ryan.

He smiled.

On the crest of a great wave of nausea, Ryan turned and fled out the front door. For a moment, he stood at the railing adjacent the steps to the parking lot and sobbed. Hot tears burned his cheeks against the biting February air as he coughed and cried. The betrayal and humiliation twisted his stomach, and he could feel his heart beating violently, trying to break free of his chest. The loss of his truck and his house he had taken in stride, but the loss of Darren felt like assured destruction. The foundation upon which he'd based his life— his future—was crumbling around him, and as if to drive the point home, his knees buckled.

He shook his head and focused on breathing, then steadied himself enough to walk down to the parking lot. It was going to be a long walk home, but he didn't care. All that mattered at the moment was getting as far away from here as possible. He was halfway across the lot when he heard frenzied footsteps behind him. Turning, he saw Max bundled in his pea coat, sprinting forward.

"Ryan! Ryan!" Max came to a stop, winded. "Come on; I'm going to take you home. It's freezing out here. Where's your coat?"

"I didn't bring one." He folded his arms across his chest, realizing how cold he was in his thin sweater.

Max threw his hands in the air and said, "Come on, my car is over here."

~*~

The ride home was mostly silent. Max drove slowly and smoothly, letting Ryan cry—offering neither words of condolence, nor condemnations about Darren and Brandon's behavior. Ryan appreciated the silence, and by the time Max pulled into the parking lot behind The Garden, he'd composed himself.

"Do you want me to come up?" Max asked, softly.

Ryan wiped the remnants of his tears from the corners of his eyes. "Yeah, I'd really like that—for a minute or two."

Inside his bedroom, Ryan flopped heavily onto the mattress. The apartment was quiet—for once it seemed his roommates had gone to a party elsewhere instead of hosting their own—and Ryan was thankful. He looked at the clock. One forty-eight in the morning. Max laid down beside him and rested his head on Ryan's chest—candy apple red hair smelling of pine trees and meadows, and clean, masculine things. "Is this alright?" he asked.

"Yes. Thank you for bringing me home."

Max threw his arm across Ryan's middle. "I'm sorry you had to see that. *No one* should have had to see that."

Letting out a cross between a sob and a laugh, Ryan replied, "No one should have had to see me react that way. I just don't understand why he did that to me. It's not as if he doesn't know how I feel."

Max sighed and began to withdraw his arm, then thought better of it. "Oh, Mister, I meant what I said. You can do better." He rolled off Ryan's chest and propped himself on his elbows. "He isn't any good for you."

Ryan sat part-way up with a pained expression on his face. "What do you mean?"

"I mean he's bad news! Listen, I'm not the only one who thinks so. We all—"

"Who is *we all*?"

"It doesn't matter—a bunch of us in our group. You're something really special, Ryan—a real diamond in the rough. You're smart and funny, and innocent—"

"Naïve?"

"I didn't say naïve. You're—untainted. You're going to do great things. And the thing is, Darren doesn't see any of that. We all know how you feel. For God's sake it's written all over you. Everyone in that room held their breath when they saw what was going on—because they were worried about how you'd react. Darren uses you. Can't you see how he feeds off your attention? He has a totally negative impact on you—squashes the things that make you shine."

Ryan sank back down into his pillow. "I can't believe I'm hearing this."

Max placed his head back on Ryan's chest. "I'm sorry to say it. You've got so much to give. Why don't you give it to someone who'll appreciate it?"

"Can we just lay here for a minute?"

"Of course."

"Thank you, Max. I don't know what I'd have done without you tonight."

"Anytime." He paused. "Mister—"

"Yes, Max?"

"Never mind."

Max left twenty minutes later, promising he'd call to check up in the morning. For the following hour, Ryan lay sleepless watching the ceiling fan turning overhead. Slowly and methodically he mulled over the events of the night—Darren's mood, the icy attitude at the party, and of course, the great betrayal. He picked up the phone several times and started to dial the number, but it wasn't until close to three-thirty that he completed the call.

"Hello?" Darren's voice was heavy with sleep.

"Hey."

"What's up? It's late."

Ryan laughed. "Yeah, it is. Are you alone?"

"Last I checked."

"So, what was all that about, tonight?"

"Ryan, can you just let it go?"

"I don't want to *let it go*."

Darren sighed. "Fine. I was just drunk, okay? I didn't want to be rude to him."

"Rude? I don't think courtesy extends to letting someone molest you in front of your friends."

"Okay, this conversation is over, goodbye—"

"Wait!" Ryan shouted. Then he softened his voice again. "Wait. I'm sorry, I just—"

"I'm really too tired for this, Ry—"

"People think you're bad for me—that you have a negative impact."

Silence.

"Darren?"

"What people?" he replied, finally. Ryan thought he could hear genuine hurt in his voice.

"Just, people we know."

"I can't talk about this right now. I'm sorry, Ryan."

"Darren, please—" Ryan started. It was already too late. The line was dead.

CHAPTER 4

When Ryan woke at ten the next morning, the world seemed to have reset. Uncommonly brilliant light spilled through the paned windows of his bedroom, and when he rose to look out of them, everything he could see was covered in a thick layer of soft, fresh snow. In the cloudless sky above, the sun radiated bright and hot despite the month, conducting a tinny symphony of drips and drops melting from the rooftops of the city outside. The room, with its eastern exposure, was too warm. He swung open a pair of windows, leaned his head outward and breathed deeply. The cold air stung his lungs and widened his eyes, and he laughed. Saturday night had been cruel, but this Sunday morning—it seemed—spoke of redemption.

He closed his mouth and swallowed. Last night's gin still soured his breath, leaving an aftertaste of humiliation. A sudden, desperate need to expunge the flavor overtook him, so he closed the windows again and headed for the kitchen.

From a high shelf in the pantry, he pulled down a battered white coffee machine and set it on the kitchen counter. Although he liked the ritual of drinking coffee, he didn't do it often. This morning, however, he needed it, hoping it could erase the flavor of the terrible night. He filled the reservoir, pulled a can of French roast from the freezer, and set the machine to brew.

When it was finished, he put a couple spoonfuls of sugar and a generous amount of milk into the bottom of an empty mug. He topped it off with the steaming black liquid and took a seat at the little dining set Cara had gifted him from Elizabeth Street. With his elbows on the table, he grasped the mug tightly between his hands, closed his eyes, and inhaled deeply.

The aroma triggered a memory.

It was January again—a year ago at Asbury Drive—a quiet night alone at home with no plans. Steven had called wanting to come over, and he'd sounded so strange—almost desperate.

The doorbell rang, and Ryan jumped up off the couch. As he scurried down the steps to the front door—the house on Asbury was a split level—he wondered if he should've turned down the music playing in the living room. It was too late now—outside Steven was ringing the bell incessantly. Ryan considered making him wait, just for fun, then thought better of it and opened the door. Steven stepped hurriedly in, and a boy Ryan hadn't seen before followed behind him.

"Oh! It's freezing out there!" Steven exclaimed. "It's not just the temperature. The wind is howling like a mother—"

Ryan laughed. "Hi, Steven." He looked beyond his friend to the new boy, and hoped his eyes didn't give away his surprise. He was beautiful—shorter than Ryan with a thin, triangular face and artfully spiked straw-colored hair. His eyes—a color between green and grey—sparkled. Afraid he had appraised his new guest a moment too long, Ryan stepped around Steven, held out his hand and said, "Hi, I'm Ryan."

The new boy smiled. "Darren. Nice to meet you. Fuck it's cold!"

Ryan laughed and told his guests they could take off their jackets and hang them on the hooks by the door. The apartment was warm, so he beckoned them up the stairs into the living room. Darren asked where he could find the bathroom, and Ryan directed him down the hallway.

Steven collapsed into a chair. "He's something, isn't he?"

Ryan laughed. "Yeah, he is! Where did you find this one?"

"Online. Same place as always."

"Of course you did. I was a little surprised to see you already had company though. When you called I assumed it would just be you."

"It's alright, isn't it?"

"Of course it is! But if I'd have known, I would've told you I was busy tonight. Shouldn't you two be out somewhere together—alone?"

Steven turned his shoulders inward and forced a smile. "Yeah, probably, but—you know how I get freaked out in the beginning. It's just so intense, one on one! I don't think he's really into me *in that way* and I get so stuck in my head. Anyways, if he can't hang with my friends what's the point in even—"

Taking a seat on the couch perpendicular, Ryan reached over and put a hand on Steven's shoulder to quiet him. "It's fine Steven, really. You've got to stop being so hard on yourself. I mean, I'm not much better, but hell! We'll just have fun tonight, alright?"

"You're a good friend, Ryan." He was quiet for a moment, then, noticing the music for the first time he scowled. "Wow, you really know how to entertain. You're listening to *this* again? How about something a little more—lively?"

Ryan blushed. The plaintive sounds of William Ackerman's acoustic guitar filled the room too loudly as they mixed with the various synthesizers that were a signature of his New Age sound. He stood and walked to the CD changer to switch the disc.

"Don't change it," came a voice from behind him. He turned around to find Darren had returned. "This is 'Processional,' isn't it?"

Ryan's eyes widened in surprise. "You know this song?"

"Yeah," Steven echoed. "You *know* this song? I don't think we were even born when this stuff was made."

Darren laughed. "It's not *that* old, I don't think. It's Windham Hill—the label I mean. I had a Windham Hill sampler I used to play every night when I went to sleep as a kid. Leave it on; I haven't heard this in forever."

Steven groaned.

Smiling brightly, Ryan said, "How about I just turn it down a little?" Steven looked cold and slightly miserable. "Do you guys want some coffee to warm up? I keep a can of French roast in the freezer for a really cold day like this. We could put some cinnamon in it."

"Yes please!" Steven exclaimed, instantly reanimated. He turned to Darren. "Ryan makes the best coffee."

"That sounds awesome," Darren said. "If you don't mind."

Ryan blushed a little. "No problem. I'll get right to it." He rose from the chair and headed into the kitchen. Darren followed.

"So, Ryan, Steven has a lot of great things to say about you. What's your story?"

As Darren watched him, he felt his heart rate quicken, and his hands fumbled as they reached for a filter in a cabinet. Darren was shockingly beautiful, and there was an incredible kindness in his eyes that warmed Ryan far more than the coffee would. Coming closer, Darren reached in front of him to pull the empty carafe off its base and fill it. The nearness caused Ryan to hold his breath for a moment. He bit down on his tongue to dampen the excitement he felt—Darren was here as Steven's date, after all.

Beyond the kitchen, he could see Steven still sitting in the living room alone. More loudly than necessary he said, "You've been talking about me again? Why don't you come in here and join us?"

When there was no immediate response, Ryan knew Steven was in his head again. He'd seen this before. Something must have happened earlier in the night, either real or imagined—a momentary lapse in eye contact or a perceived sense of disinterest—that switched on Steven's warning lights. Now he'd all but written Darren off as a viable prospect. His heart was enormous but fragile, and Ryan knew that even the simple action of Darren accompanying Ryan to the kitchen—rather than sitting with him in the living room—was breaking it into pieces.

Finally, Steven responded. "I'm still trying to warm up. I can't move right now!"

Having filled and replaced the carafe, Darren silently mouthed a question. *What's his problem?* Ryan smiled compassionately and tilted his head toward the living room. Darren's eyes widened in under-standing, and he smiled in turn. He touched Ryan's shoulder lightly—*thank you*—and left him alone in the kitchen to finish the job.

When the coffee was done Ryan brought them each a mug, and friendly conversation started in earnest. He did his best to keep fo-cused on topics Steven liked in an effort to draw him out of his shell—video games, pop music, and the trials and tribulations of be-ing a business student. At first, it worked, but as the night wore on, he found it increasingly difficult to keep his friend engaged.

William Ackerman's 'Conferring With the Moon' began to play, and Darren smiled. "What is that instrument?" he asked.

A high, tremulous melody floated over a recurring guitar theme. "It's called a lyricon," Ryan replied. "It's a wind synthesizer. Think of like—an electric piano inside of a clarinet. It responds to the force of the player's breath and the fingerings."

"It's amazing!"

"Yeah, a really beautiful instrument. They don't make them any-more. I mean, I think there are new wind synthesizers, but the lyr-icon was the original."

"You seem to know a lot about this. Are you a musician?"

As the conversation continued, Ryan was aware of Steven retreating further. Occasionally he contributed a well-timed nod of the head or a short laugh, but eventually, he stopped altogether.

It was getting late. Darren excused himself to the bathroom again.

"You need to snap out of it," Ryan said to Steven.

His friend smiled weakly despite his mood. "I'm fine, Ryan. I screwed this one up though, didn't I?"

"I don't think so. I mean, it's not too late. Just dive in. Talk to him. Talk *with* us!"

"Nah, I think we'll call it a night soon. Anyways, it seems like this one is for you."

Ryan blushed in spite of himself. He'd been thinking the same thing for a while now but wouldn't have dared to say it. "Oh, come on, Steven."

He winked, and this time his smile was genuine. "I didn't grow up listening to Salisbury Hill or whatever the hell it's called. I can't talk with the two of you about how beautiful lyricons are. That's really an instrument? To me it sounds like a bunch of nerdy songwriters renting out a convention center for a weekend."

Ryan laughed. "Hey, he didn't exactly know what it was either."

Shaking his head slowly, Steven said, "It doesn't matter. I think the two of you would be really good together—"

The telephone rang, and Ryan was jettisoned back to reality. Asbury Drive was ancient history. He set his mug down on the table and rushed into his bedroom to pick up the receiver. "Hello?" he said.

"Hi, Mister. Are you doing okay?"

He exhaled. "Max. Yeah, I'm fine—feeling a little introspective."

"Do you think you want some company today? I could come over, or we could go out somewhere. Dinner or something to keep your mind off—" Max didn't finish.

Ryan smiled. Max was a good friend. "I would love to, but I have to work at noon. Maybe later this week?"

"Okay. Let me know."

"I will. Bye, Max."

"Bye."

Keeping the receiver with him, Ryan looked at the alarm clock before leaving his room to sit back at the table. It was 10:50 am. He picked up his coffee and realized he must have reminisced for longer than he'd thought because the liquid inside was lukewarm at best. He sipped it anyway and looked out the windows. The snow was melting quickly, and the streets would be a mess. He needed to leave soon, but shuddered at the thought of riding his bike through all that slush.

Hoping she wasn't busy, he pushed the talk button on the telephone and dialed his mother.

"Hello?"

"Hi Mom."

"Oh, hi Ryan, what's up?"

"Are you busy?"

"No—not really."

"Okay, well—I need a favor. I have to be at work by noon, and things are looking a little sloppy out there for me to be on my bike. Do you think—you could take me in?"

His mother laughed. "Of course. I'd love to. Haven't seen you in a while—"

He could feel himself blush. Even though The Garden was a short seven blocks from his parents' house, he hadn't seen his mother since the night of the accident. "I know—I'm going to get changed and then I'll walk over, okay?"

~*~

Work was predictably slow; there was little incentive for people to go swimming on a cold, sloppy Sunday afternoon in February, but Ryan didn't mind. He had plenty to do adding and canceling classes in advance of an upcoming session of swimming lessons, and the work—though tedious—helped keep his mind off Darren.

Halfway through the afternoon, Jay came in for a short lifeguarding shift and regaled Ryan about the party he and Mark had gone to the night before. Jay was turning out to be nice enough, but wasn't great at talking about anything other than himself. Typically, Ryan found this trait to be annoying, but today he was grateful to hear about the beer and the girls and the extra-good pot, because it was yet another reason not to think about his own situation.

It was only toward the end of the afternoon—the pool closed at six—that he allowed himself to dial his voicemail. He hoped desperately for a message from Darren but found the inbox empty. Going home to be by himself probably wasn't the best option, so he dialed Max's number and asked if the offer of dinner was still on.

Max picked him up from work, and they went to eat at a fast food noodle place. He was happy for the distraction, and after the meal, Max invited him back to his apartment. They shared a half bottle of cheap red wine, and for the hour they spent on Max's little sofa, Darren was the furthest thing from his mind.

Now, back in his bedroom at The Garden, Ryan brushed his teeth twice to cleanse his mouth of the dark stains left by the bargain Shiraz. He was exhausted. After turning down the sheets, he pushed the shuffle button in iTunes and collapsed into bed.

As the computer speakers started playing something by George Winston, he reached behind and flipped the light switch on the wall in an effort to extinguish the day. Above the bed, the ceiling fan turned—humming softly on low—illuminated only by the lights creeping through the windows from the street outside. As the blades slowly spun, they cast their shadows eerie and blue about the room, growing longer and shorter, then longer again as they moved. Finally alone, with no distractions left, Ryan felt his eyes begin to well up, then forced the tears down again.

He'd been strong today, and he could remain so. He wasn't sure when he decided he wasn't going to be the one to reestablish contact, but having made his decision, he owed it to himself to stand by it. Breathing deeply, he forced his mind blank.

Dido started to sing 'See You When You're 40,' and pulled him back again. The song was black and desolate, and he couldn't stand it. He sat up sharply and reached for the telephone beside the bed. Dialing his voicemail again, he prayed there would be a message—that Darren had called while he was at dinner and said what happened at the party was all a misunderstanding.

No new messages.

Dido sang on, more of a whisper than anything else. He scowled, unsure whose side she was on tonight, and scrambled clumsily out of bed to hit the skip button.

Although the next few days brought no word from Darren, they got easier. It wasn't a matter of missing him less; Ryan simply grew more resolute. During the days, he went to work early and stayed late to swim, or the reverse if he was closing. Tuesday afternoon he met Steven for lunch, and Wednesday night he went to see his parents and brother and sister.

Late at night when he was finally, unavoidably alone, he put Céline Dion's French albums on repeat. He missed Darren sitting at his computer while he fell asleep—listening to Echoes with John Diliberto, or pulling strange tracks off the far corners of the internet. But in his solitude there was hope. How sweet would it be when Darren came around? He could see Darren sitting there again with his back turned, clicking away at the keys. That would be the reward for his perseverance—that their old routine could resume, no longer taken for granted because they'd traversed this difficulty together.

It was a good idea—keeping busy and avoiding things they enjoyed together—but was ultimately untenable. By Thursday evening, when he failed to drum up plans to keep himself occupied—when Darren *still* hadn't called—he took a moment to realize he couldn't keep this up forever. He hoped Darren couldn't either.

The night offered nothing but emptiness and temptation. Twice, he picked up the phone and started dialing before forcing it back down onto its base. He had to open the pool the next morning at five-thirty, so he switched the lights off early and prayed for a dreamless sleep.

The morning came too soon. When his alarm began to buzz at four forty-five he almost ripped the cord from the socket, rose groggily, and stumbled out to the main bathroom. After a quick shower, he bundled up tightly, threw his old black messenger bag over his shoulder, and commenced the quick two-mile bike ride to work.

The opening shift was a particular kind of hell—a long slow march out of the gloomy depths of morning, where every advance of the minute hand on the clock was a hard-won battle against heavy eyelids. He simply wasn't cut out for it—for being awake that early—so he was grateful he only had to do it once a week. His lifeguard didn't show up, and repeated calls from the office telephone remained unanswered.

With a weary resolution, he climbed up into an elevated lifeguard chair as the first bright-eyed swimmer emerged from the locker room. Her face beamed as she waved and dove happily into the pool, breaking the water's still, glassy surface. The gutters of the pool—dry all night—hissed and roared as their thirst was slaked, and the gentle, rhythmic percussion of freestyle arms cutting through the water met Ryan's ears like a lullaby. No other staff was scheduled until eight thirty, so he settled in for a long morning of solitude.

By six forty-five he was quickly losing the fight to keep his eyes open. After one particularly dramatic nod forward he shook himself awake, fearing the next time he might actually fall out of the chair. He sighed. It was nearly two hours before anyone else would arrive to take over. Relief was nowhere in sight.

Minutes passed, and the hands on the large clock over the diving well crept closer to seven o'clock. His head was nodding more frequently now as the sky began to imperceptibly lighten through the skylights above. His eyelids were leaden, and suddenly closing, and then—

"It looks like I got here just in time!"

Ryan's head shot back up, and he looked quickly left and right for the sound of the voice.

"Down here, creeper." Darren stood beside the chair, smiling broadly with a cup of coffee in each hand.

"What? What are you doing here?" He shook his head as he climbed clumsily down from the lifeguard chair—surely the weight of the morning had finally gotten to him, and he was dreaming. He knew it wasn't a dream though. Dressed in a faded pair of blue jeans and a fleece shell, it was clear that Darren wasn't here to swim, but he *was* here.

"Well, I haven't heard from you all week, so I thought I'd stop by." He handed a cup to Ryan.

Continuing to eye him suspiciously, Ryan put the cup to his lips and sipped gratefully. "This will be my second coffee in a week." He scowled. It was French roast with a hint of cinnamon.

Darren poked him in the ribs. "Oh, you rebel. It's good for you, and it looks like you need it today."

"You didn't really answer my question. I mean, I'm glad to see you—I think—but you could have just called me. When is the last time you saw this side of 10 a.m. voluntarily?"

"It's a fair point. I actually haven't been to bed yet."

"Well, that explains why you're so chipper. What the hell have you been doing all night?" Ryan thought he could detect the faintest scents of liquor and some kind of smoke.

"A little bit of this, and a little bit of that. It doesn't matter." Darren set the coffee cup he'd kept for himself on the pool deck and placed his hands squarely on Ryan's shoulders. In a more somber tone he continued, "But what does matter—is that I'm sorry." Ryan started to speak, and Darren shushed him quickly. "No, let me finish. First of all, what I choose to do, or—let be done to me? It's my own business. I realize the timing wasn't great, but these things are hard with you. It's really hard to say that I might be interested in someone because I know—"

"Darren—" Ryan protested but was shushed again.

"But you are important to me, Ryan. Don't let anyone tell you that we shouldn't be exactly as we are together. And that being said, I'd like to be through with everything that happened last weekend and never bring it up again. Okay?"

Ryan was silent for a moment, considering. "I'm really worried about you, Darren." He fought back tears. "Something is wrong, and you're not telling me. But if you need to put that party behind you—"

"I do."

"Then I can forget about it too." He put down his coffee and hugged his friend tightly. He held it, expecting Darren to push away, but smiled when the embrace was allowed to linger.

When Ryan finally let go, Darren said, "I really missed you."

"I missed you too."

"So, my parents are coming up next weekend."

"Oh?" he said, perhaps too excitedly. He'd met Darren's parents, the Hendersons—Alice and John—at a party at their house south of Denver the previous fall.

"Yeah, we're going to breakfast that Sunday before they head home. I know it's a little over a week away, but—they asked me if you wanted to come."

"I'd love to. Where?"

"Well, I've got this great idea. It's kind of a surprise. We'll pick you up at nine?"

"Sounds great!"

Any fatigue Ryan felt before his unexpected reunion evaporated quickly. Holding out and waiting for Darren proved to be a success, and for the rest of the day, he felt like he was walking on air. The remainder of his shift went quickly, and he was back at The Garden shortly before two. He took a brief nap, and then later in the evening called Steven to invite him over for pizza.

"How was your week?" Steven asked with a mouthful of pepperoni.

"It was alright."

"Did you stick to your guns about Darren? You said Tuesday you weren't going to call him. I bet that worked out."

Ryan laughed and shoved him from across the table. "It did as a matter of fact! It was touch and go for a while though."

"Then you're a better man than I! So, when did he finally call?"

"Actually, he stopped by work this morning—said he'd been up all night."

Steven rolled his eyes. "No one is surprised."

"He asked me to breakfast next Sunday morning with his parents!"

Steven swallowed sharply. "Okay, okay, let's not get ahead of ourselves."

"What do you mean?"

"I know you, Ryan. Do you think that's a good idea?"

"Of course! It's only breakfast."

"That's not the way you're making it sound. I bet you've been hearing wedding bells in your head all day. What, do you think he's going to like, ask for their approval?"

Ryan scowled. "I know it isn't like that. I meant what I said. It's only breakfast." As the words came out of his mouth, he wasn't sure he believed them.

~*~

The anticipation of the breakfast date with the Hendersons caused the following week to pass slowly. Ryan continued to swim before or after work and spent more time than usual at his little Yamaha keyboard. Tuesday night Darren stopped over for a little while in the evening, and on Thursday Max took him to dinner again.

Finally, the weekend arrived. Saturday was Ryan's day off, so he spent the day cleaning in case Alice and John wanted to come up for a few minutes before they left for breakfast. All the while, as he vacuumed and scrubbed, he reminded himself of what Steven said—he couldn't read too much into this. On the surface, he understood it was an innocent invitation, but deeper down he couldn't help but attach a greater meaning. He worked on, and by the evening the walls of the apartment above The Garden shined as white as their stained, tired paint would let them, and a dozen scented candles temporarily made the apartment smell like a field of wildflowers instead of a dingy pool hall. When it was done, he smiled contentedly.

Jay and Mark were away for the weekend—gone back home to Colorado Springs to see their families—so there was no danger of a random party ruining his hard work.

He hardly slept in anticipation of the event. By seven-thirty on Sunday morning he'd already showered and shaved—the latter was something he only needed to do once a week—and dressed smartly in a pair of cream-colored slacks and a light-weight, faded blue sweater. He shaped his unruly hair—desperately in need of a cut—into soft, neat curls that satisfied him immensely.

With nothing left to do, he made a small pot of coffee and waited, wondering if the black stuff might turn into a habit. After he'd had two cups—it was nearly nine, and he could feel himself sweating in nervous anticipation—he sat at his keyboard and picked at the melody of a Sarah McLachlan song. Finally, at two minutes past, he heard his doorbell ring. He jumped up, rushed to the apartment door and opened it.

"Hi, honey!" Alice said. Her arms were outstretched, and she wrapped them tightly around Ryan's middle. She was a short woman with a medium build, and her arms pinned Ryan's to his side closer to his elbows than his shoulders. Since the first time they met, he'd been entranced by the constant sense of warmth and welcome that Alice exuded. He leaned his cheek lightly down on top of her voluminous honey-colored hair. It smelled of exotic herbs and tea leaves.

"Hi Alice, it's nice to see you again," he replied as she let go. Behind her, John stood a foot and a half taller, smiling ear to ear. He held out his hand, and Ryan shook it.

Darren, who stood next to his mother, shrugged his shoulders and said, "Should we go?"

Alice gave him a scornful look. "No! I want to see this apartment where you're spending so much of your time these days."

Darren grimaced at Ryan, who just smiled. "You're in luck! It's not usually this clean. I live with a couple of train-wrecks!"

Looking past him, Alice pushed through the open door with a fluidity and grace that caught Ryan off guard. "Oh, it's okay, Sweetie. Don't you think I've seen a college bachelor pad before?" At this remark, both Ryan and her son blushed involuntarily before following her deeper into the apartment.

From the kitchen, Ryan took over, giving a brief tour. The Hendersons remarked positively on the plethora of windows and praised the open space. After hearing several times about the apartment's potential, Ryan and Darren ushered Alice and John back onto the porch.

"So where are we going?" Ryan asked.

"Oh," Alice replied, "didn't Darren tell you? We're going right downstairs!"

"The Garden?"

"Yeah, have you eaten there yet?"

Before Ryan could reply, Darren punched his shoulder lightly and answered for him. "No, he hasn't."

Alice laughed. "Well, neither have we. There's a first time for everything!"

Downstairs, Ryan expected a long wait—The Garden was popular with the Sunday brunch crowd. A pretty Irish-looking girl greeted them just inside the door. "Welcome to The Garden!" she said, with clearly forced enthusiasm. Ryan appraised her and smiled to himself—she looked just as new-age as the restaurant purported to be. Her ears sagged slightly under the weight of several surgical steel earrings, and there were green and yellow ribbons—the colors of the university—woven through her curly auburn hair. "Table for how many?"

Alice chuckled softly. "Four, please. Is there a wait?"

The girl—she wore a nameplate that read 'Meredith'—rolled her eyes. "No. You made it before the church crowd, and all the sane people are still in bed." She grabbed a stack of menus. "Follow me this way, puh-lease."

Alice chuckled again. "It sounds like maybe you don't want to be here this morning?"

"Me? No! This is the happiest place on earth!" Meredith pointed to a table with a look of cold disinterest. "Enjoy your meal."

Once seated, Alice opened her menu and said, "She's rude, but I like her."

Darren groaned. "You would, Mom."

A few minutes later a waiter came, and orders were placed. Ryan mentally convulsed a little as he ordered what would be his third cup of coffee in as many hours. Alice and John exchanged the obligatory pleasantries with their son. There were questions about school and Darren's apartment and how the weather differed up here from south of Denver, and no one was really invested too much in the answers.

Ryan tuned out the chatter for a moment to observe the contrast between the restaurant and his home above. The differences were remarkable. The floor consisted of large, gleaming red floor tiles and the walls were painted a deep forest green with bands of pistachio. Delicate and tasteful miniature chandeliers hung over every table, glistening and spreading sprays of refracted yellow light around the room. The effect was bright but intimate, unlike the apartment above, which was perpetually dark and relied on floor lamps for illumination in the common areas. But it was the ceiling of the restaurant that was truly arresting. In place of the dirty plaster tiles he was used to seeing, a layer of white garden lattice hung, suspended as a false ceiling. Through the diamonds of open space, between the crisscrossed wood, several massive pothos plants wove their way in and out, over and through—a living canopy that seemed to embody the restaurant's ideals of earth, health, and life. The ceiling above was painted black, and strands of white Christmas lights glittered and shined through the leaves below them. The place ought to change its name from 'The Garden' to 'Eden,' Ryan thought.

And they ought to call the apartment above 'Purgatory.'

He heard a chuckle. "Hello in there?" Alice was smiling. "Where'd you go, Ryan?"

He coughed a little. "Sorry. I got lost in my thoughts for a minute. It's just amazing how different this place is than my apartment on top."

"I'll say," she said. "So, have you thought any more about school?"

"Going back?" It appeared it was his turn for the obligatory questions. He blushed. "Well, yeah. I think about it. Maybe this fall."

John looked at him sternly. "I'm not sure what you're waiting for."

Alice shoved her husband lightly and smiled. "Everyone does things in their own time. But hey, if you start soon, you'll probably still beat Darren through."

"Oh thanks, Mom!" her son scowled.

She shook her head. "So, how is the apartment upstairs. You like it?"

"Oh, yes. I mean, it's absolutely filthy," Ryan replied, "but I think I'll definitely stay there. My roommates are moving out at the end of the summer, so I'll be able to fill it with whomever I like. That should take care of the problem."

"Really?" Alice said in a suspiciously meaningful way. "How much do you pay?"

"It's nine-fifty total, so three-seventeen a piece."

John coughed.

"You're kidding. We're paying six hundred for Darren's room at Admiral's Park. He should move in with you!"

John coughed again. "Today," he said, quietly.

Alice looked at Darren and asked, "Well?"

"He *did* offer it to me," Darren replied. Then he shrugged.

"And you said?"

"That I'd think about it."

"And now?"

"I'm thinking about it."

Alice scowled and Ryan had to try not to laugh. The expression was identical to the one he'd seen on Darren's face on so many occasions. "Well, don't wait forever." She looked at Ryan. "You might fill the rooms before he's done thinking about it, right, Ryan?"

"Right," he said, smiling.

With the obligatory questions out of the way, conversation moved to more pleasant things. The food arrived, and Alice and John regaled the boys with stories of their last dive trip to an island off Honduras. They were planning to go again in October, and were hoping to have Darren come along. In no time the plates were finished, and then taken away. John paid the check to the mild protest of the boys, and breakfast was over. Alice and John said their goodbyes to Ryan, and Darren wished his parents a safe drive home; he was going to stay with Ryan for a while longer.

Back upstairs, Ryan sat on his bed, and Darren opened iTunes on the computer. He put on an album they'd heard on Echoes in the fall, and turned the computer chair to face Ryan.

"Yes," he said.

"Yes, what?"

"Yes, I'll move in."

Ryan's heart tried to leap out of his chest. He briefly wondered if it was what Darren had said, or the three cups of coffee. "Really?" There was a slight tremble in his voice, and he swallowed hard.

"Really." Darren smiled. Then in a more serious tone, "But there have to be some understandings."

"Like what?"

"Like understanding that we are not—"

"Not—" there was that tremble again.

"We are not a couple. I mean, I don't know what we are. But we're not that. Not right now."

"Okay," Ryan sighed. "We're not a couple. Right now."

"Maybe not ever. I don't know. But sometimes I might want to date. Sometimes I might want to have people over. And once in a while, I might need to do things by myself. But, it should be okay, because we'll still be together."

"Still be Ryan and Darren?"

Darren laughed. "Yes. Can you handle that?"

"Yes. I can handle that."

Turning his head slightly to the left as if to indicate the true weight of the situation, Darren asked again. "Can you *really* handle that?"

"Yes."

"Then it's done." He smiled.

"Now we just need one more roommate!"

"Actually," Darren said, "I have an idea about that one."

"Oh?"

"Yeah, the LGBT office at school puts people interested in transferring here in touch with current students. Yours truly has been talking to this kick-ass girl over instant messenger for a while. I think she's in Ohio."

"Oh?" Ryan said, skeptically.

"Yeah. She's a cute little lesbian named Shelly."

"Shelly?"

Darren laughed. "Is there an echo in here? Yeah. She's coming to town over spring break in a couple weeks to look at places. We might as well show her this one, and if you like her—if I like her as much in real life as I do on the computer—we can offer her the third room."

Ryan considered for a moment. "That sounds fine to me. What a queer little house we'd be—"

"She's awesome. You'll love her." Darren was silent for a minute. "There's one other thing."

"What?"

"Let's have a party! Here. We'll celebrate our good news."

"Okay." Ryan smiled excitedly. "When?"

"How about next Saturday?"

Ryan plucked the phone from his nightstand. "Great! Let's see who is around."

CHAPTER 5

The following morning, Ryan felt a lightening of his spirit as he turned his calendar from February to March. A new month meant new possibilities, and he was content to leave February behind to languish in the cold. It was March now, and his conversation with Darren the previous morning meant that everything was about to change for the better.

It was early when he wandered out of the bedroom to take a shower, but the bathroom was occupied, so he set about making a small pot of oatmeal, humming happily to himself. Just as the cereal started to thicken, the bathroom door opened and Jay stepped out, wrapped tightly in a towel.

He glared at Ryan suspiciously. "Hey man, are you *humming*?"

Ryan laughed. "I guess I am. Good morning."

"The fuck it is! I never really took you for a morning person. I'd give my left nut to go back to bed right now, but I have class in a half hour."

"Yeah, I usually don't love the mornings myself. But I don't know—this morning I just feel good."

Jay shook his head. "Good for you, man—fucking weird, but good for you." He started to walk away.

"Oh hey! Jay!"

His roommate turned. "Yeah?"

"Do you or Mark care if I have a party here on Saturday night?"

Jay smiled. "You? Party? Bring it, man." He shook his head again. "Fucking weird—"

Ryan spooned the oatmeal into a bowl and took a seat at the table. He was relieved Jay hadn't objected. After all, he wasn't just planning a party—he was marking a turning point. Everything he'd wanted since that first incredible night at the house on Asbury Drive was suddenly attainable. It was within his grasp, and it was worth a celebration like nothing he'd ever thrown.

But even through the anticipation, deep in his mind, Darren's voice taunted. *Can you handle it?* He shivered involuntarily and then laughed to himself. Of course he could handle it. Five months from today he and Darren would finally be living under the same roof. Then it would only be a matter of time before Darren finally came to terms with the fact that he was in love with Ryan too.

Breakfast finished, he set the empty bowl in the sink and walked into the bathroom. After undressing and turning on the shower, he took a moment to regard himself in the mirror. His long, tightly curling hair looked tangled and frayed as it stood awkwardly atop his head and hung heavy around his ears. He scowled at his reflection— he was sure Brandon never looked like this in the morning. Then he scowled further as he turned away and stepped into the shower. Those kinds of self-destructive thoughts belonged to a version of himself he was no longer willing to indulge. It was March now, and change was in the air.

He needed to call Max.

By Thursday evening nearly everything was ready. The pantry was filled with chips and crackers, salsas and dips. In the refrigerator, bottles of soda and other non-alcoholic mixers competed for space against Jay and Mark's immense stockpile of canned beer. The only thing left was the alcohol, and that would be provided by Darren and the other guests.

Ryan took a quick survey of the pantry to determine if there was anything he'd forgotten, and then, satisfied, pulled down a box of shells and cheese for his dinner. He set a pot of water on the stove to boil, and a moment later the phone rang.

"Hello?" he answered, plucking the phone from where it rested on the kitchen counter.

"Hey," Darren said at the other end of the line. "Do you have dinner plans?"

"Oh!" Ryan was surprised; Darren had been conspicuously absent for most of the week. "Well, I just put a pot of water on. I'm making shells and cheese, but I can double it if you want to come over."

"Yeah, I'm still at school working on this project for my nutrition class, and I really need a break. Plus, I haven't seen you all week."

Ryan smiled. "Just let me grab a bigger pot. How long until you get here?"

"Ten minutes?"

"See you then."

By the time Darren actually showed up fifteen minutes later, the water was just beginning to boil. He walked slowly into the kitchen and set a slender paper bag on the counter before removing his signature grey fleece shell.

Ryan looked at him, distraught. "You look like shit. Have you been sleeping?"

Darren rolled his eyes, but it was true. He was a shadow—his face gaunt and his skin too white. The darkness around the edges of his eyes had returned, and he looked worse than the night they went to Steven's on Valentine's Day.

"I'm fine," he said. "I'm just tired, but I'm sleeping alright."

"Really? There was that morning you came to see me at work and you hadn't slept yet. What was that all about?"

Darren threw his hands in the air and stepped close. He wrapped his arms around Ryan from behind and held tightly as Ryan pretended to struggle.

"Really," Darren answered. "I'm fine—just stressed about this project and—some other stuff." He let go.

Ryan turned and said, "What other stuff?"

"It's the empathy thing." He was quiet for a moment. "Lately it's felt harder to shut it out. I've been trying to find ways not to think about it but—"

"And I suppose you believe in unicorns too?"

Darren laughed, but he looked disappointed. "I don't expect you to get it."

Ryan opened a second box of shells, removed the gooey cheese packets, and poured the pasta from both boxes into the boiling water. Then he turned and put his arms around Darren, holding him tightly to say he was sorry. He let go after a few seconds and proceeded to throw the boxes in the trash.

Darren plucked one back out of the bin and looked at the nutrition label. Ryan stirred the pasta and said, "So, tell me about your project."

"Well, not much to tell, but my Nutrition professor would be pissed if he knew this is what I was eating for dinner. I can't wait!" Darren walked to the pantry and came back with a couple of wine glasses. He pulled a bottle of sauvignon blanc out of the paper bag and then dug into a drawer looking for a corkscrew. "Want some?"

Ryan looked up from the stove. He'd never had a sauvignon blanc before. "Yes please!"

Darren poured two glasses and put them on either end of the dining table, then proceeded to set out a couple of plates and forks, and an oven mitt as a trivet. After Ryan drained the pasta and mixed in the delicious synthetic cheese goo, he brought the entire pot over to the table, set it on the oven mitt, and deposited himself in a chair. Darren raised his eyebrows and said, "Buon Appetito!"

Ryan laughed and took a sip of his wine. He liked it—sour, cold and citrusy. "Dig in!"

"Oh, wait!" Darren practically jumped out of his chair. "I need to use the bathroom quick, plus we forgot something!" He rushed into Ryan's room and came back a minute later with the trusty old boom box. Ryan smiled as Darren switched it on and pressed play.

His smile grew, stretching nearly to his ears. "Conferring with the Moon," he said. "William Ackerman."

A momentary splash of pink colored Darren's ghostly white cheeks. "Yeah," he said. "I've just been thinking about that night that we met. Can you believe it's been over a year already?"

"No," Ryan confided. "I actually feel like it's been longer—in a good way. I feel like we've lived a lifetime together."

"Ha! And look at where we've ended up. We're going to be roommates! Did you think for an instant this is where we'd be?"

A warning light was flashing somewhere in the back of Ryan's mind. Only a few minutes ago Darren had looked sullen and tired. Now he was acting more alive than Ryan had seen him in ages, as though a switch had been thrown to reanimate him. He dismissed the feeling of foreboding and brought his mind to the question Darren posed. No, he never thought this is where they'd end up. He thought by this point they'd be something greater than friends. But this was a step in the right direction. When he replied, "No, never," he wasn't exactly lying.

Dinner was beyond excellent, in the way the worst foods on the best days can be. Ryan had two glasses of wine, but Darren limited himself to one. Afterwards, they cleaned up and reminisced about their time together—the great adventures they'd had and the millions more to come. Darren held his newfound whimsy and told Ryan all about the tropical resort he'd buy when he was done with school, and how Ryan would go to live there. He could run a restaurant, and in the mornings they'd swim in the ocean. Ryan could learn to SCUBA dive, and then they'd go to Honduras and Curaçao and anywhere they liked with Alice and John.

At one point Ryan excused himself to the bathroom, and when he came out again, he thought his heart might explode with love. The aroma of French Roast and cinnamon filled the air. Darren smiled from the kitchen holding two mugs in his hand, and Ryan felt his knees threaten to buckle beneath him. *This*, he thought, *is what it will be like.* This is how it would be when Darren finally admitted that he loved him too—every day this wonderfully romantic and easy. Darren was on the precipice now, ready to step forward at any moment and declare himself. Ryan could hardly sip his coffee in anticipation of where the night would go next.

But shortly after nine Darren rose unexpectedly and reached for his fleece.

"What are you doing?" Ryan asked.

"I have to get home and finish my project." Ryan was still seated as Darren leaned over behind him and lightly grasped his shoulders.

"Oh." He stood up as Darren walked toward the door. "That just seemed so sudden."

Darren laughed. He looked slightly tired again, though not as tired as when he'd first arrived. "I'll see you tomorrow though, right? We're going to start getting things ready for Saturday."

"Right."

Darren stepped halfway into the hallway and then turned around. Wearing his grey fleece—the very same he'd worn the night they met—Ryan found it difficult to distinguish if what he was seeing was the present, or if he was back at Asbury Drive again. Darren was beautiful standing there with his straw-colored hair shining in the floodlights above the kitchen, and Ryan marveled—not for the first time—at how his grey-green eyes sparkled. He looked intently at his friend and drank deeply of the image, feeling it was important to imprint this on his mind. It was impossible to tell how long this gaze went on, but it must have been forever, because Ryan memorized the knowing smirk—the secret smile—Darren wore in that moment. It was enigmatic—Mona Lisa in a beautiful twenty-one-year-old boy.

Darren laughed and broke Ryan's trance. "Over a year?" he said from the doorway. "I can't believe how much we've done." He turned and lifted one hand in the air as a parting gesture before disappearing into the short, dark hallway beyond.

Ryan said nothing. Later he'd wish that he convinced Darren to stay, but by the time it crossed his mind to protest, Darren was already gone.

~*~

When the alarm went off at a quarter to five, Ryan leaped out of bed and practically skipped to the bathroom, pleasantly aware of the absence of his normal Friday morning fatigue. As he stood under the hot shower he smiled brightly—Max was picking him up from work so they could execute the plan they'd concocted at the beginning of the week. It was going to be an extraordinary day.

He couldn't wait to see Darren's reaction.

Work went smoothly—the morning lifeguard showed up this week—and in no time, it was nearly noon. Coming down off the guard stand, Ryan took a moment to call Darren. The phone rang five times before voicemail picked up. He waited for the beep, then said "Hey, it's me. I hope you got your project done. I want to know what time you're planning to come over to start setting up—can't wait for tomorrow night! Give me a call back at the pool until one-thirty." He rattled off the pool office's number and hung up.

When Max pulled up outside the pool in his dark blue Pontiac, he was wearing an enormous smile. Ryan climbed into the passenger seat and chuckled. "Look at you," he said. "You're grinning ear to ear!"

Max drove slowly out of the parking lot and nodded his head. "Aren't you excited, Mister? This is going to be one hell of a makeover!"

Ryan smiled, despite his annoyance that Darren hadn't called him back. "It's going to be amazing, Max!"

"Are you nervous at all?"

He considered—the transformation they'd planned was certainly bold. "Maybe about the ears, I guess. I don't do so well with needles."

"Well that's a hell of a needle! It's going to be worth it though. People are going to drop over when they see you tomorrow."

"Do you think?" He ran a hand lightly through his hair, enjoying its length and curl. "I guess maybe a little part of me is worried that I'm, I don't know—"

"Worried that—"

"That it just isn't me."

Max laughed. "That's how I felt the first time I dyed my hair this fire-engine red! But now I like to think it's kind of my signature. Don't worry. Piercing your ears and cutting your hair seem pretty drastic, but really? They can be undone in a heartbeat. If you don't like the earrings, take them out! And your hair is going to grow."

He sighed. "Thanks, Max."

"No problem! Thanks for letting me be a part of it! I'm practically having a joygasm just thinking about how awesome this is going to be!"

"Joygasm?" Ryan laughed.

"Oh yeah. It's my word of the week! It's like the real thing except no men need be directly involved."

Ryan looked at his friend, quizzically. "Ha! You've always got men involved." When Max didn't immediately respond Ryan considered a minute. Actually, Max hadn't mentioned anyone in a while. "Who are you seeing now, anyways?"

Max shook his head vehemently while still keeping his eyes firmly on the road. "Nope. Not seeing anyone at the moment."

"Oh, come on! I don't believe that for a minute!"

"Well, there's someone I'd *like* to be seeing."

"And the problem is—"

"He just hasn't figured it out yet, Mister." He grinned at Ryan and winked. "How about some music?" He turned on the radio, and Céline Dion started into the first chorus of 'The Power of Love.' He looked at Ryan again and said, "I just love her."

Ryan giggled. "Me too, but you already know that."

A few minutes later they arrived at the hair salon Max had selected. While the hairdresser washed Ryan's hair and massaged his head, Max read through an outdated copy of People Magazine. But the moment it came time for the actual cutting to commence he watched, transfixed.

Ryan's hair had been on the longish side since his senior year in high school. There were only a few people that knew him now who'd ever seen his hair short. He couldn't help but feel self-conscious as the damp, dark curls fell like rain onto the floor, because Max's eyes studied the process so intensely. When it was done, he hardly recognized himself. His hair was cropped close around the sides of his head, and on top, the hairdresser had constructed a set of soft, messy peaks that looked less like hair and more like architecture.

Max whistled. "Wow-ee, Mister! You look—"

"Hot?" The hairdresser finished with a grin. She smiled proudly and then pointed her finger squarely at Ryan. "Now, don't you *ever* let your hair get that long again. I want to see you back here in four weeks, honey, or else!"

Ryan grinned, and Max assured her that he'd be back, even if Max had to kidnap him. They left the salon and got back into the car.

When they arrived at the piercing parlor, Ryan discovered he was far more terrified than he thought he'd be. "I don't know if I can actually do this!" he groaned as they walked up to the door.

Max squeezed his hand. "Sure you can! I'll be right next to you."

Inside, a thin, heavily tattooed woman stood behind a glass display case containing hundreds of earrings of various styles and materials. "Good afternoon, gentlemen," she said. "How can I help you?"

Ryan hesitated, suddenly overwhelmed. Max pushed him gently forward and said, "This one wants to get his ears pierced."

The woman raised her eyebrows and smiled. "By the look on your face, I'm guessing you're a virgin." Ryan choked, and the woman laughed. "To piercing, I mean."

"Um," he sputtered. "Yeah, first time."

"Okay, well it's not going to be that bad. Why don't you start by picking a pair?" She indicated a corner of the case. "These here are fourteen gauge. I think that's a good place to start."

With Max's assistance, he selected a pair—steel rings with a small black ball—and the woman led him to a chair. He gripped Max's hand tightly as he felt a sharp pinch in his right earlobe.

"Are you okay?" Max asked. "You're halfway done."

The woman nodded. "Yeah, you're doing great. One more." She moved to his other side and before he could brace himself there was another sharp pinch.

He caught his breath. "Was that it?"

The woman laughed. "Well, now I just need your money." She eyed them coyly as she led them to the counter. "You know, you two are really cute together."

Max chuckled. Ryan blushed as he handed her his debit card. He was too embarrassed to tell her that they weren't a couple.

A few minutes after four, Max pulled into the parking lot behind The Garden. Ryan asked him if he'd like to come up, and he agreed. Once inside the apartment, Jay met them with a cry of "Holy shit!" and Mark made a vulgar cat call. Ryan smiled and exchanged pleasantries—knowing he'd been paid a pair of high compliments—before leading Max into his bedroom.

He stepped into the adjacent bathroom to look in the mirror.

Max followed, and over Ryan's shoulder said "You look absolutely stunning, Mister. People aren't even going to believe it when they see you tomorrow."

Ryan grinned. "I know." Indeed, he was delightfully surprised by the image reflected in the mirror. His face, which he'd always felt was too round, looked thinner. He enjoyed seeing his cheekbones and his ears—so long covered or detracted from by the mop of his unruly hair. Now his face looked pristine. He lightly touched the sculpture of hair on top of his head and said, "I don't know if I can recreate this."

Max put a hand on his shoulder. "Sure you can. You saw her do it, and you bought a jar of the stuff she put in it. It'll take a little practice, but you'll be fine."

Ryan turned around and gave Max a long, tight hug. "Thank you for taking me around today." He let go and walked back into the bedroom, where he plucked the phone off the nightstand and dialed his voicemail.

No new messages.

"Is there something wrong?"

He frowned and sat on the edge of his bed. "Yeah. I mean, it's nothing really. Darren hasn't called me back today, and I've left him a couple of messages."

"I hate that. Did you two have plans?"

"Sort of. He's supposed to come over tonight and help set up for tomorrow—prep some food things."

"I wouldn't worry about it too much. He's probably had a busy day, or maybe he just forgot his phone at home this morning."

"You're right."

"Hey, I have to get ready to go to dinner with my roommates. We'll probably be done by eight, so if you need some help after that—if he still hasn't called you back—I can come over."

"Thanks. I'll let you know." Then Max left, and Ryan dialed Darren again. There was still no answer, and he was starting to worry.

~*~

At six there was a knock on the bedroom door. Ryan was sitting at the keyboard constructing a melody, but hearing it, he stopped abruptly and sighed with relief. *Darren,* he thought, *finally.* "Come in," he called.

When the door opened it was Steven who stepped inside—his face long and his eyes darting around the room. "Darren isn't here?"

Ryan's stomach dropped through the floor. He swallowed hard and felt an eternity pass in the time it took his Adam's apple to move from the top of his throat to the bottom. He coughed a little and then said in a voice just above a whisper, "No. Have you heard from him?" Steven's face grew darker still. More loudly, Ryan continued. "Oh, what's going on? Why do you look like that?"

Steven shook his head slowly back and forth. "No one has heard from him. I was sure he'd be here but—"

Ryan stood up and rushed past Steven to the telephone. He dialed his voicemail hoping that somehow he'd missed a call while he was playing, or when he'd stepped out to use the bathroom. His heart lifted when the electronic voice declared he had one new voicemail and then sank again when the voice on the recording was Steven's. *Is Darren there?* He hung up the phone and looked at his friend. "What do you mean no one has heard from him?"

Steven sighed and sat at the edge of the bed, looking out the windows. "He had two shifts at the LGBT office today—he picked one up in the morning, and then had his regular shift in the afternoon. When he missed the first one, the office director assumed he overslept. But when he missed the second one—"

Ryan's voice caught in his throat, but he managed to squeak, "He missed the second one too?"

"Yeah," Steven said. "And then the director made some calls. He missed his classes today, also. I was there at the time. I told him I was sure Darren would be with you. I called, and when you didn't answer I came right over—"

Pressing his hand to his forehead, Ryan closed his eyes. He suddenly realized he was sitting on the floor and wasn't sure how he got there. Steven's hand came to rest gently on his shoulder. "What're we going to do?" Ryan asked of no one in particular.

"I think we should call the police."

Ryan thought about it for a moment. "No." He was surprised by the resolution in his voice. Turning his face up toward Steven he asked, "Did you drive here?"

"I did."

"Then we need to go to his house. Maybe he just freaked out and needed a day to himself. He's been struggling with some things." Steven's eyes grew large and panicked, and Ryan amended. "No, no. Nothing like that. Darren would never hurt himself." Even as he said the words, a trickle of uncertainty broke through the dam of his belief. Darren had been acting strangely.

"Are you sure?"

Ryan stood. "Yes. Come on, we'd better go."

The night was bitingly cold. Steven started the car, and a tense silence settled over the vehicle as he drove through eerily deserted streets toward Darren's apartment. It was Friday night in a college town, and there should have been more cars on the road. Ryan distracted himself from his growing fear by considering reasons for the apparent desolation—it was too early for students to be out, or it was too cold. Beyond the foggy windows of the car, small banks of dirty snow lined the streets like spectators watching a funeral procession—alternating in color between orange and blue, reflecting street lights and the glow from the moon respectively. Traffic lights slowed their progress, turning red one after another in a clear attempt to spite them. The journey of no more than two miles seemed to disregard time to such an extent that when Steven pulled into the Admiral's Park complex, Ryan didn't know if it had taken ten minutes or two hours.

"Go to the left," Ryan said.

Steven jumped at the sound. "Okay?"

"Building M." Ryan pointed. His spirit swelled a bit as he said, "Darren's car is here. At least we know he didn't run off, right?"

Steven tried ineffectually to laugh as he guided the car into an empty spot beside Darren's grey '92 Subaru. He turned off the engine and turned to look at Ryan. Swallowing hard, he said, "He'd better be there, or I'm going to kill him when we find him." Both boys looked up through the windshield toward Darren's apartment on the second floor. The windows were dark except for a blue glow coming from Darren's room.

Ryan shook his head and forced a smile. "He's there—has to be. We're going to walk up the stairs to the second floor, ring his doorbell, and he's going to answer. Then I'm going to rain hell-fire down on the little asshole for scaring us like this!"

Steven laughed in spite of himself. "Language, Mister Gregori! Where'd you learn to have such a foul mouth?"

"I prefer to save the expletives for when I really mean them." He opened his door and stepped into the night. Steven followed, and Ryan led him up the stairwell on the outside of Building M to apartment 201. "Here goes!" he said, before looking squarely at Steven, and pressing the doorbell.

A minute went by, and there was no answer. This was not the result he had hoped for. He'd convinced himself that Darren would be inside, just waiting for them to come by. The alternative—the idea that something was truly amiss—was so awful that he hadn't allowed it to fully form in his mind. He felt panic grip his heart and begin to constrict his throat as he pressed the doorbell repeatedly. The panic worsened. He gasped for air and started pounding on the door, first with one fist and then with both. The effect rang through the freezing night air like a desperate, plaintive tribal beat and still, there was no answer. His vision swam with tears as he pounded with greater force. The panic overwhelmed him, and the real world started slipping away. He felt as though he was merging with the night.

Then a hand pulled him back. Steven wrapped his arms tightly around Ryan's middle and whispered unintelligibly in his ear.

"No!" Ryan sobbed. "Let go! Let me go!"

Steven shook him. "Ryan!" he said, more forcefully. "Someone is coming. Didn't you hear her?"

He quieted immediately, and sure enough, on the other side of the door he heard the exasperated voice of a woman—a girl, Darren's roommate Emily. The muffled, muttering voice was accompanied by the sounds of entry—deadbolts clicking back, chains sliding off their tracks—and then the door opened.

Emily was very short and thin, barely clearing five feet, but her presence in the open doorway was palpable. She glared at him and said, "The building had better be on fire, Ryan! I was sleeping!"

From behind him, Steven said, "It's not even seven yet."

Emily put her hands firmly on her hips and stood on tip-toes to scowl back at Steven. "I have almost a double course load, so I sleep when I can." She returned her gaze to Ryan, and he could feel her anger fall instantly away. His face was drawn and he knew she could see the lines of tears streaked across his face. "Oh my God." She said. "What's wrong?"

"Is Darren here?" Ryan asked, barely controlling the quaver in his voice.

She looked backwards as if she expected to see him. "No. I haven't seen him all day."

"I need to come in." Pushing past her before she had time to move out of the way, Ryan rushed into the apartment and down a small hallway to Darren's room. The door was closed, and when he tried to turn the knob, he found it locked. Feeling adrenaline course over-whelmingly through his veins he backed up slowly. Turning his shoulder toward the door, he prepared to ram it.

"Wait!" Steven cried. Ryan felt his friend's hand again, and his heart nearly burst as the energy driving him forward was suddenly bottled, leaving his muscles to absorb the impact meant for the door. Steven pulled out his wallet and retrieved a library card. Vaguely in the background, Ryan heard Emily's voice on a telephone, giving her address. Steven knelt in front of the door and looked back at Ryan. He smiled weakly. "Believe it or not I know how to do this." Seconds went by as Steven moved the card between the door and its frame. There was a click, and the door swung open and inward.

Later, Ryan would wish he had waited on the other side of the door a few moments longer. Stepping through it, he was like Lewis Carrol's Alice, through a looking glass. He would wish he'd taken the time to relish the place he'd been, because once through he could never go back again. But in the moment, he did not wait. He did not step gingerly through the looking glass as Alice would have done, but instead went barreling through like a brick, leaving nothing but shards of his former life in his wake.

The room was dark except for the blue glow—an aquarium screen saver on the monitor of Darren's computer in the corner of the room. Ryan did not immediately turn on the light because there was no need, he could see him. Darren was in his computer chair, but as Ryan looked, he realized that was not exactly right. Darren wasn't *in* the computer chair. He was collapsed backward over it. One of his legs had lifted and was caught under the desk in front of him, and part of his back still rested on the seat, but his upper body draped down until his head nearly touched the ground. Both of his arms extended above him and his hands rested palm up on the carpeted floor. As Ryan looked at his face—mouth and eyes wide open—he could tell, even in the dark, there was something wrong with his skin.

Behind him, Steven flipped the light switch before letting out a sound like he was being strangled. Ryan could feel his heart racing, and forced himself to breathe deeply as he examined the scene again. He saw Darren's cell phone sitting next to his computer keyboard. It had been easily within reach. Then he looked again at his friend. His face was purple—a milky, deep lilac—and a congealing mixture of blood dripped—more black than crimson—from his mouth onto the carpet below. Hours of being in this position had caused the blood in his body to seek the lowest points, no longer moving under the direction of a beating heart. The pressure must have ruptured something inside, and now the fluid that once animated him leaked out, threatening a slow and steady exsanguination.

Emily entered the room while crying into the phone. "Okay, I can do CPR I think. I just have to push, right? And breathe? Ryan!" He turned to look at her, with the receiver pressed against her ear. "We have to get him on the ground."

It seemed ludicrous, but maybe there was a chance. He moved forward and gripped Darren's hand. The skin felt cold and gummy, and he forced himself not to recoil. Steeling himself, he pulled forcefully, and the body gave barely an inch. It was stiff and unyielding, and he let go. He exhaled and turned to Emily, letting the reality wash over him. Shaking his head slowly he said, "It's too late, Emily."

"Ryan!" she screamed. "You have to get him on the ground! You have to—"

"Emily!" he screamed back. Her eyes widened, and he continued more softly. "Emily. I teach CPR as part of my job. He's gone. Just tell them to get someone here fast. Please." Amazed by the composure in his voice, he gripped whatever strength he had left and walked slowly out of the bedroom.

Steven followed. Ryan sat on the couch in the living room, and it wasn't until Steven was seated beside him, holding his hand, that he could feel the river of tears building behind his eyes. He looked at his friend and said, "Steven, you have to promise me something."

"Anything," Steven said, holding back his own tears.

"You have to promise me that we won't become victims of this. This is the kind of thing that could really—" he didn't finish.

Steven blinked and replied, "Okay." Then they cried.

~*~

The following hours were a blur. Police came. There were photographs to be taken and reports to fill out. When a nice female officer asked Ryan to write a statement, he could barely write his name. He stared blankly at the sterile police form for twenty minutes until finally the officer returned and offered to write it for him. He gave a confused dictation of the events leading up to the discovery of Darren's body, and then Ryan, Steven and Emily were escorted out of the apartment so that the coroner could prepare to move the corpse. On the way out the door, Ryan asked if he could call Darren's parents, and the officer told him it was being taken care of. Steven made a couple of phone calls with his cell phone, but Ryan was too dazed to pay attention to who he was talking to.

The manager of the apartment complex was contacted, and arranged a room at a nearby hotel for Emily to stay in for the night. After a brief and otherwise useless chat with a pair of police-commissioned grief counselors in the Admiral's Park office, Emily went on her way, and Ryan and Steven returned to the car. The clock said it was half past nine, and they rode in absolute silence, still crying quietly, all the way back to the parking lot behind The Garden.

At a quarter to ten, as they walked up the steps to the apartment door, Steven said, "I made a few calls. I thought you might not like to be alone tonight. I know I don't want to be."

Ryan nodded that it was fine, and he no sooner opened the door than Max ran forward from the kitchen and threw his arms around him.

"Oh, Mister—" Max began. But he didn't finish because Ryan buried his head in his shoulder and started to sob uncontrollably again.

After composing himself, Ryan walked through the short hallway past the kitchen and into the dining area. He sat on the floor, and

Steven and Max sat beside him. More phone calls were made, and by the time the clock reached eleven, there were ten bodies seated in a circle on the floor. Quietly, Ryan began to give his account of the evening's events. He spoke slowly, but no one pressed him to hurry. If he forgot a vital piece of information, Steven gently stopped him and filled in the missing details.

Then the story was done, and he shuddered. He hated that he already thought of it as just a story—something that could have happened to somebody else. The pain ebbed for a moment and was replaced by a calm detachment. He kept looking at the hallway off the kitchen, expecting Darren to walk through it at any time. But he knew it wouldn't happen. This was just denial; the beginning; the first stage of grief.

Ryan's mother arrived around midnight. He wasn't sure who called her, but he was glad beyond words when she held him. He did not retell the story, but simply held on, silently.

When the others left, Max offered to stay behind. He tucked Ryan into bed. Holding his hand, he said, "I'm going to stay here tonight, Mister. I'll be sleeping on the futon in the living room if you need anything."

Ryan squeezed his hand tightly and whimpered, "No. Please stay with me." So Max pulled up the covers and slid beneath them. He and Ryan lay on their sides, and Max held him tightly until Ryan fell into a fitful sleep.

CHAPTER 6

When Ryan opened his eyes, he was in the little red bedroom at Elizabeth Street again. Through the skylight overhead, a soft reddish-peach hue cast the room in a warm light. He basked in it as he stretched—the golden moments of gloaming—and wondered what time it was. In a few minutes either the day would ripen to the full brilliance of morning or descend into the darker violets and cobalts of the coming night. It didn't matter; at the moment he was happy, and the light was a gift.

He placed his feet on the warm wood floor and stood, stretching again. Then he pulled on a pair of shorts and a shirt and walked out of the bedroom, down the short hall, and into the living room beyond.

Everything was as he remembered it—the rubber tree and the pothos, the deep grey overstuffed furniture and the large mirror over the sofa. The wooden blinds were open, and more of the beautiful pink light spilled through the windows and the skylight above, bathing everything in its exquisite, marshmallow-soft hues. The room was love and security, and he was here again! It didn't matter how. Everything was perfect, except—

He felt the hairs raise on the back of his neck. There was an odor. Something like—gasoline. A sound in the kitchen caught his attention—liquid hitting the tile floor. He walked toward the door and caught his breath.

Darren stood, smiling sadly with a red plastic gas can held to his chest. He sighed and swung it forward, dousing the walls of the kitchen. Looking directly at Ryan he shook his head slowly. "I'm sorry, Ryan. You should go."

"Darren! What are you doing?"

"I'm sorry. It has to be done."

Ryan rushed forward and reached for the gas can, but Darren deftly evaded him and moved into the living room, swinging his arms and dousing the gasoline as he went. He swung wide, turning in a full circle, wetting the walls and the floor. Then he moved to the sofa and poured hard, saturating the cushions. Ryan caught his shoulder and pulled him back, but it was too late.

The gas can fell to the floor, empty.

Darren turned and looked at him again. There were tears in his eyes as he folded his hands and began to fidget with his thumb ring. "Ryan," he said. "Please go. Please, just go."

Ryan grabbed the inside of his elbow and started pulling him toward the front door. "Why did you *do* this? Come on; we need to get out of here."

Darren shook himself away. "No. Sorry." He pulled a book of matches from his pocket. "Please. Go."

Ryan advanced again, but Darren placed a hand on his chest and pushed hard, shoving him away. He lit a match and tossed it onto the sofa. With a mighty *whoosh* the cushions roared aflame. The fire spread with supernatural speed, climbing up the back of the sofa and catching the places on the wall that Darren had doused.

"Darren!" Ryan cried. The fire was still climbing, already licking the ceiling with its serpent tongues of flame. "Darren! Let's go!"

Darren shook his head one more time, more sadly than before, then laid down on the sofa and let himself be engulfed by the flames.

"Darren!"

There was a feeling of wet lips on his forehead and a voice saying "Mister?" He opened his eyes and Max kissed him again, directly above his left eyebrow. "Oh, Ryan. It's only a dream." He turned his head groggily to the left and found his pillow was wet with tears.

Sitting up, he asked, "Where am I?"

"You're at home, safe and sound."

According to the alarm clock, it was a quarter to eight in the morning. He blinked several times and then looked at Max, laying on his back. "So, it all really happened? Darren really—"

Max didn't speak, instead turning his lips into a compassionate smile. Ryan felt something well up inside him. As Max lay there, with his piercing blue eyes—devoid of glasses—and candy-apple red hair disheveled by sleep, Ryan was sure he'd never seen someone so beautiful. He felt an unexpected urge to feel Max's lips pressing against his own. He wanted desperately to lean forward and taste them.

But then he thought of Darren and remembered why Max was here. As quickly as the urge had come, it was gone.

He climbed out of bed still fully clothed and walked into his little bathroom to wash his face. When he came back out again, Max had left the bedroom, and Ryan heard noise from the kitchen. When he moved into the dining area to investigate, Max was behind the kitchen peninsula getting the coffee pot ready. He began weeping again and forced himself to say, "Stop!"

Max turned with a filter in his hand. "What's wrong, Mister?"

"Not today. I couldn't stand coffee today."

"Alright." Max started to make a pot of oatmeal instead. Shortly after the water he'd set on the stove began to boil, he said, "Oh!"

Ryan—sitting at the dining table—looked up from his thoughts. "What?"

"What do you plan to do about the party tonight?"

In the chaos, Ryan had completely forgotten. He groaned. "Oh no! How could I even consider it?" Suddenly he felt overwhelmed. His voice quavered as he said "Oh Max, how am I supposed to call all those people and tell them it's off? I'm going to have to explain over and over—"

Max left the cereal to thicken on the stove and wrapped Ryan in a tight embrace. "Alright, alright now. Just breathe." He was quiet for a moment. "You know, you could still have it. I'm sure most of the people coming already know about last night—these things spread like wildfire." Ryan shuddered at the reference. "People are going to want to come together—to grieve. It might as well be here, right?"

Ryan considered. "I don't know. I see what you're saying, but I'm in no condition to be a host."

Max guffawed. "I don't think you could be a bad host if you tried. But if that's all you're worried about, I can help out. I'm sure Steven will want to play a big part too—he was there, after all. Between the three of us, I really think we could do it."

Ryan chewed his lip for a moment. The last thing he needed was a party, but he also knew he didn't want to be alone. Finally, he sighed. "Alright."

"Alright."

When the phone rang toward the end of breakfast, Ryan was relieved to be distracted from the meal. Even though Max had only given him a small bowl—complete with brown sugar and cinnamon—he barely managed to eat a quarter of it. Now it looked up at him, defiant and cold, sticking together like modeling clay. He answered with a quiet "Hello?"

"Ryan? It's Alice, honey." Her voice was unsteady. In the background, he heard the low rumble of the interstate. "I heard that you found—" her breathing turned heavy and she couldn't finish the sentence.

There were so many things he wanted to say, but his lips couldn't form the words. He wanted to tell Alice how sorry he was, and how much he loved her son. He wanted to say he regretted he didn't see it coming—that Darren hadn't looked worse when he left on Thursday night because he might have stopped him. He wanted to express how deeply he hurt and to tell her it was his fault, even though it couldn't have been. But he said nothing. Instead, he focused on his breathing. On the other end of the line, hers slowed down, and he knew she understood all of it without hearing a word.

"Honey?" she said, momentarily composed. "Honey, John is driving us up right now. Do you think I can come and see you? Are you working today?"

"No, I'm not working," he said. "I'll be at home when you get here." The question struck him as odd. He hadn't even considered work yet. Even if today hadn't been his day off, there was no way he would've been able to go. The pain inside him was screaming, and he wasn't sure he could ever go to work again.

"Alright, honey." She swallowed a sob. "We'll be there in about forty-five minutes."

Ryan hung up the phone and looked at Max. "Darren's parents are coming over. They're probably going to have questions."

Sighing, Max replied, "Wow. Are you going to be okay with that?"

"I think so."

"Do you want me to be here?"

Ryan thought for a moment. "No, you don't have to be. You've already done so much for me, Max." He felt a warmth blossom in his cheeks as he realized the truth of the statement.

Max smiled. "Alright. When they get here I'm going to go home, take a shower, and pick up some clean clothes. Then I'll come right back here so you don't have to be alone. Does that sound alright?"

"Yes. Yes it does."

The doorbell rang a short while later. Max grabbed his keys and gave Ryan a quick hug, then let Alice and John into the apartment on his way out. Ryan rose from the dining table and met Alice in the kitchen. John was right behind her. She was dressed in a bright floral blouse covered by a thin teal jacket, and comfortably loose, dark brown pants. Bright, chunky beaded jewelry hung loosely around her neck with pieces of turquoise, hematite, and glazed terra cotta strung throughout. Large but elegant silver hoops hung from her ears, and her voluminous hair was as expertly coiffed as anytime Ryan had ever seen her. The overall effect was joyous and light, with a touch of eccentricity, so it was only her face that betrayed the turmoil raging inside.

She wrapped her arms tightly around him, and neither spoke, choosing instead to cry softly and let the chemical rush of their mutual grief bind them together. He clung to her because she was the mother—the one who'd brought Darren into the world. She clung to him because her son was gone, and in that moment Ryan was the closest thing tying her to the world in which he had lived. In truth, they were practically strangers, having met only a handful of times before, but by the time they disengaged from one another, they'd become something very different.

Family.

After taking a seat at the little dining set, Alice rested an elbow on the table and breathed deeply. After a short time, she looked at Ryan with tears in her eyes. "They're saying they think it's cocaine?" As she said this last word, her head rolled in an exaggerated circle.

Ryan looked surprised. "What?" The idea was at once ludicrous and completely plausible. He remembered the sunken eyes and the sudden bursts of energy and reanimation. It would also explain why he hadn't seen it coming. Drugs were an alien concept to him—even alcohol had been a mystery until recently. He'd never have suspected—*didn't* ever suspect—something like cocaine.

"The police told us they found a bag of white powder and all the other things too—a little mirror and razor blades—"

"I can't believe—"

Alice pushed away from the table and threw her hands in the air. She rose and started pacing. "How stupid could he be?! He knew I didn't care if he experimented a little bit. Hell, I did some ridiculous things when I was his age." She stopped pacing and looked at Ryan. "Did he ever tell you he had a weak heart?"

Ryan shook his head. "No."

"He was born several weeks premature. Nowadays that wouldn't matter, but in the early eighties—"

John cut in. "We were just lucky to get him home. He turned out to be a healthy kid, but his doctor told us there'd always be a little damage."

Alice sat back down and continued. "I wouldn't say *damage*. It wasn't like that." She composed her voice to the best of her ability. "He could exercise all he wanted—that was good for him. But he had to be—careful."

"Okay."

"I mean, marijuana, that would be one thing." Her face turned from neutral to irate. "But cocaine? Do you have any idea what that does to your heart? Hell, if he needed something to, I don't know—cope? John and I would've paid for an *unlimited* supply of marijuana. Pot hasn't ever killed anybody provided they used it responsibly."

Ryan felt uncomfortable. "I'm sorry, Alice. I should've seen something. I should've known—"

Her face softened. She reached out and placed her hand on his and said, "I'm sorry, honey. Darren always had this secretive side. For as friendly and outgoing and *open* as he was there were things he wouldn't even tell *me* about. And I'm not exactly the most judgmental of mothers." After a moment, she asked, "Are you doing okay?"

His eyes welled up with tears again, but not because of Darren—not directly. He was moved beyond measure as he considered what a strong and wonderful woman Alice Henderson was. After losing her only son, he couldn't believe she had it in her to ask how *he* was doing. "I don't know," he said. "I really don't."

She touched the corners of his eyes gently with her fingers. "Let it out, honey. Trust me, none of us have even begun to cry all the tears we'll shed by the time this is over. We'll be staying up here for a few days to make preparations. We need to talk a little bit about memorial services, and I know Darren would want you to be involved."

~*~

Alice and John left The Garden at noon, having to meet with a funeral director a half hour later. It was decided that there would be two memorial services—one at the University tailored mostly toward Darren's friends, and a more private family service the day after in Denver. In the few minutes Ryan had to himself before Max returned, he called and checked in with his mother. He assured her that he was coping—at least for the moment—and then called Cara at work. She was shocked to hear the news, and before Ryan could ask, she offered to cover his shifts for the next week.

When Max returned around one o'clock, Ryan was thankful for the company. Steven was in tow, looking drawn and tired, and Ryan briefly wondered if anyone had stayed with him last night. He felt a sharp stab of guilt as he realized he didn't even know at what point Steven had left. Tonight, he assured himself, he'd do better to make sure Steven was taken care of.

Between intermittent bursts of tears—mostly Ryan's—the boys spent the afternoon chopping vegetables and cubing cheese. The prep seemed to take forever, but he was thankful for the distraction.

When Jay and Mark walked through the door just after three, Ryan was surprised to see them. He realized with a sudden discomfort that Steven's whereabouts last night weren't the only blank in his memory. Had he seen his roommates?

Jay approached him first. "Hey man, you look like a zombie. You were pretty out of it last night when we came home. Your friend Max here told us—" he was quiet for a moment. "Aw, shit! How are you holding up, man?"

Ryan pushed the cutting board he'd been working with off to the side. He'd chopped a small mountain of fresh broccoli, and as the board moved, a few rebellious florets leaped for the ground. He looked at his roommate. "I'm doing alright."

"You're still having your party tonight, yeah?"

Ryan smiled weakly. "I wasn't sure at first, but I think it's important. People need a place to grieve." He opened his arms to indicate both the space and the bowls of fruits, vegetables and cheeses he and the other boys had already prepared. "Plus, I had all this food, right?"

In an uncommonly intimate gesture, Jay placed his hand on Ryan's shoulder. "You're a good man, Ryan." He turned to Mark. "Dude, do you want to come over here?"

Mark walked over slowly. In each of his hands, he held a gallon jug of wine—one sangria, the other merlot. He hefted them onto an empty space on the counter and said, "These are for you, dude. We're not gonna be around tonight, but we wanted to contribute." He extended his hand and Ryan shook it.

"Thanks, guys."

Guests were due around seven, so shortly before five, Max encouraged Ryan and Steven to nap. His head barely touched the pillow, and suddenly it was six thirty and Max was waking him again.

Little by little the guests arrived. Each, in turn, paid their condolences to Ryan as though he was a widower, and it touched him that so many people understood the depth of affection he had for his departed friend. By eight, almost everyone had arrived, and in spite of the circumstances, the apartment held an unexpected atmosphere of levity. The occasion retained traces of its somber core, but the guests' countless amusing stories of Darren's exploits slowly and surely drowned the underlying sadness in a sea of laughter.

Shortly after nine, over the soft roar of conversation, Ryan heard the doorbell ring. It was odd—the door was unlocked, and all the other guests had known to walk in. He extricated himself politely from his companions and walked down the short hall from the kitchen to the front door.

Brandon waited on the other side.

Shocked, he stepped out onto the wide deck and closed the door behind him. The bitter wind howled—winter was refusing to give way to the impending spring—and pulled his arms in tight to his chest. Brandon was wrapped warmly in a pea coat, scarf and hat. He didn't look happy. Indeed, even in the dark Ryan could see that his eyes were tired and red.

After a moment of silence, Brandon spoke. "I heard from some people at the LGBT office that you were—" he trailed off. "Oh, shit. I'm sure I'm probably the last person you expected to see here tonight."

Ryan was suddenly furious. "Yes. I'm kind of wondering what you're doing here. The last time I saw you, you completely humiliated me. I think you should probably go." He started to turn back toward his door.

"Wait!" Brandon exclaimed. Ryan turned to face him again. There was anger in the other boy's eyes. "How could you say that to me— tell me to get lost? I have a right to mourn too."

"Yeah? Well, mourn elsewhere. You hardly even knew Darren— except maybe what it felt like between his legs."

Brandon deflated. "Hardly knew him?" He started to pace. "Ryan, I also came here to apologize to you for that." He shook his head. "Hardly knew him? I guess he didn't tell you after all."

Ryan's eyes grew wide. He was shaking from the cold. "Tell me what?"

Brandon stopped moving, and Ryan could see his eyes were wet. "Darren and I have been dating since right before Christmas." Ryan said nothing, so Brandon continued. "At first it was just hooking up— he'd come over late at night. It was simple. We probably should have left it that way."

"I don't believe this," Ryan said, under his breath.

"Well, you need to hear it."

"Why? So you can humiliate me again?"

Brandon shook his head. "No. Just hear me out. It was supposed to stay simple. Darren didn't want to get involved for some reason, but the more I saw him, the more I started to want something—more. I was tired of only seeing him late at night—really late. Anytime I'd try to get him to spend some real time with me he'd just make up some excuse. By the end of January, I'd had it. I told him I felt like he was keeping me a secret—like he was ashamed, or something."

A light clicked in Ryan's head. "Was he with you on February first?"

"Yeah. I told him if he wouldn't see me in the light of day, I was done. So we spent the day together." He turned his head slightly. "Why did you think of February first?"

Ryan's face was flush with anger. He didn't feel the cold anymore. "He was supposed to help me move in here. He didn't return my calls all day."

Brandon sighed. "Well, I'm sorry for that, too. Of course, I didn't know. I thought things were going to get better after that, but then it just went back to how it was before—only seeing me late at night. I didn't understand who, or what he was hiding me from. Then Valentine's Day was coming up. I wanted to take him for a romantic night on the town, but he said he had that stupid party to go to. I tried to convince him that he could miss *one* party—it was Valentine's Day! Finally I caved, but told him I was going to go too. He got so angry—"

Ryan was crying. "Please, stop. I don't want to hear about this anymore. I really can't stand—"

"No, Ryan. You're missing the point."

"The point? The point is that he chose you over me and never even bothered to tell me about it. What did he think I was going to do? Instead of just being honest, he let me run all over the place professing my love and looking like a total idiot."

"No," Brandon continued. His voice was deceptively calm, but Ryan could see tears freezing as they streaked across his face. "That isn't the point at all."

"God, what an asshole! I can't believe he did this to me. I can't believe—"

Brandon's face tightened in anger, and he shouted, "Can you just shut the fuck up for a minute!" He paused. When he continued, his voice had calmed but still retained a sharp edge of anger. "I understand that you're upset—that you had this idea of a relationship with him that's turning out to be untrue. I'm sure that's hard, but can you step back and look at it from my perspective for a minute? Do you have any idea how I feel? I loved him too, you know. I loved him, and I had to hear third hand that he died. You've got all these people around you right now telling you everything is going to be all right, and where am I? I'm left in the fucking shadows again."

Ryan swallowed. "Brandon, I'm sorry, I—"

"Sometimes I wonder if it wasn't you he really loved, and that hurts even more. See, when I went to that *fucking* party, I thought he'd told people. I thought everyone knew we were seeing each other. Sure, my behavior was a little bit vulgar, and I regret that, but I wasn't trying to hurt you. You weren't even a thought in my mind. I was just so happy I didn't have to hide anymore. But the truth is, I backed him into a corner and didn't even know it. When you rushed out the door and Max went after you? That's when I understood everything." He closed his eyes and pressed his fingers lightly against the lids. "I waited until the party was over, but then we had a huge fight. I told him I didn't want to see him anymore until he told people the truth. I was hoping we'd get back together, because I really cared about him, and we started to make up about a week later, but then—"

"But then time ran out," Ryan said, softly.

Brandon walked forward and put his arms around Ryan, who was shivering now more than ever. "I'm really sorry, Ryan. I don't know what was in his head that kept the two of you from being—more than friends. I also don't know why he couldn't tell you about us. Right now I feel like I was never more than an afterthought. Can't we just have a truce? I'm sure seeing me hurts you, but can't we hurt together?"

Ryan let Brandon hold him for a few seconds longer and then said, "I'm sorry I judged you so harshly without—knowing the facts. This feeling I have right now—knowing everything you just told me—is worse than anything. I think it hurts even more than the knowledge that he's—"

"No. Don't. You don't have to—"

Ryan swallowed again. "But I know it's not your fault." He pushed away and forced a smile. "You'd better come inside. It's really fucking cold tonight."

~*~

After the party ended, Max and Steven stayed the night. Ryan slept peacefully without dreaming, and when he woke the next morning, he felt rested. He was still upset by his conversation with Brandon, but in the end, he realized he was going to have to let it go. Darren had loved him, albeit strangely, and that was how he wanted to remember things. Max made coffee and oatmeal, and after breakfast Ryan told him it was alright if he and Steven went home—he wanted a little time to himself.

Alone for the first time in nearly forty-eight hours, he sat quietly on his bed. With his eyes closed, he allowed his mind to swim through the memories and painful emotions of the past year. The love and loss, the betrayal and forgiveness—all of them washed over him less like scenes in a movie and more like bursts of vibrant color and mellow greys.

When he opened his eyes again, he looked instinctively toward the keyboard against the wall. It drew him off the bed, and when he sat down and switched it on, he was surprised he hadn't thought to do it sooner.

He set the patch to 'Slow Strings' and held a chord with his left hand—F major, the IV chord in the key of C. It was his favorite. Then he moved to A minor, the vi chord, and back again. He repeated the chords, and then with his right hand, he laid a mournful melody atop. He grabbed a notebook filled with staff paper out of his desk drawer and wrote it down. With undaunted confidence, his fingers returned to the keys and he let the music flow through him, pausing from time to time to transcribe the work. Each note he committed to paper raised his spirits a little higher. Hours passed, uninterrupted, and when he finished, he played the entire piece all the way through and cried. At the top of the first page of staff paper, he wrote the title. Elegy.

~*~

Alice called late in the afternoon. Darren was set to be cremated the next morning, Monday, and she and John had set up times for the two memorial services. The one at the University would take place on Thursday in a lovely old stone reception hall converted from a hundred-year-old girls' dormitory. The service in Denver would take place the following day.

After the necessary details were relayed, Alice asked, "Honey? We're going to head over to Admiral's Park now to start cleaning out Darren's room. Is there anything there that you might like? Most of it I think we'll donate, but we wanted you to be able to keep anything you think is important."

Ryan considered the question seriously for a minute and then said, "I don't even know. I'm sure there is some memento—" he paused. Then it struck him. "Alice, do you think I could have Darren's thumb ring? It's just a cheap little thing he found some-where but—"

"I know exactly what you're talking about. Absolutely you can have it, honey."

"Do you—think you need some help?"

"Oh, Ryan, we wouldn't dream of burdening you."

"It's no burden. It would probably be good for me to get out of the house and it might help me—process."

"Well, we'd love it, honey. We'll come by and pick you up."

It was already dark by the time they reached Admiral's Park, and Ryan shuddered inwardly as they walked up the flight of steps to apartment 201. This is where everything had changed, and his life as he knew it had ended. As John fit the key into the lock, Ryan wondered if it had been a good idea to come here after all.

The door opened, and he and Alice followed John inside. Light switches were flipped on—Emily had not returned because the manager of the complex moved her permanently to another unit—and John went back to the car to retrieve a stack of folded self-assembly boxes. Alice and Ryan started in the kitchenette, placing in groups the items they felt belonged together. As he handled blenders, silverware, plates and bowls, he wished he could *feel* them more. The objects out of context were meaningless. He had expected an electric rush of connection as he handled Darren's things, and yet, only two days after his passing, these objects had no relationship to him at all. They could have belonged to anyone.

John worked alone in the living room and bathroom, and while he did, Ryan and Alice talked. He told her about the party and how wonderful everyone was. He even told her about Brandon. Alice said she'd like to meet him, and Ryan promised to arrange it. When he talked to her about the piece he'd written earlier in the day, she suggested he try to find a string quartet to play it on Thursday.

He admired her strength. Although her eyes were dry, he could feel the pain she dammed up behind them. The anguish was building, and he was sure she wanted nothing more than to sit and let it out. Still, focused on the task at hand, Alice moved fluidly, placing things in boxes and keeping the conversation going—light and informal.

When it was done, she looked at Ryan with an expression of accomplishment on her face. "Well, then!" she said. "That wasn't so bad!"

Ryan laughed, but he wasn't sure he meant it. "No, not so bad at all. Now we just have—"

"The bedroom." She said the word with an air of mock foreboding, perhaps to mask the emotional gravity of the task—the returning to the place everything had changed. "Are you ready, honey?"

"Yes," Ryan said, starkly aware of the hollowness of the statement.

They walked down the hallway to Darren's bedroom, stepped inside, and turned on the light. Alice took hold of Ryan's hand. Although the room was filled with things—clothes, books, compact discs, furniture and decorations—all of it was lost to them. Instead, their eyes fixed directly at the dark spot on the carpet next to the computer desk. For a moment Ryan felt his body was not his own as the spot drew them both silently forward. He wondered again if it had been smart for him to come here.

Still holding his hand, Alice sat forcefully, devoid her usual grace. She pulled Ryan down across from her and closed her eyes—sealing equally behind her lids the pain of the moment and the conflagration that had been growing intensely since the moment they'd walked through the door. With uncanny certainty—indeed instinctually—she guided the hand that held his toward the stain on the floor. As their entwined fingers touched the spot of dried blood and fluid that had spilled from Darren's lifeless mouth, Ryan was surprised he did not recoil. Instead, he let his hand rest, as Alice's did, on this physical remnant of this man he'd loved. There were still moments now— fewer than before—when Darren remained a real person in his mind, and not the amorphous concept Ryan's denial was forcing him to become. This was a moment of reality, and he held on with all his might. He understood this was all that was left. Darren's body was about to be nothing but ashes, but this mass of organic matter seemed in the moment to be a holy grail—a whisper of life, memorial, and eternity that held Darren to an earth he had forsaken for places beyond.

"He's here in the room. I know he is," Alice whispered.

"I know he is," Ryan replied, feeling tears once again warm the inner corners of his eyes. "Right here."

He didn't believe it though. His idea of eternity was different than hers, and while he was sure neither was accurate, in the end, it gave him comfort. Exhaling deeply, he imagined the scene that had confronted him two nights previous, but pushed his mind farther back to envision the moment Darren had passed.

Consciousness gone, Darren had exhaled his last breath. All that was left of his being was his heat—ninety-eight-point-six degrees that stood in contrast to the sixty-eight of the room. Slowly and steadily that heat—the energy which had animated him—was stolen by the air. It dissipated outward to the walls like concentric ripples across a still and silent pond. The brisk March breeze outside the apartment would certainly have picked up a bit of that energy and spun it upward—almost endlessly—into the sky above the city. How long could it have been before the remnants of his warmth heated—imperceptibly—a molecule of water in the air that would fall as snow over the eastern plains of the state? That water—that heat—would melt into the Platte, finding its way eventually to the Missouri, then the Mississippi and finally the Gulf of Mexico. Wasn't it then possible for that heat to help the photosynthesis of a single alga before being eaten by plankton which would be devoured by fish swimming out into the Caribbean? Darren—an infinitesimal piece—would become part of the great vast ocean. The chain would go on indefinitely until some part of what once made him washed up equally upon the shores of France and Japan.

That was eternity.

CHAPTER 7

As the days trudged forward, the preparations for the first memorial service kept Ryan going. Alice and John attended to the outside details—reserving the space, hiring a caterer, choosing flowers, and printing small memorial programs—but left Ryan to arrange most of the substance.

He wasn't sure what a traditional memorial service was supposed to look like, but he had a clear vision of how he wanted to pay homage to his friend. It was going to be simple, but beautiful. He arranged for people to stand and speak—sharing stories and memories. He'd introduce each in turn and say a few words in-between, or play a song Darren had loved. At the end, Alice and John would speak, and Ryan would say his final words.

He'd give Darren a parting gift. With Max's assistance, he'd contacted a string quartet at the University; a playing of 'Elegy' would close the service.

Finally, Thursday morning arrived. The service was scheduled to start at ten-thirty, so Ryan woke up at eight. After climbing out of bed, he threw a couple sticks of cinnamon in the bottom of the coffee pot, set the machine to brew, and headed into the bathroom for a long, hot shower. Once he was dry again, he cleaned his ears around the still-healing piercings with a small bottle of alcohol and a couple of cotton swabs. The coffee was done, and the cinnamon had sufficiently soaked, so he put on a pair of sweatpants, poured himself a cup, and sat at the dining table.

He was surprised he didn't feel nervous. As he slowly sipped the coffee, letting its warmth spread through him, he settled into an extraordinary calm. He'd prepared well for the service, and though the ache of loss was still new and raw, he felt very nearly happy for the first time in a week.

After finishing the first cup, he poured another. Today, he understood, was a mandatory turning point. After the memorial services were done, life would shift slowly but steadily back to normalcy. Strangely, he didn't want this period of focused pain and grief to end, but he understood that the world was going to move on with or without him. He could no more halt the forward progression of his life than he could stop the advances of a glacier. The very nature of existence was a mandate to move forward. The options were simple—go on, or be crushed by a world that didn't care if it left him behind.

He remembered the promise he'd made with Steven. They wouldn't become victims of this situation.

Finally, it was time to dress. He and the Hendersons had decided that black clothing would be strictly forbidden—today's service was meant to celebrate a life lived in color. He chose his favorite cream-colored slacks and a bright blue button-up because it was the boldest thing in his closet, then went into his little bathroom and rewetted his hair. Using a little of the product he'd purchased, he shaped it into soft peaks that were the equal of the treatment the hairdresser had given. He smiled at himself and exhaled deeply. It was time to begin.

When he arrived at the reception hall, its beauty took his breath away. The room was an interior courtyard in the shape of a tall, vast square, with a polished stone floor. Marble columns around the edges supported a wraparound balcony on the second story, where giant windows on all four walls let brilliant sprays of sunlight fall into the room below. In the center, an ornate fountain surrounded by tropical flower arrangements bubbled and shimmered in the sun. Caterers were setting up large round tables with crisp white tablecloths, and in one corner of the room, a small stage with a podium had been erected, from which Ryan and others would speak.

It was just after ten, so only a handful of people occupied the space. Alice saw Ryan immediately, and rushed over with a small box in her hand. She hugged him tightly and said, "Oh, honey! Good morning! How are you feeling?"

"Strangely calm, actually. I expected I'd be a mess today."

"Well, you've worked really hard on this. I think it's going to turn out well. I'm glad you're feeling calm."

"Thank you," Ryan said. Alice handed him the small box she'd been holding. It was no larger than a deck of cards and covered in deep blue velvet. "This is for me?" he asked, surprised.

"Of course, honey. Open it!"

With great caution, he lifted the lid of the little box and gasped. Inside, Darren's thumb ring was strung onto a thin, silver chain. "Oh, Alice. You didn't have to do this."

She smiled widely, and he could see a dampness at the corners of her eyes. "I know it will mean something to you. Will you wear it today?"

"Of course." He pulled the necklace out of the box, and undid the little clasp. He wrapped it around his neck and tried to affix it, but found his fingers fumbled behind him.

"Oh, I'll do that," Alice said as she moved behind him and secured the necklace. She stepped back around to the front and surveyed him up and down. "That's just perfect." She held her arm out and indicated the reception hall. "What do you think?"

"It's great." Just then, he saw Brandon walk in through the doors to the hall, and smiled. "Alice, there is someone you need to meet." He took her hand and led her in the other boy's direction.

They met by the fountain. Brandon's eyes widened slightly, and he clasped his hands in front of him. "Ryan," he said.

"Brandon, this is Alice, Darren's—"

She reached forward and wrapped both of Brandon's still-clasped hands in her own. "Oh, I'm so glad to meet you. I'm so glad to know—" but she couldn't finish, suddenly overcome.

Brandon swallowed hard. "I'm glad to meet you too. I wish it could have been under—different circumstances." His voice quavered. "I really loved—"

She inhaled sharply and blinked with bleary eyes. "You know, as a mother it's not supposed to work out this way. And I've just been left with all these questions, and you think—you think about all the things you've done and the experiences you've had that your child will never have. And it's just so—" she laughed in spite of herself. "It really sucks. And the thing with Darren that hurt me the most was that he never dated. He never got to feel the rush when it's all new, and all possibilities—the excitement and the butterflies. But then Ryan told me about you and—and I was so relieved that he got a little bit of that after all."

Brandon was crying now. Alice wrapped her arms around him, and they held each other tightly. Ryan felt his tears coming too—he'd wanted so badly to be Darren's excitement; the butterflies. He wanted to cry out *I offered him all of that and more*, but this was not the time or the place. Today wasn't the day, and Darren was gone. It didn't matter anymore.

At the far end of the room, he saw Max slip in through the doors, and was relieved to have an excuse to walk away before he was consumed by darker thoughts.

Just before ten-thirty, Alice stood behind the podium and called the room to attention. The crowd had grown to nearly a hundred people, and she had to struggle to make her voice cut through the dull roar of conversation. "Hello everyone," she called. "Hello, excuse me please!" The conversations halted, and she sighed. "If you'll all be seated, we'll begin." Slowly but surely, everyone assembled found their chairs and turned them toward the stage. Ryan seated himself at a table near the front, next to Brandon and John. Alice joined him, and Max and Steven found seats nearby. After the room appeared to have settled, Alice looked at Ryan and smiled. "Okay, honey, go ahead and begin."

The service moved forward easily between speakers and the musical selections Ryan had chosen. The speaking was divided between affirmations in the belief of a restful, peace-filled beyond, and amusing stories about Darren's various antics as both a child and an adult.

Near the end, Alice and John rose and walked to the stage. They held hands in front of the podium, and the entire room caught its breath as she began to speak. "To suffer the loss of our only child has been, and will continue to be, an event to shape the lives of John and me for years to come." She cleared her throat ineffectually. "I could stand here for hours and speak about how wonderful our son was— how truly precious and unique—but I don't need to do that. Each and every one of you is in this room today because you already know." She was quiet for a moment. "I want to thank you all for the support you've given us during this last week, and will continue to give in the weeks to come. Like I said, I could talk forever, but I just want to say—" she looked up at the ceiling, "—Darren, honey? We love you." She extended her hand in Ryan's direction and beckoned him forward.

When he reached the stage, Alice nodded, and he turned to face the room. In the far back corner, the little string quartet had quietly assembled, unheard, with instruments at the ready. Ryan raised his head slightly and said. "We have just one last part of our memorial service today. I have always found that music is the medium through which I best process my emotions. Earlier this week, I was driven to write a short piece—something which could encapsulate both my own grief, and the joy I've felt from being able to have Darren in my life. If you would allow me the honor, a string quartet from the University has agreed to play it for us here today. This is, in a way, a parting gift for our dear friend." He smiled and lifted his hand to the quartet, indicating they could begin. He took Alice and John's hands, and they were seated.

Although the quartet sat in the far corner of the reception hall, when the string bass began the first somber tone of Ryan's 'Elegy' the room filled with rich, dark sound. The cello followed, and then the viola. Finally, the violin crowned the opening chord and the world melted away. Ryan briefly marveled at the way that strings, when combined, have a unique power to penetrate even the toughest of human souls. Barely thirty seconds into the piece, he could hear audible sobs coming from every table in the hall. Indeed, he held back his own. The melodies and harmonies swept through him, and he could scarcely believe that he was responsible for this heartbreaking collection of sounds. The Yamaha keyboard had done his 'Elegy' little justice, and as he listened, he discovered a level of raw emotion to the piece he had not known existed until this point.

The piece built to its climax and in the end dropped to almost nothing as only the violin sang out the last refrain. When it was done, no one moved or spoke.

After what must have been a full minute of silence, Alice stood and faced the room. She did not try to hide the tears in her voice.

"Thank you, everyone. Please, feel free to stay here as long as you like. The caterers have brought in an amazing spread. Please. Eat."

~*~

The following morning Ryan rode with the Hendersons to their house south of Denver to attend the second memorial service, and at Alice's urging, he agreed to stay over for the weekend. Truthfully, he was thankful to remain in her company—the bond growing between them was strong, and when he was near her he could feel the familiar warmth her son had so often exuded.

Still, by the time John drove him back north on Sunday night he was glad to be returning to some semblance of normal life. Monday morning arrived, and he greeted it with relief. Though he still grieved—he didn't know if he could ever reasonably be expected to stop—he was ready to leave the intensity of the previous week behind. He hoped that returning to work would provide a much-needed distraction.

His shift started at one, and he planned to walk to the pool, so he was showered and changed by eleven thirty. The day was bright and beautiful, and for the first time this year, it held a promise of the warmth of spring to come. The doorbell rang as he was packing up, so he shoved the work shirt he'd been neatly folding into his bag and went to the door.

His heart sank when he realized the girl standing on the other side was Shelly from Ohio.

"Are you Ryan?" she asked, extending her hand. She was short, with foppish, dark-brown hair, and eyes such a deep shade of ebony they were almost black. A loose polo with fat horizontal stripes in navy and mustard hung over her slight frame, and would have made her look amorphous if she hadn't tucked it into her baggy blue jeans. The entire outfit was cinched together with a broad leather belt.

He bit his lip as he shook her hand. "Yeah," he said, "I'm Ryan."

"Shelly. Pleased to meet you." She let go, tilted her head to the side and spread her arms with palms up. "Hey," she continued. "I'm looking for Darren? His phone has been off for a week, and I'm kind of, you know—pissed." She laughed, but looked worried. "I'm here on spring break from Ohio. I'd been talking to him online and—"

Ryan tried to smile, but he couldn't. It was awful that she didn't know, but then, no one would have thought to tell all the people on Darren's online buddy lists. He cut her off. "You'd better come in."

He turned from the door, and she followed behind. When they stepped into the kitchen, she started taking in the scene. "Well, it's kind of dirty," she said. "But I bet I could clean it." She looked at Ryan. "So, is he here?"

Ryan swallowed hard. "I'm sorry, Shelly. Darren died very suddenly a little over a week ago."

"Oh, shit!" she said, and then laughed. Her eyes narrowed, but Ryan thought she looked worried. "You're just fucking with me, right?"

He walked around the kitchen peninsula to the dining table and picked up a small piece of paper. When he returned to her, he handed it over. "I wish. This is one of the programs from the memorial service we held here at the University."

She took the paper and held it lightly with her fingertips as though it were very fragile—or very dangerous. "Oh, wow. I didn't—"

Ryan put his hand on her shoulder. "I'm really sorry. I should have thought to contact you. He told me that you were coming, but in all the chaos I completely forgot. I'm really glad you found me."

Shelly handed the program back, and looked relieved to be free of it. She crossed her arms and said, "Well, yeah. Me too. Luckily there's only one restaurant in this town called The Garden." She moved into the dining area and seated herself in one of the chairs at the table.

"Shit, I don't know what I'm going to do. I was really counting on this place—the whole reason I came here this week was to see it. Shit. Darren made it sound like it was a done deal."

He sat down across from her. "Well, it *is* a college town, so there are tons of places for rent. How long are you here? I've got a phone book and can look up some realtors."

She shook her head and looked very upset now. "No, no. That's too complicated. See, my whole thing is that I really wanted to live with gay people. I'm just like—I'm more comfortable that way. There's no way I can afford a one bedroom, and finding roommates for a two or three bedroom here after I go back to Ohio—"

Ryan cut her off again. He had an idea of what she was trying to do, and he wasn't prepared to agree to live with her based on only a few minutes of interaction. "Well, you found Darren through the LGBT office at the University. I'm sure you could go over there today and meet a few people in real life. Even if no one is looking for roommates yet, they might have some ideas."

Perhaps sensing that he was on to her, she tried a more direct approach. "Well, you're still going to have rooms available here, right?"

"Well, yeah. But, Shelly, the thing is that I don't know anything about you. I mean, I'm sure you're a nice girl, but I can't just decide right here and now."

"Why not?"

"Shelly, I just lost my best friend. Today is going to be the first day I go back to work in over a week. I'm sorry, but—"

"Hey, wait!" She stopped him. "I get it. But look, this is how I see things. Darren thought you were pretty awesome, right? He told me all about you—your music, your job. He said you're an amazing cook. There were a million things, but mostly he was really excited to live with you. I mean, I trust his judgment." Ryan nodded slowly, feeling himself being pulled against his will. She was quiet for what seemed like an eternity. "Do *you* trust his judgment?"

He felt his face begin to flush. It infuriated him—the way she talked like she and Darren were old friends. *I trust his judgment*, she'd said, almost accusatorially. He swallowed hard to contain his anger before he answered. "Yes, I do trust him."

"Well, if he were still alive, I'd be moving in here pretty much no questions asked, right?"

He hated to admit it, but even if he hadn't liked her, Darren would have persuaded him to let her move in. "Right."

She raised her shoulders and dropped her neck toward her chest in an effort to be cute. "So, come on. What do you say?"

It wasn't her fault that he died. He weighed his options, and in the moment, chose the one he believed was the right decision. "There are two bedrooms that'll be available August first. You should come pick one out."

~*~

Work was just the relief he was hoping for. During the periods when he had to lifeguard, he found the act of watching the lap swimmers move endlessly up and down the lanes to be calming. He counted their strokes from one end of the pool to the other, then back again, over and over, allowing his mind to become delightfully numbed. When he wasn't lifeguarding, he busied himself with clerical work, and the afternoon passed quickly. His coworkers must have sensed his reluctance to talk, because no one bothered him much. In fact, aside from a few questions about the memorial services, people kept their comments limited to how nice he looked with his new earrings and fancy hair.

The pool closed at eight thirty, and Ryan—who'd ridden his bike after all—was home by nine. He wasn't looking forward to spending the evening by himself, so he was happy to hear that he had one new message when he dialed his voicemail. Pressing the receiver to his ear, he expected to hear Max's voice, or Steven's.

"Hello, Ryan," the message began. "It's Brandon. . . I guess I'm still not your favorite person, but I'm feeling. . . down tonight. I was wondering if you wanted some company. If you get this, and you're feeling the same way, why don't you give me a call back?" He gave his number, twice. "Anyways, take care."

The message ended, and Ryan pulled the receiver away from his ear, holding it delicately as though it might suddenly grow razor teeth. Initially, the thought of spending time with Brandon was repulsive, but as he considered the alternatives—he'd probably listen to Echoes by himself and drink too much of the wine leftover from the party—he decided it might not be so bad after all.

There was no reason they shouldn't be friends, or at least try. After all, it wasn't Brandon who'd wronged him. Darren should have said something about their relationship. Now that he was gone, Brandon, like Shelly—like Ryan himself—was a sort of orphan. He dialed the number, and soon after, Brandon was on his way.

Fifteen minutes later, the telephone rang. Ryan picked it up and said, "Hello?"

"Hey, it's Brandon. I'm outside."

"Alright, you can come on up. The door is unlocked."

Brandon paused. "Actually, I was thinking we could go for a drive."

"A drive?"

"Yeah. I know this amazing place where we can talk—just chill. I think you'll really like it."

Ryan considered for a minute and then said, "Okay, I'll be right down." He hung up the phone, grabbed a light jacket and headed out the door.

Brandon was waiting in his car—a smaller black SUV—at the base of the steps leading up to the deck. He climbed in, and Brandon said, "Hey, thanks for calling me back."

Ryan buckled himself into the passenger seat. "It's no problem." The radio was tuned to a country station, turned down low. He exhaled deeply as he picked out a few words from the song. After a few moments he asked, "So, where are we going?"

As Brandon pulled out of the parking lot, he looked at Ryan. His face was impossibly sad, but he smiled anyway. "Larimer Canyon. Have you ever been up there?"

He considered. Larimer Canyon was in the foothills just outside of town, but Ryan never thought of it as an actual canyon—like the bigger ones to the north and south that led into the heart of the mountains. It was just a narrow road with a little creek running beside between the hills. "Yeah, I've driven through there a few times. My dad did some work up there for a while."

"Driven through? But have you ever been to the top?"

"I didn't really think there *was* a top. It just kind of runs into another road. I mean, I guess it crests."

Brandon shook his head. "No, no. There is a top. Wait and see."

Brandon drove the SUV west through quiet streets. The traffic lights cooperated, and soon the vehicle reached the edge of town. The houses fell away, giving up to the few rows of farm and patches of open land that huddled close to the foothills above. The night was inky black, and the moon—only a quarter full—did little to illuminate the world below. Only a few silver wisps of cloud graced the night sky. Brandon turned the car north, and then a few minutes later back to the west up a steep hill. Ryan looked around him and felt the magic of this place. This narrow corridor of land was a transitional zone between two worlds—the majestic Rockies above and the endlessly flat eastern plains below, which stretched with little interruption all the way to Pennsylvania.

He looked out his window and said, "I've been here a few times. There is a beautiful pioneer cemetery just on the right, here."

Brandon looked in Ryan's direction. "I didn't know that. I'm surprised you can even think about—"

"Cemeteries?" Ryan finished. "Well, Darren isn't in one. I think Alice and John want to spread his ashes at sea."

Brandon sniffed, sharply. "That would be nice." His voice quavered. "They're great people. I'm glad I got to meet them."

Ryan turned his gaze straight ahead. "Yeah, I really enjoy them. They've kind of become family."

The road turned and climbed to the crest of the first foothill and then dipped into a valley beyond. After a few minutes, Brandon turned the SUV right and followed a road that led into the picturesque center of a tiny town called Bellvue. He turned the vehicle once more, and they began their ascent into the canyon.

As Bellvue gave way to the wilderness beyond, Ryan looked around again. It had been years since he'd traveled this road, and he was surprised to see how the steep, mountainous hills closed tightly in around him, tighter than he remembered. In places, the bows of the ponderosa pines and Douglas firs that blanketed the mountainside hung down close enough to the road to almost touch the top of the SUV. The road narrowed sharply, and Brandon reduced his speed as he took a series of tight turns through the blackness. At times the headlights—the only things making sense of the world ahead—showed nothing but the sharp curve of the road as the towering walls of rock around which it was wound obscured everything beyond. Ryan held his breath without knowing it—the twisting road and the absolute dark of the night made him nervous. It wasn't until the way ahead finally straightened that he exhaled completely. The world opened to an unexpected patch of meadow for a moment before the road plunged them once again into the forested canyon.

"We're almost there now," Brandon said, his voice barely above a whisper. The trees thinned, and the road turned to a series of steep switch-backs.

Through the windshield, Ryan could see an army of stars in the nearly cloudless sky above. "It is very beautiful up here."

"Just wait. It gets better." The vehicle reached the place where the road crested. Ryan expected Brandon to keep driving forward, down the other side, but instead turned onto a dirt road he hadn't noticed. "This is the road that leads to the *real* top."

"So why did you want to come here?" Ryan asked. The vehicle shook and rattled slowly across the unpaved road surface.

"I brought Darren up here a few times."

"I see," Ryan replied, sullenly. He suddenly hated being in the car with Brandon. If they weren't so far outside of town, he'd have told him to pull over so he could walk home. It felt like a trap—now he was going to be forced to endure Brandon reminiscing—and this far from home there was literally no escape. What was he expected to think they'd done up here, anyways? He imagined Brandon pointing out all the places they'd laid in the snow and had each other.

"It's nothing like that," Brandon said. Ryan was glad the interior of the SUV was dark, because he felt himself blush. He hoped he hadn't been speaking his thoughts out loud. Brandon continued. "I imagine you don't want to think about our time together at all—I wouldn't if I was in your shoes—but this place wasn't about the romance. Or the sex."

Ryan laughed, bitterly. "Well, what's left then?"

"The person," Brandon responded, flatly. The road—if it could even be called such a thing—narrowed to a single lane. One edge pressed up against rock, and the other fell off into an impossibly steep drop. Brandon continued, both driving and speaking more slowly. "I was such an idiot. You see, I couldn't read the signs. This was the only place I could take Darren where he would just be himself—really open up to me." He laughed. "If you'd have asked me a couple weeks ago, I'd have said I loved Darren Henderson." His voice quavered again, "But how can you love somebody who won't—who doesn't—let you see them for who they truly are? Do you beg? Do you drive them up a mountain twenty miles outside of town? Or are you just wasting your time?"

Ryan didn't feel like speaking, but when Brandon let the silence stretch, he replied, "I don't know."

"Well, I don't either." After a moment, his voice grew more excited. "Hey, we're almost there. You have to close your eyes when we go around this next curve, okay?"

"Oh, no way!" Ryan laughed. "You're going to drive us right off the edge."

Brandon stepped hard on the brakes, and the SUV came to a dramatic stop. With authority, he said "This car isn't moving until your eyes are closed. I'll blindfold you if I have to. I'm not going to drive off the edge, trust me. I just want the view to be a surprise."

He thought it was crazy, but Ryan agreed. "Alright, my eyes are closing. I'll even put my hands over them." He did as he promised and the vehicle started forward again. He felt it turn twice and then head up a moderately steep slope. Finally, the world flattened out, and Brandon parked the SUV.

"Alright," Brandon said. "You can open your eyes."

Ryan did so, and Brandon swung open his door and stepped into the night. The SUV was parked in what passed for a small dirt parking lot. Out the front of the vehicle, at first, all Ryan saw were trees. To the left, there was a bright glow, and as he turned his head, he gasped. A large cinderblock building with dull yellow lights placed at intervals atop its outer walls sat protected behind a high, chain-link fence. Next to this was erected a massive steel radio tower. Several giant white discs affixed to the sides glowed a deep blue in the limited moonlight. The entire structure reminded him of a collection of flying saucers caught in an industrial spider web. He opened his own door and moved lightly out of the vehicle, closing it behind him. Icy wind whipped around him, and he shivered.

Brandon called, "This way!"

Ryan turned around and caught his breath. As he looked down the road from which they'd come, the trees fell away revealing an uninterrupted view of the endless plains beyond. Brandon was standing a little ways down the hill, and Ryan rushed to meet him. When he did, he was out of breath, but he didn't mind. The combination of the view and the frigid air was exhilarating. Even from this distance, Ryan could clearly pick out the streets of the city, lined with twinkling yellow lights in an expansive grid. Farther beyond, a faint strip of white and red lights—headlights and tail lights respectively—marked the interstate just outside of town. Off slightly to the right and farther into the plains, he spied another patch of yellow light that he assumed must be Greeley.

Brandon sighed. "It's stunning, isn't it? If the night is clear enough, you can see all the way to the outskirts of Denver. And if you look the other way—" he pointed left, to the north "—you can almost always see Laramie, and Cheyenne Wyoming."

"This is amazing." Ryan drank in the scene again. "It really is."

"I went to Los Angeles once when I was a teenager. They have this road in their own foothills. It's called Mulholland Drive. From there you can see the entire city, all the way to the ocean. I remember being so amazed, but this is even better."

"Still, that must have been an incredible thing to see."

Brandon reached in the pocket of the light jacket he wore and pulled out a pack of cigarettes in a green box. He removed one, fished in the pocket of his jeans for a lighter, and lit it. He extended the pack to Ryan and said, "Want one?"

Ryan recoiled a bit. "I didn't know you smoke."

Brandon shrugged. "There are worse things." As he exhaled his first drag, the hot air between his lips made a soft hissing sound. The smoke expired into the night in a gently curling cloud. He inhaled again. "Darren smoked now and again."

Ryan rolled his eyes and hoped Brandon couldn't see in the dark. "That's great. Of course he did." He remembered briefly the Friday morning Darren had come to see him at work. Hadn't he smelled of smoke and liquor?

Even in the dark, Ryan could see that Brandon looked worried as he exhaled again. "I hope you don't think less of me—I can put it out if you want."

Ryan shook his head. "No need. I'm less judgmental than people make me out to be. I won't preach at you."

The other boy dropped the half-finished cigarette into the dirt and snubbed it with his foot anyways. "People think you're judgmental?"

Ryan considered. "Well, maybe not judgmental. It's just that I have a reputation for being kind of prudish when it comes to these things. I don't smoke, I've never done any kind of drugs—I drink more than I used to, but I never even had a drop until last fall. Like I said, it's just a reputation. I'm the good kid, you could say."

"So, people think you're not very fun." The way Brandon phrased his words, it was a statement, not a question.

He felt uncomfortable. "I think people enjoy my company. Most of my close friends are the same way. But the broader spectrum of people I know? That's one of the reasons Darren and I made such a good team. Between the cigarettes and cocaine and whatever else I don't know about that was probably right in front of my face—he brought the fun in the sense you are talking about. I suppose I'm more the regulator."

Brandon laughed. "How do you feel about people thinking of you that way?"

This was getting too deep. He hardly knew Brandon, and his level of discomfort was mounting. "I don't really want to talk about this."

"Well, we have to talk about something. Come on, Ryan, it's a valid question. And trust me, I'm not judgmental either."

"I don't really care if people don't think I'm fun. The people I spend my time with enjoy me, and that's what matters."

"Okay. Do *you* think that you're fun?"

Truthfully, he didn't. And on some level, wasn't that part of the attraction to Darren in the first place? Darren was *fun*—constantly challenging Ryan to step outside of his comfort zone, but still accepting him just as he was. Indeed, Darren embraced everyone without judgment. He'd treated each person as though they were the greatest human being he'd ever known, and did his best to express that to them in his own way. It could be something as simple as praising an eccentric, twenty-year-old new aged guitar recording, or as generous as offering an apartment to a worried, over-eager girl from Ohio.

Ryan was not fun. Ryan did not accept change easily, and was too content with his banal routines to strive for something more.

The more he thought about his life, the more he recoiled. His spirit had no sense of adventure. After high school, he'd been accepted to multiple universities. In the end, if he was honest, he turned them down not so he could focus on his music, but so he could stay at his job. He moved to Asbury Drive and disliked it so much that when Elizabeth Street became available—a chance to live in his old neighborhood—he took it without hesitation. Indeed, even his unending fixation on Darren could probably be described as having less to do with love and more to do with comfort. He had grown used to Darren, and Darren's inherent sense of adventure electrified him. The constant, nagging heartache and romantic rejection were simply par for the course as long as he could remain static. He looked out again at the spectacular view below and felt a twinge of sadness. From this place, he could see his entire world, and although it was beautiful, it was small.

Finally, he responded. "No, I don't really think that I'm fun."

Brandon considered for a moment. "And how do you feel about that?"

"I don't know why I'm telling you all of this. I hardly know you—"

Walking forward, Brandon placed his hand gently on Ryan's shoulder. "Just answer the question," he said, softly.

"I'm not very proud of it."

"So, change." Brandon said it so simply that Ryan couldn't refute its possibility. "You're what—twenty?"

"Nineteen."

"Big deal. I have one more year of school, and then I'm out of here. I'm going to see the world, and I'm going to own it. What's stopping you from doing the same?"

"Brandon, it's not that easy. I've made choices—"

"Bullshit. Make different choices. I'm not telling you to take up smoking or do cocaine. With Darren dying, life just knocked you down and gave you a fresh start, with a fresh perspective."

Ryan didn't speak, and Brandon just stared at him. Finally, he said, "I think I need to go home now."

"Have I upset you?"

"No," Ryan said, truthfully. "I've upset myself."

They walked slowly back to the SUV and climbed inside. Brandon turned on the engine, and slowly turned the car around to begin heading down the hill. As they left the parking lot, he said, "Do you think that we can be friends?"

Ryan was crying almost imperceptibly. He wiped his eyes and looked in the other boy's direction. "I think I'd really like that."

PART TWO:

METAMORPHOSIS

CHAPTER 8

In the weeks that followed, Ryan was haunted by both the view from the top of the canyon and the realizations it evoked; his world was small, and there was no one to blame but himself. Through a series of decisions and indecisions masquerading under the guise of comfort, he'd spent the last two years fencing himself into a life he wasn't sure he wanted anymore. Suddenly, his every motivation was shrouded in doubt. Did he really choose to take time away from school to write his music, or had he simply wanted to keep his job and the familiar routine he'd established with the City? Was Asbury Drive truly so terrible, or was Elizabeth Street more attractive because it was in the neighborhood where he grew up?

Then, a thought occurred to him which he could barely acknowledge. Was Darren really so incredible, or was he simply the one who was always there?

Whatever the answers, there remained one certainty. He no longer liked the choices he'd made. The time was ripe for a change, so he quietly gathered his transcripts, wrote an essay, and sent his application to the University. It was the right choice, and he'd expected to feel something—a sense of pride—when it was done. There was nothing; just a rattling echo of progress reverberating inside the now-familiar hollowness of the shell he'd become.

Reluctantly, the nights grew shorter than the days and March bled into April. The winter was vanquished. Buds fattened on trees and layers of clothing fell away as early blossoms and cool spring rains perfumed the streets. Though the spirits of all those around him soared on a great vernal lift, Ryan remained unaffected. He watched the awakening of the world absently, feeling nothing except the dull ache of loss. Sometimes he wondered if he'd ever feel anything again.

One otherwise unremarkable Thursday night, Ryan received a knock on his bedroom door. Groggily, he rose from his computer chair, walked across the room and opened the door.

Steven stood on the other side. "Hey," he said, "I was thinking I hadn't seen you in a while so I thought I'd stop by. I need a study break."

Ryan smiled as warmly as he could manage. "Yeah, sorry. I've been a little off the radar. Come on in."

Steven did so, cautiously. The bedroom was a minefield of un-washed laundry. A few dirty plates were piled on the computer desk, and the air smelled stale and recycled. As he sat gingerly at the edge of Ryan's bed, he said "Have you been outside tonight? It's friggin' beautiful!"

Ryan collapsed into his computer chair. "No. Is it?"

"Yeah, it's like, sixty-five degrees. Unseasonable. Maybe you should—open some windows in here?"

In spite of himself, Ryan blushed. "Yeah, sorry it's kind of a mess."

"Oh, I just assumed your washing machine was broken."

He rose again to open the windows. "The washing machine is fine. I think I'm the one that's broken." He sat on the bed next to his friend and reached for Darren's thumb ring, still hanging on the chain around his neck. He put his smallest finger through the band and be-gan to roll it with his thumb.

"You're still wearing that thing, huh?"

"It brings me some comfort." He sighed.

"Or maybe it weighs you down?"

Ryan felt his face heat with anger. He looked sternly at Steven and breathed deeply before speaking. "What am I supposed to do, Steven? It's only been a month." He softened his tone. "I'm just so sad. I mean, I don't sit around and cry all day—it's nothing like that. I just—sometimes I feel like I'm in this entirely alone."

Steven guffawed. "Alone? Ryan, I was right there with you. Darren was my friend too. I'm sad. I'm sad all the time. Hell, I was sad long before Darren died and I'll probably still be sad long after this is all just a distant memory."

"Steven—"

He gripped Ryan's hand forcefully. "Do you remember what you said to me that night? Right after we found him? You said to promise that we wouldn't become victims of this situation. I wasn't exactly sure what you meant by that at the time, but—"

Ryan shook his head slowly. "You're right. I'm not doing the best job keeping that promise, am I?"

"No, not at all. I guess that's alright as long as you snap out of it—get yourself back on course. Did you hear from the University yet? Are you in?"

"No, not yet. Soon I hope."

"Well, that was a step in the right direction."

Ryan smiled. "Yeah, it's time, isn't it?"

"It is. Hey, like I said, I kinda wrote the book on being sad, so I'm not exactly the best at this but—"

"But?"

"Do you remember when we met?"

Ryan considered. "Yeah," he chuckled. "That damned website."

It was September a year ago. He'd only been at Asbury Drive a few months. Most of his high school friends had gone off to school in Boulder, or Denver or out of state, and he'd started to get lonely. The idea of embracing the bold new world of online dating had been daunting, but it seemed like the only solution. How else was he supposed to meet other young gay men? Where was he supposed to go? With great reluctance, he'd signed up on a website and pieced together a profile.

Steven smiled. "I was the first person to contact you, wasn't I?"

Ryan nodded. "Yeah. And remember how nervous I was? You messaged me for what—two weeks before I agreed to meet you?"

"It seemed like longer at the time. Oh, man—I was so fixated. Ha! You put up that picture, and I think I invented a whole life for us. By like, the third message I could already see us with the white picket fence and a couple of kids and a big fluffy dog. It was excruciating waiting for you to agree to meet up. But I just knew, if I were persistent enough, you'd come around."

"And then I did." He laughed. "I have to be honest though, Steven. It's probably good I didn't know about all of that at the time. It's a good thing you didn't send me real estate listings or anything."

Steven laughed as well. "Believe me I was tempted! Hey, a boy can dream, right? Do you remember how *the date* went when you finally agreed?"

"How could I forget? Oh, I still shudder when I think how stupid I—"

"No, no. You weren't stupid." He considered. "Well, maybe a little stupid. I mean, I blind-sided you when I went in for that kiss. I'd thought we were on the same page, but then, I was already planning our wedding, so maybe I was the stupid one."

"Steven—"

"But anyways, the point is, what you did after that? Do you remember how upset I got? I just lost it. I started bawling right there on your couch on Asbury Drive. You know it wasn't the first time I found myself in that situation. Rejection is my oldest, dearest friend.

And you just—you just put your arms around me and held me. You asked me to calm down. You asked what was wrong."

Ryan laughed again. "What else could I have done?"

"A million things! You could've been cold and told me to leave. You could've laughed at me. Maybe you could've gone down the list of why it would never work between us. That's happened to me before, you know. I'm not thin enough, my arms are too scrawny, my hair is too dark, I'm too tall, I'm not tall enough, my laugh is annoying, my eyes are too close together—"

"Whoah, Steven. Your eyes are spaced perfectly fine. And all the rest of it? Fuck 'em. I mean, it's easier said than done—you know I've had my fair share of—"

"Exactly!" He clapped. "Ryan, that's pretty much exactly what you said to me that night. And I stopped crying then, and I looked at you and—that's when I really fell in love with you. I mean, not romantically, but with the person. That's the moment I knew I'd met someone who was going to be one of the best friends I'd ever had. And then you stood up, and you said—"

"I said, what do you think of Cyndi Lauper?"

"Right! And I was like—what?"

"And I made you watch that music video. I told you it always cheers me up."

"And it did cheer me up. Lately, I've been thinking about that. Because you're always the happy one. You're the one who is always making *me* and everyone else feel better, right? Well, now our roles are reversed. So I think, if I was moping around in a garbage pit of a bedroom withdrawing from the world around me? My dear friend Ryan Gregori would tell me that I should focus on something good and celebrate the little things in life—the modest victories and the small pleasures. Does that sound like something you'd say?"

Ryan laughed. "Yeah, it kind of sounds like something I'd say."

"Maybe you should spend some time with your piano, or whatever."

"Or maybe I should just spend some more time with my friends." He smiled. "Oh, Steven, I wish you were around all the time. I already feel a lot better."

He was quiet for a moment, considering. Then cautiously he said "Funny you should say that. I'm facing kind of an unrealistic rent hike if I renew for next year. I was thinking maybe—"

Ryan leaped off his bed. "Steven! What a great idea!"

"I wasn't so sure of this place when you first moved in, but now that I've spent a little more time here—"

"Steven, say no more. The third bedroom is yours!"

"Excellent, well that's settled then." He looked around. "I hope the state of this room isn't indicative of how we're going to live together—"

Ryan chuckled and started gathering up the clothes piled on the floor. "Yeah, I guess it's time to start cleaning things up."

~*~

The following afternoon, Ryan returned home from his opening shift to find a letter from the University in the mail. Quickly, though with a great sense of nervousness, he tore open the envelope and looked at the contents inside.

He'd been accepted.

Despite his lingering grief, the occasion called for a celebration, so he called Max and asked him to come to dinner. They set a date for six, and after Ryan was off the phone, he rushed to the grocery store to pick up the necessary ingredients.

When Max arrived at six-fifteen Ryan was already prepping in the kitchen.

"Hello, Mister!" Max said enthusiastically.

Ryan turned from where he was carefully chopping an onion and caught his breath for a moment. Max looked absolutely stunning. His hair was recently cut, and its vibrant candy-apple red looked to have been freshly dyed. He'd left his glasses at home in favor of contact lenses, and his striking blue eyes gleamed as though they were lit from within. His light blue T-shirt clung snugly around his small chest and trim middle, and the low-rise fit of his dark blue jeans showed off his shape to great effect. In one of his hands he held a jug of deep purple sangria, and in the other, he carried a vibrant bouquet of spring flowers. Above all, his smile was electric.

When he found his words, Ryan said, "Max! You didn't have to do all that!"

Max set the wine and the flowers on the counter and wrapped his arms around his friend. "You deserve it, Mister! I'm really proud of you for deciding to go back to school."

He hugged him back and felt a deep and sudden longing. He allowed the embrace to linger until he felt Max's arms release. "You are too good to me."

Max took a step back and gave him a stern look. "Like I said, you deserve it. You look happier than I've seen you in over a month."

"Well, I'm not sure I've made it all the way back to happy, but I've got a reason to celebrate, right?"

"Mhmm. Have you got a vase for these?" Max indicated the flowers.

"Oh, yes." Ryan pointed to the pantry. "Right in there. Do you mind taking care of them while I get this started?"

"Not at all!"

"Thanks."

Max retrieved the vase from the pantry, removed the flowers from their plastic wrapping, snipped the ends with a pair of kitchen shears and arranged them. After adding the little packet of flower food, he filled the vase in the kitchen sink and moved around the peninsula to place them in the center of the dining table. "So," he said, "What are we having?"

"Carbonara."

"What?"

"It's this amazing Italian pasta dish. Last fall I watched this celebrity chef make it on TV, and since then I've done it a few times. I don't know how closely my version resembles his anymore, but I think you'll like it."

"Can't wait!"

Max started recounting his day while Ryan set a pot of water to boil and sliced raw bacon into tiny, sticky pieces. As he slowly rendered the fat in a giant skillet, the room filled with a warm and decadent scent. When the bacon was cooked perfectly, Ryan removed it and added the onions he'd diced to the grease. Max poured two glasses of the cheap but delicious sangria, and Ryan dumped a box of linguine into the now boiling water.

As he moved the onions around the pan, he asked, "So, who are you seeing now?" Max laughed, and so Ryan said, "You know I always have to ask."

Max laughed again. "Well, I'm still waiting for someone to wake up and smell the coffee!"

"He's elusive, huh?"

"I'll say. But I have a feeling I'm closing in."

Ryan pulled a ladle from a drawer and added a bit of the boiling pasta water to the skillet. The liquid hissed and steamed. "You're very patient."

"Well, Mister, good things are worth waiting for, right?"

The pasta was done, so Ryan drained it in a colander before dumping it directly into the skillet and turning off the burner. He added the bacon back in and removed a couple eggs, shredded parmesan cheese, and a bunch of fresh parsley from the refrigerator. After briefly chopping the parsley he added it to the skillet with a generous amount of parmesan. He cracked the eggs over the sink, separated the yolks with his hands and threw them directly into the skillet, allowing the whites to drop into the drain below. He tossed the entire dish with a pair of kitchen tongs, added some freshly ground pepper and, when finished, stepped back to survey his work.

"Now," he said, "doesn't that look delicious?"

Max stared, wide-eyed. "It does look beautiful. I'm confused about the eggs though."

Ryan used the tongs to start plating. "They coat the pasta and work with the cheese to create this really luxurious, velvety sauce. Trust me; you're going to love it."

Max moved to the dining table, and Ryan brought the two plates of pasta, seating himself opposite.

He raised his wine glass and said, "Here's to school."

Max shook his head but raised his glass anyways. "No, Ryan. Here's to you."

The meal was delicious. After two more glasses of wine, they moved to Ryan's bedroom—freshly cleaned—and Ryan put iTunes on shuffle. Sitting next to each other, legs folded on the bed, they talked easily. Ryan realized with a smile he was actually *happy*.

Halfway through their fourth glass, the computer started playing 'See The Sun.' As was her habit lately, Dido's words were relevant; the track was about moving on after loss, being happy for time together even when it's over, and letting light back into life. Beneath the melodies and harmonies, Ryan could feel the nearness of Max, and it filled him with immeasurable joy. Wasn't he the one, more than all others, who strived to pull Ryan out of his grief?

Max let the conversation die off and placed his hand on top of Ryan's. When the song ended, there was only silence. Breaking it, Max said, "What happened to the music?"

Ryan shivered at the electric feeling of Max's fingers on top of his, but he didn't move. He looked at his friend and smiled. "It's not over yet. There's a secret track after a minute or so of silence."

"That was a beautiful song," Max said, softly. "I don't think I've heard that one before." The silence stretched on until finally, she began to sing again, this time about possibilities overlooked—about realizing the one we ought to be with was right there the whole time.

Their eyes locked and Ryan felt himself suddenly drowning in Max's icy blue gaze. It pulled him deeper as their faces drew together. He could feel the warmth of Max's breath and smell the sweet dark wine as he exhaled. The moment stretched on, tenuous, until suddenly Max bridged the distance.

The kiss was simultaneously gentle and deep. At first, Ryan's lips held rigidly, but then his body relaxed, and he felt them open. Their tongues touched and he was overcome by the sensation of the gently probing, delicate exchange—his eyes closed and he was somewhere else entirely. The world felt pink and warm and bright. The kiss stretched on, and Ryan held to it until Max reluctantly pulled away.

"Wow, Mister," Max said. "I have been waiting for that forever."

Ryan stared, dumbfounded. Struggling to find words he said, "I can't believe that just happened. I didn't know—"

Max laughed and kissed him on the forehead. "Yes you did. Who do you think I was expecting to wake up and smell the coffee?"

Suddenly, Ryan felt an overwhelming surge of guilt. His left hand disengaged from Max's and gripped the thumb ring hanging around his neck. He caught a brief flash of surprise in Max's eyes before quickly letting go and reaching for his hand again. Finding it, he was certain the other boy's fingers withdrew almost imperceptibly at his touch. As quickly as the guilt had come, it was gone again, but he feared the damage was done.

"No, no," Ryan said. "I didn't know. I mean, I guess I'm an idiot." He knew it was the wrong thing to say—that he needed to tell Max how much he wanted this—but no other words formed on his lips.

Max looked worried. "No, you're not an idiot, Mister." He stood, seeming to avert his gaze. Rising as well, Ryan took Max's face in his hands and kissed him again. This time it was Max's lips that hesitated. It lasted only a few moments before Max pulled away. Though he smiled, Ryan could read the hurt in his eyes. He laughed. "Wow, I think I'm a little drunk. I should probably head home."

Ryan opened his mouth to speak. There was nothing he wanted more desperately than for Max to stay, but his breath escaped his lungs without a sound. Max was moving toward the bedroom door, and then he was out walking toward the kitchen. Ryan followed, trying harder to find the words. Finally, he called out, "Max!"

The other boy turned and smiled briefly. "Dinner was excellent, Mister. I'll call you tomorrow, okay?"

Deflated, Ryan replied, "Okay." Max disappeared into the dark hall beyond the kitchen, and a moment later the sound of the front door opening and closing announced his departure. He was gone.

Ryan walked solemnly back to his bedroom, undressed and climbed into bed, defeated.

His eyes opened to a brilliant light. He stood on a dirt path lined with enormous weeping willows whose long, limber tendrils glowed lime green as they swayed gently in the breeze. The humid air was cool and lightly scented with apple blossoms. He laughed as he turned his face up to a cloudless blue sky and felt the warm embrace of the sun on his skin. In the distance, the sound of gently churning water called him forward.

At first, he walked slowly, but the sun and the breeze energized him until soon he was running. The path turned and hugged the bank of a narrow brook. A few yards further the willows gave way to towering apples whose pale pink blossoms fell all around him like snow.

The path turned abruptly right and the brook ended in a small pond. Ryan stopped suddenly and gasped. At the edge of the water, Darren sat on an ornate black metal bench, his golden hair shimmering in the sunlight.

Accelerating forward, Ryan raised his hand and called "Darren! Darren, what are you doing here?"

Darren smiled, knowingly. "Hey there, creeper! I thought I might find you here."

Ryan scowled. "I don't know why you always call me that."

Darren slid to one side of the bench. "Do you want to sit down? The view is awesome."

Ryan nodded slowly and took a seat beside his friend, grinning uncontrollably. Darren was right; the view was spectacular. The water in the pond was perfectly still, and it reflected beautifully the apple blossoms and the willows that grew on its far side. A patch of lily pads completed the scene, and Ryan felt suddenly that he must be inside a painting by Monet. He sighed contentedly and then said, "You still didn't answer my question. What are you doing here?"

Darren shook his head. "Everybody's got to be somewhere, right? I thought this place was as nice as any."

"Sure it is. But—"

A cloud Ryan hadn't noticed before drifted in front of the sun and cast the world in sudden shadow. Darren shook his head. "You're unbelievable, you know it?"

"Unbelievable?"

"I'd say I was disappointed in you, but I never liked Max much anyways."

"What do you mean?"

Darren laughed heartily. "I mean you really fucked it up, didn't you?"

Ryan reached for the thumb ring and squeezed it tightly. "I don't know what came over me. I mean, it's all I wanted."

"Apparently not."

"No, it is. I just—I didn't expect it, that's all."

Darren clucked his tongue. "Well, that's your first problem. He couldn't have made it clearer—for months! You really didn't see any of the signs?"

"Clearly not!"

"Whatever you say. It's too bad."

"Hmph! Well, I can fix it if I want to."

Darren laughed again. "Right, but you don't want to."

"Who says I don't?"

"You don't. I see the way you hold that damned ring—so did Max." He shook his head in wonder. "Even in death, I've still got you in my yoke. Maybe they were right, and I wasn't any good for you after all."

"Darren—" now he was pleading. "Darren, don't talk like that. Please—"

Darren smiled. The cloud drifted on, and the sun illuminated the pond again. "I have to go in a little while. What do you say we just sit here and take in the view?"

"Wait, why do you have to go?"

He shook his head. "You can't dream forever—"

The next morning Ryan awoke uneasily. Both his encounter with Max and the conversation with Darren in his dream left him unsettled. He was going to have to deal with the Max situation one way or another, but he feared Darren was right—he wasn't ready to let go yet—so when Max called mid-morning, they simply exchanged pleasantries, but neither mentioned the kiss. When Ryan hung up the phone, he kicked himself for letting another opportunity to express his feelings go to waste, but took some comfort in the belief that perhaps the timing wasn't right.

~*~

A further distraction from Ryan's grief-driven introspection came a few days later when Cara announced she was planning to run a Water Safety Instructor course in the middle of May. He was overjoyed by the news. Though he'd been approved to start the process of becoming an Instructor Trainer over a year ago, this was the first time the opportunity to begin his training had arisen. He accepted the invitation to co-teach and turned his grief aside to devotedly study his materials.

He prepared well, and on the first day of class—Friday, May 14th— he arrived early and walked into Cara's office with an air of confidence. He sat heavily in the chair opposite her desk and smiled.

Cara looked up from a stack of paperwork. "Hey, Ryan!"

His smile broadened. "Are you ready for this?" he asked. "How many people have we got?"

"Well," she examined the topmost sheet from the stack of papers. "Turns out there was a lot of interest, and since you're assisting I let fourteen register."

He opened his eyes wide and whistled. "I think when I took the class a few years ago there were only six of us."

Rolling her eyes, Cara placed an elbow heavily on the desk before laying her head against the hand it supported. "I know. I'm surprised at the interest because I feel like we can never get these things to run. But I'm really happy we have so many because summer lessons start in what—two? Three weeks? I still need more people on staff, so I'm hoping we've got some good candidates in this class."

"Plug them right into the system?"

Cara laughed and said, gruffly, "Plug 'em in!" She stood briskly and gathered her materials. "Ready to go set up the room?"

"Absolutely."

An hour later as students started trickling in, Ryan handed each a folded piece of paper—a 'name tent' Cara called it—and instructed them to find a seat, write, and display their name. They trailed in slowly—the typical mix of high school and college students looking for part-time work. The final student to walk into the room looked oddly familiar, and the sight of her gave Ryan pause. She was a girl of about Ryan's age with beautiful, curling auburn hair that she'd tied back into a coarse pony-tail. Her ears were filled with various gauged surgical steel earrings—both hoops and horseshoes, and on one side Ryan even saw a long steel bar through her cartilage. When he handed her a name tent, she looked at him for a long second as if trying to place him, but said nothing and walked to take a seat. As she found her chair, Ryan stared, still puzzled. Cara cleared her throat and stood.

"Good afternoon, everyone! My name is Cara Holmes." She looked politely at Ryan.

"And I'm Ryan Gregori."

"I am a Water Safety Instructor Trainer, and I'll be conducting this course. Ryan is an Instructor Trainer Candidate, and he will be assisting me for the duration as he works to become a full-fledged Instructor Trainer." She paused for a minute before continuing. "If you haven't already done so, please fill out your name on the name tent Ryan has given you, and turn it so that we can see. It'll avoid embarrassing moments where I call you Josh when your name is really John—or Martha when you're actually Margaret." She rolled her eyes. "I'll tell you; I'm terrible with names." The room laughed nervously. "So, here's how we're going to start. You know my name, and now I'm going to tell you what motivates me to be here. The first lesson you need to learn—and this applies to teaching anything—is that it is important to understand the motivation of your students if you ever expect to reach them—"

When she finished, Ryan spoke briefly about his own passion, and then the students in the room each took a turn. The introductions wound their way backward until they finally reached the oddly familiar girl in the back. She rose out of her chair with an almost musical fluidity, clasped her hands before her and lifted her head slightly. On her name tent, she'd written her name in purple with impossibly curving cursive letters.

"Hi, everyone," she began. Ryan was transfixed, still trying to place her. "My name is Meredith Gardner. I'm twenty-one years old, and I'm a student at the University. I guess what motivates me is in two parts. First of all, I just left a ridiculously awful job, so I need a new one if I'm going to stay afloat." She laughed, and the room laughed nervously with her. "The second part is that I really love kids. I think people have this idea that I'm kind of hard—you know, some kind of ice queen—" she laughed again, and this time the room did not follow suit. "—But honestly I'm not. I had a lot of swimming experience growing up, and now I think this is what I want to get into." She smiled politely and then took her seat.

Cara laughed from her chair. "Well, nice to meet all of you. Meredith, what was your ridiculously awful job?"

Meredith raised her brows and opened her eyes widely. In an ominous voice, she said, "I was a hostess at this God-awful restaurant."

Finally, it clicked. Meredith had seated Ryan and the Hendersons at The Garden. He smiled at the memory—Alice had loved her.

"Well," Cara said, "I'm glad you've seen the light!" There was a pause. "Now, to get started, Ryan is going to come around and hand each of you a copy of the syllabus for this course." Ryan rose and took a stack of papers from their folding table and started to distribute them around the room. "The first thing you'll notice," Cara continued, "Is that at the very top of the page, there is an email address and phone number listed for each of us. If you have any questions whatsoever outside of class hours, please feel free to contact one or both of us."

Class continued, and after Cara painstakingly outlined the syllabus and further expectations of the course, she announced that everyone was to get changed and meet on the pool deck for a prerequisite swimming test. She stood up and left the room, and the students filed out behind her. Meredith was the last to walk toward the door, and as she approached, Ryan stood and said, "Hello!"

Meredith looked at him suspiciously. "Hello?"

"You used to work at The Garden, right?"

Her eyes grew worried. "Oh, shit," she said. "I stuck my foot in my mouth, didn't I?" She rolled her eyes. "You probably love that place. Shit! I almost always recognize the regulars."

Ryan laughed. "Oh, I'm not a regular. I've actually only eaten there once—a couple months ago. The food was kind of bland. I guess you made an impression though because before your introduction I was struggling to place where I'd seen you before."

She cocked her head and looked at him slyly. "Do you have some kind of photographic memory or something? Or are you just a creep?"

Ryan laughed again. "No, not normally—to either question. I was there with a friend and his family." He swallowed sharply. "Unfortunately, he died about a week later. I think I've got everything that happened that last week permanently imprinted." He paused. "But we all thought you were really funny."

162 | GREGORY JOSEPHS

She pressed her lips tightly together as Ryan studied her eyes. After a moment, she said "Well, I'm sorry to hear that." She waited to see if he would speak again, and when he didn't, she said, "I guess I'll see you on deck." Smiling softly, she turned and walked out of the room. Ryan gathered his things, locked the classroom door, and followed.

Everyone passed the prerequisite swimming test, and class continued until late in the evening. Ryan slept soundly, and arrived bright and early the next morning—Saturday—for the second day of the course. Cara took care of most of the lecturing, but Ryan got his opportunity to get into the finer aspects of teaching when later in the afternoon Cara put him in charge of conducting the first of four practice teaching sessions.

When he returned home on Saturday evening he was exhausted, but content. There was still sangria left from dinner with Max, so he poured himself a glass. Jay and Mark were home as well, sitting in the living room at the far end of the apartment. Mark had recently purchased 'Return of the King' on DVD, and he and Jay had been watching it non-stop ever since. Ryan rarely sat in the living room—indeed often forgot it was there—and tonight was no exception. Deciding he couldn't handle hobbits, he took his wine and relaxed in his room.

Around eight o'clock, the phone rang. Ryan didn't recognize the number on the caller ID, but he answered it anyway. "Hello?"

"Hi, is this Ryan?" It was a girl's voice.

"Yes."

"Ryan, it's Meredith Gardner from the WSI class?"

He was surprised. "Oh, Meredith. Hello. What's up?"

"I figured I'd try you before Cara. I'm such an idiot. This afternoon when I was changing after class I must have left my materials on one of the benches in the locker room. The pool is closed now, so

I was wondering if you have an extra set. I need to do my reading and write a lesson plan for my practice teaching tomorrow."

He considered. "Hmm, well, I don't have an extra set, but I suppose I could loan you mine for the night. We'll find yours tomorrow morning."

She sighed with great relief. "Oh, thank you! Where do you live? I'll drive anywhere. God, I'm such an idiot."

Ryan chuckled. "You're not going to believe this. I actually rent the apartment above The Garden."

She laughed sharply, and the distortion over the phone made Ryan wince. "You're shitting me, right?"

"No, not at all. Just park in the lot behind the restaurant, walk up the stairs to the deck, and you'll see my front door. Where are you coming from?"

"About five blocks away. I'll be right there, and thank you so much." She hung up the phone, and as he replaced the receiver, he smiled.

Ten minutes later the doorbell rang. Ryan rushed from his room to see Jay headed toward the door. "Don't worry," he said. "It's for me."

"Oh?" Jay said, meaningfully. "Got company, man?" He raised his eyebrows.

Ryan rolled his eyes. "Hardly. It's a girl from the WSI class at work."

"Is she hot?'

Ryan laughed. "Fuck off!" He smiled, knowing Jay would take his words in jest.

"I'm just saying, man, don't go turning on us now!"

Ryan raised a middle finger behind him and walked through the hall from the kitchen to the front door. He opened it and began to smile at Meredith, standing on the other side, but quickly changed his expression when he saw that she was soaked. It was raining furiously, and she stepped quickly inside.

"Jesus Christ!" she exclaimed. "Where the hell did this come from? I checked the weather this morning, and there was a ten percent chance of rain."

Ryan stared, wide-eyed before he said, "Hold on, let me grab you a towel." He rushed to the bathroom, grabbed a clean towel, and when he returned, she was standing dripping in the kitchen.

"Christ," she said. "This place is a shit hole." Ryan extended the towel, and as she took it, she added, "No offense, of course."

"None taken. Was it raining when you left your house?"

"No, I was about halfway here. I figured I'd walk because it was so close, and then the sky just opened up out of nowhere."

Ryan bit his lip and surveyed her up and down. She was tall for a girl—slender but with moderate curves. He considered and then said, "Could I get you some dry clothes?"

She looked at him skeptically. "Do you keep a spare women's wardrobe?"

"No, but I have a dryer. I can give you a clean pair of sweats and a kind of baggy sweater to wear while your clothes dry—that is if you want to wait it out." He was quiet for a moment, then shyly added, "You don't have to worry about—I'm—"

"Gay?" she asked. Ryan blushed. "Obviously. I'm sorry, but it's no big secret to me."

From the far end of the apartment, Jay called "Hey, new girl! You'd better not turn him."

Both Ryan and Meredith laughed at this. Finally, she said, "Do you have anything to drink?"

"Half a jug of sangria." He blushed suddenly, realizing she'd probably meant something other than alcohol. "Or, I mean, water. I think there might be some soda."

She smiled wickedly. "Water might have been fine, but since you offered, I'll go with the sangria. You'd better get me those clothes."

Ryan brought her the pair of sweatpants and sweater he'd promised, and while she changed in the bathroom, he poured her a glass of wine. After she emerged—she looked like she was swimming in the baggy garments—they put her wet things in the dryer. Over the course of the next hour, they sat at the dining table, and he outlined for her the contents of the next day's lesson and sat with her while she read. He answered her questions, and when it was time for her to write her lesson plan for the next morning, he went into his room to check the weather.

Meredith finished her lesson plan just after her clothes were dry. She changed back and sat down to finish her second glass of wine. Ryan poured himself a third. "Thank you," she said.

"Anytime. Sorry about the rain." He looked out the windows into the dark beyond. "It looks like it's stopped for now."

"For now?" she asked.

"Yeah, I just checked the weather and it looks like it's going to rain all day tomorrow. It's going to make for a messy ride in."

She raised her eyebrows. "You don't have a car?"

"I did until about January. Nasty car accident."

She raised her eyebrows further. "Your fault?"

"No," he replied shaking his head slowly. "Just some idiot running a stop sign."

"Shit. You've had a tough year so far, huh?"

"Well, what doesn't kill us—" he didn't finish.

Meredith raised her glass and drained the rest of its contents in a single swallow. "Phew!" she said, rising. "I should get going. Long day in the pool tomorrow, right?"

"Right," he said, standing to walk her to the door.

When they reached it, she turned to him. "Thank you again for your help tonight—and for the clothes and wine."

"Like I said, anytime."

She was quiet for a moment. "Do you want a ride tomorrow? I'd be driving in anyways, but since it's going to rain, you could consider it a thank you."

"Well, sure. I have to be there a little earlier than you though. Class starts at nine, would it be alright to get there by eight-thirty?"

"Not a problem," she said, opening the door. "I'll be downstairs at eight-fifteen."

"Thanks, Meredith." He smiled.

"Goodnight." She stepped outside and closed the door behind her.

Ryan returned to the dining table and finished his glass quickly. A few minutes later he put himself to bed, content. He liked Meredith— she was sharp and unusual—and hoped dimly that he might forge a friendship with her. He slept like a rock.

The next morning, Meredith arrived at eight-fifteen exactly. As Ryan walked down the steps from his apartment to the waiting car below, he caught his breath. Meredith's vehicle was a light blue Subaru sedan—perhaps even the same model Darren had driven. A thick coating of dirt and grime on the outside withstood even the rain and left the car looking grey, just as Darren's had been. As he pulled open the passenger door, he shivered at the resemblance. He climbed inside, and Meredith smiled, oddly.

"You look like you've seen a ghost," she said.

Ryan forced a weak laugh. "I guess you could say that." She waited a moment for him to continue, and when he didn't, she shook her head and started to drive. There was music playing softly. It was cold and electronic but somehow familiar. As she pulled out of the parking lot and into the alley leading to the street, Ryan said, "Can you turn this up a little bit?"

She did as he asked and then replied, "Not much of a conversationalist this morning?"

He shook his head. "No, no. I just feel like—" he stopped talking to listen.

He remembered Valentine's Day; bare branches against a stale orange sky and traffic lights reflected on snow banks. *I love this part— everything comes twice as fast.*

"Feel like—" she prompted.

"I know this song!"

"Congratulations," she said, flatly. "Actually, it's pretty cool that you do. A lot of people don't. It's a band called Kosheen. I think they're British. They're probably my favorite. How do you know them?"

He smiled sadly. "Just someone I used to know."

She turned her eyes from the road to look at him for a moment. He expected her to speak, but then she returned her gaze to the street ahead and let the silence between them be filled with the aching sound of the rich female vocals.

He stared out the windows at the bleak watery world beyond and gave in to his sorrow as Meredith drove on through the rainy streets of Ryan's new world. It was a world without Darren, and it was filled with artifacts—reminders that he had been and was no more. Unable to regard the dismal mood of the weather outside any longer, Ryan closed his eyes, and for a few moments, the world was quiet around him.

CHAPTER 9

When Meredith stepped out of Cara's office, Ryan breathed a sigh of relief. It was minutes from closing time on Sunday, May 30th, and he was drafting an instructor schedule for the session of swimming lessons slated to start the following Tuesday morning. Seeing her, he let the pencil fall from his hand and pushed away from the lifeguard desk with an exaggerated sigh.

Meredith looked at him, quizzically. "Tough day?" she asked.

He threw his hands in the air. "I'm really glad that tomorrow is Memorial Day. I'm going to need a day to rest before lessons start on Tuesday. I just have no idea which classes to assign people. You're teaching next week, so help me out. What do you want?"

She stepped forward and looked at the schedule he'd been working on. "Hell if I know."

"Oh, great. Thanks."

She shrugged. "Why don't you just give me one of everything, then I can figure out what my preferences are for next time around."

"Alright—that's not really helpful." The office phone rang. "Hold on one second, I need to get this." He pulled himself back to the desk and picked up the receiver. "Aquatics, this is Ryan."

"Hey man, it's Jay," said the voice at the other end of the line. "You're almost closed, right?"

Ryan looked at the clock hanging above the desk—five-fifty-two. "Yeah, about eight minutes. What's up?"

"Man, Ryan, you have to get home fast. There's some girl here—Shelly? She says she talked to you and she's moving in?"

Ryan laughed. "Oh yeah, sorry, she's fine. I meant to tell you guys I already have people lined up for when your lease is done in August. She probably just wants to look around again. I don't know why she's in town though, she lives in Ohio."

Jay's voice was grave. "She must have missed the August part. She showed up fifteen minutes ago with a moving truck and some yapping fucking dog. You've got to get here fast, man. Mark locked the door, and she's refusing to get off the deck. If she doesn't leave soon, he says he's going to call the police. He's pissed, man."

"Shit," Ryan said, softly. "I'll be there as quickly as I can. Just tell Mark to hold off on the police. I'll figure this out."

"Alright, see you soon." Jay hung up the phone.

Ryan replaced the receiver and turned slowly to look at Meredith. When she saw his face she whistled and said, "Wow. Bad news?"

"My new roommate is trying to move into my house two months early."

"Ouch, and I'm guessing you didn't know anything about it?"

"No, not a thing." He groaned and slapped his hands on the desk. "And now I'm going to have to clean it up."

Meredith shrugged. "Seems pretty cut and dry to me, don't you think? She needs to figure something else out until those two oafs move."

He was silent for a minute, considering his options. Finally, he asked, "Meredith, are you going straight home?"

She laughed. "Nope, I'm hitting the town at six on a Sunday night."

"No need for sarcasm."

"Actually," she said "I *am* going out tonight, but that's not until late. I'll give you a ride. Come on, get packed up."

Fifteen minutes later, Meredith parked her car in the lot behind The Garden. Jay had exaggerated a bit—Shelly hadn't brought a moving truck, just a rented trailer attached to her blue Honda SUV. Meredith turned off the engine and asked, "Do you want me to come up with you?"

He shook his head. "Oh, no. That would be really embarrassing. Anyways, this isn't your fight."

She laughed. "I never said it was." For a moment she said nothing, then continued. "Well, fuck what you want anyways. I'm coming. You never know when I'll come in handy." She pushed open the driver side door and stepped out into the sunny late afternoon. Sighing inwardly, Ryan followed.

Shelly was sitting on the floor of the deck at the top of the stairs. When she saw Ryan and Meredith's heads appear on approach, she leapt up and rushed forward. Smiling brightly she stood diminutively before them and said, "Thank God you're here. Like—ugh. They won't let me in."

Ryan's brow furrowed as he considered her. She looked the same as she had on their first meeting—spiky, short mahogany hair, and a baggy men's striped polo shirt tucked into loose dark jeans, cinched with a belt. Her deep brown eyes gleamed in the early evening sunlight. Before he had time to speak, he felt movement around his leg and jumped. A small dog—a cocker spaniel with a dishwater white coat—was sniffing his ankle. Reading his surprise, the dog hopped backward and started yelping painfully.

Shelly laughed. "Oh, don't worry about him. His name is Mars, and he's a sweet old thing. I've had him for ten years now, since I was eleven."

Ryan sighed with exasperation. "You didn't tell me you had a dog."

"Yes I did."

He shook his head. "No, I'm pretty certain that you didn't."

She shrugged and extended her arms. "You had a lot on your mind. You probably just let it slip."

Beside him, Meredith laughed quietly to herself. Both Ryan and Shelly glared at her, and she pulled her neck inward like a turtle trying to hide in its shell.

Ryan pulled his hands through his hair and asked, "What are you doing here, Shelly?"

"I'm trying to move in. I thought that was pretty obvious with the trailer and all."

"When you were here in March I told you that the room would be available on August first. Or was I so distracted that I let *that* crucial piece of information slip as well?"

"Look," she replied. "My lease in Ohio is up tomorrow. I didn't have anywhere to go, and with Mars—I can't just couch hop, you know? He's old. He needs a solid routine."

Ryan looked at Meredith and said, under his breath, "This is unbelievable." He turned back to Shelly. "So, you thought the best option was to show up here and hope for the best? What about your family?"

"Dad is in L.A. Mom is in Chicago."

Feeling increasingly frustrated, Ryan threw his hands in the air. As he struggled to keep his temper under control—he really didn't want to deal with this right now—he forced himself to speak calmly. "Chicago is in Illinois, which is the second state over from Ohio. Hell, you probably had to drive *through* Chicago to get here. Why couldn't you stay with your mother for two months?"

Like a frightened but dangerous animal that had been backed into a corner, Shelly's eyes glimmered, and she pulled her shoulders slightly inward. The adrenaline coursing through her veins practically made the air crackle with explosive energy. When she spoke, Ryan detected a slight quaver in her voice. "I really don't want to get into that right now. Let's just say it wasn't really an option, okay? Look, I'll pay whatever. Can you just talk to the guys inside?"

Ryan swallowed sharply. "Shelly, this is Meredith. Meredith, this is Shelly. Can you two please stay together out here? I need to talk to Jay and Mark."

"Of course," Meredith said, quietly. Shelly nodded.

He walked to the front door and pounded on it, forcefully. "Hey, guys? It's Ryan." A few moments later the door opened a crack, and then wider still. Ryan stepped inside and closed it forcefully behind him.

When the door opened again a few minutes later, Shelly and Meredith looked up expectantly from where they'd been sitting. Ryan stepped forward with Jay and Mark beside him. "Shelly," he began. "After some deliberation, the guys have agreed to let you stay here with us for the interim."

She leapt up from where she'd been sitting. "Oh, thank you so much. Thank you!"

"Wait," said Mark, sternly. "There are some fucking conditions."

Shelly's expression changed from joy to something more sober. "Such as?"

It was Jay who continued. "Listen man—err, I mean—whatever. Listen, Shelly, the place is pretty full already. We're going to let you sleep on the couch, but anything non-essential has to go to storage."

"I don't have a—"

"A storage unit? You're going to need to get one. Like, tomorrow."

She was quiet. Then, "Anything else?"

"Yeah," Mark said. "You're going to need to pay a quarter of the rent, and it's due on the first—two days."

After another silence, she swallowed hard. "Anything else?"

This time Ryan spoke. "Sort of. I'm way more forgiving than these two—" they each nodded at this "—and it's pretty shitty showing up here unannounced. You could have at least called to check first. If you cause any issues, they are going to ask you to leave, and there won't be much that I can do about it. Technically I'm only subletting until August, so I don't have any authority. Can you agree to all of this?"

She nodded slowly. "Yes. Thank you very much. I'm really—I'm really sorry."

Jay and Mark nodded in return and walked back into the apartment.

Now Meredith rose from where she was sitting and turned to Shelly. "Do you want some help bringing up some clothes? Also, I have a small storage unit not far from here. Maybe you can get one in the same facility."

"Thank you," Shelly said, grasping Meredith's hand firmly. "Thank you."

~*~

An hour later Shelly finished arranging her essential items, and Mark and Jay's tempers had cooled slightly. Still, the atmosphere of the apartment above The Garden was tense, and slowly but surely each of Ryan's roommates found a reason to leave. Shelly excused herself, saying she wanted to meet up with some girls she'd been talking to from the LGBT office on campus. Confused as to why she hadn't tried to room with one of these girls during the interim, Mark and Jay headed to a bar in a huff. By eight o'clock, Ryan and Meredith were by themselves, except for Mars the dog, who was taking quite a liking to Ryan and refused to be more than five feet away at any given time.

Sitting at the dining table with a can of Miller Light she'd found in the refrigerator, Meredith said, "So that was pretty wild, huh?"

Ryan propped his elbows on the table, covered his face with his hands and groaned. "I don't even want to think about what I've gotten myself into. I knew from the first time I met her that something was a little—off?"

"Then why did you agree to let her live with you?"

The flat manner in which Meredith asked the question suggested saying *yes* to Shelly hadn't been the only option. He knew why. "Darren," he said. "Darren was talking to her before he died and thought she was really cool. He was planning on having her live with us next year anyways."

Meredith rolled her eyes and set the can of beer on the table. "It always comes back to Darren, doesn't it? I'm so glad I didn't know you while he was alive, because I probably would've thought you were an idiot."

"Ouch," Ryan said, playfully. Actually, her words stung, but he was developing an admiration for Meredith's blunt honesty.

"I mean, come on!" she continued. "He thinks she's cool, so even after he's dead—totally nullifying the agreement—you still decide to let her move in? What's the reason? Is it out of respect for his memory?"

Now things were getting uncomfortable. "Look, a lot of people were—orphaned when Darren died. It's not her fault, so why should she suffer?"

Meredith leaned forward. "Ryan, it's not your responsibility, because it isn't your fault *either*. And honestly, in the future, you might want to question Darren's judgment a little more."

"Why is that?" Ryan asked, defensively. He reached absently for the thumb ring around his neck.

"Because the same kid that thought crazy Shelly was cool and would be good to live with is also the kid that thought lines of coke were good for his weak heart. Catch my drift?" Ryan looked down at the table, and she reached across and slapped him lightly on the side of the head. "Don't sulk."

He lifted his eyes and forced a smile—he was dangerously close to tears. After he was sure he could speak without sounding distressed he asked, "So, where are you going tonight?"

"Actually, I'm headed to Paradox." She grinned, slyly. "Do you want to come? I know you aren't working tomorrow."

Ryan groaned. Paradox was the seedy establishment that passed as Northern Colorado's only gay dance club. Really, it was a collection of modular trailers shoved together just outside the city limits. The owner had remodeled the giant tin cans to include a tiny bar with some pool tables and a small dance floor that was perpetually sticky with spilled drinks. The space was constantly filled with a thick haze of cigarette smoke, and they charged a five-dollar cover at the door if you were of age—seven dollars for Ryan because he wasn't.

"Sorry," he said, shaking his head slowly, "That's not really my scene, and there isn't enough liquor in this house to make it my scene tonight."

Sighing, Meredith said, "Suit yourself, prude." She laughed to lighten the mood. "You really should come though. I don't usually go to Paradox, it's not totally my scene either, but they always have an amazing night on Sundays before a Monday holiday."

"Really, I couldn't."

"Oh well. It's too bad. Maybe you'd find a boyfriend."

The ways she phrased it—flat and matter-of-fact—gave Ryan the idea that something like finding a boyfriend was simpler than he imagined it to be. He thought of Max. More than a month had passed since the ill-timed kiss and he'd still not found the courage to express his feelings.

He considered Meredith's what's-the-big-deal phrasing and asked, "How do you do that?"

She pulled another long sip from her beer. "Do what?"

"Talk about things like they're trivial. Like they should be easy."

"I'm not sure I follow."

He placed his hands on the table and pushed as if preparing to stand, then changed his mind and slumped back into his chair, defeated. "You did it twice already tonight. The first time you asked me why I let Shelly move in, as if saying *no* was nothing to sweat over. And then the second time was just now. You talked about finding a boyfriend in the same way you'd talk about grocery shopping—like I could walk down the aisles and just pull one down off a shelf."

Meredith laughed. "Well, what would the consequences have been for telling Shelly to take a hike?" When Ryan didn't answer she continued, "I bet Darren's ghost would have haunted you for all eternity for being such a prick."

"Alright, alright. That's enough." Ryan forced a laugh. "I think I'm just overly concerned about other people, you know?"

Meredith rolled her eyes, dismissing the excuse. "And as for a boyfriend? You could have one, easily. All you have to do is try."

"Try? All I did for the last year was try!"

"With Darren?" Meredith shook her head. "That's not what I meant by trying. Anyways, everything I've ever heard about Darren makes me think he was a royal asshole. No. Here is how it works. You find someone you think is attractive—inside and out is a plus, but just one or the other is acceptable to start—and you ask him out. If he says no, he can go fuck himself, and you move on to the next one. I mean, you're nineteen, and you're cute enough—"

"Cute enough? Why are we friends, again?"

Meredith laughed. "You know what I mean. But if you get a rejection, just forget about it. It doesn't matter. And the one thing I know for certain is that you can't force it. A no is a no, and it doesn't matter why. You're never going to be able to turn it into a yes. Is it their loss? Probably. Whatever, move on."

Ryan sighed. "I mean, that all sounds okay, but putting it into practice is a whole other thing."

"Well, practice is the key word there, isn't it?"

He shuddered at the implications of admitting it, but Meredith was right. He was certain she saw the look of surrender on his face before he spoke, and he knew with equal certainty by her reaction that she was going to press the issue from now on. "Yes, I suppose you're right." He thought for a minute and then smiled defiantly. "So, if it's so easy, why don't you have a boyfriend?"

She shook her head slowly. "Purely by choice. I'll admit I'm a little messed up from the last one. I could have someone else in a minute, I'm sure. But right now? Not interested."

"What happened?"

"Nope, you don't get to go there yet. I like you Ryan, but you're going to have to earn that one." She frowned. "Let's just say I've got some issues with trust."

"I see. Well, if you think you want to talk about it—"

"No, I don't thanks. Anyways, what were we talking about? Oh, you need a boyfriend!"

"You really do make it sound easy."

She clapped her hands together excitedly. "Yes! This is going to be so much fun!" She looked at him slyly. "Is there anyone you've been thinking about lately?"

He felt a warm rush as his face reddened, and he knew he'd never get away with a lie. "Well, I think there is something between my friend Max and me, but—"

She didn't wait for him to finish. Meredith moved fluidly up and out of her chair, and rushed into Ryan's room. Moments later she emerged with the telephone receiver. Smiling mischievously, she walked slowly forward and handed Ryan the phone. "Call him. Ask him to come over."

He placed the phone on the table. "Meredith—"

"Call him!" she said, more forcefully.

"Alright, I promise I'll call him tonight."

Giving a stern look, she said, "I'd like to see you do it now."

"Baby steps, Meredith. I promise I'll call tonight. Have another beer."

It was nearly ten by the time Ryan worked up the courage to call Max. Meredith had left an hour ago, and in the interim Ryan paced back and forth in his bedroom. Untangling the logic behind his lack of emotional disclosure to Max was exhausting. But Max had kissed him. Max had made it easy. Max could be the future that obliterated the past.

In his deliberations, he realized how badly he wanted this. His fears and misgivings amounted to nothing in comparison to what he stood to gain. And really, wasn't this what he'd always wanted? The truth hit him suddenly and without warning. For the first time since meeting Darren, he felt a clarity in his desires. For the longest time, he'd believed that the fire which animated him was a desire to be held by *Darren*, and loved by *Darren*. Now he realized, gratefully, he'd gotten it all wrong. Meredith's words about the simplicity of it all cut through Darren like a scythe, and now Ryan understood. In reality, the fire which animated him was a desire to be *held* and to be *loved*. It didn't matter if it was Darren. It simply mattered that it was—that it could be. He imagined Max beside him, sleeping in on a rainy day. He imagined cooking together in the kitchen. He pictured hiking and camping and birthdays and Christmas. He imagined on and on until finally, emboldened, he dialed the number.

Max picked up on the third ring. "Hey, Mister! Great timing! How are you?"

Ryan smiled to himself, excitedly. "I'm doing pretty well, and yourself? What are you up to?"

"I just said goodbye to the most amazing first date of my life! His name is Jake, and I've got a really good feeling about this one. I can't wait for you to meet him!"

Without warning, a flash flood of tears stung Ryan's eyes. Carefully controlling his voice, he said, "That's awesome! I can't wait. Well, I just wanted to check in, but I think I have another call."

"Mister—Ryan, are you okay?"

"Catch you later!" he said, as brightly as he could manage before he hung up the phone.

~*~

Ryan's tears became increasingly violent, and at times he had to focus on his breathing. Sitting on the floor a few feet from the dining table, Mars cocked his head and winced every time Ryan sobbed. After a minute or two, deciding the whole scene was pathetic and distasteful, he let out a low huff and disappeared into the apartment.

The dog's attitude didn't help matters. Ryan was angry at himself for so many reasons. Max—the embodiment of everything he wanted in a partner—had thrown himself at him, and Ryan waited a day too long to acknowledge to Max that the interest was truly mutual. He was angry because his theatrical reaction, which thankfully no one was home to witness, forced him to recognize the extent to which he was damaged. And he was angry because through it all, a voice in a distant corner of his mind told him that he could only attribute part of this damage to Darren.

A few minutes later, when the sobbing began to subside, he turned his thoughts to the whimsical. He imagined himself as a caterpillar—a tiny creature inching his way through a world whose colors were desolate and grey in the wake of Darren's passing. This constant misery was tiring, and the time had come for a profound change. He wanted to wrap himself in a chrysalis and undergo a metamorphosis of self.

He could emerge glorious with wings of orange and black; beat them against the air. He could rise above, fluttering, reborn as the Monarch.

For a moment, he felt comfort in his musings, but the emotional reprieve was fleeting. Within a half hour of his call to Max, he was subdued but lonely, so with great effort, he decided to stop feeling sorry for himself long enough to address the immediate problem. He needed company tonight.

Though Steven initially came to mind, Ryan dismissed him almost at once. He was one of Ryan's best friends—loyal, intelligent, and dryly funny—but it was difficult to predict his mood in situations like this one. It was possible that Ryan's present misery would cause Steven to reflect on his own failings at romance, and then they'd both spend the night spiraling deeper into a state of depression.

He also considered swallowing his pride and meeting Meredith at Paradox, but ultimately decided he didn't want her to see him break down if she asked the wrong questions about how the phone call went.

Finally, he thought of Brandon.

He wasn't sure he could call Brandon a friend just yet. Though the trip up the canyon had been a significant step in that direction, he remained hesitant. He still associated Brandon with a lot of pain, but in the end, he called the number anyway.

On the fourth ring, Brandon picked up. "Hello?"

In the background, Ryan could detect a dull hum of voices and what sounded like a guitar. "Oh," he began, hoping he didn't sound too surprised. "Hi, it's Ryan. Sorry, it sounds like I'm interrupting you."

Brandon laughed. "Interrupting? No, not at all." A brief silence ensued. "So, what's up?"

"Oh—nothing really. I just wanted to see what you were doing. Sorry, I know it's getting late." He laughed, quietly. "But anyways, it sounds like you're at a party or—"

Brandon cut in. "A party? No, not exactly." There was a silence again. Finally, he said, "Are you—wanting to hang out?"

"Actually, yes." He hoped he didn't sound too eager. "But like I said, it sounds like you're busy."

"Not busy at all. I'm actually kind of surprised. In fact, really fucking surprised—and excited. You picked the perfect night to call. Have you been to the Back Alley Café?"

Ryan knew the place, but he'd never been. It was a coffee shop built into the upstairs of what had either once been a proper residence or an enormous carriage house. Either way, he supposed the charm of the place was that it existed quite literally off the beaten path, tucked into an unpaved alley from which it derived its name. The best part, he supposed, was that it was just over a block away. "No," he said, finally. "Is that where you are now?"

"I can't believe you've never been! Yeah, we're on the porch upstairs. You should come."

"We?"

"Yeah, I'm here with my friends Caleb and Tom. You're going to love them!"

Ryan smiled to himself. "Okay." Moving from the dining table he poked his head into his bedroom to look at the time on the alarm clock. "So, it's about ten of eleven. You guys are going to be there for a while?"

"All night. We were thinking about going to Paradox, but we got a little too drunk last night, so we decided to stick with coffee and tea this evening. So yeah, we're staying for a while. But, Ryan, you could be here in literally two minutes."

"Yeah, I know. I just kind of want to clean up first. I'll be there shortly."

Twenty minutes later, Ryan stepped off the paved sidewalk into the seemingly utter darkness of the gravel alley that housed his destination. Halfway down he saw what he knew in daylight to be the Back Alley Café. Though the alley was dark, a mix of brightly colored lights on the far side of the café set the building into sharp contrast against the night—its facade inky-black against the backlighting. As he moved forward, he could hear jovial voices wafting up from smoky figures huddled at the base of the stairs leading to the café above. Standing at the place where the darkness ended and the light began, their bodies looked ethereal, and Ryan could sense their happiness. It drew him forward.

Each step he took toward the café brought a further spectrum of colors and sounds emanating from the side of the building. As he came within a few yards, the smells began as well—an oddly intoxicating mix of coffee, onions, cigarettes, and marijuana. Finally, he reached the line where the darkness of the alley was vanquished by the light of the café above. The smoky figures turned into actual humans—approximately Ryan's age—standing in groups of two and three. Mostly unaware of his presence, they continued speaking to each other in animated, chattering voices, only pausing their thoughts long enough to drag off the lit cigarettes each held in hand.

For a moment, he stood at the base of the slatted wood stair—not unlike his own—that led up to a porch similar to that of the Garden. But as he began to walk up the stairs, it was quickly evident that the

Back Alley Café was in an entirely different league. White tube lights curled around the hand rail invited him upward until he reached the top.

He gasped at the beauty of the porch. Eight small wrought-iron tables were scattered about with three or four chairs each. Giant houseplants—palms and fig trees and colorful crotons—had been put out for the season, transforming the space into a lush, elevated garden. Pansies and impatiens exploded with color out of the flower boxes that lined the porch railings. But perhaps most spectacular— the source of the light that had led him forward—were the dozens of colored lamps hanging from wires strung above.

Lost in his awe, it took Ryan a moment to hear a voice calling, softly at first, and then with greater intensity.

"Ryan! Over here!"

Turning to look at the farthest corner of the porch, he saw Brandon waving, seated at a table with two boys he didn't know. He waved in turn and headed forward, then sat down in a vacant chair and said, "Hello."

When Brandon smiled, Ryan shuddered involuntarily and hoped no one noticed. He was struck and sickened by how effortlessly attractive Brandon always appeared. Now, as he regarded the other boy's smile—so genuine and warm—he found himself fighting the urge to think about Darren, and the nature of the smiles he might have received.

Brandon spoke. "Ryan, glad you made it out. First things first." He indicated his two friends. "These two lovely gentlemen are Caleb and Tom."

Ryan turned his attention to the others, who smiled just as warmly. Upon first appraisal, the chemistry between them left no doubt they were a couple. He observed the way they leaned in close to one another from adjacent sides of the table while they regarded him. For the most part, they held his gaze, but their eyes kept turning to one another, almost conspiratorially, as they kept their smiles facing forward. In spite of his own romantic difficulties that night, he couldn't help but feel happy for them. They were adorable, though to Ryan's perception slightly mismatched. Where one looked slender and youthful, the other was shorter, thicker, and somewhat prematurely distinguished.

The slender and youthful half reached his hand across the table. As Ryan grasped it firmly, the other boy said, "I'm Caleb." He looked at Brandon. "That wasn't super clear, Brandon." He smiled again, and Ryan felt his heart flutter slightly. Upon further examination, he found Caleb to be nothing short of stunning. His medium, spiky hair was a deep brown, almost black, and it complemented perfectly the intense emerald green of his eyes. Though his face was somewhat gaunt and sharp—even stretched—Caleb's skin glowed in the multicolored luminescence from above.

Feeling slightly ashamed of his reaction, Ryan let go of Caleb's hand and turned his attention to the other boy. Clearing his throat, he said, "And you must be Tom."

Tom nodded forcefully and extended his hand. With a booming voice that could only be described as jolly, he said "Pleased to make your acquaintance!" Ryan considered him. Where Caleb's face came to harsh angles, Tom's was softer and round. His white-blond hair curled wildly out from his head in simultaneously thick and wispy locks, in the style of Mark Twain or Albert Einstein. An impressively bushy goatee hemmed in his mouth and protruded triumphantly from his chin, completing the picture of intelligent distinction. As they shook hands, Tom continued. "So, Brandon tells us it's your first time at the Back Alley?"

Ryan laughed, self-consciously. "Yeah. It's a shame because I only live a block away."

Brandon pushed his chair back and stood. "Well," he said, "It's time we introduced you to the place. I need something to drink, Ryan. Care to come inside and grab something yourself?"

"Sure."

Standing, he followed Brandon through a door just a few steps from the table. Once inside, his senses were forcefully accosted. The porch of the Back Alley Café seemed positively dull compared to the inside. The walls were painted in bright oranges, purples and reds. In the center of the space an enormous bar where customers ordered their coffee, tea, and food pressed up against an enclosed kitchen. The public space in the café was shaped around this central point in a square. Against one wall, a small carpeted stage—complete with a tattered upright piano—stood surrounded by giant, atrociously up-holstered couches and arm chairs. A few booths pressed up against another wall, and at the opposite corner of the room, there was a large section of bistro tables with tall chairs. Bookshelves lined the walls, and mismatched antique lamps graced most of the tables. The ceiling tiles above were each painted—some in solid colors, others as an abstract mix, and yet others as proper scenes ranging from the pastoral to the fantastical. The place was filled with people chatting and laughing as they sipped exotic looking beverages. In one of the arm chairs near the stage, Ryan found the source of the guitar he'd heard on the phone was a slightly sleepy-looking young hippie, strumming absently with his legs over one of the arms and the in-strument in his lap.

"This place is incredible," Ryan said.

Brandon laughed. "Come on, have you ever had Yerba Matté? It's basically a South American tea that gives you the kick of caffeine without the crash. They make these amazing Matté Lattes."

Ryan smiled and grabbed Brandon's hand, briefly. "Brandon," he said, quietly, "Thank you."

"For what?"

"I'll tell you about it later, maybe, but it's been a shitty night. It's good to see a friendly face."

Brandon smiled again, that same, slightly addicting smile. "No problem. Come on; Matté Latte and then you can tell the boys and me all about it."

Five minutes later, Ryan and Brandon sat back down in their chairs at the table outside, a couple of peach Matté Lattes in hand. Conversation began in the typical obligatory fashion—questions about what one another did for work or studied in school. Tom was twenty-four and had finished college with a generic liberal arts degree. Caleb was twenty-one and not currently enrolled in school because he was *figuring things out*. Ryan understood. Both worked as certified nurse's assistants in an assisted care facility for the elderly on the south side of town, and spoke of the work with a delightful amount of passion.

Eventually, the conversation turned to Ryan and his plans.

"So, you've had a couple years off and decided it's time to go back to school?" Caleb asked.

"Yeah, I think it's going to be kind of crazy. I'm glad I have the summer to prepare."

Ryan swore that Caleb fluttered his eyelashes slightly as he asked, "Prepare? How so?"

Considering a moment, he answered. "Well, you know—both mentally and, financially. I've been working full-time for two years now. I don't make gobs of money with the City, but I do alright. I'm going to have to seriously cut back my hours. And mentally? I still haven't decided if I'm going to major in music or French, or both. No matter what, I think my mind has just been out of school mode for a while."

Tom nodded understandingly. "Caleb won't admit it, but those are exactly the reasons he hasn't, um, figured it out yet."

Caleb shot him a scornful look, but before he could respond, Brandon chimed in. "Yes, yes, Tom is mister traditional four years in and out. Maybe if he'd spent a little time questioning what he wanted to do instead of diving in head first, he'd have come out with a more useful degree."

Tom guffawed with a booming cough of indignation. "Excuse me?" Then his face smoothed and he laughed again as he looked at Ryan. "Brandon is sort of right. I only harp on Caleb because I love him." With that, he reached an arm over his boyfriend's shoulder and pulled him in close, kissing him sharply on the cheek. Ryan couldn't help but notice a slight grimace on Caleb's face. In the moment, Ryan had taken Tom's ribbing as lighthearted, but the disappointed, slightly embarrassed look on Caleb's face suggested that he took it more seriously.

Tom seemed to wait for an *I love you* in return, which did not come. So, to stem the growingly awkward silence, Ryan asked, "How long have you two been together?"

Softly, smiling perhaps too widely in an effort to save face, Caleb responded. "It'll be a year in August. We've been living together since January." He looked at Tom then, and his disgraced demeanor melted away. "It's hard to believe it's been such a short time because things have moved so fast. Sometimes things just work, you know?"

Just then, Ryan noticed Brandon watching him intently. Caleb leaned in to give his boyfriend a real kiss, and when their lips met, they held it. Ryan's face must have registered a little of the emotional distress he'd been feeling earlier in the night, because Brandon cleared his throat more loudly than was necessary.

"Anyone feel like a cigarette?" he asked, rising from his chair.

Caleb and Tom broke apart, and Caleb responded with excitement, "That sounds great right about now. Ryan, you in?"

Trying to hide his disgust Ryan said, "No, sorry. It's not my thing. All three of you smoke?"

Caleb rolled his eyes. "Oh, honey, don't get preachy when you just met us." He laughed to lighten the mood. "If you're not allergic, or something, you could come downstairs to the alley and keep us company."

Not wishing to offend, Ryan obliged them and made the trek back down the stairs to the alley below, where the four of them turned into their own cluster of bodies, not unlike the ones that greeted Ryan on his arrival. After lighting up, Caleb and Tom chatted about a series of dramas at work. Brandon and Ryan laughed at the appropriate places, and inserted incredulous commentary as required.

When he finished smoking, Brandon threw his butt to the ground and smothered it into the gravel with the heel of his shoe. "If you gentlemen will excuse me, I need to go lose a little water weight. Meet you upstairs?"

Ryan and Caleb nodded, but Tom said, "Hold on, I'll come with you."

Brandon winked at Ryan and said, "I mean, sometimes it *is* a little too much for one person to hold. I can always use the help—"

This comment elicited a riot of laughter from the other three until finally, Tom said, "You should probably have that looked at. I just want some more tea." He looked then at Ryan and Caleb, whose cigarette was just over halfway burned. "Will you two be okay out here by yourselves? Caleb is a really slow smoker."

Rolling his eyes, Caleb said, "We'll be fine, honey. See you in a minute." Laughing, Tom and Brandon headed up the stairs. Caleb looked at Ryan and said, "I know we just met, but Brandon mentioned you were having a bad night?"

Ryan blushed a little and hoped Caleb couldn't tell in the dark. "Oh, yeah. I think I'm a little better now. I just needed to be around some friendly people."

Caleb pulled another drag off his cigarette and then said breathily through his exhale, "Boy problems, I presume?"

"Something like that."

"Okay, okay. You don't have to tell me. I mean, we *are* practically strangers. But whatever it is, you'll get through it." He laughed quietly and looked up at the sky. "You know, Tom and I have our issues. God knows there are times that he speaks to me and I just feel like—"

He trailed off, so Ryan said, "For me it's nothing like that. I'm just struggling with—I don't know. Knowing what I want? And when I do know what I want, they never seem to want me."

Caleb coughed and drew his eyebrows together in a scowl. "Excuse me? I've known you for all of twenty minutes, and I already know that anybody would be lucky to have you. I mean, if I weren't with Tom, I'd be all over you."

Ryan felt his blush deepen. His cheeks burned. He found Caleb to be hopelessly attractive, but this was too direct. And Caleb wasn't an option. Though he appreciated the flattery, it left him feeling soiled. And yet—

"Well—" he stammered. "Thank you?"

Caleb winked as he dropped his cigarette and pressed it into the dirt. "Come on; let's head up. You're so modest and innocent. We'll have to see more of you and see if we can ruin you a little bit."

"That doesn't really sound like a good thing."

Halfway up the stairs, Caleb considered a minute. "Maybe not. But trust me, you'll love every second of it."

CHAPTER 10

Two weeks passed between Memorial Day and the first time Max called. Ryan had just returned home from work and barely had time to sling his messenger bag onto the bedroom floor before the phone began to ring. He sighed with exhaustion—summer lessons had begun in earnest, and he was managing ten instructors and hundreds of children on a daily basis. He wasn't sure he had the energy for whoever was on the other end of the line. Letting his shoulders slump, he walked slowly toward the receiver.

Seeing Max's number on the caller ID put him into a slight panic. The phone continued to bleat as he hesitated, imploring him to answer. Finally, he touched it, gripping the receiver's sides firmly as he closed his eyes and exhaled.

Then the answering machine picked up, and he stepped away, relieved. His own voice began to play through the speaker on the phone's base, tinny and small. "Hi, this is Ryan. I can't get to the phone right now. Please leave a message."

After the beep, Max began to speak. "Hey Mister—uh, just calling to check in. I'm sort of surprised I haven't heard from you in a while. I know work is probably crazy. Anyways, um, give me a call back. Alright. Bye."

He sat heavily on the edge of his bed and covered his face with his hands. Max was a dilemma, and he wasn't sure how to proceed. At this point, it wouldn't be fair to anyone to express his feelings. In one

191

scenario, he risked driving a wedge between Max and Jake before their relationship even got started. But ultimately it was the second scenario that stayed his tongue; there was a possibility Max liked Jake *better* than he liked Ryan—that he was better off with someone less damaged. It wasn't worth the risk. A further rejection now would be a blow he couldn't withstand.

He watched the phone from across the room, knowing he should call back. Perhaps he could swallow his feelings and pretend nothing was wrong. Maybe he could muster the courage to smile and laugh as Max expressed how happy he was—for the sake of friendship.

He stood again, walked to the desk and picked up the phone. Not tonight, he decided. Maybe he could do it tomorrow. His limbs felt heavy, and he looked back toward the bed, thinking he ought to just go to sleep. Still, he was unsettled now and thought he could use some company.

He dialed Caleb.

On the third ring, there was a click. "Hello?"

He smiled with relief. "Hey, it's Ryan."

"Oh! Hey. What're you doing? Tom and I just opened a fresh bottle of vodka. Brandon is coming. Want to join?"

"Um—" he considered. "You're at home, I'm guessing?" He'd visited Tom and Caleb at their house—a little bungalow on the edge of campus—a week previous. It was about a mile walk.

"Sure enough," Caleb said.

"Vodka again, huh? You guys have kind of an unhealthy taste for the stuff."

"There you go, getting all preachy again." Caleb laughed. "Are you coming or not?"

"Alright," he said. "I'll be there in maybe twenty minutes? Don't drink it all before then."

"You'd better hurry. I can't make any promises."

He didn't return Max's call, and the following week Max tried three more times. The tone of the voicemails became increasingly frustrated to the point where Ryan couldn't bring himself to listen to them. He knew he was doing potentially irreversible damage to his friendship, yet couldn't find a way out of his paralysis. After the third call, Max stopped. It was bittersweet marking the absence of his number on the caller ID—for the second time in only a few months Ryan felt like he'd lost his best friend. Perhaps it was for the best. At this point, further association with Max would only bring everyone— especially himself—more pain.

He spent more time with Caleb and Tom and Brandon in an effort to put Max out of his mind.

He also tried to to spend time getting to know Shelly, who was turning out to be a surprisingly easy guest tenant. Although she took up almost permanent residence on one of the couches in front of the television, she didn't cause any problems. Her essential items were packed into clear plastic totes and organized neatly in a corner of the living room, while the rest went into storage as requested. He began making a point to spend a few minutes with her every night in the hope of discovering what Darren had liked about her so much.

Progress was slow, at best. While their conversations were pleas-ant, they were far from enlightening. Shelly had surrounded herself in a labyrinth of emotional walls, and reaching her—the *real* her—was going to be a formidable undertaking. He resolved to be patient and understanding, hoping it would be worth the effort in the end.

As the month began to wane, Mark and Jay got word that their new place was ready to move into a little early and started boxing their things with the intention of being gone by the beginning of July. Ryan viewed their departure with a mixture of relief and regret; in spite of their slovenly habits and generally wild behavior, they were good guys. Indeed, over the course of the spring the three of them had developed a pleasant, almost effortless co-existence. So even as he looked forward to the next chapter of living above The Garden, he knew he was going to miss them.

On the last Friday in June—the 25th—Ryan came home to find Max waiting for him on the porch. As he climbed the slatted wood stair up to his apartment, he caught a glimpse of familiar candy-apple red hair, and his breath stopped for a moment. Max was sitting in a chair near the front door, a brown paper bag in his lap. When he saw Ryan reach the porch he smiled, weakly.

"Hi there, Mister. It's been a while."

Ryan felt his face flush, and he swallowed hard to hold back tears. "Max," he said. "What are you doing here?"

The other boy set the paper bag on the ground and stood up slowly. When he answered, there was more than a hint of anger in his voice. "Oh, I don't know. I've been trying to get ahold of you for weeks now. Here I thought something was really wrong. You weren't answering any of my calls, so finally I talked to Steven. He said you seemed just fine, so I figured the problem was me, for some reason."

Ryan felt a few rogue tears break free and rushed forward, wrapping Max in his arms. "No, the problem isn't with you. It's me. It's only me."

Max pulled him tightly for a moment before stepping away. "Mister, what's going on? You've been acting funny since right before Memorial Day. You called me that night and then just—hung up. Is this a Darren thing? Did something happen?"

Folding his legs clumsily, Ryan seated himself hard on the floor of the porch. Max lowered himself down beside him before Ryan continued. "Ugh, Max, can we just forget about it?"

"No, I don't think so. Whatever it is, you know you can tell me."

He was silent for nearly an entire minute while he worked up the courage to say what needed to be said. The situation left him feeling frustrated, verging on irate. This was a moment he'd worked hard to avoid, and now it appeared all that effort was for nothing.

Sighing heavily, he began. "Max, I called you that night because I wanted to tell you how I felt—about you, and about us."

"About us?"

"When you kissed me in April, that was—I've never felt anything like that before and I *wanted* it, believe me. I don't know why I couldn't just accept it, but I've been having feelings for you since that Valentine's Day party. And I guess when you kissed me—when I got confirmation that you were feeling something too I just—"

"Mister—"

"I don't know! It's like something snapped in my brain. I wanted to believe it but I couldn't. And then you thought I didn't want it—want you—but that's the fucked-up thing. I'm not sure I ever wanted something so badly." He reached with his left hand and grabbed the thumb ring hanging around his neck, pulling on it forcefully. "And then you saw me grab on to this, like a reflex, and I think you thought—oh, I don't know! I'm just so damaged that instead of embracing what was happening and letting myself be happy, I shut down. I should have told you the next day, or the next week. I should have told you a thousand times. And then when I was finally able to—"

"Jake," Max said, and sighed.

Ryan choked on his next words. "Right. Jake. So, how could I? How could I tell you without everyone just being—hurt?"

Max shook his head, slowly. "Well, I don't know what to say. Maybe I should have been more direct. Maybe if I'd have just said something—not sprung it on you like I did that night—maybe things would've been different."

After a brief silence Ryan asked, "What are we going to do?"

"Well," Max considered, "Nothing, I guess. Things with Jake are going really well. That's probably not what you want to hear. Um—this is a mess, huh?" He laughed nervously. "To be quite honest all this really makes me question things because I still feel—"

Ryan reached out his hand and gripped Max's firmly. "Listen, Max. Whatever you're going to say, please don't. You're with Jake now, and no one benefits from thinking about might-have-beens, or what could be. Least of all, me. I don't think I could stand—" he closed his eyes and exhaled. "Just—don't say it. Okay?"

Max smiled sadly, and Ryan noticed that his eyes weren't exactly dry either. "Okay." He brightened. "Hey, I brought over a bottle of white in that brown bag. I was hoping maybe we could have a glass or two?"

Ryan grinned, letting his shoulders relax. "That would be really nice, Max. We've got some catching up to do."

"I'll say." He stood. "By the way, I think you've got a birthday in a couple weeks, no?"

"Heh. Right. I won't be a teenager anymore." Ryan stood beside him as Max picked up the paper bag and they headed toward the door.

"Twenty. Whoah. I always forget you're so young."

"You're only two years older."

"Not even. Anyways, what do you think about having a party here? We could celebrate, and maybe you could meet Jake."

As Ryan opened the front door, he paused to consider. Smiling, he said, "A party? Yeah, I think we could use a party."

~*~

"Isn't it wrong for you to be preparing your own birthday party?" Steven asked. He grimaced as he forced a paring knife through a particularly large block of sharp cheddar. The blade of the knife was too short to cut through the cheese in a single stroke, so he wrenched it up and down, over and over, in the same manner an excited child might flip a light switch on and off. It was nearly seven and Ryan had asked people to come for his party at eight. Though there wasn't much left to prepare, both he and Steven were feeling the pressure of anticipation.

Ryan finished opening the package of red plastic cups he'd been holding and set the entire stack upside down on the dining table. He looked at Steven struggling behind the kitchen peninsula and shook his head. "You're never going to get that cheese cut using that little thing. Open that drawer to your left. There's a giant chef's knife in there."

Scowling, Steven did as he requested and found that the new, larger knife cut his effort significantly. "I wish you'd have told me that earlier, considering I just moved in and don't know my way around this kitchen yet. Really though. I know you and Max planned this, so it's not a surprise party, but he could at least have taken you out somewhere while someone else got this set up."

"Nah," Ryan smiled. "You know I love this stuff. Anyways, last I checked, today is the tenth of July."

"Point being?"

"I've actually been twenty for two days now. It's not *really* a birthday party if it doesn't happen on my birthday, is it?"

Steven groaned, then said in his most patronizing tone, "Your actual birthday was in the middle of the week—a bad time for parties. So now it's Saturday, and we're celebrating today." He continued more seriously. "Regardless, I feel like you shouldn't be here right now. I wish you'd let other people take care of you a little more. You should relinquish control once in a while."

"Ouch."

"I'm not trying to offend you, but think about it."

Walking quietly to the pantry, he considered Steven's words. He pulled a pack of bulk napkins from a shelf and started back to the dining table. "I let people take care of me," he said.

Steven set the knife down and gave Ryan a hard look. "Yeah right. You turned twenty, but the way you act you might as well be forty. Do you know what I miss most about Darren?"

"No, what?" Ryan asked, his voice little more than a whisper.

"Darren was good at breaking you down, you know? You can be so reserved sometimes that—"

Ryan dropped the package of napkins on the table with a dramatic flourish. "Reserved? What the hell does that mean?" He thought he knew though. He was at the top of the canyon with Brandon again. *Do you think you're fun? No, I'm not fun.*

"Ugh, forget it."

"No, I won't forget it. Is this because I criticized how you were cutting that cheese?"

Steven didn't speak for nearly a minute. Ryan watched his face as he carefully sliced the cheddar, and knew how deeply he was considering his next words. When he finally spoke, his voice was calm. "All I'm going to say is, it would be nice to see you approach life with more of a *fuck-it* attitude now and again." Steven smiled. "It's been a rough year for you. Hell, it's been a rough year for *us*, and everyone since, well, you know—Darren. I'd just love to see you throw caution to the wind sometimes. Kiss boys. Dance on tables. Get really drunk. That kind of thing, right?"

Ryan couldn't help himself. He nearly doubled over laughing. When he finally caught his breath, he said, "Steven, you're insane. First of all, I don't dance. Secondly, I don't—"

"No, no, no! I'm not asking you to do those specific things. Just, get in the spirit. Right? It's figurative."

"Well—" Ryan felt himself blush, and when Steven noticed, he couldn't continue.

"Well, what? That was very conspiratorial, mister Gregori!"

"I mean, I do a little of that already."

Steven's eyes bulged. "What do you mean?"

"I told you I've been hanging out with Brandon and his friends a lot—you're going to meet them tonight—and they can get kind of crazy, at least by my meager standards."

The other boy rolled his eyes. "I'll believe it when I see it."

"Are you challenging me, Steven?"

He smiled, mischievously. "Let's just say I am. And if you're not falling-over drunk tonight, I win. Deal?"

Ryan hesitated a moment. He saw that Steven was about to speak—to tell him it was case-in-point—so without letting himself think further, he blurted, "Deal!"

Steven's expression changed from smug to concerned. "Really? I'm mostly just giving you a hard time, Ryan."

"I'm sure you are, but truthfully? I'm kind of trying to change some of what you were talking about. I need to learn to be more—relaxed."

"Okay. I can handle that."

"I think this is going to be a really interesting party, Steven."

He raised his eyebrows. "And you'll be—relaxed?"

Ryan grinned. "Not a chance."

Meredith was the first to arrive. Without knocking, she waltzed in through the front door at a quarter to eight with a case of Miller Light under one arm and a black plastic bag in her other hand. When Ryan gave her a skeptical look, she laughed. "Oh, don't look at me like that. I know you won't drink any of this beer. It isn't for you anyways. With Jay and Mark gone, I know anything I don't drink tonight will just sit in the fridge until next time I'm here." She set the case of beer on the counter, tore open the box and removed a can. Opening it deftly with a thumb, she took a long sip and then kissed Ryan on the cheek. "Happy birthday."

"Thank you." He looked her up and down. She was ravishing, as usual, with her bulky surgical steel piercings, auburn hair threaded with violet ribbons, and a tight, tank-top jeans combination that set off her trim figure. "And what's in the bag?"

"Ooh!" She lilted. "Wouldn't you like to know?" Slowly, she pulled out a bottle of Malibu rum and a two-liter of cola. "One of my favorite summer drinks. Shall I pour you one?"

"Yes please."

From the back of the apartment, a yipping sound announced Mars as he came bounding from Shelly's new room. Shelly herself wasn't far behind.

"Meredith!" Shelly said, perhaps too excitedly. "You're looking ni-ice tonight."

Laughing, Meredith licked her index finger and pressed it to her hip, making a hissing sound. "Thanks, Shelly. Are you enjoying having a bedroom, finally?"

"You have no friggin' idea." She looked longingly at the rum. "Make me one too?"

"Absolutely."

By eight thirty most of the guests had arrived, and Ryan started on his second drink. Realizing suddenly that he'd completely forgotten music, he ducked into his bedroom and emerged with the trusty old CD boom box. On the dining table, an impressive bar had formed from the various liquors and wines brought by the guests. He moved these slightly to make way for the boombox, and plugged it into the wall. With a smile, he pressed the play button, and the light, percussive solo piano of George Winston's 'Living in the Country' started to fill the room.

Quickly extricating herself from a conversation with Steven in a corner of the apartment, Meredith rushed over. "What the hell are you doing?" she asked.

Confused, Ryan said, "Just trying to create a little musical ambiance."

She rolled her eyes. "I'm sorry. I didn't realize there was going to be a poetry reading tonight. For fuck's sake Ryan, are you trying to kill your birthday party before it even gets started?"

"Ouch."

She began to twirl her hair impatiently. "Have you got anything more upbeat?"

"Well, I could put on Savage Garden, or Dido—"

She let go of her hair and pressed a finger to Ryan's lips. "No, no. Stupid question. Just—turn this off. I'm going to my car to get my CDs."

"Okay—"

Steven appeared beside them. "What's going on?"

Meredith laughed. "Oh, the usual. Ryan is committing musical suicide."

Ryan scowled. "Hurry up and go to your car then."

Two minutes later she returned with a small black binder full of compact discs in sleeves. Without hesitation, she pulled one and popped it into the player, handing George Winston's 'Summer' to Ryan unceremoniously.

"Be careful with that!" Ryan chided. "Just because you don't appreciate new age piano doesn't mean that I don't."

Meredith made a clucking noise and pressed play. She raised one finger, and a watery lyric began—a single line, cool and dark. The line repeated three more times and then spilled directly into a driving drum and bass intro. The voice seemed familiar, but Ryan couldn't place it until the lyrics began again.

His face lit up for an instant and then grew worried. "Is this Kosheen?" He knew it was.

Meredith smiled. "See? Already ten times the party it was two minutes ago! And before you go and get all mopey about Darren and how he's the one who first introduced you to them, forget about it."

Steven cut in, a note of caution in his voice. "Meredith, I don't know if—"

"No way!" she nearly shouted. "I'm so fucking sick of Darren." She looked at Ryan, and when she spoke again her voice was genuinely tender. "This is *our* time, Ryan. This is *my* music, not his, so enjoy it."

Ryan smiled. As usual, her to-the-point declaration gave no room for argument. "I'll see what I can do."

Just then, Ryan heard his front door open, and he turned. A moment later Max emerged from the darkness of the hallway into the bright floodlights that illuminated the kitchen. There was another boy—presumably Jake—behind him. Ryan felt a tightness in his stomach and quickly swallowed half the Malibu and Coke he held in his hand, wincing sharply as it went down.

Max smiled brightly and walked to the dining area, Jake in tow. He wrapped his arms around Ryan and said, "Happy birthday, Mister. There's someone I'd like you to meet."

After Max let go, Ryan put on what he hoped was a convincing smile and held out his hand. "You must be Jake. Welcome."

Jake shook it firmly. "A pleasure. I've heard a lot about you."

Ryan perused him discreetly. Jake was shorter than Max, with close cut, medium brown hair. His face was unshaven but neat, with light scruff around his lips and chin extending halfway up his cheeks to his ears. From the center of his face, Jake's shimmering brown eyes sat squarely against a soft, round nose. Physically he appeared somewhere between fit and average. Overall, Ryan supposed he was attractive enough, though he seemed deficient in every way compared to Max beside him.

"Oh, I'm so glad," Ryan said, alarmed by the suddenly high pitch of his voice. "Max was just gushing about you the other day. We finally had a chance to catch up."

Jake blushed slightly. "Oh, I doubt he was gushing." He put an arm around Max's waist and pulled him close. Ryan swallowed hard to suppress the crippling pangs of jealousy as his organs tied themselves in knots. "This is an awesome apartment."

"Oh, it's a little dilapidated, but it's home."

"Maybe so, but it's huge!"

An awkward silence began creeping forward, so Ryan was relieved when Meredith cut in. "Forgive our host's rudeness. I'm hoping it's just because he's a little buzzed already. My name is Meredith. You're Jake, and, Max? I don't think I've had the pleasure yet. Oh, and this is Steven—"

After the introductions, Jake excused himself to the bathroom. Max pulled Ryan aside. "Hey, Mister, I know we talked about this but, is it really okay that Jake is here?"

Ryan picked up the bottle of Malibu to refill his cup. "Max, it's absolutely fine." He wasn't sure he meant it. "Really. I'm just glad you're here."

Max hugged him again and kissed him lightly on the cheek before whispering. "I hope so. I couldn't stand to lose you over this." He pushed away and smiled.

"I learned my lesson. You'll never lose me again."

By the time Brandon and Caleb showed up, Ryan was three-quarters of the way through his fourth Malibu and cola. He and Steven were seated on the floor in the living room, deep in conversation about the improvements they intended to make to the apartment come August first. Sometime within the last hour, the effects of the rum began to wash over him. It seemed to caress gently at first—just at the edge of his senses—in the same manner the ocean caresses the shore in a calm harbor. Then, as surely as tides will rise, intoxication crept up on him, eventually pulling him down like an undertow.

A hand on his shoulder startled him, and a voice from above began to laugh. "Happy birthday, down there."

He turned to see Brandon hovering over him, smiled a little too brightly—this was certainly the work of the rum—and pushed himself to his feet. "Brandon!" he exclaimed, wrapping his arms around his friend. "I started to think you weren't coming."

Pushing away gently, Brandon smiled, conspiratorially. "Oh, just fashionably late." He indicated Caleb, behind him, whom Ryan now noticed for the first time. Then in a hushed voice, "Let's just say there's trouble in paradise."

Stepping forward, Caleb countered, "I can hear you, asshole." He smiled brightly then and opened his arms to Ryan. "How many hugs have you gotten today?"

Ryan appraised Caleb for a moment before stepping into his embrace. He couldn't quite place what it was about Caleb that he found so mesmerizing, and it filled him with conflicting feelings of guilt and desire. As Caleb wrapped his arms around him, he tried his best to ignore the decidedly unhealthy attraction, but couldn't. There was something alluring about the way the thin, angular shape of Caleb's body flirted with the line between beautiful and awkward. And his face! Caleb's features were so geometric—at once harshly masculine and softly feminine—that he was the definition of androgyny. He was unlike anyone Ryan had ever been attracted to, and that made him dangerous.

As the embrace went on, Ryan felt himself melting further into his arms—hopelessly sinking. It was magical and wicked—the taste of something forbidden and exotic—and he basked in the warmth of the sin. Allowing himself a final indulgence, he breathed deeply of Caleb's scent before pushing reluctantly away and back to the real world.

He nearly forgot the question the other boy had posed, but remembering suddenly, he stammered, "Hugs? Quite a few. Oh, and an unusual number of kisses on the cheek."

Caleb's eyes sparkled, and he laughed. "Well, I'd like to be a part of that club." He leaned in again, close, and Ryan shuddered as he felt Caleb's warm lips touch near the base of his ear. Then, soft and damp, the tip of Caleb's tongue flicked his earlobe lightly before pulling away. He caught his breath, momentarily overcome by the overtly seductive gesture. "Sorry Tom couldn't make it," Caleb said. "He's got some—stuff going on."

Brandon clucked his tongue. "Get a room you two." He looked down at Steven. "Caleb, I'd like you to meet our friend Steven. Steven, Caleb."

Somewhat removed from sober himself, Steven rose with a lack of grace and held out a hand. "So, you're the one corrupting our little Ryan?"

Caleb laughed with pleasure. "I told him when we met I was going to try to ruin him. I don't think I'm doing a very good job."

Steven winked. "He's incorruptible. I haven't noticed a damned bit of difference, except that maybe I don't see him as much now that you guys are in the picture." He winked again.

Laughing nervously, Ryan opened his mouth to speak. But before he could form words, Meredith appeared—seemingly out of thin air—and interjected. "Did I miss some introductions? I assume you two brought that luscious looking vodka? In the classy plastic handle?"

Ryan had no doubt that any vodka added to the liquor selection on the dining table was the result of Brandon and Caleb. The former began to protest in defense of the decidedly cheap grade of the spirit, but Meredith interrupted him. "Whoah, dude. I'm not judging, believe me. I walked in with a case of Miller Light." All four boys winced, and she smiled. "Oh, you gays and your loathing of cheap beer. Anyways, I'm Meredith." Everyone laughed.

The party continued, and by a quarter to midnight, Ryan was drunk. Although he felt his physical coordination slipping, he observed with a sense of pride that his mental acuity remained sharp— or so he believed. At the bottom of his fifth Malibu and cola, he found a sense of spiritual liberation. Meredith demanded shots of vodka, and Brandon and Caleb were all too happy to oblige.

"Ryan," Brandon called from the dining table, "Are you in?"

"Absolutely."

Brandon turned to Max and Jake, who were talking quietly near the kitchen peninsula. "Boys? How about you? Vodka?"

Max wrinkled his nose. "Oh, no! Vodka has never touched these lips." He laughed. "Well, that's not true. I'm not a big shots person though. Jake?"

"Oh, sure. I'll take one," Jake said. "I'm not a huge shots person either though, so I'll need a chaser."

Brandon started pouring shots into red plastic cups from the ever-diminishing stack Ryan had put out, while Caleb and Meredith moved around the apartment to see who else was interested. In the end, nine people raised a toast to Ryan's twentieth, and swallowed with wincing eyes and grimacing smiles. Afterwards, there was cheering. Ryan squeezed his eyes tightly together as they watered from the burning the vodka induced on the way down.

"Hey, Ryan," Brandon asked. "Do you mind if Caleb and I step outside to your porch for a cig?"

Shaking his head slightly against the sickly taste of the spirit, Ryan opened his eyes and said, "Of course not."

Brandon beckoned to Caleb, who was chatting animatedly with Meredith a little ways away. He began to excuse himself, and then Meredith boomed, "Are you guys going out for a cigarette?"

Laughing, Brandon answered, "Yes. I take it you want one?"

Meredith smiled. "Yeah, I don't have any of my own though, if that's okay?"

Caleb answered. "As long as you don't mind a menthol, honey, I've got you covered."

From near the kitchen door, Max clucked. "All of you smoke?"

Meredith wove her arm into Caleb's. "Don't judge, Maxy boy. I'm a social smoker at best." She looked at Ryan. "Care to keep us company?"

Max clucked again. "Ryan! Not you, Mister!" The alarm on his face was palpable.

"Seriously?" Ryan laughed. To his own ears, it sounded unconvincing. "Don't worry Max." Smiling, he followed Meredith, Caleb and Brandon out of the kitchen, through the hallway and out onto the deck.

He closed the door to the apartment behind him and looked up as he breathed the sweet, summer air. The night sky was remarkably clear. An astounding number of stars shown through the light pollution of the city. Though it was the middle of July, the clarity was more suited to January.

January. He was suddenly aware of the date. Six months to the day had passed since the accident in his truck. He expected the realization to shake him—these had been the most volatile six months of his entire life—and yet it didn't. Instead, something incredible happened. He looked at his friends—Meredith, Brandon and Caleb, standing in a far corner of the deck, slowly smoking and exhaling in drunken ecstasy. A feeling of great warmth washed through him. He was fine. He was more than fine! Everything was alright. He'd been through hell and passed through to the other side.

Then, like a tidal wave, a great longing coursed through his being—a feeling of contented anticipation—the likes of which he hadn't felt since his night with Brandon at the top of the canyon. It was a desire for something more. He realized there were no limits—he could become anything, *anyone* he wanted to be. It was time for his metamorphosis to begin in earnest. He needed to experience the world—to taste all it had to offer. He thought of Steven, inside. Ryan *did* want to kiss boys, dance on tables and get really drunk—figuratively. He wanted all of that and more.

Reacting, he marched forward and tapped Caleb on the shoulder. When the other boy turned, Ryan nodded toward the cigarette in his hand and asked, "Can I have one of those?"

Meredith, Brandon and Caleb had been deep in conversation, but now they fell silent. Caleb spoke first. "Ryan, are you serious? You hate smoking."

Ryan groaned. "Just—please? Before I change my mind?"

Caleb shrugged, pulled a pack of cigarettes from his pocket and offered one. Ryan took it, along with the lighter that Caleb produced a moment later.

Meredith frowned as she took a drag of her own cigarette. "Are you sure you want to do this?"

Ryan placed the cigarette between his lips and exhaled, deeply. "I just want to know what it's like. That's all. There are so many things—I don't know what they're like."

Meredith chuckled softly. "Do you even know *how* to smoke a cigarette?"

Now it was Ryan's turn to frown. "Don't I just breathe?"

"No, no," chided Brandon. "Look, you light it, breathe in half-way, then take the cig back out of your mouth. Then breathe in the rest of the way and hold it for a second. Right?"

Everyone fell silent again as Ryan raised the lighter. He flicked it, held the flame to the end of the cigarette and breathed deeply. The smoke filled his mouth and the back of his throat seized. Fighting the urge to cough, he pulled the cigarette from his lips and inhaled deeply. Within seconds a rush of delicious fire coursed through his veins, as though someone was injecting hot water directly into his bloodstream. As he pulled the cigarette to his lips for a second drag, his fingers and toes began to tingle. He breathed in deeply this time—delighting that his throat had already relaxed against the cooling tickle of the menthol—and exhaled slowly, with a combination of dizziness and pleasure.

Meredith shook her head. "Well, happy birthday, Ryan Gregori. I never thought I'd see the day."

He took another drag before he answered. "Don't get used to it, but neither did I."

Stepping forward, Brandon patted Ryan on the shoulder. "How do you feel?"

"Dizzy. Warm. Slightly amazing. Is it always like this?"

The other boy sighed. "No. After the first few they just calm you down and exponentially increase your risk of cancer." Ryan couldn't mask his look of alarm. He pulled the cigarette sharply from his lips and looked at it with disgust, as if Brandon's words had suddenly sobered him. "Don't worry," Brandon laughed. "One isn't going to do you in."

"Maybe not," Meredith said. "But Ryan, seriously. I can't believe you just did that. It wasn't even peer pressure it just—was."

Ryan took one last drag off the cigarette before extinguishing it and tossing the butt into the alley below. "It's not about smoking, Meredith. It's about changing. I want to be—different."

"Different?" she asked.

"Yeah, I want to kiss boys, dance on tables, and get really drunk. Figuratively." All three of his companions raised their eyebrows. He turned to Caleb. "I want you to ruin me. Just a little. I want to feel like I've lived." No one spoke. Ryan's words hung heavy with the ghost of Darren. In the weight of the statement even Meredith and Caleb, who'd never met Darren, shivered a little against the warm summer air. The silence stretched and finally Ryan said, "You never know. Today could be my last day. So, if I can help it, my world isn't going to be small anymore."

He reached with his left hand and grasped the thumb ring around his neck for a moment before letting it fall against his chest. Without another word, he turned and went inside.

CHAPTER 11

"Are you getting nervous?" Ryan's mother asked. She handed him a wet plate, which he took graciously and began to dry with an old towel.

"About what, school?"

"Well, you're starting on Monday. If I were you, I'd probably have a few butterflies in my stomach."

It was early on Saturday evening, the twenty-first of August, and Ryan had finally found the time to accept his parents' invitation to a family dinner at home with his siblings. His mother had tried to have him over for the last three weeks, but between wrapping up summer lessons at work, registering for classes, preparing for music auditions and attending school orientations, he'd been too exhausted. Indeed, even the time he normally devoted to his friends had significantly dwindled as the beginning of his first semester approached.

He placed the plate carefully in a cabinet and smiled. "I suppose I am if I think about it too much. Mostly, I'm just excited."

He turned from the cabinet back toward his mother. He watched as she stood in front of the sink, her hands deep inside the basin, scrubbing. There was something about her expression, which he caught in profile. The line of her mouth—curving only slightly at the corners—suggested something more than neutrality but less than a smile. She was thinking deeply.

"Mom," he began in a quizzical tone. "What's on your mind?"

She turned from the sink and grinned. "What? Oh, nothing. I'm just proud of you. I'm glad we were finally able to get you over here for dinner before you get all wrapped up in it."

"Well, thanks, it was delicious, as usual." He took another plate.

"No problem." She was silent a moment, and when she continued her voice was soft and wistful. "I can't believe it's practically the end of August. You're finally starting college, and your brother starts kindergarten on Monday, too. Your sister's a sixth grader! I can still remember so vividly the days each of you was born. It seems so long ago. The time—"

"Mom? Seriously. You're acting really strange." He looked at her more intently now and saw a dampness at the corners of her eyes. She was smiling, but he detected a slight quiver in her lip. Overcome with concern he quickly put down the plate he'd been drying and folded her in his arms. "Mom? Please. What's going on?"

She sniffled softly and laughed with a tear-laden voice as she pushed gently away. "Nothing, really. Oh, I don't know. You've just had a really hard year with the accident, moving and—Darren."

"Yeah, it's been hard, but things are looking up now, right?"

She laughed. "That's exactly it. Someday if you have kids—well, you always want the best for them, you know? You don't want them to suffer—you'd like to protect them from everything. I guess I was thinking about you starting school and I started thinking about family. I got a little overwhelmed. I'm just so glad that you're doing alright. It would be really nice to see you more."

He hugged her again. "I can try to make an effort."

After a moment of silence, she changed the subject. "Are you doing anything to celebrate this weekend? It's your last for a while without school obligations."

"Hmm," he replied. "I hadn't thought about it."

When he arrived back home, it was just after eight thirty. He'd allowed himself a long, meandering walk, stretching the short seven blocks between his parent's house and The Garden into almost fifteen minutes—all the while thinking about the semester ahead. His mother's excitement about starting school electrified him, and he felt an irrepressible urge to celebrate. Why not? She was right. After the weekend, school obligations would eat up much of his time, so he might as well enjoy the little bit of freedom that remained. He headed for the phone to see who might be around.

When he pulled the phone out of its base, his heart leaped. The caller ID showed a missed call from Caleb. He dialed his voicemail, and as his fingers pressed the buttons, he felt himself succumbing to an increasingly untenable desire. Over the past month his fixation on Caleb had been steadily growing, while at the same time, the guilt that accompanied his covetous thoughts was diminishing.

There was one new message. "Hi Ryan, it's Caleb. Yep, just another day on the island of despair. I swear Tom is having an affair sometimes. We were arguing about absolutely nothing, and then he went off in a huff and said he wouldn't be back tonight. Well, I say fuck it, so I called Meredith, and we're going to Paradox. You should come. She says there's no way in hell you'll go, but I bet I can convince you. Call me back."

He hung up the phone and exhaled. It seemed like Tom was never around lately, which made it easy for Ryan to succumb to Caleb's shameless flirtations. Sometimes he even returned the attention. Whether it was a mildly suggestive quip, or something that manifested itself physically—a supposedly accidental brush of the arms, or fingers touching a leg while sitting too close together—he found himself yearning for these stolen moments. Even when Tom was present, Caleb always found a way to express the dysfunction of their relationship. Every action seemed to broadcast a message. *This isn't working. You and I should be together.*

He hung up the phone and closed his eyes. The thought of Caleb pressed up against him in the dark, smoky club caused him to shudder with desire. He could imagine the sweet, mingling scents of sweat and cologne permeating the heat of their nearness. He hated dancing, and yet he'd do anything for that fantasy to manifest itself—to have the opportunity to feel that close.

His guilt surged again momentarily. Forcing these thoughts from his mind, he searched for a different justification—a better reason to go. Hadn't he marched in here, positively high on the energy of the semester to come? Didn't he want to celebrate? He smiled. What better way was there to celebrate this joyous occasion than to dance? As he dialed Caleb's number, the purely rational part of his mind asked whether he'd be so inclined to dance if it was only Meredith who'd asked.

He was able to ignore the question with remarkable ease.

After the third ring, Caleb picked up. "Ryan? What's going on?"

He felt his heart flutter, and when he spoke, he was alarmed to hear the unusually high pitch of his voice. "Oh, hi Caleb. I just got your message." He collected himself and forced his voice lower. "Are you still going to Paradox tonight?'

Caleb laughed. "Yes. Meredith *swore* I was going to have to beg you to go. Are you going to make this easy on me?"

"Believe it or not, yes. With school starting on Monday I feel like I need to celebrate."

"Celebrating school starting? That's supposed to be something you *dread*! I wish you could see my face right now. I'm pouting. Here I thought you were going to go so you could be with me."

"Caleb!" Ryan hissed. Another shot of adrenaline coursed through him and he felt a shiver of cold as his pores opened and he began to sweat.

"Right, right. Out of line, as usual. Sorry, Ryan. So, we're planning to head over at about ten. Meredith is on her way here now; do you want me to call her and we'll meet at your place instead? It's a little closer."

Ryan allowed himself a silent but luxurious exhalation. "That sounds great. I'll see you soon." He placed the phone back into its cradle and headed for the shower.

Once he finished, he dressed himself in a tight pair of blue jeans and the smallest T-shirt he could find in his closet. After spiking his hair, he headed into the kitchen, intent on making coffee. Steven was at the stove boiling a pot of water.

"It's a little late for dinner, isn't it, Steven?" he asked as he pulled a filter from the pantry.

Steven looked up from the box of macaroni and cheese he was scrutinizing. "It's a little late for coffee, isn't it, Ryan?" He paused for a moment. "Why are you dressed like a hooker? That shirt barely covers you."

Ryan laughed. "Meredith and Caleb are coming over. We're going to go *dancing* tonight."

Steven clutched his side as he erupted in laughter. From the far end of the apartment, Mars came bounding forward to investigate, with Shelly not far behind. "You're doing what?" Steven balked. "You don't dance!"

"No, I don't usually like it. But, hey, you're the one telling me I need to let loose, so what's the problem? What's that you said? You want to see me dance on tables, kiss boys and get really drunk?"

"Well, sure. Figuratively."

"So, figuratively, I'm going dancing."

As Ryan filled the coffee pot, he heard Shelly behind him. "Who-ah, you're really going dancing? Do my ears deceive me?"

He pulled a small can of French roast from the freezer. "No, they don't. I can't believe it myself. But, you know what? I'm finally going to be a student again, so I feel like I need to do something to celebrate. Are either of you interested in going?"

Shelly answered first. "Oh, no. I actually need to get in the shower. I'm headed to the bar with some girls."

"Ooh," Ryan cooed. "Any prospects."

Shelly winked. "Wish me luck?"

"Good luck. Steven, how about you?"

Scowling, Steven said, "Yeah right. I can't think of anything nicer than standing around awkwardly in a smoky club while you hang all over someone else's man."

All the levity Ryan was feeling evaporated as Steven's sharp words brought him crashing back to earth. "Excuse me?" he said, his voice barely above a whisper.

"Don't play dumb, Ryan. Tom isn't going out tonight, is he?"

"No, I don't think so."

Shelly interjected. "Sorry, what's going on?"

Rolling his eyes, Steven said, "Oh, you know, Shelly. Remember Caleb and Tom? Even a blind man can see that Caleb is baiting Ryan. I don't know why." He turned and looked at Ryan as he dejectedly poured the box of macaroni into the now boiling pot of water. "You are so much better than this. I don't know why you're bothering with him. Even if he broke up with Tom tomorrow, he still wouldn't be right for you. One of these days he's going to try something, and then you're going to fall in love with him because you fall in love with *everyone*. Then he's going to do something and break your heart into little pieces, and I'm going to be here picking them up off the floor."

Ryan was flabbergasted. Was his infatuation with Caleb really so obvious? He understood that Steven's words came from a place of love and respect, but they still cut deeply. His previous euphoria was now being replaced by rage. Who was Steven to make such accusations, anyway?

"There is nothing going on between us," he asserted. "We're just really good friends."

Steven laughed. "That may be so, for now. But you can't deny that you wish it were something more than that. Ryan, you can't bullshit me. I know you, and I've seen the way you look at him. Worse, I've seen the way he looks at you. He's bad news, Ryan. Bad news."

Shelly threw her hands in the air as she walked into the bathroom. "You guys are complicated."

Ryan began to protest, but instead, he turned as he heard the sound of the front door opening. Quickly shooting Steven a look to say that the discussion was over, he called out, "Hello?"

Meredith's voice returned the call. "Hi—i." A moment later she sauntered out of the dark hallway. "How many cans of beer do I have left in your fridge?"

Steven exhaled. "Two, I think. Don't you have your own refrigerator? In your own apartment?"

"Stevey, Stevey," she taunted. "Why so bitter tonight?" Stepping into the kitchen, she swung open the refrigerator door, removed a can and had it opened before the door was shut again. "This is perfect. I'm driving tonight, so I can't drink much—not that I like to get too sloppy when I'm dancing anyways. It throws off my rhythm."

"God forbid you ever miss a beat," Steven groaned. "And don't call me Stevey."

"Whatever." She turned her attention to Ryan. "You look cu—ute!"

He laughed soberly. "Thanks, Meredith. Why are you talking like that?"

"Like what?" she asked, innocently.

"You know, 'hi—i' and 'cu—ute,' all sort of cutesy and vapid."

"Vapid? Ou—uch." She laughed. "That one was on purpose. I don't know! Do I always have to be so sharp and dry? I'm excited! Dancing is my *thing*, and tonight we're doing it together for the first time." She turned again to Steven, who was still scowling as he stirred. "Are you coming, Stevey?"

"I'd swear you're high on something right now," he retorted. "And the answer to your question is no. I can't stand that place."

"Suit yourself." She went to sit at the dining table. Ryan poured himself a cup of coffee before sitting down across from her. She looked around. "Caleb isn't here yet?"

Again came the sound of the front door opening and closing. "I am now," boomed Caleb's voice through the hallway. He emerged from the darkness into the bright kitchen. "My ears were burning."

As Ryan watched Caleb approach, it was all he could do to keep from melting into his chair. Caleb's inky dark hair looked to have been freshly cut, and it was shaped in such a way that the term 'spiked' did it little justice; it folded gently over itself into small rigid peaks evocative of turbulent ocean waves during a storm. His emerald green eyes shimmered brilliantly above his thin, unusually glossy lips. This evening he wore a simple, baby-blue V-neck shirt over dangerously low-rise, boot-cut jeans.

Steven's voice from the kitchen broke Ryan's appraisal. "We were only saying good things, I swear."

Caleb laughed as Steven drained his pasta and returned it to the pot. "Yeah, why don't I believe you?" he asked. Before Steven could answer, he directed his attention to Ryan. "You look nice! Is that coffee you're drinking?"

Ryan attempted a scowl. "So what if it is?"

"No, no, no. We're doing this right." He held out a nearly full twenty-ounce bottle of ginger ale Ryan hadn't noticed before. "Have some of this before we go."

Eyeing it skeptically, Ryan asked, "What is it?"

"It's ginger ale with just a hint of vodka."

Ryan considered a moment before taking it. Deciding it couldn't hurt, he unscrewed the cap and took a moderate sip. It was immediately apparent that ginger ale was the minority ingredient in the bottle. He began to choke and then swallowed hard to avoid spitting the vile concoction all over the dining table. His face must have clearly shown his distress, because Meredith cackled with laughter.

"Ugh!" Ryan sputtered. "Is that straight vodka?"

Caleb chuckled quietly. "No," he said. "There's ginger ale in there—at least a quarter of the bottle."

Ryan winced and pushed the bottle back toward Caleb. "You're unbelievable. How can you possibly drink that?"

"In teeny, tiny sips."

In the kitchen, Steven poured his completed macaroni and cheese from the pot into a large bowl. "Well," he called dramatically across the kitchen peninsula, "You three enjoy your teeny tiny sips. Oh, and your night. Don't do anything—untoward." Without waiting for acknowledgment, he disappeared down the hallway and into his room, just beside the front door.

An hour later Ryan tried to climb out of the back seat of Meredith's car with an utter lack of grace. Caleb came around the side to assist him, and once he was standing squarely on his feet, Caleb chided, "I know I made you drink half of my 'ginger ale' before we left your apartment, but you at least have to pretend to be sober until we're inside."

As Meredith locked the car doors, she added, "Yeah. You'd better not fuck up my night by being 'visibly intoxicated,' understand?"

"Check and check," Ryan laughed. "Don't worry; I'm fine. Between your 'ginger ale,' Caleb, and my coffee I'm feeling pretty great, actually. I think it's just been a while since I had to climb out of a small back seat like that—I'm all legs, you know."

Caleb made a soft cat-call. "I'll say!"

Ryan looked across the dark gravel parking lot to the club beyond. He felt an immense distaste for the place; he'd only been twice before—both times at Darren's behest—and he observed with disdain that nothing had changed. It was a fairly unremarkable structure—essentially a collection of modular trailers connected together and covered in a banal, beige vinyl siding. Pairs of floodlights placed at intervals around the top of the building cast pools of blue-white light on the gravel below. There were no windows. At one corner, three slatted steps led up to a small wooden porch where a metal door provided the only entrance from the parking lot. The sole indication that the building served any purpose at all was a large, black metal sign to the left of this door that read 'Paradox' in curving white letters.

The trio passed a moment of what would have been silence if not for the dull, booming bass line of whatever track the DJ was spinning inside. Caleb pulled a pack of cigarettes from his pocket. "Either of you want one?" he said, placing a cigarette between his lips.

"Can't you still smoke inside?" Ryan asked.

"Oh, definitely," Caleb replied. He lit the cigarette and inhaled deeply. Then he pulled two more from the pack and offered one each to Meredith and Ryan. "Here, just take them. I'll have plenty more inside, but I like to prolong this moment."

Sighing inwardly, Ryan took the cigarette and then the lighter Caleb offered. "And what moment is that, exactly?" he asked. He lit the cigarette and breathed it in.

"This—" Caleb began, "This is the moment where it all begins. You listen to the bass beating through the walls, and you get excited! You wonder what the DJ is spinning. You imagine who might be inside— is it a good crowd, or is it lame tonight? You think about the people you hope to see—the ones you met last time—and about the club trolls you'd rather avoid but are destined to run into. You wonder who's going to try to pick you up, and how far you're willing to flirt, because if you're like me, you just want to dance. The night is young, and you enjoy the fresh air and the clarity because by the time you leave, if you've done your job right, nothing is clear, but everything is wonderful."

Meredith laughed between puffs of her cigarette. "Caleb, who knew you were such a poet?"

Frowning, Ryan said, "I wish I thought of it that way. Honestly, I've just never really gotten it, if you know what I mean. I've never understood the draw."

Meredith gently squeezed his arm. "That's all about to change. We'll show you."

After they had finished their cigarettes, they pulled out their IDs and headed inside. Once the cover was paid, Meredith and Caleb each got a neon orange wristband. Ryan—being too young to buy drinks—ended up with a giant black 'X' on each hand.

Inside, the main room was much as he remembered it. A long bar stood against one wall with a handful of high bistro sets and pool tables occupying the space in front of it. Beyond was a moderately sized dance floor sitting below a small stage built into the very back of the club. The black walls of the interior were illuminated with red and yellow lights, whose otherwise clandestine beams were revealed by the thick haze of cigarette smoke that wafted and curled through the air. It was looking to be a busy night because even though it was early, both the bar area and the dance floor were three-quarters filled.

Willing his voice to cut through the absurdly loud, throbbing electronic pulses of the music, Ryan remarked, "It's really busy!"

Caleb nodded delightedly. "It's the last weekend before the semester starts! Everyone is back in town after the summer!"

Grabbing both their arms, Meredith leaned in. "I love this song. Come find me on the dance floor when you're ready!"

Ryan and Caleb nodded, then Caleb said, "Stay right here! I'm going to get a drink. I'll bring you a water!"

He started to tell Caleb he didn't need a water, but his voice was drowned out, and Caleb was already at the bar. Returning two minutes later, Caleb held a clear plastic cup in each hand. Both were filled with ice and clear liquid, presumably a water and some sort of vodka concoction. He pressed one of them into Ryan's hand. "Here!" he shouted above the throbbing bass. "Water!"

Politely, Ryan put his lips around the straw and pulled some into his mouth. He was hardly surprised when it wasn't water at all, but a very strong vodka and Sprite. "Caleb," he began. "This isn't—"

The other boy shook his head vehemently and held a finger to his lips. "Yes, it is. Water. I wouldn't want you getting dehydrated now, would I?"

Ryan took the hint. "Well, thanks."

"No problem. Now come on, let's find Meredith."

Taking a step back, Ryan said, "Oh, not yet! I'm not ready. I have to prepare myself—"

"Bullshit!" Caleb grabbed him by the arm and pulled him toward the dance floor.

It didn't take long to find Meredith in the middle of the small space. Ryan grinned at the sight of her—she moved so effortlessly to the beats and pulses, shifting her weight between the music's driving hits and its back beats. The graceful yet machine-like precision with which she moved her hips and feet provided a steady foundation up-on which her arms moved freely as tools of expression. Even Ryan—who knew next to nothing about dancing—was struck by the absolute art of her movement.

As he continued to watch her, it was her face above all else that transfixed him—enraptured. Meredith was overcome.

He had to experience that feeling for himself. Beside him, Caleb started moving to the beats as well, so Ryan forced his inhibitions aside, closed his eyes and endeavored to feel nothing but the music. As he gently shifted back and forth he accepted the challenge.

He thought of all the reasons he hated the idea of dancing and be-gan to tick them off in his head. Number one was his tendency to feel self-conscious. He knew he wasn't a particularly good dancer, and in a room full of exceptionally beautiful people, he was average at best. Having acknowledged these facts, he forced his eyes open and scanned the dance floor. For better or worse no one was looking at him, judging his mediocre dancing or calling him ugly. Sure there were a handful of prematurely drunken revelers leering at the most beautiful specimens on the dance floor, but Ryan forgave them that. Indeed, for the most part, the patrons of Paradox appeared either totally self-involved, or they contained their attention to small cliques of two or three companions each.

As the current song ended, the DJ layered the next track cleanly on top. He continued moving as his brain delved deeper. His second reason for hating to dance had to do with the atmosphere. Before Darren's passing, Ryan had been staunchly conservative with his be-havior. He'd detested drinking in excess, and cigarette smoke was an absolute affront to his senses. Clearly, he realized that his attitudes had changed—were changing—rapidly. He laughed inwardly. Since the beginning of the summer, he'd pushed his alcohol intake on several occasions, and was no longer qualified nor interested in judging others by their indulgences. Furthermore, he'd smoked through at least ten cigarettes in Caleb and Tom's company. With an alarming lack of shame, he considered how pleasurable the deadly little sticks could be. At this point, counting the atmosphere of Paradox as a deterrent to dancing would be hypocritical.

He rifled through a list of further minor complaints in his head as he moved back and forth, sipping his drink. It was easy to dismiss each in turn until his only remaining source of discomfort was his lack of experience in the scene.

Meredith's voice roused him from his thoughts. "There you go!" she exclaimed. "See? It's not so bad, is it?"

"No, I'm just trying to get lost in it like you do."

"Well, keep going. You're doing great! I'm going to get a beer!" she shouted.

After she walked away, Caleb moved in close. He took Ryan's drink—essentially empty—and set it on the floor along with his own. Unsure what was about to happen, Ryan closed his eyes and tried to focus on the music, but much like his fantasy from earlier, he could smell Caleb now, and feel the heat of his nearness.

Suddenly, firm hands grasped him just below the back pockets of his jeans and pulled him sharply forward. His body coursed with electricity as he felt Caleb's hard, lean frame press against him. Then Caleb whispered into his ear, just loud enough to cut through the music. "Don't get too lost in it. Who knows what you might miss if you do."

Ryan shuddered as Caleb moved one foot squarely between Ryan's on the floor, then started moving up and down, pulling Ryan with him. The friction of denim on denim as their legs brushed together was delicious. He wanted to drown himself in the feeling of this—to sink into Caleb's skin and never come up for air again.

But then an image of Tom flashed into his mind. Poor Tom. Regardless of what transgressions Caleb claimed Tom had committed, he was innocent until proven guilty. Ryan imagined himself in Tom's shoes—the heartbreak that their actions right now could cause—and found himself sobered for a moment. "Caleb," he whimpered. "What are you doing?"

"Dancing. What does it look like I'm doing?"

"But—Tom. Shouldn't we—"

"I don't want to talk about Tom right now, Ryan. Just dance with me." Caleb laid his head on Ryan's shoulder as he continued to pull against him. Resistance melted away, Ryan closed his eyes, and danced.

A few moments passed, and then Caleb whispered something into his ear he couldn't quite hear. "What was that?" he asked.

"I said, why am I falling in love with you?"

He was too struck to muster a response. Instead, he pulled Caleb closer and experienced the moment of Nirvana he'd been seeking. The music washed over him until the entire world was nothing but Caleb's body, deep rhythmic pulses of sound, and the most extraordinary happiness. In that instant, and for the rest of the night to come, all else was eclipsed.

~*~

Staying true to her word, Meredith kept her drinking to a minimum, finishing her last beer of the evening shortly after midnight. Caleb however, having procured two more drinks for Ryan, and three more for himself, was visibly unsteady on his feet by the time the lights came on just after two in the morning.

"You'd better not throw up in my car," Meredith laughed as they made their way across the parking lot. "I know it's not exactly in mint condition, but I wasn't planning on shampooing the carpet anytime soon."

Caleb laughed drunkenly and squeezed her shoulders as he walked beside her. As Ryan watched, he wasn't sure if the gesture was intended to show affection, or to keep him from stumbling. "Oh, please. I can drink this much before breakfast and still work a double shift."

"Let's hope so." She unlocked the door and climbed inside.

No one spoke much on the drive back to The Garden, and Ryan relished the silence after so much noise. Caleb's statement—that he was falling in love with him—had been repeating in his ears all night, muffled by the driving pulses of the music. Now, with nothing but the sound of the road under the tires, he was able to replay them without distraction—looping from end to beginning over and over. Each time the sentence repeated, he felt a rush of warmth at the word *love*. It was electric—this feeling—and his body tingled with the energy of it. But despite the euphoria, a tiny, irksome voice crying in the name of self-preservation extolled worry in the back of his mind.

Tonight, Caleb had given him the validation he'd sought for so long. Even before his ill-fated love for Darren, and before the string of short-lived relationships he suffered before that, he'd been search-ing. Three little words. *I love you.* In a brief moment of clarity, he re-alized that his entire adult life—short though it may have been thus far—had been consumed by this quest. He wondered what that said about him as a person—that he assessed his own worth exclusively by the value others placed upon him.

His musings turned darker, and he thought of Tom again—how his present happiness was coming at Tom's expense. He began to ask himself whether he could really accept that. Was it worth being loved if it also meant that he'd be hated—that someone else's heart would have to break?

Why am I falling in love with you? Caleb's words resonated in his mind, continuing their endless, almost maddening loop.

He decided there was no sense in worrying about Tom right now. Nothing had happened yet. Nothing *would* happen as long as he did the honorable thing and remained strong. If Caleb's words were true—and Ryan knew with an unshakeable certainty that they were—he'd leave Tom, and then they could be together, no guilt required.

Abruptly, the sound of the road beneath the tires changed. Ryan roused himself from his musings and was surprised to see that Meredith was pulling into the alley beside The Garden.

As she gently brought the car to a stop in the parking lot, she asked, "Ryan, do mind if I use your bathroom before I take Caleb home?"

"Of course not," Ryan said as he climbed carefully out of the vehicle. "The door should be unlocked."

Climbing out of the car herself, she looked at him quizzically. "You're not coming up? This is your house, you know."

He smiled. "I'll wait with Caleb. See you in a second."

Now Caleb pulled himself out of the passenger seat. "Yeah, it's fine. We'll have a cigarette before we call it a night."

Meredith shrugged. "Whatever, see you in a minute then."

After she had walked up the stairs, Caleb produced two cigarettes. He handed one to Ryan and lit it before lighting his own. Inhaling deeply, he asked, "Did you have fun tonight?"

Ryan exhaled long and slow, turning his head upward to watch as the smoke curled and dissipated into the clear night sky. He laughed. "You have no idea. I really, really enjoyed my night with you." When he lowered his head back down, Caleb had taken a step closer and was gazing at him with a bold intensity. Ryan saw himself reflected in Caleb's eyes and shivered against the raw desire he projected.

Before Ryan could say anything else, Caleb stepped closer again. Placing his hand between Ryan's legs, he gripped firmly and pulled Ryan forward. Suddenly, he was pressing his lips against Ryan's with an almost violent intensity. His tongue forced Ryan's mouth open, and Ryan was overcome with the unexpectedly delicious taste of smoke and stale vodka. Overcome by the raw passion of the moment, Ryan flung his cigarette to the ground, and his hands moved of their own accord—one wrapping itself around Caleb's shoulders and the other reaching behind his legs to pull him closer. They pressed against each other nearly quaking with desire, holding their faces locked together until the sound of the front door opening above forced them apart.

Ryan was panting. Caleb offered him another cigarette, which he nervously took as the sound of Meredith's feet on the slatted wood steps announced her imminent arrival.

"Is that your second one already?" she asked.

"I dropped the other one," he stammered. "Maybe I'm drunker than I thought."

Looking skeptically at the barely burned cigarette still smoldering on the ground a few feet away, Meredith said, "So? Pick it up. I never took you for a germaphobe. What a fucking waste."

He and Caleb laughed nervously. "Whatever," he said. "I had an amazing night."

She smiled. "Good, me too. Come on Caleb, finish that in the car. I'm tired."

When Ryan walked into the kitchen, Steven was waiting for him.

"Did you have a good night?" Steven asked, in his most innocent tone.

Smiling cautiously, Ryan responded, "Yes, actually. I didn't think I'd have as much fun as I did. The whole club scene might not be as bad as I remember it."

Steven laughed. "I guess you get out of it what you put into it, right? I can tell you had a good time just by smelling you—liquor and cigarettes. Since when do you smoke?"

Ryan felt himself flush. "What are you talking about? Everyone smokes at Paradox. That's what you're smelling."

"No, you smell like an ashtray. It's fresh. You just had one."

Groaning, Ryan seated himself at the dining table, and to his dismay, Steven followed. "Fine. You caught me. I have one now and again with Caleb and company."

"Really? You? That's kind of hypocritical, don't you think?"

"How so?"

"You're mister CPR instructor, lifeguard, and swimming guru. It's a tough song to sing with a black lung—"

Ryan held up his hand. "Did you wait up just so you could lecture me when I got home? What's the matter with you tonight, Steven? You've been on my case all day."

"Oh, well. Forgive me if I'm concerned that all of a sudden one of my best friends has started making bad choices. I'm sorry if I give a shit!"

His temper was rising, and he felt powerless to do anything about it. "Steven! *Now* who is being hypocritical? You're the one who basically told me—as if I didn't already know—that I was too naïve, straight-laced and boring. And that's rich, by the way, coming from you. At least I'm doing something about it."

"What is that supposed to mean?"

"You know exactly what it means. I love you, Steven, I do. But for two years I've been watching you mope around like life owes you something. You've got this cycle, right? You say that I fall in love with everyone? Look in the mirror. You're constantly finding these boys who are not interested in you and making up these little fantasies that one day they'll wake up and see how glorious you are. Then, when they don't, and instead they start telling you about the guys they're interested in—because you're always just a good friend—you mope around for weeks like you've just been fucked over."

"Little fantasies?" The tears forming at the corners of Steven's eyes quelled Ryan's sudden rage. "Wow, and you don't do the same thing? You didn't do the same fucking thing with Darren—for over a year? At least I move on. But who am I to say anything? I'm just the pathetic good friend who hasn't ever had a boyfriend. It's not much to relate to, right?" He started to rise from his chair.

Ryan reached out and caught his arm. "Steven, wait! Steven, I'm sorry, I didn't mean that."

The other boy smiled weakly, and sat back down. "Yes, you did. It hurt like hell, too. I needed to hear that though, because in a lot of ways it's true."

"Steven—"

"But you need to hear this. What you're doing with Caleb—"

"There is nothing going on with Caleb."

Shaking his head slowly, Steven sighed and wiped his tears. "I don't believe you, Ryan. I want to, but I don't. You know what? Fuck it. You can smoke your brains out and drink until your eyes turn yellow. That's all on you. But Caleb? I don't care what he says to you, what he does to you, or how he makes you feel. He's in a relationship, and for people like you and me—people who want that so badly—how can you mess with the sanctity of that?"

Ryan started to speak, but Steven shushed him and continued. "And it's not even about Tom. It's not about breaking his heart. It's about you. You and I? We might be shit at this whole romance thing, but at the end of the day, if there is one thing I know unconditionally, it's that we respect ourselves. At least I do. And you did, even if you don't anymore."

"Steven, really—"

"Really, nothing. If you don't respect yourself enough to know that you deserve better than being second best—someone's toy boy, or whatever—then you've got nothing. If Caleb really cares about you, he'll break up with Tom and let the wounds scab over before he tries anything." He rose. "I need to go to bed."

Ryan pushed away from the table, stood, and wrapped his arms tightly around his friend. "Thank you, Steven. Thank you for telling me the things I don't want to hear."

"You too, asshole." He laughed. "You too."

CHAPTER 12

Ryan awoke with Caleb's words still echoing in his ears. *Why am I falling in love with you?* Last night the question—the affirmation—had acted like a powerful magic, making him feel invincible and dangerous and righteous. Even his confrontation with Steven—sobering though it had been—only temporarily broke the spell. He'd gone to sleep happy and excited, relishing the potential. With his eyes closed in the last moments of consciousness, he'd had no doubts. Soon, he and Caleb would be together. Anything else was inconceivable.

But now the morning had arrived, and he wasn't certain of anything. From outside, a cool, grey light spilled reluctantly through the windows. He'd left one of these ajar against the warmth of the night, and now he shivered in the chill, damp air that filled the bedroom. The morning was gloomy, and he knew it would rain.

Why am I falling in love with you? The words repeated again, but didn't fill him with the same warmth as the night before. He was still alone, whether Caleb loved him or not. The afterglow of Paradox and the kiss was fading, and now he was unsure how to feel.

Outside, a robin began a raucous melody that startled and jarred his ears. The incessant warbling continued until he couldn't stand it any longer. He climbed out of bed and shut the open window firmly, shivering all the while.

How to feel? What to feel?

Tenuous.

It struck him finally as he crawled back beneath the covers. The world around him was poised for a change he wasn't sure he'd like. Perhaps it was the threat of rain as the atmosphere struggled to hold its moisture. He dismissed the thought as wishful thinking; his unease had nothing to do with meteorology. Instead, there existed a sense that everything was suddenly fragile and bruised.

The consequences of last night's actions were yet to be seen, but he could not shake the feeling that damage had been done. He'd crossed a line and tasted something that was not his to taste. How could he resist? It was the ultimate indulgence of a gilded summer—a time that had been so reckless and easy. Now things were going to be different one way or another. Coming out of the shadow of Darren and the spring, these past months had been a bright spot of sunlight. Perhaps if he hadn't given in to his longing—hadn't allowed Caleb to lead him across that line—it could have gone on. But not now the clouds had rolled in.

It was fitting. Today was his last day before becoming a full-time student again. Today the summer was over.

Laying on his back, he wondered if he should call Caleb. It wasn't too early. There was a chance he was awake. And the call could be innocent! Wasn't it reasonable to check in and make sure he'd gotten home alright? He supposed he could accomplish the same thing by calling Meredith, but that wasn't really the point. Slowly, he sat up again and rubbed his hands together for warmth. No. It was best to let Caleb initiate contact. A little glimmer of last night's certainty returned. Surely it wouldn't be long—he was bound to hear from him today.

He pulled on a pair of sweats and a shirt, and headed into the kitchen to make coffee. After pouring a cup, he sat at the dining table and held the mug with both hands, letting it warm his fingers. Yes. Surely he'd hear from Caleb today. How could he not? The whole night—the kiss especially—had been seismic. It wasn't an event to be ignored.

Steven emerged sleepily from the hallway, and once again Ryan felt a sense of things being damaged. He should tell Steven about the kiss and ask him for advice. There would be disappointment, yes, but Steven could ground him—remind him again about the sanctity of relationships.

Standing in the kitchen, Steven blinked. "Coffee," he said. "Do you mind if I have some?"

"Of course not," Ryan replied.

Steven filled a mug and then took a seat at the dining table. "How are you feeling this morning?"

"I feel—I don't know. I feel like I'm on the edge of something—like I might fall off at any moment. But I mean, not physically. I'm not hung over. I'm just—"

"You're feeling guilty." It wasn't a question, but it wasn't an accusation either.

Ryan considered. "No—not guilty." He realized suddenly that it was true. Perhaps he ought to feel guilty. That might be preferable to the mixture of apathy and unease that presently took its place. It was shameful maybe, but he didn't feel an ounce of remorse for what he and Caleb had done. He considered whether he should tell Steven what had happened after all. If he didn't feel guilty about it—if he couldn't even feign it—perhaps it was better to keep quiet. He smiled. "Like I said, there's nothing going on."

"Okay—" Steven said. "What then?"

Ryan shrugged. "Maybe it's just school starting."

"Maybe." Steven frowned.

Ryan returned to his bedroom a short while later and remained there for most of the day. He occupied his time mindlessly at the computer, all the while distractedly waiting for Caleb to call. The rain began to fall at noon, and he felt his spirit begin to fall with it. As the afternoon stretched on, he started to feel a faint twinge of frustration.

He couldn't imagine what was taking so long.

By the evening he began to feel a shift as his apathy was replaced by a dull ache. The important thing, he realized, was to remain hopeful. If Caleb didn't call today, there would be a legitimate reason—the timing wasn't right, or maybe Tom hadn't been home to talk. The night dragged on, and his optimism slipped away; he felt more isolated than ever. Classes started the following day—his first, Music History, was at seven-thirty in the morning—so he put himself to bed early, utterly dispirited.

Surely Caleb would call tomorrow. Or the next day.

Surely he'd call.

~*~

Caleb did not call the next day, or at all the following week. Ryan's dull ache grew sharper as his resolve strengthened. He would not be the one to initiate contact. Instead, he did his best to turn his attention to his studies and re-acclimate to the world of academics.

This was no easy task. It was the middle of September before he completely adjusted to his new routine. Balancing fifteen credits with thirty hours at the pool was difficult. His average day began with Music History at seven-thirty in the morning and didn't end until the pools closed at eight in the evening. Most nights he was barely able to get through his homework before falling asleep, but by the time the leaves started to turn, he found himself hitting his stride—tired beyond belief, but coping.

As the month stretched on, so did Caleb's silence. Ryan felt the whole situation slipping through his hands. Any promise of their potential together was quickly fading—a product of both Caleb's absence and Ryan's distraction. On more than one lonely night he considered calling—abandoning his resolve—but found he was too drained from the day to mount the emotional effort. The situation needed to be dealt with eventually, but it seemed like there was always a better time.

On an otherwise unremarkable Wednesday evening, Ryan sat on his bed, trying to read for a Music History test the next morning. He was so exhausted that it took him twenty minutes to realize he'd been scanning the same two paragraphs over and over again. Frustrated, he stood up and headed into the kitchen for a glass of water.

Steven was reading at the dining table. Looking up from a textbook he'd been engrossed in, he cocked his head and remarked, "You look pissed off."

Ryan laughed as he filled a glass at the sink. "Oh, I'm alright. I just can't believe how tired I am, and I've got reading I have to finish before tomorrow. I can't seem to get anywhere with it though."

Considering a moment, Steven said, "Well, maybe you need a change of scenery. In fact, have you done *anything* but go to work and school since the semester started?"

Ryan raised his eyebrows. "No, actually."

"Maybe you should head over to the Back Alley. You know, grab a table and some coffee, and then dive in."

"You don't think I'll get distracted?"

"Nah, it's what? Ten-thirty? Most of the people there will be studying at this hour. You might have to drown out a few conversations, but at least you'll feel like you're doing something—not just school work."

"Thanks Steven." Ryan smiled. "I'll give it a try, especially considering I'm not getting anything done here."

Fifteen minutes later, Ryan dropped his backpack on the table of an empty booth and headed toward the counter at the Back Alley Café. He ordered a peach Matté Latte and settled in with his textbook and a spiral notebook in which he'd been taking notes.

At first, he was able to drown out the noise of the place, but five pages later he began to pick up on voices coming from neighboring booths. A discussion on botany piqued his interest, and his focus was suddenly and irrevocably lost. He closed the textbook, looked at his nearly full Matté Latte and sighed. This was a good experiment, but it was clear he'd never get his reading done if he stayed here. Taking a sip of his drink, he decided that when he finished it, he'd head back to his bedroom to try again.

As he slowly swallowed, he looked around, and the memory of his first visit to the café overtook him. In many ways that had been a perfect night. Every experience was new—the beginning of a real friendship with Brandon, meeting Caleb and Tom, tasting Yerba Matté, and of course the Back Alley Café itself. That, he realized, was the beginning of his glorious transformation—the first step in becoming someone other than the boring, naïve Ryan Gregori he'd always been. He smiled at the memory and settled back into the booth, contented.

It didn't last long, however. He continued to think about that first night—how magical it had been. He thought about following Brandon and the boys down to the alley and standing with them while they smoked. Then he remembered Brandon and Tom leaving him alone with Caleb, who'd been so kind.

Then he thought about Caleb.

Suddenly he was sure that Caleb cared nothing for him. Clearly, he'd chosen Tom. The situation was black and white, and once again Ryan was left with nothing and no one. Once again, Ryan *was* no one.

He was momentarily overcome with a suffocating sense of help-lessness. All the feeling and the processing he still needed to do re-garding Caleb weighed down on him, and he could no longer ignore it. He wanted to let it crush him—to succumb to it, a victim. He wanted desperately to let himself be the boring, naïve, pathetic Ryan Gregori he'd always been. The desire to wallow in self-pity and cele-brate the injustice of another failed love affair was so strong, he bare-ly resisted. The moment was coming—swiftly—when he'd break. He felt flushed as tears began to build up in the corners of his eyes.

How could this have happened—that he'd read the situation all wrong? That kiss in the parking lot—the heat of it—had been so au-thentic. It was truth. In a sea of uncertainty, that moment of lips and tongues dancing together in the night was a lighthouse. It had been absolute and real, and whatever else transpired between then and now, there was this one, ultimate certainty. It had happened, and Caleb had meant it.

Caleb didn't care? Maybe not now, but he had then. Ryan laughed inwardly at his foolishness.

As he took another sip of his Matté Latte, a lyric began to form in his head. He reached for the spiral notebook and was amazed by how effortlessly the first verse flowed out of him.

I can endure that I'm going to fall in love with you
I can endure seeing you with him
I can withstand waiting for something to come of this
And I understand the burden of your guilt—

He reread the lines several times, feeling their internal rhythm. Rolling them quietly over his tongue, he smiled at the structure, en-joying the emphasis on the early rhyming words—endure, endure, withstand, understand. Then he continued—

—You don't need to ask me to
I will be the stro-ong one
I'll put my arms around you
While you tell me he's the wro-ong one

But let me be ho-onest
The one thing I can't do
Is forget about you—

The words were rough, but he thought he was on to something. He paused for a moment. When was the last time he wrote lyrics? It invigorated him in a way he'd forgotten. The song needed a chorus—something painful. He swallowed the last of the Matté Latte. A few loose tea leaves that had settled to the bottom of the glass caught in his throat, and he coughed. He thought of the suffocating helplessness he'd felt a few minutes before, when he decided that Caleb had forsaken him. Inspiration struck, and hastily he scrawled—

—Don't let this become
A mutual unrequited attraction
I experience a stro-ong reaction
When you're not near
It's like anaphylaxis—

He reread the verse and chorus in their entirety and smiled. Perhaps the flow was a little coarse on the eyes, but he was certain when he set it to the music already forming in his head that it would make perfect rhythmic sense. Suddenly exhilarated, he stood brusquely, deciding to have another Matté Latte after all. He headed to the counter smiling.

After paying for his second beverage, he turned back toward his table and felt the smile fall from his lips as he froze in terror. Tom was sitting in the booth with a small pot of tea, reading his lyrics. Ryan began to tremble and forced his hands still as a small, milky wave of Matté Latte freed itself from his glass and splattered on the floor.

Testing his voice underneath his breath, he walked slowly forward, manufactured his most innocent smile, and called out, "Tom! What are you doing here at this hour?"

Tom looked up from the lyrics, squinted his round eyes and smiled. He laughed, and his wispy white-blond hair moved erratically. "Hi, Ryan. I tried to catch you when you got up, but I figured I'd surprise you."

Ryan kept his smile intact as he slid into the booth opposite Tom. "Ha! Well, I *am* surprised." He looked at the other boy, still dressed in his blue work scrubs. "I'm guessing you just got out of work?"

There was sadness in Tom's eyes when he answered. "Yeah. Caleb is working the overnight tonight. I didn't feel like being alone yet." When Ryan didn't speak—he was waiting for the inevitable accusations—Tom looked down at the lyrics. "These are—interesting. You're still hung up on that guy from the beginning of the summer, I guess."

A tidal wave of relief washed over him as Ryan laughed and closed the spiral notebook. Tom thought the lyrics were about Max. "Well, not really. I just felt like I needed to write something. It was the first situation that came to mind."

Tom seemed to be focused on his breathing. He took a long sip of his tea and exhaled. "Maybe you can help me with something."

"What's that?"

"Well, I'm sure you know that Caleb and I have been having our issues. Most of the time I don't think it's anything major. We get into arguments, and I'll be the first to admit I have a temper—"

Ryan nodded. "These things happen."

"But lately I'm worried. I think there's someone else. He's just been more and more distant, especially these last few weeks."

Ryan swallowed hard, feeling cold sweat on his forehead and beneath his arms. "Well, that doesn't necessarily mean there's someone else."

"No—" Tom mused. "It doesn't *mean* there's someone else. But look. A few weeks ago on a Saturday, we got into this huge argument. I can't even remember honestly what it was about. I just blew up. I went to stay with some friends for the night. I guess you and Caleb and that girl—Meredith? You went to Paradox. The next morning when I got home, Caleb was just—"

Ryan waited patiently for him to speak again, and when he didn't, he was compelled to fill the silence. "Tom, maybe he was just upset that you went off like that. I'm sure you apologized."

"Of course I did. Believe me; I know how Caleb gets when I upset him. But this was something different. He was troubled, and I got the impression it didn't have anything to do with me. I got to thinking. Did anything—happen at Paradox?"

Ryan felt his cheeks warm, and there was no doubt that Tom noticed. He stammered, "Between us? No, of course not! Caleb, he—"

Tom started laughing ferociously. When he calmed himself, he spoke with more than a glint of malice in his eyes. "No, of course not between the two of you. I'll admit I did have a moment when I thought the two of you might be—" Ryan swallowed hard. "It's just, he's always talking about Ryan this and Ryan that." Tom chuckled. "I wish you could see your face right now. You look like a goddamned tomato! But seriously, I know you'd never do something like that.

And the two of you have gotten so close, I thought maybe you'd have seen something—or he'd have mentioned someone. Was he talking to anybody?"

Ryan tried to laugh, and took a large sip of his Matté Latte. "Meredith and I were with him basically the entire time. If he met someone, it wasn't that night. But, Tom?"

The other boy raised his eyebrows. "Yes?"

"Caleb loves you. I know he does. Whatever the two of you are going through right now, I'm sure it'll pass."

"I sure hope so. I'll be the first to admit that I'm not a perfect boyfriend. Caleb isn't either. But I love him—he's the best thing that ever happened to me." There were tears welling up in his eyes now. "If I ever lost him, I don't know what I'd do. So, please, if you think of anything, or if you see anything—"

Ryan reached out his hand and grasped Tom's firmly. His heart was breaking to see Tom like this. His eyes drifted to the cover of his spiral notebook, and in that instant, he understood that the only relationship he could ever have with Caleb was scrawled onto those pages. Whether or not they were suffering a *mutual unrequited attraction*, his agony was nothing compared to what Tom was feeling right now, or would be feeling if the affair ever truly manifested itself. After tonight, for all their sakes, he wouldn't think about Caleb anymore.

"Of course, Tom. You two will work through this. If I hear anything, I'll let you know."

Tom wiped his eyes. "Thanks, Ryan." He'd finished his tea. "I should get going. Clearly, I'm not actually fit to be in public right now." Ryan smiled as Tom rose up out of the booth. "You're a really good friend, Ryan. That guy you're writing those lyrics about—Max, or whatever? He doesn't know what he's missing."

Ryan smiled sadly. Max, or whatever. "Thanks, Tom. Have a good night." He finished his drink, packed up his things and headed home.

~*~

"I'm surprised you didn't want Caleb to come," Meredith said as she accelerated down the onramp. It was Saturday night again, and she'd convinced Ryan to go dancing at a club in Denver. She promised that the crowd was mixed—offering plenty of male attention for both of them—and Ryan acquiesced, feeling like he needed to get out of the house. "You've been *all about* Caleb lately."

He considered his words carefully. "I think I've seen enough of Caleb for a while."

Meredith gasped as she merged onto the interstate. "There's something going on between the two of you, isn't there?"

Ryan choked. "You don't know what you're talking about."

"I knew it! Oh, shame on you Ryan Gregori!"

"Meredith, there is nothing going on."

"But you're avoiding him? Please, Ryan. I'm not an idiot."

He sighed. "Fine. I was dealing with some—uninvited emotions regarding Caleb."

"Uninvited emotions? Sometimes I swear you're an alien. What's wrong with just saying you *want him*?"

"Seriously, Meredith? Call it whatever you want. But it's over now. I've put all that behind me, and I just don't think I should see him for a while."

She was quiet for a minute. "You're a big fan of avoidance, aren't you?"

"What do you mean?"

"I mean, you hate to put yourself in any situation where you might end up emotionally compromised. You'd rather cast off your great new friend because of a little crush than put in the work to redirect your relationship with him."

"Oh great, is this whole drive going to be a therapy session?"

"I'm serious, Ryan! Look, you still haven't told me all the details about the Max situation this summer, but from what I've gathered, that was the same thing, right? You felt vulnerable, didn't know what to do, and so you put off dealing with it. And what about Darren— though I hate bringing him up—have you really dealt with that yet?"

"What's to deal with? I moped around for half the spring and then realized it was time to move on." His words were flat and unconvincing.

She sighed with exasperation. "Time to move on? First of all, you can't put a timeline on grief. Secondly, yeah, I know you've come to terms with the fact that he's dead. But have you spent any time considering what you might learn from the situation? Have you tried to figure out why Darren had such a hold on you in the first place? Are you treating your current relationships the same way you treated your relationship with Darren? Or has that changed?"

"Meredith, I can't handle this right now."

"Case in point. Well, forget about Darren for the moment. You have to deal with the Caleb situation. Deciding not to ever see him again isn't exactly a viable option. Like it or not, he's my friend too, now. Your paths are bound to cross, and I'll be damned if I'm going to plan my life around making sure the two of you don't see each other when I want to hang out."

He was starting to get angry. "So, what am I supposed to do? It's been hard enough to control my feelings when I don't see him. How am I supposed to do it when I do?"

She thought for a moment. "Have a party. Everybody loves parties at your house. Have a party, and make sure that he and Max, and anyone else you're having feelings for is there. I'll be there too, of course. Then, you just start to retrain yourself. Put these people in a totally different context. Tell yourself they're just your friends. Oh, and you can invite some people you don't know very well—maybe from school. Getting to know them better will distract you from your *scary feelings.*"

"Now you're taunting me."

She laughed. "Maybe a little bit. Really, though. You're going to see Caleb again someday. Why not make it on your terms? You can paint him in a different light."

"Ugh," he groaned. "And you'll be there?"

"Mm—hmm. And so will prudish Steven. He won't hesitate to throw some cold water on your hot coals."

"Hey, that's not fair. Steven isn't prudish."

"Okay, maybe not, but little Stevey sure makes a damned good foil for the devil on your shoulder."

Ryan laughed because it was true. "Okay, a party? I'm thinking fondue."

"Of course you are. Of course you are."

"And what about you? Do you have any demons you'd like to in-vite? Anyone *you* need to paint in a new light?"

She was quiet for too long. When she spoke her voice was soft, and Ryan struggled to hear her over the sound of the tires on the road. "More like, wash in turpentine."

"What?" he asked.

"It's a long story."

"We've got a long drive ahead; we have time."

She shook her head. "I don't want to talk about it."

"You're a big fan of avoidance, aren't you?" He mocked, playfully.

"Touché. You're right, I *am* avoiding it, but that's just because I've dealt with it already. That's what I tell myself anyways. I don't like to bring it up because it makes me think maybe I haven't really dealt with it as well as I thought. So yeah, consider the subject *avoided.*"

"Oh, come on, Meredith. You know everything about me and what I've gone through. You've got to give me something."

She groaned. "You're not going to let this go, are you?"

"Nope."

"Fine. It's my ex. We were together for a long time, and it ended badly about a year and a half ago. He moved away and left me with a bunch of trust issues. That's it, end of story."

"End of story? That's not even a *story*. Why did it end? Where did he move?"

"It doesn't matter. I'm done talking about it for tonight."

Ryan wanted to protest, but the tone of authority in her voice left no room for argument. Instead, he said "Okay, well, that's something I guess."

She turned her face and smiled at him. The inside of the car was dark, but even in the dim light from the dash, he could tell the smile was filled with genuine warmth. "Let's talk more about this party."

~*~

The following day, Ryan made arrangements for the party, and spent the week preparing. He chose the evening of Friday, September 24th. The guest list was substantially smaller than that of his birthday, but he made certain all the key players would be there. Max and Jake confirmed right away. Brandon also agreed to come, provided he could bring a guest. Caleb and Tom were the only holdouts. Ryan was afraid they were going to decline, but then he returned home on Wednesday night to a message from Tom saying they'd be there with bells on.

Most Fridays, Meredith taught a private lesson at the pool until six. The night of the party, Ryan arranged to leave work early, and after Meredith finished teaching, she threw a pair of sweat pants and a hoodie over her wet bathing suit and drove them back to The Garden. Once inside the apartment, she headed straight for the shower with a set of clean clothes while Ryan began chopping vegetables for the fondue.

Steven emerged from the hallway, squinting into the bright flood lights of the kitchen. "Here you are again, preparing for a party."

Ryan laughed. "Were you sleeping?"

"It was a long week. Who is in the bathroom? I have to pee."

"Meredith. She didn't shower at work because we just wanted to get here."

Steven groaned. "That girl needs to start paying rent. Can I use the bathroom in your room?"

"Of course." Steven began walking toward Ryan's room, but before he entered Ryan called out. "Oh, Steven. You're not planning to sleep through my party, are you?"

"I wouldn't dream of it. Besides, I've been asleep for four hours already; I'm going to be up all night."

At seven-fifteen, Brandon and his guest were the first to arrive. As usual, the door to the apartment was unlocked, so he waltzed into the kitchen unannounced with his companion behind him. Ryan looked up from the cheese he was grating as Brandon whistled. "Look at you, our little domestic goddess!" He walked forward and kissed Ryan lightly on the cheek. He indicated his companion, standing shyly behind him. "Ryan, this is Peter."

"Pleased to meet you," Ryan said.

"You too," The other boy replied, quietly. He was tall and narrow with thin, straight blond hair that fell lightly over his pimply forehead. Soft grey eyes sparkled behind medium-rimmed oval glasses as he reached out his hand and shook Ryan's. "Brandon's told me a lot about you." He chuckled in a deceptively low voice.

Ryan wanted to laugh and make a comment about Brandon liking them young, but he bit his tongue. This kid looked like he was sixteen. Instead, he said, "Good things, I hope."

Brandon punched him lightly on the shoulder. "Only good things. Peter is a freshman who happened to walk into the LGBT office when I was studying the other week—" he nudged the other boy, "—all scared and lost like a little puppy dog, right, Petey?"

Peter laughed nervously. "I dunno if I was *that* awkward. I just wanted to see what the place was about. I never really had any gay friends. But Brandon was so nice. And you're really nice, Ryan. Thanks for letting me come tonight."

Ryan beamed. "Of course!"

Brandon cleared his throat. "Anyone feel like a glass of wine?"

While Caleb and Tom remained conspicuously absent, the remainder of the guests arrived by seven-forty-five. Meredith took over DJ duties while Ryan and Steven took time to catch up with their guests and make sure wine glasses were filled. During one joint trip to the kitchen for refills, Steven pulled Ryan aside. "Hey," he asked, "What do you think of that new kid?"

Ryan laughed as he poured from a jug of sangria that Max brought. "What? Peter? He seems nice enough, but maybe a little shy. Why? Do you *like him*?" he taunted.

Steven blushed slightly. "He *is* kind of cute—pimples and all."

"Don't you think he's with Brandon?"

It was Steven's turn to laugh. "Are you kidding me? He's not Brandon's type at all."

Just then, Ryan noticed the duo in question walking toward them. "Speaking of—" he said quietly. "Hey, Brandon, where are you two going?"

"Smoke break," announced the other boy. Without stopping his forward momentum, he produced an unopened pack of cigarettes and lobbed them at Ryan. "Come on, let's go."

Ryan caught them and then withdrew his shoulders guiltily. Feeling as though he'd been caught in the middle of a crime, his eyes darted around the apartment wondering who'd seen. He wished Steven hadn't been next to him, but he audibly exhaled when he noted that Max was at the far end of the apartment.

Steven groaned. "Seriously?"

Ryan offered him an apologetic smile, then turned back to Brandon. "Why did you throw these at me?

Finally, in the door to the hallway, Brandon stopped. "Those are for you—the whole goddamned pack. Now you don't have to ask for them."

"I don't want a whole pack."

Brandon clucked his tongue. "No one is telling you to go crazy. I don't care if those last you the night or the next three months. Just come on, Petey needs a cig."

"You go, I'll be right there."

The moment they were out of earshot, Steven chided, "You had better not make a real habit of this, Mister Gregori."

"I won't, I promise." He turned to walk into the hallway, but a thought occurred to him. "Steven, have you seen Shelly at all?"

"No, actually. I think she's here though. I saw her before people started arriving."

Ryan groaned. "While I'm out there, do you think you could drag her out of her room? It's a party, for God's sake."

"Will do. Enjoy your cancer stick."

When Ryan stepped onto the porch two things were immediately evident. He could tell by how closely Peter stood to Brandon that he was hopelessly infatuated. It was also apparent by the look of relief Brandon displayed at seeing Ryan that he didn't share Peter's sentiments. Ryan opened his fresh pack of cigarettes and lit one. Only after he took his first, long inhale did he notice that he and Peter were the only ones smoking.

"Brandon?" he asked. "Where's your cigarette?"

"Oh, you know I got all the way out here and realized I need to pee." Ryan wasn't certain, but he could have sworn that Brandon winked. "I'll be right back!" He brushed past Ryan and slipped inside.

Peter stood some distance away, slowly smoking with a dumb grin on his face. Not sure what to say, Ryan filled the silence with the first thing that crossed his mind. "So, you're a freshman?"

"Yeah." The other boy responded in his surprisingly low voice.

"Me too. I took a couple years off, but it's good to be back in school."

Peter exhaled with a long hiss. "So far I think it's okay. I was pretty lonely. The guy I'm sharing my dorm room with isn't very nice, and I haven't really met a lotta people yet. I guess I'm kinda shy, so when Brandon started talking to me in the gay office—is it alright I call it that? Anyways, when he started talking to me—it's made a big difference. He's really great, you know?"

Ryan chuckled. "He *is* pretty great. He's helped me out a few times when I've been feeling down." He looked again at Peter's dumb expression and saw what Steven had seen. A dull pang of pity started to throb in the center of him. There was no way Brandon was interested in this kid, and Peter didn't have a clue. It wasn't that Peter was unattractive—far from it if you could look past the pimples and the thin hair—it came down to confidence. Brandon had an enviable knowledge of himself—who he was as a person and where he stood in the world. By comparison, Peter was just a lost little boy.

"So you know what I'm talking about," Peter said. "When we're together, I just feel like I could do anything." Ryan frowned suddenly, and noticing, Peter asked, "What's wrong?"

"Oh, nothing." He forced a smile. It wasn't true though. He'd seen this exact situation before, only last time it wasn't Peter and Brandon, it was himself and Darren. He thought of the year he'd spent chasing after Darren—the feelings of legitimacy and invincibility that filled him anytime Darren was around. Is this how it had looked from the outside—just some poor misguided kid, blindly begging for the affections of someone who was never going to love him in the way he wanted? He felt he knew Brandon well enough to know he'd shower Peter with nothing but kindness, but that's where it would end. On a higher level—a romantic level—Peter had nothing to offer Brandon as he was today. Ryan wanted desperately to tell him—to save him the heartache—but stilled his tongue to save Peter's spirit.

"I'm just—really lucky," Peter said.

Ryan smiled sadly. "You *are* lucky. And now you'll have me too." He meant it. Of course, he'd just met Peter, but seeing the parallels between their lives was enough. He resolved then and there to advocate for him in any way he could.

The echo of car doors slamming closed in the parking lot distracted them momentarily. Ryan searched for something else to say, but the sound of heavy feet on the stairs up to the porch caused them to turn. Wispy white-blond hair appeared from below, and then a face, smiling brightly.

"Hello!" Tom bellowed.

Ryan pulled hard on his cigarette as Caleb appeared next. He felt his blood run hot, searing its way through his body all the way to the tips of his fingers and toes. *Friends.* Caleb was his friend, and nothing else. He closed his eyes for a moment in an effort to summon his resolve. When he opened them again, he smiled as warmly as he could manage and opened his arms. "Hello!"

Tom hugged him tightly while Caleb stood a short distance away, looking at the ground. "Better late than never, right?" Tom said.

Ryan laughed lightly as he stepped back. "Or maybe you're right on time. We didn't start eating yet, or anything." He looked past Tom and met Caleb's eyes briefly. "Caleb. Welcome."

There was sadness in Caleb's eyes, and more than a little fear. "Ryan. Sorry it's been so long. You're—settling into school alright?"

"I am." He swallowed. Then, remembering, he turned toward Peter. "Oh, um, Peter! These are my friends Tom and Caleb."

Peter exhaled a thin blue cloud of smoke. "Nice to meet you."

"Nice to meet you too," Caleb replied. "I actually need to use the bathroom. Catch you guys inside? Come on, Tom."

Tom scowled. "Go ahead. I'll have a smoke with them first."

"Aw, come on, babe. I'll come out with you later. Maybe you can get me a drink?"

Tom shrugged. "Alright. See you in there then." He smiled again and followed Caleb into the apartment.

When the door was closed Ryan exhaled with relief, then turned back to Peter. "They're nice. You'll like them. But—sorry. What were we talking about?"

"Yeah," Peter said. "They seem nice. What do you think is taking Brandon so long?"

Ryan smiled to himself. "I don't know. He probably got distracted inside."

"Well, I should go find him." Peter extinguished his cigarette and headed for the door. Ryan followed close behind.

Back inside, Meredith and Steven cornered him in the kitchen.

"Shelly is refusing to come out," Meredith groaned. "She won't say why, just that she needs to be alone right now."

Ryan shrugged. Shelly's behavior was odd—she tended to delight in social situations—but it didn't bother him too much. "That's her right, I guess. I skipped out on quite a few parties when Mark and Jay lived here."

Scowling, Steven retorted, "But I bet Mark and Jay's friends weren't banking on seeing you. Everyone here really likes Shelly, and I don't understand why she's being so rude."

"I just feel bad for the dog," Meredith said. "I can hear him yipping at the door off and on. Little Mars wants to see what's going on out here."

Ryan shook his head. "She'll come out when she's ready."

As the party progressed, Ryan set up the fondue station. He had two pots in the center of the table—one filled with oil and the other with cheese—around which he put plates of raw meats, vegetables, fruits and bread. In bowls at the four corners of the table, he set out sauces—mustard, soy sauce, chili paste, and ranch dressing. When everyone's glasses were filled, he invited his guests to start eating, and conversation flowed casually as the partygoers took trips back and forth between the dining table and the living room.

Halfway through his third glass of wine, Ryan stood alone at the table, watching his guests in the living room. Somehow Meredith snuck up behind him, and he jumped as she playfully pinched his side.

"How are you doing?" she asked.

"Oh, fine."

She turned her head to the side and scowled. "No, I mean with the demons. You're supposed to spend tonight retraining your brain, remember? So, you look at Max, and you look at Caleb, and you think *friends*."

He considered the question honestly for a moment before answering. "Really, I think I'm doing fine." As he spoke the words, he looked at Jake, leaning in close to Max. He was genuinely happy for them. Then he looked at Caleb and Tom, who were laughing together. It looked like their relationship was improving, at last. In a real moment of unadulterated goodwill, he realized it was enough for him that Max and Caleb were both here. Maybe a romantic relationship with one or the other would come to pass one day, but in the present, it sufficed that they were his friends. He also remembered that he didn't suffer his feelings alone. Both Max and Caleb had expressed an interest in him, and even though no one could act on that attraction, Ryan derived comfort from knowing that somehow, he'd earned their affections. "I mean that, Meredith. Everything is okay."

She smiled. "I'm really glad to hear it. In other news, what do you think of Peter?"

"Ugh, why is everyone going on about Peter?"

Meredith laughed. "Well, Brandon brought him for you."

"What?"

"Oh, come on Ryan. Remember I said we should try to get some new people here tonight? I knew you weren't going to do it, so I talked to Brandon early in the week. We both agree it would be good for you to spend some time with someone who is nice and available, and it's pretty clear that Peter is in the market for a boyfriend. I wish you were too, but God knows you aren't ever going to fucking do anything about it."

"Meredith, that kid is smitten with Brandon."

"So go make him be *smitten* with you! Jesus Christ, have some fun! You need to settle down with someone for a while so you can get out of your fucking head."

He felt himself start to blush. Angrily he retorted, "No one asked you two to be matchmakers."

Meredith shrugged as she walked back toward the living room. "Hey, what are friends for?"

He started to follow her, then noticed Caleb staring at him intently from the circle of guests on the floor. His eyes pleaded with Ryan, and the message was clear. *Don't move. I want to talk to you.* Sighing, Ryan stepped back and rested an elbow on the kitchen peninsula. Caleb quietly excused himself from Tom, stood, and made his way toward where Ryan waited.

As he approached, Ryan asked, "Are you enjoying the party?"

"It's great."

Ryan could see in the other boy's face that he was searching for the right words, but couldn't find them. Caleb continued to stare, looking more and more desperate, while out of nowhere Ryan felt his temper rising. He tried to remember his resolve and look at Caleb as any other friend—to channel the goodwill he'd felt only moments before—but the pain and anger handily eclipsed his better nature. Apart from the awkward greeting on the porch, this was the first time he'd had any interaction with Caleb since their ill-fated kiss, and all the emotion he'd compartmentalized was bubbling—frothing forward. With his fists clenched in frustration, he found himself seconds away from screaming.

"I'm so sorry," Caleb whispered.

Three simple words.

Ryan's rage deflated in an instant. "What?" he asked.

"I said I'm sorry. I'm sorry I never called you or—"

He sighed. "Caleb—"

"Listen. I just need a little more time to sort things out. What I said that night—that I was falling in love with you? I meant it. It's only—things are so complicated with Tom. But if you can just be patient a little longer—"

Ryan smiled and repressed the urge to laugh. Caleb couldn't have his cake and eat it too. He felt a resurgent strength in his convictions, and when he spoke, he meant every word. "Caleb, stop. I think we're better as friends." Ryan wrapped his arms lightly around Caleb and held him. The moment might have turned awkward, but from the living room, Meredith bellowed a command for them to come back to the party and stop being antisocial.

Glasses were filled one more time as the partygoers talked and laughed. Max was particularly interested in how Ryan's music classes were going, and promised to attend Ryan's first Wind Ensemble performance in a few weeks. The conversation moved easily from topic to topic, and eventually everyone became aware that they were mildly drunk. Brandon and Peter left shortly before eleven, and it was clear by the sleepy looks on the faces of the remaining guests that the party was winding down.

Just as Meredith stood to get ready to leave herself, Shelly's bedroom door opened and she stepped into the living room with Mars on a leash. She was dressed in baggy sweats and an oversized hoody. Her eyes were sunken and red, and her normally olive complexion was slightly more green than usual. The whole party fell silent at the sight of her—haggard and weary.

"Don't stop on my account," she said, her voice cracking softly.

Meredith stepped forward. "Shelly, are you alright? Have you been crying?"

She attempted a laugh. "I'm fine. Mars needs to go out." Without saying another word, and diligently avoiding eye contact with anyone, Shelly shuffled through the remaining guests and exited through the kitchen.

After the sound of the door indicated she made it outside, Meredith sighed. "She looks like shit! I wonder what's going on?"

Max looked at Ryan, "Have you ever seen her like this, Mister? Did something happen?"

Truthfully, Ryan was puzzled. He knew Shelly harbored a certain darkness, but the four months they'd been living together hadn't been long enough for him to discover its source. "I don't know. I haven't been able to get her to open up." He looked imploringly at Steven. "She's been pretty happy though, right?"

Steven nodded, drunkenly. "—As a clam."

Shaking her head, Meredith said, "I'll bet it's nothing. Maybe just girl problems. She'll be fine. Ryan, walk me out?"

Ryan agreed, and stood to accompany Meredith to the door. While she retrieved her bathing suit and sweats, he stood by the dining table. Returning a moment later, she said, "Great party! I'm really proud of you for facing the demons like this. Do you feel any better?"

He smiled. "Actually, yes. I think I'm done with boys for a while."

She groaned. "That is not the point. The point is to—"

The door slammed and Shelly came stomping into the kitchen with Mars in the lead. As she walked past the dining table, head down and scowling, Mars changed his course and leaped up toward some leftover raw meat on the table.

"Mars!" Shelly cried as she pulled forcefully against the leash.

"Whoah!" Meredith laughed. "Easy there. It's just some meat."

Shelly stopped and looked at the table. She whirled around to face Ryan with wild, incredulous eyes. "Is that hot oil? And raw meat? Left unattended?"

Ryan smiled. "Well, it *was* a fondue party. I wish you'd have come out. And no, I don't think the oil is hot anymore."

She pressed her lips tightly together, took a menacing step forward and shoved him sharply. "What the fuck is wrong with you?

You could kill Mars! What if he knocked that over? Are you trying to fucking *deep fry* my dog? And the fucking meat? Are you going to pay the fucking vet when he gets worms?"

Ryan was flabbergasted. "Shelly—"

Meredith stepped between them. "Listen sister, you need to calm down! Mars is fine. We'd never let anything happen to him. Anyways, the poor dog was in your room all night."

"Are you telling me how to take care of my animal? I've had Mars for ten years!"

"No, I'm just telling you you're overreacting."

There was a deafening crack as Shelly slapped her, hard and fast across the cheek. Meredith stepped back, stunned. Pointing a quavering finger, Shelly hissed, "Fuck you!" She pointed at Ryan. "Fuck you too." Turning, she dragged a whimpering Mars back toward her bedroom. As she moved through the silent guests, she boomed, "Everyone get the *fuck* out of my house!"

"Last I checked this wasn't just *your* house!" Ryan called. The only response was the slamming of her bedroom door. He looked at Meredith. "Are you okay?"

"I'm fine," she said. "Hopefully that'll leave a mark—I'll come up with a hundred amazing stories as to how I got it."

In the living room, the guests were standing up, so Ryan walked quickly forward. "Wait! You guys don't actually have to leave."

Max put his hand gingerly on Ryan's shoulder. "I think it's time, Mister. Thanks for a great party. Sorry about how it ended."

Five minutes later, everyone was gone.

CHAPTER 13

"Shelly finally apologized," Ryan said as he slowly chewed his pasta. "It only took two weeks."

Meredith raised her eyebrows in acknowledgment, but she did not look at him. She was trying to get the attention of the waiter. "No shit, huh?"

"Yeah, I was as shocked as anyone, the way she's been avoiding me."

Picking up her fork again, Meredith began to absently twirl spaghetti through the tines. Ryan watched as the fork went around and around. Even after she formed a tight little nest the fork continued to spin, the ends of the noodles whipping and slapping against the rest of the pasta on the plate. He wondered how she could stand the sound—soft though it was—and he frowned. She'd been distracted like this for most of the night, and he was waiting patiently for her to tell him what was wrong.

He let a few more seconds go by before he cleared his throat. Startled, her eyes widened, and she half smiled. "Sorry, I got lost there for a minute. So, did she say why she reacted the way she did?"

Ryan's frown grew deeper. "No, not exactly. She hinted that it was something to do with her family—she had a bad conversation, or someone said something that upset her—I don't know. She plays those cards so close. Do you remember the day she moved in? I mentioned her mother, and she totally freaked."

Meredith nodded, still not making eye contact. "Absolutely." Finally catching her gaze, the waiter ambled across the restaurant. Before he could ask what she needed, Meredith raised her empty wine glass and said, "I'll have another, when you get a chance? Thanks." Having accomplished her objective, she looked at Ryan for the first time in minutes. "So, did she say what was wrong that night?"

Ryan shook his head. "You didn't hear a word I said. Forget about Shelly. I need to know what's wrong with *you* right now."

He smiled compassionately in an effort to hide his worry. Earlier in the day when Meredith came into work to teach a couple of private lessons, her somber mood had been palpable. She finished a half hour before closing and practically begged Ryan to go to dinner with her. He explained, regrettably, that he didn't think he could—it was the first Thursday in October, and with his reduced hours due to school, money was getting pretty tight. He offered to make her dinner at home instead, but she dismissed his reservations and told him she'd pay if he would come along. Considering her odd mood, he agreed. It was clear something was bothering her, so after the pool closed, she drove them to a small Italian restaurant in the Old Town district of the city. Throughout the dinner, she managed to talk about everything and nothing, and Ryan got the sense she was only half present.

Meredith sighed. "Ugh, where is that wine?"

"Oh come on, you've already had two glasses. Why the need for all this liquid courage? Hmm? Out with it!"

She groaned. "I got an email today."

"An email?"

"Yeah, from my ex, Andrew."

It was Ryan's turn to raise his eyebrows. "It's the first time I've heard you mention him by name."

"Yeah, and it's only the second time you've heard me mention him at all."

"Fair enough. I guess you're finally ready to talk about it though. Do I get the full story now? What was in the email?"

"It's really complicated." She let out a long, slow exhale. "We started seeing each other in high school. After we graduated, we both moved up from Denver for college. Things were great at first. After freshman year we got an apartment together. I thought everything was good until it turned out he didn't have any money."

Ryan stifled a laugh. "What do you mean? Why didn't you know this before you signed the lease?"

"I don't know! I was young and stupid? To be fair, I don't really know what it's like—or I didn't anyways. I won't lie, my education is completely taken care of by my parents. They're paying for school, and deposit enough money into my account every month that I can pay my rent and have a little left over. The only reason I work now is to subsidize what they give me. I know I'm lucky—really lucky. But Andrew's parents just didn't have the means. He was working a little, but I don't know. Maybe he squandered his money, or maybe there just wasn't enough. Whatever the reason, three months into our lease he wasn't able to make his half of the rent."

The waiter walked up with a fresh glass of deep red wine. Meredith snatched it greedily from his hands and took a long sip before she continued. "Well of course, I panicked. I was on the phone with my parents pleading for more cash. They came through, but were pretty disappointed in Andrew. He promised—*promised*—it would never happen again. He was going to work more, or change his spending, or whatever—"

Ryan interjected. "Let me guess; it happened again?"

"Yes! Month four he was fine, but then it came time to pay December rent, and he couldn't. Well of course, humiliated, I went to my parents again. They told me that this was the last time. Andrew swore, he *swore* he had it under control. We made it to February before I had to take a shitty retail job to cover what he couldn't. And before you get all smirky, thinking *oh, poor little rich girl*, I'm talking twenty hours a week. That's tough! I don't know how you're doing thirty and taking a full course load."

He shook his head. "Yeah, it isn't easy. Free time is hard to come by."

"So, obviously this whole situation put a strain on our relationship. I'll admit I got bitter. I mean, you know me, Ryan. I don't put up with shit, and I'll say it like it is. I just don't understand why he didn't try harder. I started to feel like he was taking advantage of me. And then, here's the real kicker! In April of that year, I came home sick from class one day, and he had some girl over, 'studying.' They were sitting on the living room floor. She had a book open in front of her at least. But when I walked in the door it was pretty clear that the only thing he was studying was her breasts, because he had his hands inside her shirt."

Ryan blushed. "My God, what did you do?"

Meredith laughed and took another large gulp of her wine. "What do you think I did? I told him to fuck off and get out of my house—I was the one fucking paying for it, after all. I told her she was something even I won't say in public, and then I cried for a week. I have never, *never* felt so betrayed. Later he tried to make some excuse about how his judgment was clouded—he was just trying to work through all the conflict we'd been having."

Reaching across the table, Ryan took Meredith's hand. "Wow, I'm so sorry." He remembered vividly the pain he'd felt when he witnessed Brandon and Darren together at Steven's Valentine's Day party. Then he thought of Caleb and Tom and almost involuntarily withdrew his hand. He was quiet for a moment, and then, meekly he said, "I'm surprised you can be my friend after going through something like that."

Her brow furrowed. "Excuse me? What do you mean?"

"Well—Caleb. And even Max! It seems like I'm constantly in love with these men who are taken."

She laughed. "Well, you were in love with Max before he was taken. And Caleb is such a flirtatious little shit—how are you supposed to feel? Anyways, it's not like you've actually done anything to compromise their relationships."

"Right, that's true." The words fell out of his mouth, dry like sand. It was the first time he'd ever lied to Meredith. He felt tiny beads of sweat on his forehead and hoped she didn't notice. He was glad she didn't know the truth about what happened with Caleb, but he immediately regretted the dishonesty. Needing to slake his sudden thirst, he reached for his nearly empty glass of water and swallowed the rest of it in one long draw. He looked longingly at her half full glass of wine and wished he was old enough to order one for himself. After clearing his throat, he asked, "So, what was in the email?"

She rolled her eyes. "I get one every couple of months. I try not to read them—sometimes I don't—but today I couldn't help myself. It's just a whole lot of bullshit. He moved home after that semester—transferred to Boulder and commutes in every day. It's always the same. He misses me. He's so sorry. There hasn't been anyone since. He always asks if he can see me."

"Do you want to see him?"

"Of course I do! We were together for so long. I loved him. I probably still do, but I just can't. I've dated a few people since then but—"

"It's not the same?"

"Right. Ugh, anyways, I was pretty upset about it today, so I'm glad you came out. I needed the company."

Ryan smiled. "Of course."

On the walk from the restaurant back to Meredith's car, Ryan pulled a pack of cigarettes from his pocket and lit one unceremoniously. Meredith coughed in surprise and said, "You're carrying them with you now?"

Exhaling a pale blue mentholated cloud, Ryan sighed. "It's terrible. I bought a pack a couple days ago."

She squealed with delight. "I shouldn't be condoning that behavior, but I'm proud of you. Give me one?" Ryan did. "How's all that going, by the way—the education of Ryan Gregori?"

He looked at her quizzically as he took another drag. "School is fine. The hardest thing is just managing my time."

Meredith clucked. "Not *that* education. I'm talking about the stuff outside the classroom. I'm talking about the *ruination* of Ryan Gregori."

"Oh. Kind of at a standstill? It's pretty hard to dance on tables, kiss boys and get really drunk when all I do is go to school, work, and sleep."

"Huh, well that's going to need to change. I've got a few ideas up my sleeve."

"Great," Ryan groaned. "I can't wait."

She shoved him jovially. "Do you have plans for Halloween?"

"Not yet?"

He looked at her cautiously, and though it was dark he could have sworn she winked. "Well, now you do."

"Oh? What do you have in mind?"

"Well, there's this thing at Paradox." They reached the car and she fumbled in her purse for her keys. "But it's not a normal night. This promoter who works in Denver is bringing up some big DJ. It's going to be a mixed crowd, so not all the same boring queens that are usually there. It's a big deal; there hasn't been a night like this up here in a couple years."

"Okay—"

After extinguishing her cigarette, she opened the driver's side door and climbed inside. He followed her and once he buckled she continued. "And I can probably convince Caleb and Tom to come too. Maybe Brandon."

Something was going on. "Why are you selling this so hard?" he asked.

She bit her lip and smiled. "Well, there's just one little catch."

He laughed. "I knew it! What? What is it?"

"Well, I've been planning to go to this for a while—since I found out about it last month. I was going to ask you to go anyways but—"

This was unlike the Meredith he knew. She was nervous. He shook his head and said, "Alright. Out with it."

"In the email from Andrew today? He said he's going."

Ryan sighed, and his shoulders relaxed. "Meredith, you can't go then. Let's go out somewhere in Denver if that's what you want to do."

Suddenly angry, she made a fist and slammed the side of it into the steering wheel, causing the car horn to bleat in protest. She tilted her head all the way back and sank into the seat. "That's just it," she said. "I can't *not* go. I was planning to do this before I knew Andrew was going. I can't alter my life just because he'll be there. I mean, he should know better. He should stay away. But if I stop doing the things I like because of him? Then he wins."

Ryan nodded slowly. "When you put it that way—"

"He fucking *wins*! And if there is one thing I can't stand—it's losing." She sat up straight again and took a moment to smooth her hair. More composed she turned to look at him again. "So, please say you'll come?"

He wasn't sure he could refuse—not now. He smiled. "Of course I'll come."

~*~

The following Saturday morning Ryan took his time getting out of bed. The early autumn light woke him first at eight, but he rolled over and pulled the covers more tightly against the crisp October air flowing in through his open windows and drifted back to sleep. Sometime after nine, he woke again and relished the simple pleasure of watching the ceiling fan above his bed spin in slow, silent circles. Today was the only day of the week without obligations—no work or school—and he planned to enjoy it the best he could. He was considering trying to fall asleep again when there was a sharp knock on his bedroom door.

"Ryan?" It was Steven, his voice faintly muffled through the wood and walls. "Are you awake?"

He groaned. "Yes Steven. What is it?"

"Can I come in?"

Ryan sat up and quickly pulled on a pair of shorts and a shirt sitting on the floor beside his bed. "Yeah, go ahead."

Steven opened the door, stepped inside and shivered. "Ugh! It's freezing in here. Why are all your windows wide open?"

"I like it cold, what's the big deal? This is the best time of year for sleeping with the windows open." He watched as Steven shook his head before awkwardly sitting on the edge of the bed. When he didn't speak, Ryan asked, "So, what's up?"

Small patches of color blossomed on Steven's cheeks. "Well, Peter is coming over."

"Oh?" Ryan let the end of the word rise upward in a conspiratorial tone. "Do tell! You really like him, I guess."

Steven couldn't hold back the sheepish grin that spread across his face. "Yeah. He's still pretty hung up on Brandon, poor fool. But I just thought maybe I'd try to start spending some time with him and, you know—"

"Well, I think that's great! What are you two going to do? It's supposed to be a beautiful day. The leaves are peaking—"

Steven laughed. "Last I checked, we don't live in Vermont. If by peaking you mean half of them are gold, the other half are brown, and not many of them have blown away yet, then yes! The leaves are peaking."

"Come on Steven, it's all relative. Anyways, you didn't answer the question. Hiking? A romantic lunch at a little cafe?"

"Actually—"

Ryan waited, but Steven didn't continue. "Actually—what?"

"Actually, I was hoping we could all study together."

Throwing his hands in the air, Ryan sighed. "Study together? What, like all sit around and read books and take notes?"

"Yes," Steven said. "Exactly like that."

It was his turn to laugh. "Okay, I know I'm pretty bad at this myself, but seriously?"

"Please? I'm just trying to, you know, get a gauge on him—see if it's really worth pursuing. When he gets here will you please just come out and sit with us? I promise next time I'll plan something really one-on-one—something more date-like."

"Ugh, fine." He smiled.

"Thanks Ryan, I really need this."

Peter arrived just before lunch time. Ryan and Steven were already sitting on pillows on the living room floor with books spread out around them. Hearing the front door open, Ryan looked expectantly toward the hallway. A few moments later Peter emerged with a

large backpack hanging from one bony shoulder. In spite of his nervous gait as he walked toward them, Ryan smiled at his appearance.
Since the first time they'd met two weeks previous, Peter's acne had
diminished, and though his hair was still thin and fine, some sort of
product gave it a pleasant volume today.

Steven stood and embraced him clumsily. "I'm really glad you
could come."

Peter dropped the backpack onto the floor. "Thanks for having
me. Any excuse to get out of the dorms. I was really glad when you
asked, because I was trying to make plans with Brandon all week, and
he just won't get back to me."

Ryan shivered, trying his best not to remember a handful of similar situations with Darren. He wanted to tell Peter that the sooner he
moved on, the sooner he'd be happy. Instead, he put on his brightest
smile and said, "You're welcome here anytime. Steven was really excited you were coming."

Peter raised his eyebrows as Steven shot Ryan a scornful glance.
Clearing his throat, Steven said, "Yeah, I just get really sick of looking
at Ryan all the time." Everyone laughed. "Pull up a pillow!"

Peter did as Steven suggested, then wrestled a history text from
his bag. He opened it clumsily, adjusted his glasses and began to read.
Ryan looked at Steven and smiled before turning his eyes back to his
own music history book.

Though the next hour proved to be productive, Ryan was grateful
when the phone started ringing in his bedroom. At the second ring,
he quickly abandoned his textbook and leaped to his feet. "Excuse me
a second, gentlemen," he said before bounding off to answer it.

Nearly breathless despite the short distance, Ryan plucked the
phone from its base and answered "Hello?"

"Hey Mister," Max said at the other end of the line. "You sound like you just finished running a marathon. Is everything okay?"

"Oh, yeah," he laughed. "What's up?"

"I'm headed to the mall—need some new sweaters I think. Do you want to go?"

Ryan considered. "That sounds great, but I agreed to spend the afternoon with Steven and—Peter. We're um, studying on the living room floor."

Max clucked. "Leave those two there. Steven just doesn't want to be alone with him, am I right?"

"You got it. I think he *really* likes him."

"So, come on! What do you say?"

"Well—how soon are you planning on going?"

"I could pick you up in maybe forty-five minutes? An hour at most."

Ryan smiled. "Okay. Then I can break the news to Steven, and he'll have time to come up with a Plan B."

"Plan B?" Max laughed. "He's going to have an utter meltdown. You might as well ask if they want to go as well."

"Good idea. Alright, see you soon, Max."

"Sounds good. See you soon."

Ryan replaced the phone on its base and walked, smiling, back to the living room. Steven looked up from his textbook and scowled. "What was that?" he asked.

"Oh, just Max."

"Just Max? What did *he* want?"

"He's going to the mall in a little while and asked if I wanted to go."

Peter's head jerked up suddenly from the book he was engrossed in. "The mall? I haven't been to the mall in for—ever! What did you say?"

"I said I'd go. You two are welcome to come as well."

Steven folded his arms over his chest and scowled even deeper. "I thought we were going to study."

At this, Peter leaned sideways and shoved him playfully. "Oh, come on, Steven. We got a good hour in. And Max isn't here yet. We can study until then, but don't you think it'll be fun? Maybe I can pick up some of those jeans Brandon always wears."

Ryan rolled his eyes involuntarily. No one seemed to notice, so he smiled and said, "Yeah Steven. Give the books a rest."

Peter added, "If you wanna, we can study more later."

Steven threw his hands in the air. "So, you're both going then?"

Peter fluttered his eyelashes. "Please Steven? Come on."

"Ugh," he groaned. "Alright."

A little more than an hour later Ryan climbed out of the front seat of Max's car and shivered against the cool mid-October breeze. The others followed, and he said, "This is definitely sweater weather."

Max chuckled as they began the long trek across the parking lot. "Yeah, I love this time of year. I hope I find some good stuff." He looked back toward Steven and Peter, a few steps behind. "What about you, Steven? In the market for anything?"

"Nope," Steven grumbled. "I'm just here for the company."

"Hmm, you must really like us. Or at least *some* of us. I know this isn't really your thing."

Steven choked, and Ryan nudged Max lightly to say enough was enough. There was no harm though; Peter seemed oblivious to the reference. Now Ryan spoke. "Peter, what about you?"

"Huh?" He seemed to be in another world.

"Is there anything in particular you're looking for today? You said something about jeans."

"Oh," he laughed. "Yeah, sorry. I was trying to remember what brand of jeans Brandon wears. I'd really like a pair for myself."

"Why?" Steven asked.

"I dunno. He always looks so good in them. I thought maybe—I dunno. Maybe he'd notice?"

Steven looked down at his feet and said nothing, so Max replied instead. "Well, maybe. I don't think he'll like you any better because you're wearing the same clothes though."

As they reached the entrance to the mall, Peter pulled a pack of cigarettes from his pocket. "You guys go ahead," he said, lighting one. "I'll find you inside. Ryan, do you want one?"

Ryan blushed and guffawed. He was mortified at the idea of Max seeing him smoke. "Oh, no thanks. I'll um—I'll stay out here with you though until you're done."

Max scowled at Ryan. "You'd better not, Mister. That's a nasty habit. See you two inside then. Come on, Steven, I want to talk to you."

Once they were alone, Ryan turned his attention to Peter. "Sorry," he said. "I don't smoke all the time, and around certain people—"

"No, I'm sorry," Peter replied as he slowly exhaled. Ryan could smell the smoke and it ignited a powerful craving within him. "I hope I didn't get you in trouble."

"No, no." He shook his head. "Everything should be fine." He was quiet for a moment. Then, "So, you really like Brandon. Like *really* like him, huh?"

Peter couldn't contain his smile. "Oh yeah. He's probably the most incredible person I've ever met. When he's around me it's like—I dunno. Nothing can go wrong, you know?"

"Have you told him any of this?"

"Oh no! I could *never*. I'm waiting for him to figure it out—make the first move. It's gonna happen soon, I can feel it."

Ryan frowned. "And what if it—doesn't?"

"Well, I dunno. I haven't even thought about that." He looked worried. "Do you know something?"

"No, not exactly. It's just that—I feel like Brandon is usually pretty direct. I'm just saying—" he bit his lip. "Hey! What do you think of *Steven*?"

Peter furrowed his brow, took another drag off his cigarette and then dropped it to the ground. He smothered it with his foot as he exhaled slowly. "Steven? Oh, I like him. He's odd but funny."

"He is *both* of those things. I think you guys should make an effort to hang out more moving forward."

"Okay—" Peter began walking toward the entrance.

"I don't know. Maybe you'll find you have a lot in common."

When they found the others, Max was rifling through a pile of sweaters in The Gap, while Steven stood some distance away disinterestedly looking at a rack of button ups. Max showed Ryan and Peter his finds then checked out, and they moved together back into the mall. After popping in and out of several more stores, they reached the food court and settled on a late lunch of assembly-line Chinese food.

Sitting at a small table, Max smiled as he slowly stabbed at overcooked sesame chicken with a plastic fork. "Has anyone got Halloween plans yet?" he asked.

Peter and Steven both shook their heads no. Ryan said, "Meredith wants me to go to this thing at Paradox that night. I guess some promoter is coming up from Denver and they're going to have a big-shot DJ. And her ex is going to be there, so I told her I'd go—for moral support."

"Hmm," Max said. "You've been spending an awful lot of time with her. Alright though, can't be *that* much of a big-shot in that tired old tin can, but you already agreed. Too bad, Mister, I was thinking about having a Halloween party at my place."

Ryan frowned. "That sounds so much better."

"Hey!" Steven exclaimed. "Just because *Ryan* can't go doesn't mean you shouldn't do it! I don't have any plans yet. Peter, you'd go, wouldn't you?"

Peter nodded excitedly. "Yeah. You'd invite Brandon too, right?"

Max smiled sadly. "I really don't know Brandon that well. I'd be surprised if he doesn't have other plans already. But yeah, he could come. Why don't *you* invite him?"

"Okay! Is it gonna be a costume kinda thing?"

"Oh yeah, of course!" He looked at Ryan. "What about you, Mister? Do you need a costume?"

He frowned. "Yeah, I think I'm supposed to have one. I don't even know where to begin."

"Well, there's one of those pop-up costume stores here in the mall. We could all have a look. And then if maybe you decide you'd rather spend the night with us—"

He shoved Max playfully from across the table. "Of course I'd rather spend it with you, your timing is just bad."

"It wouldn't be the first time." Max winked, and Ryan felt himself blush.

"Okay okay," he said. "No need to lay it on so thick. Finish your food, and then we can take a look. Hey, where is Jake today, by the way?"

Max turned his eyes down toward his sesame chicken. "Oh, I don't know. I'll probably see him tonight."

Steven smirked. "Sounds like trouble in paradise."

"Nah," Max replied in a flat tone. "Jake is fine."

When the meal was finished, Max led the way to the costume shop in a far corner of the mall. Ryan approached hesitantly—his eyes were accosted by the garish window displays. Manikins dressed as sexy cats and bloody vampires stood ominously on a bed of plastic autumn leaves with giant rubber spiders and glowing jack-o-lanterns at their feet. Behind them, styrofoam headstones displayed messages such as *best prices in town* and *costumes to die for.*

"Well," Max said, ducking under the fake spider webs that framed the doorway, "This is it!"

"Ugh," Ryan replied. "Like I said, I don't even know where to begin."

The walls of the store were lined floor to ceiling with shelves holding bins of costumes. In the middle of the floor, clothing racks and carousels supported odds and ends on hangers—shirts and pants and what Ryan could only assume were capes.

"Dig in!" Max said. "Just look around and see if anything speaks to you."

Peter rushed past excitedly. "This is gonna be so much fun." He immediately found a bin containing togas and rubber grape leaves. "What do you think, guys?"

Steven answered first. "I think you're going to be cold." Max shot him a look to say *you can do better,* so he cleared his throat and amended, "But, uh—*very* sexy."

"Really?"

"Yeah," Steven said. "I guess if that's what you're going for, why not try the gladiator costume in the next bin over?"

"Ha! I'm not even gonna consider that a serious suggestion. I'm way too scrawny to pull that off."

"Okay, well, the toga is a strong maybe then. Let's keep looking." Steven smiled gratefully at Max, then nodded his head as he followed Peter deeper into the store.

Ryan sighed and let his shoulders slump. "This is all so overwhelming."

"I think you need to get yourself into the spirit of things," Max replied. "So, what are you thinking? Giant gorilla suit? Mario or Luigi? For myself, I think I'd make a pretty hot *Where's Waldo*."

"Ha! You *would* be a pretty hot Waldo. But um, I know you're joking with those others. It's hard because I'll be dancing. I don't know. These all look like great *party* costumes."

"Hmm," Max said. Then he smiled widely. "I shouldn't be helping you out with this, Mister—not when you're going to skip *my* party to go *dancing*. I still can't believe that's what you're into these days. I remember a time not too long ago when you wouldn't be caught dead in a place like Paradox." He shook his head slowly. "However—"

"However?"

"I have an idea!" He grabbed Ryan's hand and pulled him to a clothing carousel midway toward the back of the store. Several varieties of black pleather pants hung from clip-on hangers. Some were shiny while others were matte. All of them, however, looked quite tight around the legs. "Here!" Max proclaimed. "Why don't you go as like, a sexy devil?"

Ryan eyed him skeptically. "You want me to wear *those*?"

"Well, yeah! Then we'll find you a top. I'm sure there are some clip-on devil horns around here somewhere."

"No way, Max. No way in hell. Look at how *small* they are!"

"Come on, what are you, a 32 waist? Hold on—" he began turning the carousel. Partway around he plucked a pair and handed them to Ryan to hold. "Okay, you're going to try those on in a minute. Now for a top—"

Ryan followed Max from rack to rack as he thumbed through torn, bloody tee shirts and pleather jackets. Finally, when Max stopped and clapped his hands together excitedly Ryan asked, "Did you find something?"

"Oh yes! This is *perfect*. It's perfect!" He pulled a red fish-net shirt from a carousel and handed it to Ryan. "Just put a black tee underneath, or a tank top. Oh, it's going to be *amazing*!"

Ryan frowned. "Isn't this for—women?"

"Oh, who cares? Go! Try it all on!"

"Max—"

"You're going to have to trust me on this one, Ryan. You've put your faith in me before—remember the earrings and the hair? Go. I'll meet you at the changing room with the others. They need to see this!"

"Ugh," Ryan groaned. "Alright." He walked awkwardly to the back of the store and let himself into the single changing room.

He removed his shoes and jeans, then regarded the pair of shiny black pleather pants Max had selected. He was doubtful they'd fit. He held the pants in front of him and undid the zipper. First, one foot went through, then the other. He pulled them upward and felt the material sticking to the skin of his calves and thighs. With a twist and a dancing, side-to-side shimmy, they came the rest of the way up to his waist. He inhaled slightly and pulled his belly inward, then found he was able to easily fasten the button at the top—around the waist at least it was a perfect fit. He pulled the zipper and exhaled.

Next, he pulled off his sweater, but kept on the plain white shirt he wore underneath. Putting the fishnet shirt over his head, he found he needed to stretch it slightly to fit over his shoulders. The delicate netting gave way easily, and he pushed his arms through, feeling the unfamiliar texture of the fabric—if he could call it that—mold tightly to his skin.

The pants were warm—hot even—and extraordinarily tight around his legs. However, as he examined his reflection in the mirror, he couldn't help but smile. They looked *really* good. He turned slightly, enjoying the way they exploited his shape from behind. Max was right about the shirt as well. The stretching emphasized the broadness of his chest while giving a little color. Certainly, he'd need to wear black underneath. A tank top was a good idea. The overall effect was so shockingly sexual, he barely recognized himself. He smiled, enjoying the feeling.

Then as he turned to the door, he experienced a great wave of self-consciousness. His friends were waiting on the other side, and the knowledge left him feeling naked. Perhaps this outfit was too much—what if it was horrible? If it was bad—if they reacted poorly— would they be able to un-see it, or would Ryan the *sexy devil* be imprinted forever on their minds?

"Come on in there!" Max said from the other side of the door.

Ryan took a couple deep breaths. "Okay, promise not to laugh?"

"Promise."

He opened the door. Max, Peter and Steven stood in front of him with wide eyes and slack jaws.

Max's face turned upward into a crooked smile. "Wowza, Mister! Do a turn for us. Wow! You look—"

Steven cut in. "He looks like a transvestite parading as a French whore!"

"No—" Peter said, dreamily. "He looks *hot*!"

Folding his arms across his chest for what must have been the hundredth time that day, Steven shook his head. "Why would you want to objectify yourself like that?"

Ryan's eyes widened. "I don't know—it's just for fun, right? Max picked it out and I thought—"

"Oh, don't listen to him," Max said. "You look *great*. It's very sexy. I'm just disappointed this is the only time I'll see you in it—"

"Max—"

"I know, I know. Sorry, Mister—just having a little fun."

Ryan closed the door and quickly changed back into his real clothes. As he folded the black pants over his arm, he noticed the price tag for the first time—$39.99. His eyes widened. He checked the tag on the shirt—$19.99. It was all too expensive.

When he opened the door again Max was waiting for him on the other side. In one hand, he held a pair of red clip-on devil horns and in the other a can of silver hairspray. "Look!" he said. "I think they'll go together really well. You spray this stuff on and it'll make your hair stiff and shiny silver for the night. Then just clip these on, maybe put on a little makeup and you'll be good to go!"

"Makeup? Really?"

"Yeah, I'm not talking about rouge or anything—nothing girly like that. Maybe just some dramatic dark eyeliner or some silver mascara."

"Whoah," Ryan said, his tone somber. "I don't know, Max. I don't think I can afford this costume. I'm already at sixty dollars with the clothes, and if you add these things—it's going to come to almost a quarter of my rent."

Max placed his hands on his hips and shook his head slowly. "I'm sure you spent more than that on food for that last party you had. You can swing it. You *should* swing it, Mister."

"I know it's just—" He wanted to tell Max how he barely made rent for October. The reduced hours at work were starting to take a toll on his bank account. He stopped short though—he didn't want Max to think he was poor. Instead, he said, "Never mind. You're right. It'll be worth it, won't it?"

"Mhmm! Now, what am *I* going to wear?"

~*~

Ryan spent the evening reading in his room. Though he'd enjoyed his outing with Max and the others earlier in the day, he was concerned about falling behind in his studies—his bank account wasn't the only thing suffering from a lack of hours in the day. Sometime close to midnight he closed the books for the night and stepped into the kitchen for a glass of water before bed.

As he drank slowly, he noticed a light on in the living room. Steven had gone to bed, and he hadn't seen Shelly all day, so he placed his empty glass on the counter and walked to the far end of the apartment to investigate. The living room was empty. He was about to switch off the light, but then he heard—

Crying.

It was soft, but unmistakable—coming from the other side of Shelly's bedroom door. He let his hand fall from the switch and listened more closely. It was definitely Shelly. For a moment he thought about letting her be, but considering her erratic behavior of late, he changed his mind.

He tip-toed up to her door and rapped on it softly. "Shelly?" he asked. She didn't answer, but the sounds of crying stopped. He waited fifteen seconds before he knocked again. Still, there was no answer. "Shelly, can you open the door, please? I'm—I'm concerned about you." When she still did not respond, he grew more determined. "Shelly, I'm not going to leave you alone. I'm going to stand here and bother you until you open the door."

His persistence was rewarded. From the other side, he could hear shuffling. A moment later the door opened inward, and she stood before him, eyes puffy, red, and wet with tears. Mars bounded outward and ran a few circles around Ryan's legs before sitting squarely beside him.

"What?" she asked. There was a slight crack in her voice. "Now I'm going to have to take the dog out. He already went out for the last time tonight."

Ryan frowned. "Shelly, what's wrong? What's going on with you, lately?"

"It doesn't matter. Don't worry about it."

"Here," Ryan said, indicating the futon in the living room. "Come sit, please? Look, I'm not always the most—perceptive person on earth. My best friend had relationships I never knew about and ended up snorting himself to death. I had no idea about any of it. Then my other best friend dropped all these hints that he was interested in me and I didn't pick up on *any* of them. Then it was too late. But I'm trying to change that—I'm working really hard to see both the forest *and* the trees, you know? And I know something is going on with you. I've *noticed* for once, so please, won't you sit here and talk to me?"

Reluctantly she followed. Once she was seated, Ryan waited as she wiped her eyes. After considering her words, she finally spoke. "It's kind of really hard to talk about? It's hard because—in my mind, like, if I'm really thinking about it, I know nothing is wrong. But sometimes I just feel so—" She took a moment to gather her thoughts. "It feels so pointless. Like, what am I doing? I go to school; I walk the dog. I do homework; I eat, I sleep. Sometimes I watch reruns of shows I've seen. And it's so bleak."

"Why is it bleak?" he asked.

"I don't know!" She was frustrated. "It just *is* sometimes. Not all the time. I have good days. Look, I think it's clinical, but still. I wonder why I try. I'm not ever going to be good enough."

He laughed, innocently. "Good enough for *what*?"

"For *anything*! Not good enough for love, for my parents, for the world—for myself?"

He placed his hands on hers. "I've been waiting to hear you say the 'P' word. What's going on with that, anyways—your parents?"

"Aw man, Ryan—" she started to sob again. "It's so fucked up! Like, they're separated, you know that. My dad—he cheated on my mom *so many times*. Finally, she got sick of it and kicked him out when I was like, fourteen. He moved to LA, and it was just her and me. But then like, I came out, right? It was the summer before my senior year of high school. I almost didn't—my mom is *so* Catholic, but I thought, you know—it was just her and I for so long and we were so close. I thought she'd deal with it. But instead she—she kicked me out too. She sent me to live with my dad. I had to leave all my friends—my whole life! Aw man, I *hate* my dad. I hate what he did to her, and I couldn't believe she was sending me there. And the really fucked up part is that he didn't care that I was a lesbian. He didn't have a problem with that *at all*. So, like, yeah. It's really complicated."

"Wow." Ryan exhaled, suddenly aware he'd been holding his breath. "Yeah, that's a lot to deal with. I can't even imagine. Did something happen with one of them recently? Is that what this is about?'

She stood up, shaking her head. "I can't talk about it anymore tonight, Ryan. I'm just too tired." She looked at the dog. "Mars, come on, let's go outside." Then she attempted her best smile. "I appreciate it though. I'll probably be better tomorrow, and maybe, I don't know. Maybe I can talk more about it then."

Ryan stood as well. He wrapped her in a tight embrace—something he'd never done before. "Okay," he said. "Get some rest." He released her, and she began to walk to the front door with Mars beside her. Before she disappeared into the hallway beyond the kitchen, he called out. "And, Shelly? Anytime you need to talk, okay? Anytime! We need to look out for each other."

She smiled again. He thought this one was genuine. Then she waved and disappeared into the darkness.

CHAPTER 14

From where he stood in front of the bathroom mirror, Ryan heard the front door slam. He adjusted his hair one more time and then stepped out of the bedroom just as Meredith walked into the kitchen. She wore a pair of tight black pleather pants nearly identical to his own, a violet cummerbund, and a particularly revealing black silk button up which she'd fastened to just below her breasts. Her normally softly curling auburn hair was teased into a wild but deliberate frenzy, and on the top of her head, a crooked witch's hat completed the ensemble.

"Wow!" he said. "You look amazing! And if you lose the hat at some point you'll still make a pretty convincing pirate!"

She scowled. "Fuck you. Don't be an asshole tonight, alright?" She walked to the refrigerator and pulled out a can of beer.

He frowned. "What's wrong? Are you nervous about Andrew? Just like you told me—if you can't be yourself and do the things you want to do, he wins."

After swallowing half the can, she set it heavily on the counter and looked back at him. "Yeah, I'm nervous about Andrew. *Of course* I'm nervous about him. I haven't seen him in a year and a half. And yeah, you're right about what I said. It's just—it was easier to say it."

"Than to do it?"

"No, moron, than to translate it into Swahili."

He raised his eyebrows. "And you're worried about *me* being an asshole tonight?"

"No, you're right. I'm sorry, I'm not trying to be mean. I'm just stressed." She finished the beer and went back to the fridge for another. "After tonight I'll feel like myself again. I think this has been hanging over me for too long. I wish he hadn't told me he was going—he could've just shown up."

Ryan laughed. "That probably would've ended badly. And anyways, it's not like you have to hang out with him. Maybe you won't even see him."

"In that tiny little place? He's going to be looking for me." She regarded the second beer in her hand and opened it disdainfully. "I wish Caleb and Tom were here already. I could really use some vodka."

"Well, I'm sure they'll be here soon."

She looked at him, seeming to see him for the first time. "Those pants look great on you. The boys are going to eat you up in those."

He blushed. "Yeah? If you say so. I'd better get the rest of it on. Excuse me."

He headed back into his bedroom and emerged a minute later wearing the red fishnet shirt over a black tank top. Meredith whistled. "And you said Max picked this costume out for you?"

"Yeah, I still feel bad I'm not going to his party tonight."

"Oh, get over it. You'd probably just end up pining after him and then sulk your way home after seeing him hang on Jake all night."

"No—" he shook his head vehemently. "I really am happy for them. I've moved on." He thought his voice sounded convincing enough, and mostly he believed it. "I think he's disappointed that we haven't been spending as much time together though."

Meredith shrugged. "Didn't you say there was something for your hair? Some silver spray?"

"Oh, yeah!" He retrieved it from the bathroom and wrapped a towel around his shoulders to keep the spray from getting onto his clothes. "Do you mind?"

"Not at all." He bent slightly forward as she shook the can and sprayed it all over his head. When she was done, she said, "Perfect! Now, just don't touch it for a few minutes."

The front door opened again, and Tom's big, booming voice announced his arrival. "Happy Halloween!" A moment later, dressed as Indiana Jones, he stepped into the kitchen with his hands on his hips. His shirt was all the way unbuttoned, and he pressed his broad, hair-covered chest forward. "Howdy!"

Meredith clapped. "Oh! It's perfect! You look so *rugged*! And where's our little fairy?"

From the darkness of the hallway, Caleb's voice cooed sweet and high, "Right here, darling!" Tom stepped forward, and Caleb followed him into the kitchen.

Ryan caught his breath and felt all the longing he'd arduously suppressed return. Caleb wore his signature, tight, low-rise jeans and a long white tank top. Extending from his back were a pair of thin, shimmering, blue and white butterfly wings. His face was dusted with glitter, and mascara extended his fluttery eyelashes to twice their normal length. A curly silver tiara rested atop his head, encircling a rigid peak of dark, shiny hair. But more than all the rest, it was his lips that were truly arresting. A clear, glittery lip gloss caught the light and set them on fire.

"Caleb!" Meredith shrieked. She rushed forward and threw her arms around him.

"Careful!" he said. "Don't crush my wings! If you do, however will I *fly*?"

She laughed. "You both look *amazing*! And what do you think of *Ryan*?"

Caleb peered around her and Ryan swore his eyes dilated as his shining lips curved upward into a wicked smile. "I think Ryan is—delicious. Wow."

Tom guffawed and walked forward, wrapping Ryan in a tight embrace. His strong hands clapped Ryan firmly on the shoulders. "Yep! They're going to eat you up tonight!" He let go. "Caleb, you've got that vodka, don't you?"

"Oh yes!" Caleb replied.

"Give me some, oh God *please*," Meredith said.

As Caleb began pulling glasses out of the pantry, Ryan frowned and said, "So, who is driving, by the way?"

"I am," Tom said. "I have to work in the morning, unfortunately." Then louder, "I'll still have some now though, babe, before we go—just a little."

Meredith raised her head. "And you are, Ryan. You'll drive my car. I don't plan on being in *any* state to operate a motor vehicle."

He scowled. "Well, what about me? You're all able to drink when we get there."

Caleb diluted the vodka with a little ginger ale and handed glasses to Meredith and Tom before taking a long sip from his own. "Oh, don't you worry, honey. I mixed up a twenty-ounce *soda* for you to drink in the parking lot before we go in. And then, of course, I'll be getting you lots of *waters* from the bar."

Meredith shook her head. "Not tonight you won't. This isn't a normal night—I'm sure security is going to be heightened."

Caleb clucked. "Oh well, it's a good thing I made it strong then." He winked at Ryan. "You'll be alright." He was nearly finished with his drink already. "Okay ladies, drink up! Let's get this party started!"

~*~

Forty minutes later Ryan parked Meredith's car at the edge of the gravel lot outside Paradox, and Tom's car pulled in beside them. The night was cold but bright—a familiar stale orange sky had spread over the front range, and a few small flakes of snow began to fall on the windshield. He looked at Meredith and smiled. "Okay, are you ready for this?" he asked.

"As ready as I'll ever be." She reached down between her feet and produced a twenty-ounce bottle of ginger-ale. "Are you ready for Caleb's special brew?"

Ryan took the bottle, unscrewed the cap and laughed. "I'm never ready for Caleb's special brew." He took a sip and choked. "Ugh! It's practically paint thinner! I can't drink this!"

"Well, you'd better. It's the only alcohol you're getting tonight." She looked across the parking lot to where two bouncers stood beside the front door. "Like I said before, they're upping their game tonight. Just plug your nose and—bottoms up!"

"Ugh." He tilted the bottle back and took a long, laborious swallow. The vodka burned, causing him to shudder. He forced another large gulp and fought to keep from gagging.

Caleb and Tom were outside the car now. They lit cigarettes, and Caleb knocked on the window. "Come on, slowpokes! This fairy needs to spread her *wings*!"

Meredith laughed. "Ryan is um—hydrating. Cool your fucking jets, Tinkerbell! Smoke that slowly and we'll join you in a minute." She looked at Ryan and the bottle, which was still half full. "Go on then, chug it!"

Ryan sighed and tilted the bottle back again. Closing his eyes tightly, he took three large, quick gulps. His body convulsed, and he was certain he was going to vomit. Still, with his eyes closed, he breathed deeply. His mouth filled with saliva as he repressed the urge to heave.

Meredith clapped. "Whoah, Ryan! Nice work. Come on, you need a cigarette."

"Ugh, I don't think I can."

"No," she said. "You *need* a cigarette—to mask the smell of that rubbing alcohol when you give the bouncers your ID. Come on, let's go!" She opened the car door and stepped into the night.

Slowly and reluctantly he followed. He accepted the cigarette Caleb offered him, and upon his first exhale he said, "I really might be sick. Caleb, that was *terrible*."

Tom clapped him hard on the shoulder. "You'll thank him later. Now, let's get to it, yeah?"

Caleb was only half finished with his cigarette. "Just hold on, Doctor Jones. Listen, this is my favorite part."

"Oh, right," Tom said. "The *anticipation*."

Ryan closed his eyes and listened, remembering from his previous visit how Caleb cherished the moments before entering the club. The *thump, thump* that resonated through Paradox's thin metal walls was more pronounced than the last time, and he smiled. It was nice. He finally understood the allure, and when he opened his eyes, Caleb was smiling too, looking at him.

"You get it now, don't you?" Caleb asked. He dropped his cigarette into the gravel and ground it with his heel.

Tom guffawed in his particularly jolly way. "I hope *someone* does, because I still don't. Come on, you rapscallions! That morning shift is coming fast, and I only get two drinks tonight. If you three lollygag much longer I'll have to cut it down to one!"

Ryan extinguished his cigarette and turned to Meredith, who was unusually quiet. He took her hand and squeezed it gently. "It's going to be fine," he said.

She pulled her hand away. "Don't you *dare* coddle me, Ryan Gregori." Though she scowled, Ryan thought he caught a glimmer of a smile. "Come on, let's go inside." Then she turned and marched purposefully toward the door.

The bouncers gave them no trouble, and two minutes later Ryan stepped into the dark, smoky club. It was just as he remembered it, except tonight it seemed a little brighter and a little cleaner. The space was packed with bare-chested vampires and werewolves, scantily-clad sorceresses and the odd dominatrix. The majority of the crowd was still men, but Ryan guessed at least a third were women. As he followed his friends through the crush of bodies toward the bar, he felt a firm hand on the back of his pants, and he jumped. When he turned, a tall blond Legolas winked and smiled before disappearing into the crowd.

Flattered, he exhaled and allowed his ears to adjust to the intoxicating *thump, thump* of the music.

The line at the bar was long, and since he couldn't order anything anyways he shouted to his friends, "Meet me on the dance floor!" As he turned away, he saw Caleb say something to Tom and then follow after him. He pushed his way through the throng of people and found a tiny spot near the corner of the floor.

The music enveloped him—rhythmic, pulsing and wordless—and he started to move his feet.

Then Caleb was in front of him. Reaching forward, he worked the tips of his fingers into the pockets of Ryan's pants and pulled him close. Caleb leaned his head forward and whispered into Ryan's ear above the music, "What are you thinking about?"

He shuddered. He wasn't thinking anything good. He could smell Caleb now, and feel the place where his hot breath tickled his ear. He felt the warmth of Caleb's legs against his own as they moved in time to the beats. There was a delicious friction as the netting of his shirt moved against the cotton of Caleb's tank top, already beginning to dampen with a light, clean sweat. He wanted to pull him tighter, and once again had an idea that he could happily sink into Caleb's skin and drown there. He thought he'd moved past all this. Desperately, he tried to remember the night at the Back Alley when he resolved to move on—to remember Tom's pain, suspicion and fear. He tried to remember Steven reminding him that all relationships are sacred—how could he mess with the sanctity of that?

He tried to remember the fondue party a month ago—that he'd told Caleb they were better as friends.

It was all so easy to forget. In the moment, all that mattered was Caleb—his nearness again. He leaned forward and whispered back. "I'm happy."

"Are you?" Caleb asked.

"Are *you*?"

Caleb smiled. "I am right now."

Suddenly Ryan felt a body begin grinding into him from behind, and then Tom's booming voice, "You two didn't waste *any* time!" He laughed heartily. "Here's your drink, babe!"

Caleb took the drink and then Ryan turned. Tom took a sip of his own—it looked like beer—and smiled brightly. He looked so happy that Ryan felt a little ashamed of himself.

"Sorry," Ryan said. "I was just really excited to get started. I guess the line at the bar went faster than I thought it would."

"Yeah," Tom replied. "Not too bad." He looked around. "There are a lot of hotties here tonight, huh? Too bad I've only got eyes for one!"

Ryan laughed nervously. He was pretty sure he only had eyes for one himself. However, the spell was broken, and he felt a little of his resolve returning. Caleb was a forbidden fruit, and anyways, Tom was here tonight. Even if he wanted to give in to his wicked desires, it was impossible. He looked around. "Hey, Tom, did Meredith come with you from the bar?"

"Oh yeah, but—" he looked side to side expecting to find her. "I don't know where she is now though."

"Hmm, alright. Excuse me; I'd better go find her."

He made his way toward the bar and began scanning the crowd, looking for her hat rising above the heads of the dancers. When he didn't see her, he turned back toward the entrance and finally caught a glimpse of her in a corner near the restrooms.

When he got closer, he noticed the man she was talking to—tall and well-built, with short, dark hair. Ryan guessed from his costume—dark jeans, a black button shirt and a black cape lined with a shiny red fabric—that he was going for some type of vampire. She was gesturing wildly, even angrily, and Ryan watched as the man tilted his head back and folded his arms.

It had to be Andrew.

He stepped purposefully forward, intent on coming to her aid, but was forced to stop for a moment as the first wave of intoxication overtook him. The room spun a little, and he laughed; his head felt light, and he experienced a momentary lapse in focus. When he regained his bearings, Meredith was still gesturing wildly. Andrew caught her hands in his and pulled her forward. Ryan was ready to jump to her aid again, but before he could move, Andrew was kissing her. He watched as her body relaxed and folded against him.

The kiss endured, and Ryan tried unsuccessfully to pull his eyes away. Finally, after ten or fifteen seconds, Meredith freed her hands and shoved at Andrew sharply. As she began to turn in Ryan's direction, he quickly pivoted and began to walk back to the dance floor.

He was halfway back to Caleb and Tom when he felt her hand on his arm. "Ryan!" she said. He turned. "What are you doing?"

"Oh! There you are! I was looking all over for you. Tom said you were following him back from the bar, but you never made it. I thought maybe you'd run into—"

"Andrew?" She rolled her eyes. "Oh, did I ever. What a fucking Neanderthal! I asked him why he was here—what was he trying to accomplish?"

"And?"

"And he said the usual. He misses me. Nothing is the same without me. He's *changed*. Blah-blah-fucking-blah. Well, I've changed too. I'm not an idiot. I learned my lesson, and I'm not ever going to let someone take advantage of me again. Especially not *him*."

She was quiet for a moment, so Ryan said, "Anything else?"

Her eyes widened. "What do you mean?"

He breathed a sigh of relief. She hadn't seen him watching. It was clear she didn't want him to know about the kiss. "Just, did he say anything else?"

"Oh, no."

"So, now what? Is he going to leave? Is there anything I can do?"

"No, I'm sure he's going to keep trying. I just need to get hopelessly drunk so I can ignore him. He's here with a couple friends, so maybe if I can turn on my ice queen routine, he'll get the hint after a while." She looked down at her hands. "Oh shit!"

"What?"

"I set my drink down when I was talking to him." She turned back toward the restrooms and stopped. "Oh, fuck." Andrew was walking toward her again, drink in hand. She looked quickly at Ryan. "This is him. Be polite."

Andrew reached her and smiled. "You forgot this."

"I should dump it out," she said. "You probably slipped something into it." She took it anyways and sucked greedily on the straw. Ryan hoped she was joking.

Andrew looked at Ryan, and for a few seconds, an awkward silence ensued. Finally, he said to Meredith, "Who is your friend?" Before she could answer, he reached his hand out to Ryan and said, "I'm Andrew, nice to meet you."

Ryan grasped his hand and shook it meekly. Andrew's grip was too strong, and he winced. "I'm Ryan. Good to—meet you."

"You've heard great things, right?" He laughed, then turned back to Meredith. "Hey, I'm going to go find the guys. Don't be pissed I'm here, okay? It's really nice to see. I'll leave you to your friends, but I'm coming back."

Meredith attempted a scowl, but Ryan thought he noticed the slight twitch of a grin at the corners of her mouth. "Whatever," she said, turning on a heel. "Come on Ryan, let's dance."

They rejoined Caleb and Tom, and Ryan did his best to get lost in the music. As Caleb's special concoction took further hold, he found he was increasingly unsteady on his feet. He focused on the beats and felt better—almost fluid—as he moved back and forth in time to the pulses.

The night progressed without incident, though Meredith was clearly distracted. Ryan watched as every few minutes she scanned the room looking—almost hopefully—for Andrew. Every time she located him—in some corner with his friends—the expression on her face turned from anxious anticipation to disappointment. He smiled at her unease. Even Meredith had her weaknesses; she wasn't over Andrew yet. Perhaps she'd give him another chance.

By midnight, Caleb and Meredith were on their fourth drinks. Tom—who'd had his last beer an hour previous—was getting restless. He grabbed Ryan and pulled him close, moving up and down with an almost mechanical precision. "This would be a lot more fun if I was still drinking," he said. "Look at those two; they're sloshed! Meanwhile, I'm practically sober again."

Ryan laughed and pushed away slightly. "I'm sloshed too." He meant it. At least his intoxication had plateaued.

Tom frowned. "We might have to go soon."

"Go?"

"That shift at six in the morning is coming fast—"

Suddenly Caleb was beside them. He draped an arm over each of them clumsily, and in doing so, a substantial quantity of his drink leaped out of his cup and landed on Tom's bare chest.

"What the *fuck*!" Tom exclaimed.

"Oopsie!" Caleb replied.

"You're out of control! That needs to be your last one. I just told Ryan we're going soon."

Caleb withdrew his arms and turned his nose to the air. "I'm not going anywhere until they *kick* me out! Anyways, don't you see those flyers they're handing around? There's an *afterparty*!"

"Afterparty? Don't you tempt me, Caleb. I'll drag you out by your fairy wings if I have to. Fuck. I need to go to the bathroom and wipe this shit off. The soda in whatever the hell that was is already making me feel sticky." He turned and marched off in a huff.

Caleb started to dance close again, and Ryan eagerly pressed up against him. He closed his eyes and lost himself in a smoky female vocal.

"I love this song! It's so good!" Caleb said. "This DJ—"

"Mhmm" Ryan replied, pulling himself closer still.

When he opened his eyes again, Meredith was watching him with a queer expression. He was about to speak, but then Andrew appeared beside her. She turned toward him, he grasped her hips, and they started to dance. It took only moments for their movements to orchestrate into a perfect harmony, and Ryan could not detect an ounce of resistance left in her.

Suddenly Tom was standing beside him. "Every time I step away, you two are like magnets! Or a moth and a flame!" He laughed, but there was an edge of malice. "Or flies and shit. Mind if I cut in, Ryan?"

"Of course not!" He let go and walked slowly back up to the level of the bar. It was time for this game he was playing with Caleb to end. Though nothing had happened—except for that one long goodnight kiss—the situation was becoming dangerous. He worried about disappointing Meredith, and he was sure Tom suspected something now even if he didn't before. He lit a cigarette and smoked it slowly as he watched the dance floor. Though Caleb and Tom still danced together, Caleb kept turning his head to look at Ryan. There was an intensity to his gaze that made him shudder.

Suddenly he'd had enough. He extinguished the cigarette and pushed his way back onto the dance floor, but not in the direction of his friends. Instead, he found a spot on the opposite end, as far away as he could get, and let the music take him again.

He couldn't be sure how much time passed—a handful of tracks at the least—until Meredith found him. There was a sense of urgency on her face as she gripped his wrist and pulled him across the floor up toward the bar. "Where the hell have you been?" she asked.

"I just thought I'd strike out on my own for a little while. You guys were—occupied."

She shook her head. "Oh, you mean Andrew? Ryan, this is harder than I thought. I'm still so angry, but then he's there in front of me, and I just remember how much I loved him."

"Love him," he said.

"Huh?"

He placed a hand on her shoulder. "Meredith, I saw him kiss you at the beginning of the night. I didn't mean to—I wasn't spying or anything. But you should've seen the way you just melted into him."

"Oh—"

He laughed. "It's alright."

"It isn't alright! You don't know how much he hurt me. Why am I giving in this easily? I'm Meredith-fucking-Gardner! I'm tough and strong, and I'm better than this."

"Maybe, but you're also human." He was thinking of himself now.

"He wants me to go with him tonight. Can you believe the nerve?"

"Maybe you should."

She shoved him hard as she fought to repress a smile. "What? Whose fucking side are you on?"

From behind them, Caleb said, "Whoah!" He approached with Tom, looking glummer than ever. "What's going on over here, you two?"

Ryan smiled brightly. "Andrew wants Meredith to leave with him."

"Ooh!" Caleb cooed. "Scandalous. Meredith? You said?"

"I said no fucking way!"

Tom spoke. "Well, speaking of leaving with someone, it's time for our grand exit. Always a pleasure, guys." He tipped his hat. "Come on, Caleb."

Caleb put his hands on his hips. "I told you I wasn't going right now, Tom."

"Yes, you are. Come on; you're drunk and it's late."

"Meredith?" He fluttered his eyelashes. "You wanted to go to that afterparty they're advertising, didn't you?"

She grimaced at Tom and then answered. "Yeah, that's where Andrew wants to go—at first."

Tom crossed his arms tightly. "Caleb, I really need you to come home with me." He pulled his cell phone from his pocket to look at the time. "It's almost one-thirty. Things are going to wrap up here in a few minutes anyways. Come on."

"Tom," Caleb said, flatly. "I am not going. I'll get a ride home from the afterparty with one of these two."

"I'm not going to ask again."

"Then don't. I'll see you when you get home from work."

Caleb turned and started to walk away. Enraged, Tom took a couple quick steps toward him, grabbed his wrists and spun him around. They stared at each other for a long moment. Tom was shaking with fury. Perhaps sensing how intently Ryan and Meredith were watching, he calmed himself slightly and released Caleb from his grip. Without speaking, he turned and headed out the door.

"Oh, hell no!" Meredith said after Tom was safely away. "Caleb, are you alright?"

"Yeah," he replied. "I'm fine. I feel a lot more sober all of a sudden though. It's probably last call, right? I'm going to have one more." He looked at Ryan, "You'll drive me back, won't you?"

Ryan felt suddenly sober himself. The last of the ginger-ale was finally wearing off. "Yeah, of course."

~*~

They stepped out of the club and into the parking lot a few minutes after two. The stale orange sky had gone, leaving behind a clear, starry night and a thin layer of crisp, fresh snow. The world looked white and pristine.

Caleb shivered as he lit a cigarette. "I wish I had a jacket that fit over these damned wings. So then, afterparty, right?"

Andrew slipped his hand into Meredith's. She leaned heavily against him. "Well, that *was* the plan, but Mer here is looking pretty tired. You had a lot tonight, huh?"

"Fuck you!" she said, smiling. She tried to push away but was too unsteady on her feet, and she slipped a little on the snow. Andrew caught her and held on while she steadied herself again. "I look drunker than I am."

"Maybe, maybe not. Still, I was thinking maybe we'd just—go hang out at yours? Just the two of us?"

She rolled her head in a large circle. "Fine, but don't get any ideas. You've got that flyer, right? With the address of the afterparty?" Andrew nodded that he did. "Give that to—Caleb. Ryan?"

"Yes?"

"You'll drive my car back to—my apartment in the morning?"

"Yeah, sure."

"Okay, I'll call you. Let's go, Andrew."

"Okay," Andrew said. "I'm over here." He handed a neon green flyer to Caleb and then started to lead her off in a different direction. "Goodnight, guys."

"Goodnight," Ryan said.

They reached Meredith's car, and Caleb leaned against the passenger door as he continued to smoke. A car drove past and beeped its horn; Andrew was in the driver's seat, and he waved as he turned left out of the parking lot onto the main road. Ryan waved back, then turned to Caleb. "So, where is this afterparty, anyways?"

Caleb crumpled the flyer in his hand and tossed it on the ground. "I don't want to go to the afterparty after all."

"What?"

He dropped his cigarette and wrapped his arms up over Ryan's shoulders. With his face close, noses almost touching he said, "Take me home?"

"Alright—Tom'll be happy—"

"No, not there—"

Caleb withdrew and opened the passenger door. Without speaking, Ryan walked around to the driver's side and climbed in. He turned the key in the ignition and cranked the heat, suddenly aware of how cold he was. After fumbling for a minute, he turned on the windshield wipers and watched as the light, dry snow fluttered off the front of the car, opening up his view.

As he backed the car out of the spot and headed toward the road, he looked at Caleb, smiling with his eyes closed. He turned left and drove slowly—the plow hadn't come through yet—and felt his mind boil with conflict. The choice Caleb presented him with was suffocating. He knew what he wanted to do even though every fiber of him said it was wrong. Still, didn't he deserve this? All he wanted was love, and here was Caleb, offering it to him again. And didn't Caleb deserve it as well? Ryan was appalled by Tom's behavior tonight—by the barely contained violence in him. That was something Ryan hadn't expected.

The road climbed a short hill, crossed a railroad track, and then he stopped the car at a red light. He closed his eyes for a moment and considered Caleb's proposition. Right now he was innocent—innocent of everything. He wondered if he was really willing to give that up—to sully himself and their friendship. The kiss at the end of August—he understood that didn't really count. It hadn't manifested into anything more. He'd been so strong since then. He heard Steven's voice in his mind saying he was just a toy boy. He remembered Meredith's intent gaze as he and Caleb danced too close together. He thought of the malice and the unspoken accusations in Tom's voice and eyes. If he went through with this, those accusations wouldn't be false anymore. He wondered if he could live with that—if he could face those people tomorrow, or ever again.

The light changed to green, and he stepped lightly on the gas. Caleb opened his eyes and smiled, then rested his left hand on Ryan's thigh and squeezed gently. Ryan looked at him for a moment and asked, "Are you sure this is what you want to do?"

"There's nothing else I want right now."

A couple minutes later, Ryan stopped the car at another red light just at the edge of the campus. He was quite literally at a crossroads. If he turned left, he could take Caleb home. The Garden, on the other hand, was just a few blocks straight ahead. He felt the warmth of Caleb's hand still resting on his thigh as he waited for the light to change. It was time to commit to a decision.

When the light finally turned green, he hesitated, then drove straight ahead. A great feeling of relief washed through him. For better or for worse the choice was made. He turned the wheel and guided the car into the alley beside The Garden, then into the parking lot where he brought it to a rest beside Shelly's snow-covered SUV. He turned the key and exhaled, then slowly opened the door and stepped out into the night.

The parking lot was a pristine sheet of white snow, disrupted only by the tire tracks from Meredith's car. It was beautiful and clean, and it filled him with an overwhelming sense of peace. Caleb climbed out of the car and stood beside him, producing two cigarettes.

"It's too cold for this," Caleb said, "But I don't want this moment to end." Perhaps reading Ryan's thoughts, he said, "I love the first snow." He lit his own cigarette, then Ryan's, and looked up toward the apartment. "Do you think everyone is asleep?"

"I don't know," Ryan replied. "I was thinking the same thing." He looked at Steven's window on the wall that faced the deck. It was dark. Then he realized Steven's car was missing. "Max's party must still be going. Steven isn't home."

Caleb shrugged as he exhaled. "Oh well, doesn't matter."

"Are you worried about—"

When he didn't finish, Caleb looked at him sternly. "What's there to be worried about? We decided not to go to the afterparty, but we weren't ready for bed yet. I'm just here to hang out with my friend, right?" He dropped his cigarette. "Come on, it's cold."

As they walked across the parking lot, Ryan thought he should be feeling more nervous. Instead, he was eerily calm. The sound of the snow grinding against itself as it compressed beneath his feet was oddly satisfying, and as they started up the steps to the apartment above, he smiled.

Once inside the kitchen, he paused. "Would you like something to drink? I think there's probably some beer—"

Caleb reached out with one finger and pressed it lightly against Ryan's lips as he shook his head slowly. Without speaking, he turned and walked into the bedroom. Ryan followed cautiously; his former calm was fleeing fast, and a sudden explosion of nerves threatened to cripple him. Exhaling, he stepped into the bedroom and closed the door.

Caleb grabbed his hands and pushed them over his head, pinning Ryan against the door. He kissed him savagely, forcing his tongue in and around. The taste of stale vodka and smoke filled Ryan's mouth just as it had done the last time, and he welcomed it. It was the flavor of sin and indulgence. It was everything he'd never been and everything he could become. It was the flavor of his freedom and the loss of his innocence. Caleb tasted of selfishness and lust, of danger and possibility. Ryan began to kiss back—to engage in the passionate dance of tongues. It was reckless and wicked and utterly, unforgivably delicious.

Suddenly they were turning. Caleb gripped the black tank top underneath Ryan's fishnet shirt and pulled it forcefully up and over his head. Ryan fell back into his bed and closed his eyes, momentarily overcome. There were other sounds then—zippers opening and fabric sliding down and away. Then Caleb laid on top of him, covering him in his bare skin. The weight of him pressed Ryan downward, and he thought this was it—finally, he was drowning under Caleb's skin. He opened his eyes, and Caleb's face was so near to his own. He reached his lips upward, open, and felt Caleb's tongue again—

When it was over Ryan laid on his back, breathing slowly. He could not remember ever feeling so happy. Even with his couple of short term boyfriends in the time before Darren—it had never been like this. He turned toward Caleb, also prostrate, and smiled. Caleb rolled over onto one elbow and kissed Ryan on the forehead, then stood up and started to dress.

Ryan frowned. "Why are you getting dressed?"

"I have to go home. If I'm not there when Tom wakes up—"

"Oh, but it *so* late! Couldn't you just say I was too tired to drive you home? Come on. Please stay."

He smiled sadly. "That would be more trouble than it's worth. Give me a kiss before I go?"

Ryan sat up. "Well, don't you at least want me to drive you?"

"Nah, I could use the walk."

"You don't even have a jacket, Caleb."

"It's not that far."

"Please?"

Caleb shook his head. Ryan thought he detected sadness in his eyes. "Can you just kiss me?"

Ryan stood. He wrapped one arm around Caleb's shoulders and kissed him lightly. "Call me when you get home?"

"No. I won't want to wake Tom. I'll call you tomorrow, alright?"

"Alright—"

Caleb turned and opened Ryan's bedroom door. He stepped quietly into the apartment and then he was gone.

CHAPTER 15

The aroma of coffee and cinnamon filled Ryan's nose, and his eyes opened to a brilliant light shining through the skylight overhead. He sat up in awe, marveling at the way patches of sunlight on the bedroom wall turned the paint a blinding shade of red. He laughed a little; he was back in the house on Elizabeth Street again, and it was wholly intact. The fire that had consumed it last time he'd been here seemed now to be nothing more than a bad dream. He pulled on a pair of shorts and a shirt he found lying on the floor and walked out of the little bedroom.

When he reached the living room, his heart leaped. All of Cara's furniture was back just as he remembered it—even the plants hanging in the front windows were just the same as they'd been. There was no smoke or scent of gasoline. The television was on, playing some old BBC comedy.

A white envelope sat conspicuously on the otherwise bare coffee table. He walked forward, ready to pick it up, but was distracted by a commotion in the kitchen.

He stepped through the door and Darren was waiting for him, grinning from ear to ear. He held a cup of coffee in his hand and extended it gingerly. "French roast?" he asked. "It's got cinnamon. You didn't have any milk though, so I hope it's alright that it's black."

Ryan took the cup and held it in both his hands, enjoying the warmth. "No," he replied. "I don't mind." He took a sip and grinned. "This is amazing! What are you doing here?"

Darren walked slowly to the coffee pot on the counter and filled a mug for himself. He tasted it and nodded with approval. "Oh," he said, "I just wanted to stop by to say congratulations."

"Congratulations? What are you congratulating me for?"

"Haha, come on, creeper. You know."

He shook his head. "I don't! Tell me!"

"Nah, don't play dumb. You know."

"I really don't. You're actually starting to upset me a little."

Darren shrugged. "Okay, I'll play." He grinned. "Congratulations on finally getting exactly what you've always wanted."

"What I've always—" he let his voice trail off, thinking. "Oh! You mean Caleb?"

"Well, yes, Caleb. But more specifically, *love*. Come on; let's sit down on the couch. This show I'm watching is great."

"Okay—" Ryan followed him back into the living room. Darren sprawled out on the couch, setting his coffee cup on top of the white envelope. Ryan sat in the overstuffed armchair and folded his legs.

"So, what did it cost?" Darren asked.

"Cost?"

"Yeah, what did it cost to finally get *love*?"

He laughed. "It didn't cost anything. Love is free."

"Well, that's what I always thought, but in this case, is it?"

"Of course it is. You can't buy love."

"Alright," Darren said. He picked up his coffee again and nodded toward the envelope. "By the way, I found that taped to the door when I came in. I guess it's probably for you." Ryan started to reach for it, but Darren snatched it away. "Oh! So hasty! Are you sure you want to read it right now? We could wait awhile—watch the rest of this show and then maybe find some old movie or something."

"Well, yeah! Of course I want to read it now. It could be important."

Darren nodded gravely. "Oh, probably. Well, why don't I read it to you then."

"I can read it—"

"No, no. Allow me." He set his coffee down again and tore the envelope open. He pulled out a single piece of lined paper, unfolded it, and raised his eyebrows. "Alright, here goes. Ahem. Dear Ryan, thank you so much for taking such great care of my property. It's wonderful to know there is someone else out there who loves my property as much as I do. I appreciate that you put the lease in the mail, but unfortunately I've returned the original to you unsigned."

Ryan swallowed hard. Darren was looking at him, intently. "Go on," Ryan said.

"Are you sure? We can read the rest of it later."

"Please."

"Alright. It continues: I'm sure you're a great guy, but I wish Brandon would've told me a little more about you when he brought you into my life. I have a pretty strict vetting process, and sadly you didn't make the cut. Unfortunately, I've come to see that your happiness comes at my expense. I'm glad you love my property, but I love it too, and I'll be moving back into it shortly. I know it's wrong of me to kick you out at the beginning of winter like this, but in the end, you didn't have any right to be here in the first place. Please vacate the property effective immediately. So sorry for the inconvenience." Darren shook his head sadly. "Then it's simply signed *Tom*. Who is Tom? I thought the landlord's name was John."

Outside, someone started pounding on the door, and Ryan reached for the thumb ring around his neck. Suddenly he couldn't breathe. A voice was calling through the door—the sheriff, would he please open up? There was an eviction order. He needed to leave right now. Would he please open up? He looked at Darren who just shrugged.

~*~

He woke suddenly in a cold sweat. In his sleep, he'd been holding onto Darren's thumb ring so tightly that his fingers ached and throbbed. He released it now and lightly rubbed at the indentations the hard metal left in his skin. Overhead, the ceiling fan spun slowly while a thin, watery light poured through the windows opposite his bed. He was not back at Elizabeth Street. This was the Garden—the present. Elizabeth Street and Darren were ancient history.

The aroma of coffee filled his nose—triggering a queer olfactory déjà vu—so he sat up and pulled on some clothes so that he could investigate.

When he opened his bedroom door, he found Steven in the kitchen, just filling a mug. He turned to Ryan and gave a weak smile. "Good morning. Are you—alone?"

"Alone?" Ryan felt a warmth blossom around his neck.

"Yeah, who'd you bring home last night? Or didn't he stay? Or was it Meredith? Is she sleeping in there? Her car is in the lot."

He swallowed hard. "I didn't bring anyone home last night. She was too drunk, so I took the car." He hated that he was lying to Steven. He didn't want to, but he was still in the afterglow. He could still feel Caleb's body against his and remember the thrill of finally giving in to his desires. Even now, hours later, he felt as though phantom hands caressed him, moving firmly and confidently across his skin. To tell Steven the truth now would mean disappointment and accusation. He couldn't stand the thought of the lecture to come, or the idea that Steven might think less of him.

"You didn't?" Steven frowned and Ryan thought he saw something more than disappointment in his friend's eyes. "You know, you're covered in glitter. It's all over your face."

"It is?" He was caught now. There had to be a way to explain it. He laughed, and his voice sounded shrill and foreign to his own ears. "Oh, well there *was* this guy." His mind raced, searching for a scapegoat. "He was dressed as Legolas, you know, from Lord of the Rings. I made out with him for a little while. He was very persistent."

Steven relaxed a little. "A glittery elf from Tolkien? Hmm, well I guess you got drunk and kissed boys then. Any dancing on tables?"

"No, not just yet. I'm saving that one." He breathed a long sigh of relief and sought to change the subject. "How was your night? You got home late."

"Oh, it was good. You know, the usual. Jake was hanging all over Max, who seems like he's kind of over it. Then Peter was there, and I thought that was going to be good. I was hoping maybe he and I would get a little one on one time. We did, but he spent the whole damned evening going on about Brandon this and Brandon that. He didn't bother to show up—Brandon I mean—but he might as well have been sitting right between us the whole night. I did the only thing I could to cope. I drank and drank. In the end, everyone left, but I was too drunk to drive home, so I slept on Max's couch for a couple hours until I sobered up. Overall it was a waste of a night because this morning I'm still as single and hopeless as ever. Today's got some promise though."

"Oh?"

"Yeah, it sounds like the Brandon thing came to a head this morning. I don't know what happened, but Peter called and he was balling. Actually, I could barely understand him—he sounded pretty inconsolable. He's coming over in a little while, and then I'm sure he'll tell me all about it. At least I *think* he's coming. I really only understood about every fourth word."

"Oh," Ryan laughed. "Is that why you're making coffee? I was wondering. You'd don't ever drink coffee."

"Unless you make it." Steven smiled, and this time it felt a bit more genuine. "Do you want some?"

"Yes, please."

"You know we don't have any milk though, I hope it's okay that it's black." Ryan's brow furrowed in confusion, and Steven looked at him with concern. "Are you alright? I can jump in the car quick and go get some."

He shook his head. "No, it's fine. I just had a moment of—déjà vu? Second time this morning already, actually. But yeah, black is fine." He touched the thumb ring hanging around his neck and looked around, half expecting to see Darren. Was this still a dream? He shook his head again. "Will you just pour me a cup and leave it on the counter? If we've got company coming, I'd better get in the shower. I'm going to need to take Meredith's car back to her in a little while anyways."

"Alright," Steven said. He was looking at Ryan intently—oddly.

"Thanks Steven." He said, then walked into the bathroom and closed the door.

When Peter arrived a half hour later, Ryan and Steven were sitting at the dining table, each sipping on a second cup of coffee. Steven stood and met him in the kitchen with an awkward hug. Under the bright floodlights, it was easy to see that his eyes were red and his face was long.

Letting go, Steven appraised him. "Do you want some coffee?" he asked. "We have a half a pot still."

"No," Peter replied miserably. He walked around the peninsula, pulled up a chair at the little table and sat heavily.

Ryan frowned. "What's wrong?"

"Brandon."

Steven seated himself again and placed a hand lightly on top of Peter's. "I couldn't really understand you on the phone. Tell us what happened."

Withdrawing his hand, Peter folded his arms and rocked slightly in the chair as he exhaled long and slow. "Well, remember Max said I could invite Brandon to his party? Well, I did, and he said he was gonna come. But then," he looked at Ryan. "I told Steven about this last night. At the last minute, he sent me a text message yesterday. He said he was feeling really sick and he wasn't gonna make it. I said I'd bring him soup. I didn't need to go the party. I wanted to hang out with him." His voice quavered slightly, and he sniffed loudly as his eyes began to wet. "He said—he said he was just gonna go to sleep early, that he was really upset he couldn't go to the party, but I should still go and have fun."

"Okay—" Ryan said.

"So, this morning I thought, I dunno, I should go over there and see how he was doing. I bought some bagels and orange juice. I walked all the way there—it took me probably twenty minutes. Well, I got there, and I knocked on the door. No one answered, but I knew he was home because his car was there. So I knocked again and again."

Ryan felt a sudden chill. This story was familiar. He looked at Steven and knew that he felt it too. He was impatient. If something had happened to Brandon—

Peter continued. "Finally, I heard him." Ryan and Steven both exhaled audibly, and Peter looked at them with confusion. "Oh, did you think—"

Steven shook his head. "So, he's fine?"

"Fine?" Peter said with more than a hint of anger. "When he opened the door he was wearing a pair of sweatpants and nothing else." His voice quavered again. "I could see into the apartment, and behind him, on the couch, I could see there was—another guy. And all he had on was a pair of boxer shorts."

Steven whistled softly. "Oh, Peter." He reached his hand out to touch Peter's arm, but Peter shrugged him away. Spurned, Steven looked down at the table. Quietly he said, "Then what happened?"

"Then he just kinda—he smiled—smiled like he felt sorry for me. Well, I just turned around and started walking. He called after me, but I didn't turn around. I didn't need my nose rubbed in it, you know? I dumped the orange juice out in the snow, and then I just started—"

He was crying again. Ryan looked intently at Steven and tipped his head slightly in Peter's direction. Taking the hint, Steven gently wrapped his arms around Peter's shoulders, and when Peter didn't resist he held on a bit tighter and laid his head against his chest.

The front door opened again, and Ryan turned his head toward the entrance to the kitchen. A moment later Meredith emerged from the short hall, looking ragged. Her hair was matted in places, and it curled wildly in others. He had an idea she hadn't showered yet, and her face looked slightly swollen.

She appraised them and drew her lips into a thin smile. "Well, look at you three. If it isn't Stevey and Petey—what a pleasure on a Sunday morning."

Steven lifted his head from Peter's chest and sighed. "I hate when you call me Stevey. And of course you're here. We should talk to the restaurant and see if they'll close in the deck. It could be a fourth bedroom for you."

Meredith shrugged and started to pour a cup of coffee for herself. "This smells great, do you mind if I have some?"

Steven groaned. "Well, since you're already pouring it, I guess not."

Meredith walked over to the dining table and tousled Steven's hair, causing him to cringe. She pulled up a chair and sat with a grace that was incongruent with her appearance. "So," she said, "What's going on here?"

Ryan smiled sadly. "Peter went to surprise Brandon this morning and found him with—company."

She rolled her eyes. "Men are pigs, Petey. All of them, present company excluded." Then she amended. "Actually, you three are probably pigs too, I just don't have to deal with it because I don't have the right parts." She placed her elbows heavily on the table and took a long sip of her coffee. "Oh well, it's a good thing actually."

Peter looked at her, incredulous. "How so?"

"Peter," she said. "Listen. We all know how much you like Brandon. God, *everyone* knows how much you like Brandon. Even *Brandon* knows how much you like Brandon. Didn't it ever strike you as funny that he hasn't made a move?"

"Well, I just thought maybe he was waiting—like, biding his time."

"Biding his time for what?"

"I dunno, the right moment?"

She shook her head. "Look, I might be an ice queen a lot of the time, but underneath this frozen exterior, believe me—I have a heart of gold. I feel for you, buddy, I really do. But I'm not going to coddle you like these two. Brandon might like you as a friend. In fact, I'm sure he does because he's a sweet guy in the end. But you just aren't what he's looking for. I'm sure this hurts—kind of like ripping off a bandaid—but it's sudden and quick, right? And then it's over."

Peter stuttered, shocked by her brazen honesty. "R—right."

"So, embrace the pain and then let it subside. He can still be your friend, but you've got to be honest with yourself. That's all he's ever going to want. Sorry if I'm a bitch for telling you, but someone had to."

Ryan looked at her sternly. "You're in a mood this morning. You don't have to be so harsh, Meredith."

She raised her eyebrows. "Ryan, you know I'd say the same thing to you. In fact, I'm pretty sure I have. Do either of you disagree with me? With what I said?"

Steven shook his head slowly. "No, you're right I guess. You just delivered it so—"

Peter smiled weakly. "No guys, it's alright. She's right, and I appreciate the straight talk."

"Thank you!" Meredith replied. She smiled, self-satisfied.

Ryan looked at her again. "What are you doing here, by the way? You said you were going to call and then I'd drop your car off."

"I did call, and you didn't answer."

"I must've been in the shower."

"Doesn't matter—what's the point? I only live a few blocks away. The walk did me good. It's actually shaping up to be a pretty nice day out there. Most of the snow from last night has already melted. How was the afterparty?"

"Oh, we didn't end up going." His voice was quiet.

"No? Caleb seemed really pumped about it. I mean, after that blow up with Tom he was pretty determined to keep partying."

Steven coughed, "Caleb?"

Ryan shook his head. "Well, he changed his mind I guess. I took him home."

"Ugh," she groaned. "I should've made you wrap him in plastic. I bet he got glitter all over my car." Steven's eyes widened in astonishment. Meredith laughed. "You guys should've *seen* his costume!

He was like a goddamned glitter fairy! Glitter wings and glitter lip gloss and glitter all over his face. It was really over the top."

Steven smiled sadly. "Yeah, I bet it was a sight to see." He looked at Ryan for a long second and then turned to Peter. "So, I guess you didn't have breakfast yet. Want to get something downstairs?"

"Alright," Peter said.

Meredith sighed. "We'd join you, but I have no desire to show my face in that place ever again. I kind of told them what I thought of them after I quit, so enjoy!"

Steven laughed half-heartedly. "Alright then. Come on, Peter." They stood and walked through the kitchen, down the hall, and out the front door.

"He seems like he's in a stellar mood this morning," Meredith said as she drained the last of her coffee. "So, where are my keys?"

"I'll get them," Ryan said. "But first, aren't we going to talk about last night? About Andrew?"

She bristled slightly. "There's really nothing to talk about."

"I think there is."

"You do? What do you think there is to talk about?"

"Well, everything—all of it. You're still in love with him, Meredith. Even after what he did, you're still in love with him."

She smiled, turning one side of her mouth higher than the other. "It seems that way, doesn't it? And you know, for a little while I might have agreed with you. We were together last night, and it felt so—it felt like it used to. And then he took me home, and before you ask, yes, I slept with him. God, that was my biggest mistake."

"Why?"

"Because this morning when I woke up, and he was next to me I just—I was repulsed. I was disgusted with him and with myself. It's alright. Sleeping with him was probably exactly what I needed. I didn't realize until last night that I've been so lonely, and like you, I thought I was still in love with him. That's why I didn't want to see him. That's why I was so nervous. I was sure last night was going to go exactly the way it did—he was going to show up, and I was going to lose all my resolve, and then in the morning I'd want him back, and of course, he'd say yes—"

"But?"

"But instead I realized how much I *don't* want him. Our relationship was so one-sided. I did all the loving. I paid all the bills, and ultimately, I'm the one who suffered when I found him with that girl. I'm not saying people can't make mistakes—nothing is black and white. But Andrew? He made too many mistakes. You can't have love with that much dishonesty and lack of trust. And the worst part of it is I think somewhere I lost my respect for him. When I was working all those hours to make up his part of the rent—he just didn't try. And when I woke up next to him this morning? I remembered that old familiar feeling I had toward the end of our relationship—the loathing and disgust."

"So, what happened?"

"When he woke up I handed him his clothes and explained in no uncertain terms that this was the last time we were going to see each other. I told him not to call or write. I wished him well, and I closed the door—for good. And now? I feel *so* much better."

"Wow." He believed her. He knew by the stubborn set of her chin and the sudden light in her eyes that it was true. She'd had a revelation, and he was happy for her. "So, now what?"

"Well, I've got some errands to do, which is why I came for the car. Do you want to come along?"

He shook his head slowly. "No, thank you. I think after last night I need a quiet day to myself." Really he didn't want to leave the house in case Caleb called.

"Alright," she said. "Suit yourself. Oh, by the way—"

"Yeah?"

"You know I'm going away the week of Thanksgiving? We always spend the holiday with some family in upstate New York. I know it's a few weeks away, but would you mind driving me to the airport? You could keep the car for the week. Use it for whatever."

"Really?"

"Yeah, of course!"

"Sure!" He was excited. He had a lot of time off between school and holiday pool closures. Maybe he'd try to drive down and visit Alice and John for a night.

"Great," she said. "It's a deal. Now, where are my keys?"

For the rest of the morning and the early part of the afternoon, time slowed to a crawl. Ryan waited patiently in his room for Caleb to call and busied himself by cleaning and organizing his closet. He stripped his bed of sheets and gathered clothes to be washed. Around one-thirty, he made a quick lunch and sat by himself at the dining table with the phone next to him just in case.

He remembered that Tom's shift started at six that morning. If he worked eight hours, he'd be off at two. When Ryan finished the meal, he decided he'd waited long enough and dialed Caleb's number in the hope of getting him before Tom got home from work. After five rings the phone went to voicemail. He didn't leave a message.

Perhaps Caleb was still sleeping—it was not outside the realm of possibility. It must've been four in the morning by the time he got home, and it had been a night of heavy drinking. Perhaps Tom woke him before he went to work and he had a hard time falling back to sleep. The possibilities were endless.

A little voice in the back of his mind didn't agree though. He remembered the last time he waited for Caleb to call; in the end, he never did. Once more he dialed the number, and once again the call went to voicemail. His spirits fell as he hung up the phone. He recalled the widening of Steven's eyes when Meredith mentioned the glitter. Surely Steven made the connection. He'd been so cool as he rose and ushered Peter away to breakfast. Then he thought of Tom's thinly veiled accusations the night before. They'd been false then—practically unfounded. *Every time I step away you two are like magnets—or flies on shit.* Today everything was different. His innocence was gone, and he was suddenly—oppressively—overcome with guilt. The afterglow was replaced by a terrifying sense of desolation as he realized he'd traded his integrity for a little over a half hour of pleasure.

Yet, if Caleb called, everything could change. If he'd just pick up the damned phone, it would all melt away. Ryan needed him now, didn't he understand that? There was a righteousness to their actions, and there was some dark truth in their clandestine love. If only Caleb found the courage to bring it into the light, Ryan knew the guilt—for both of them—would evaporate. They'd shine brilliantly together, and the whole world would see that their affair was beautiful and right—that they should be as one.

Still, the phone was silent.

As the afternoon marched slowly toward evening, Ryan tried distracting himself again. He had a short essay to write in French, and for a while, the work engrossed him. Thoughts of Caleb waited patiently at the edges of his mind, asking politely to be let back in, but he managed to ignore them. He was about three-quarters of the way through a first draft when the phone rang. He reached for it excitedly but then set it back down when the Caller ID showed it was an 800 number. His concentration broken, the formerly patient thoughts donned the skins of barbarians and started storming the gates. He stood, and then collapsed on his bed in frustration.

He laid there for some time, watching the ceiling fan overhead spin in endless circles. After the silence was too much to handle, he sat up again and walked to his computer. He set iTunes to shuffle and laid back down as a track by Kosheen started to play. He exhaled deeply as the rich, dark, female vocals he'd fallen in love with began the verse. The song was desolate, like his mood, and it was absolutely perfect. It drew him in, and after the first chorus he began to focus on the words; it was a song about waiting for someone to leave his lover.

There passed a moment—a serendipitous coupling of the band's lyrics and his own emotions—when he took some small comfort in the knowledge that his present situation was, in fact, a common one to human existence. Though his heart ached and he was very much alone, there was nothing unique about his pain. He started to drift off to sleep, coming in and out. He thought he'd better get up—there was more work to do—and it was still possible Caleb might call—

A light knocking on his door brought him back. He sat up and quickly paused the music. "Come in," he called.

The door opened, and Steven stepped inside. His face was drawn. He looked around as if the bedroom was a foreign environment and then said, "Can you write a rent check? With Halloween I forgot about it, and now we're already a day late. I want to run them downstairs in the morning before class."

"Oh," Ryan said quietly. "Sure." He walked to his desk and pulled out his checkbook. He tried to remember how much money he had in his account—there was a slight chance he was short. As he wrote out the amount, he remembered with relief that Friday was payday. His rent checks were never cashed in a timely manner, so he figured he'd be fine. He tore the check out of the book and handed it to Steven.

"Thanks. Oh, and can you get your clothes out of the dryer? I've got some stuff waiting in the washer." His tone was cold and dry.

"Yeah, of course."

Steven turned and started walking away. His icy attitude cut sharply, and Ryan wasn't sure if he could stand it. "Steven—"

Steven turned back and looked at him, expression blank. "What?"

He didn't know what to say. What *could* he say? He searched his mind quickly for something—anything to keep him. "How is Peter?"

"Peter will be fine. He's upset but he'll be okay. Is that it?"

Suddenly Ryan was angry. "No, that's not it. Why are you acting so cold?"

"I think you know the answer to that."

"No, I don't." He did though.

"I think you do, Ryan. I think you do and you're not ready to talk about it. I guess when you are you'll know where to find me." He started to walk away again.

"Steven—"

He turned again. "Or maybe you *are* ready to talk about it?" His voice shook with anger. "You lied to me today. Why did you do that? Answer that question, and we'll talk."

Ryan wasn't ready to give it up—not yet. "Steven, really. I didn't lie. I didn't—"

"Bullshit! That's absolute bullshit, Ryan! I knew you were lying from the very beginning. Do you know how? When I got home last night, there was that nice fresh snow on the ground. Nice fresh snow with two sets of footprints leading from Meredith's car, all the way up the stairs to the front door. I thought, wow, Ryan really lucked out at the club. Wow, this is going to be *so* good for him. Maybe it'll turn into something. And then this morning when I asked you about it, and you denied it—I don't know. I thought maybe you were just being shy about it—discreet somehow. I'll admit I was disappointed because after everything we've been through—after Darren and living together and our friendship *before* Darren—I thought we could tell each other anything. But I bit my tongue, and I let it go."

"Steven I—I'm sorry—"

"No you're not! You were willing to deny it just a second ago. Then, when Meredith mentioned Caleb's costume—"

"The glitter," Ryan said, defeated.

"Yeah, the *glitter*. I suppose now you're going to tell me you two just sat in here and listened to music and braided each other's hair."

Ryan's tears came fast and with the violence of a flash flood through a canyon. He sobbed. "I'm sorry, Steven. I'm *sorry*. I don't know why I did it. I could've taken him home. I almost just took him *home*. But he wanted this to happen and so did I—so badly and I—"

The anger on Steven's face melted away and was replaced by a look of deep compassion. He stepped forward and sat on the bed, then pulled Ryan's head down onto his chest. "Alright, alright," he said. "Get yourself together. Come on, just breathe. I've done enough of this already today."

Ryan laughed despite his sobs. "I just thought—I don't know. I thought I deserved this. Don't I deserve to be happy?"

Now Steven laughed and pushed away slightly. He looked at Ryan seriously and said, "Of course you deserve to be happy. But Ryan, look at yourself. Are you *happy*?"

He shoved him playfully. "No, I'm not fucking happy." The tears were slowing now. "But I could be. If he would just call. You should have seen Tom last night—there is this *violence* in him."

"Violence or not, I told you before, and I'll tell you again. Caleb isn't the one for you. And you know what? It's not just a matter of circumstance. Even if he was single right now. Even if he'd never even *met* Tom, he still wouldn't be right for you."

"What do you mean?"

"Come on, Ryan. What do you even see in him? Where is the attraction?"

"Well, it's hard to explain."

Steven stood up. "See? It shouldn't be! I mean, what do you two even do together that could possibly form a foundation for love? The way I see it, the only time you ever spend with him is with either Tom or Meredith, and you're just drinking and smoking and dancing and God knows what else. Do you know his favorite color? What about his dream job? Did he have any pets growing up? What's the last book he read?"

Ryan shook his head, slowly. "I—I don't know."

"Okay, how about Max?"

"Well, yeah. Red, of course, like his hair. Um, he wants to be in IT. I think he mentioned a dog—I know he wants to get another one when he's done with school. I don't know about books. Why are you asking about Max? He's in the same situation as Caleb—off limits."

"That may be so, but what you've got there? That's a foundation. You know who Max is as a person, and that's a legitimate basis for attraction. See? With Max it's more than just the pretty face. With Caleb? And that's the other thing. I'm not saying you have to have a type, but Caleb doesn't really seem to fit your pattern. He's really very odd looking, don't you think?"

Ryan laughed in spite of himself. "He is a little more—androgynous than others I've been attracted to."

"So, do you think," Steven said. "Do you think that maybe the attraction to Caleb is really just about the *attention* from Caleb?"

"Maybe you should forget that business degree and go into psychology."

"I'm serious though, Ryan. Could that be it?"

"It could be." Honestly, he didn't know. He'd never considered *why* he was attracted to Caleb before. "I'll have to think about it, but—what am I going to do right now?"

"What do you mean?"

"I mean, I'm in this *mess* now."

"Well, the way I see it, it doesn't have to be a mess. Right now, the only three people that know what happened last night are you, Caleb and me. I'd bet a kidney that Caleb isn't going to say anything. Apart from its effect on you, and the fact that you *lied* to me about it, it's not really any of my business either. Their relationship is probably doomed, but I'm not going to hasten its demise by saying anything. You should probably tell Meredith since you lied to her as well, but I doubt she'll stir up too much trouble. The one thing I am certain of, however, is that it has to end. Now. If he calls you—"

"No, you're right. If he calls, I'll tell him it can't happen again."

"Do you *promise*?"

"Yes," Ryan said. He hoped it was a promise he could keep.

~*~

"You've been unusually quiet this trip," Meredith said.

Ryan let up off the gas and slowed the car as he took the exit. Three weeks had passed since Halloween and today was the day he was taking Meredith to the airport. She was right, of course. He was preoccupied. Caleb never called, and Ryan had resigned himself to the fact that he was never going to. Really it was for the best. He was moving on—trying his best to put it all behind him—but his dishonesty about the situation to Meredith still hung over his head. He'd spent the entire drive thinking about the best way to tell her. Now, as he guided the car down the curving, endlessly turning exit ramp, he was running out of time. They were nearly to the terminal.

"Yeah," he said. "I'm sorry. Something has been bothering me."

"No shit. Well, are you going to tell me what it is?"

"Yeah." He exhaled. "I don't think I can see Caleb anymore."

"Oh? Are you still dealing with your *scary feelings*? I don't think that should be hard anyways. I've only talked to him once since Halloween. Mostly he doesn't return my calls. Tom probably has him locked up in the basement."

"Well, yes and no. I think I was still dealing with them, but now—"

"Oh, cut to the fucking chase, Ryan."

"Alright. I wasn't honest with you about that night. The night of Halloween. I—I didn't take him home."

She bristled visibly. "I see."

He was about to tell her the rest of it, but then he looked at her. He could see the tense line of her jaw as she sat in the passenger seat, and her hands were clenched. He wanted desperately to be honest, but he knew instantly that her reaction was going to be less than understanding—it would only make her think of her own situation with Andrew. Now was not the time after all—not right before a holiday away with her family. "Don't worry," he said. "Nothing happened."

Her body relaxed, and she laughed. "You had me worried there for a second."

He laughed as well, and hoped it sounded convincing. "No, nothing happened. I mean, something almost did. There was a—tension."

"A tension?" She raised her eyebrows.

"Yeah but—I don't know. I haven't talked to him at all since that night, and not for lack of trying. He just won't return my calls. I don't know if maybe Tom found out we didn't go to the afterparty and assumed—"

She waved her hand dismissively. "Don't worry about it. It sounds like it really is for the best." She paused. "And thank you for your honesty. I had a feeling from the beginning that there was more to the story." They were very close to the terminal now. A giant blue statue of a horse with glowing red eyes glowered down at them as Ryan drove by. "I've always hated that fucking thing," she said.

"The horse?" Ryan asked. He didn't like it either. Tonight its angry, glowing orbs seemed especially accusatory.

"Yeah, it's so creepy. It's like a hell horse." She changed the subject. "So, are you going to go visit Alice and John?"

"Yeah, I think so."

"Alright, don't crash the car."

"I won't."

"Oh! I almost forgot. I'm way overdue for an oil change. I really should've gotten it done before we headed down here today. I'm sorry, if you're going to drive it down again to see them, and then to pick me up, can you just get that done for me? I keep some cash in the glove box—I think there's a couple hundred in there."

"That's a lot, Meredith. Why do you keep so much?"

"I never know when I'm going to need it, so it's there in an emergency. I think the oil change usually runs about thirty dollars. Just use that."

"Alright." They were at the terminal now. He pulled the car over to the right, underneath the sign for her airline. "Here we are."

She smiled. "Here we are." She climbed out of the passenger seat and retrieved her luggage from the back. "Have a great holiday, Ryan."

"You too," he said.

She turned and walked into the airport.

CHAPTER 16

Ryan's father set the large platter of sliced turkey in the middle of the table and took his seat. "Alright," he said. "Let's eat!" The spread was enormous and beautiful with all the Thanksgiving classics present and accounted for: mashed potatoes, green bean casserole, and stuffing shared the table with homemade cranberry sauce, sweet potatoes, corn, and his mother's special fresh-baked rolls. There was also a large bowl of salad and a near-to-overflowing gravy boat.

Aunt Carol laughed heartily. Then, in her warm Wisconsin accent she said, "Aw, it's all so goddamned beautiful I almost don't want to touch it!" The exuberance in her voice always made Ryan smile, and he was glad that she and her husband Charlie were in town for the holiday.

Conversation floated along as the family ate. There were seven of them in all—Ryan, his brother, sister, and parents, and Carol and Charlie. Between discussions about the weather in Wisconsin, who was dying and who was getting divorced, Carol delighted the table with ridiculous stories about the people she encountered in her former work as a receptionist at a medical clinic. Of course, those days were over. Charlie had recently inherited a large sum of money, and though they were only in their mid-fifties, neither she nor Charlie ever had to work again.

Halfway through dinner she turned to him and asked, "So, how is school going? Glad to be back at it, finally?"

He smiled. "Yeah, it's tough balancing the school work and my job, but it's going alright." It wasn't exactly the truth. Really, he was barely getting by, both financially and academically. "I'll be glad when finals are over in a few weeks, and I get a break for a while."

Carol clucked. "Well, that's good. I still think you should've gone to school back home." Ryan laughed inwardly. He and his parents had lived in Colorado since just after he was born, yet Carol still insisted on calling Wisconsin their home. "How long've you got off?"

"Oh, about a month, I think. Classes won't start again until the end of January."

Charlie chimed in. "Well, maybe you oughta come out and see us then—if you need a break."

"Oh!" Carol said. "That's a great idea!"

"Heh." Ryan laughed. As much as he loved the snow and winter, he couldn't think of anything more depressing than northern Wisconsin in January. "Thanks, but I don't think so. I mean, I'd love to, but I'll be working."

"That's a shame," Charlie said. "Hey, is that old truck still clunking along?"

"Oh—" Ryan began to say. He looked down at his plate.

His mother cleared her throat and sat forward in her chair. "Oh, Charlie. I thought I told you, I'm sorry. There was an accident at the beginning of the year. Someone ran a stop sign in the dark. Thank God no one was hurt, but the truck—it didn't make it."

Charlie shook his head slowly. "Damned shame. We had some good years with that truck. She was what, fifteen years old? Carol? When did we get that thing?"

Carol nodded. "Yeah, I think that was about 1989. Did you get another one? I mean, probably not a truck I'm guessing, but a car?"

"No," Ryan said. "I don't really need one right now. I just bike and walk, and that's usually fine."

"In the *winter*?"

He chuckled. "Well, yeah. I'll get a ride sometimes if it's really bad."

"Well, if you say so! I guess you had a pretty rough year. Your mom told me about your friend that died in the spring—probably a sore subject, sorry. You look like you came through it alright though." She smiled compassionately.

Before he could say anything, his mother winked at him and cleared her throat again. "So," she said, "Where are you two headed next?"

"Oh!" If it was possible for her to look any happier than she already did, Carol brightened. "Well, Alaska I think!"

"Alaska?" his mother asked.

"Oh yeah! Charlie and I were sitting on the veranda this last summer—must've been August, maybe even the end of July. Anyways, it was hotter than hell and so damned muggy, and we just turned to each other and said, we gotta get outta here! So I said, where should we go? I mean in the winter when you want to get away from the cold—that's easy. Florida, Arizona, whatever. But where the hell do you go in the summer to get away from the heat? Well, Charlie says, Alaska!" She laughed boisterously. "And I said, Alaska? And he said, yeah, let's go right now. We'll bring our lawn chairs and Hawaiian shirts and sunglasses and go sit on a goddamned glacier!"

His mother's eyes widened. "Wait, you didn't—"

Charlie laughed, and his big, booming guffaws filled the dining room. "No no no, not this year. We might've gone, but the next day the rain rolled in and broke the heat, and the rest of the summer was a lot milder."

Carol raised one finger. "Yeah, but we sure fell in love with the idea. So, this summer coming up I think we're gonna leave around the end of June and come back sometime in August."

Ryan smiled. "That sounds amazing!"

"Oh yeah, it's gonna be great! Well, we'll see I guess. It's not set in stone yet—we need your cousin Julie's husband to take care of the yard and whatnot, and he's being a bit of a stick in the mud."

"Why?" Ryan asked.

"Hell if I know! All we need him to do is come and cut the grass once a week—maybe stop by a couple days after work and water the flowers."

Ryan's mother tipped her head slightly to the side. "Doesn't Julie live an hour away from you? That's kind of a lot. I don't know if he's exactly being a stick in the mud."

Carol's eyes widened. "We would do it for *them*! Anyways, that's what we're working on." She looked at Ryan. "Although—Ryan, you could come and stay. You'd take good care of the place while we're gone, right?"

He laughed. "Sure I would, but I can't. That's my busiest time of year at work."

"Well, we'd pay you a little, wouldn't we Charlie? You could get a job for the summer back by us if you needed more. At least say you'll think about it."

"Alright," he said to appease her. "I'll think about it."

~*~

The following morning, Ryan pulled Meredith's car up to the garage door of the Quick Lube and turned off the engine. He yawned loudly—the kind of deep, satisfying yawn that causes the body to tense all the way down to the toes before releasing in a blissful rush of oxygen to the blood. It was early, and he was in desperate need of coffee, but he wanted to get on the road as soon as possible. The thought of seeing Alice and John—he hadn't seen them since the memorial services—was both exciting and terrifying. He leaned over to the glove box, pulled out a white envelope filled with cash, and stuffed it into the inside pocket of his jacket.

As he stepped out of the car into the brisk morning air, a stout middle-aged man dressed in greasy overalls ambled up to him with a clipboard in hand. The man smiled. "Good morning, what can we do for you?"

"Just an oil change, please."

"Alright," the man nodded. "Synthetic regular okay?"

"Yeah, just the basic stuff."

The man peered into the car. "Keys in the ignition. Alright." He handed Ryan the clipboard. "Fill this out and then take it to the receptionist in the office over there. There's coffee in there if you'd like. It'll be about thirty minutes."

Ryan nodded. "Thank you."

He walked the short distance to the office—a small white building attached to the garage with a couple large windows facing out to the street. The inside was clean and bright and warm, but it smelled strongly of motor oil. Four other customers waited in mauve, vinyl-covered armchairs with their noses stuck into outdated copies of People Magazine and Popular Science. A small TV mounted to the wall in the corner of the room played the morning news—it was Black Friday, and already two people were confirmed dead after a stampede at a big box store in Ohio. Beneath the TV sat a water cooler and a small cabinet with a coffee pot on top. The pot was nearly full, and Ryan sighed with relief.

As he headed eagerly toward the coffee, a young blond receptionist smiled at him from behind her desk near the back wall. "I'll take that when you're done," she said.

He looked at her and smiled in return. "Okay, thank you."

When he reached the coffee pot, he took a styrofoam cup and filled it most of the way with the hot black liquid. He took a small sip and winced—it was far too strong. For a moment, he wondered if there had been a mistake; maybe the pot accidentally got filled with used motor oil. He looked disdainfully at the cup before adding three single serve containers of creamer, then stirred it with a thin red straw and sipped it again. It was palatable—just barely. Still, he was grateful. He yawned and took a seat in a vacant armchair to fill out the form on the clipboard.

He brought the completed form to the receptionist who perused it briefly before clicking away on the keyboard of an aging computer. "Alright," she said. "That'll be thirty-five dollars. I'll call your name when the car is ready. How would you like to pay?"

"Um, cash," he replied. He removed the envelope from his jacket pocket and opened it carefully. Inside were eleven crisp twenty-dollar bills—two-hundred twenty dollars—two of which he handed to the receptionist.

"Thank you," she said. A cash register popped open, and she handed him a five. He immediately placed it back into the envelope, which he then returned to his pocket. She handed him a receipt. "Shouldn't be too long."

"Thanks."

He returned to his seat and his motor-oil coffee and sighed. His left hand lifted and grasped the thumb ring hanging around his neck. Really, there was no reason to be nervous about seeing Alice and John. To say that he'd put the whole ordeal of Darren's death behind him would've been a lie, but he'd made great strides toward moving on. The thumb ring, of course, served as a constant reminder that his friend was gone, but it was also a comfort. Hadn't it served a similar purpose for Darren as well? How many times had Darren rolled it around and around in times of stress? How often had the simple act of making contact—of engaging it—brought him peace? Ryan released the ring and felt a little better. It was his ring now, but its cathartic power lived on.

On the little television, a reporter stood on a snowy mountainside, bundled tightly in a large jacket and knit hat. Next to him were two skiers—a man and a woman—smiling deliriously and holding hands.

The reporter spoke. "While many eager holiday shoppers braved the cold and waited in line for *hours* outside in the dark this morning hoping to get the best deals, Luke Richards of Aurora had something else in mind. He woke Ashley, his girlfriend of four years, at four-thirty this morning and drove three and a half hours to Aspen. They waited patiently for the mountain to open and then caught the first lift of the day. At the top of the slopes, Luke had a question for Ashley."

The reporter held his microphone in front of the man's face. "I asked if—" he looked at the woman, dreamily. "I asked if you would be my wife."

The reporter quickly moved the microphone back to his own mouth. He turned to the woman. "And you said?"

"I said *yes!*" She exclaimed, causing a little audio clipping. "Of course! I can't imagine my life without him."

Ryan tuned out the rest. It was too depressing. The story reminded him just how lonely he was. He thought about Darren again—all the things they'd done in the time they spent together. He hadn't been lonely with Darren, even though it was all strictly platonic. Then he considered Caleb. Nearly a month had passed with no word, and when he thought about the situation, his mind always came back to the last conversation with Steven. Why was he attracted to Caleb in the first place? What did Caleb bring to the table apart from attention? Was attention enough to fill the void—the loneliness?

He looked again at the happy couple on the television. They were turning now and skiing away. He resented them a little—resented what they had. One day he hoped to marry and have his own happily ever after, but considering the current state of his life, he couldn't even imagine it as a possible reality. He drank his coffee absently and waited as he tried desperately to turn his mind to brighter things.

A short while later the receptionist called his name, and he headed back out to the car. After replacing the envelope of cash in the glove box, he reached for his backpack in the back seat, pulled out a travel case of CDs, and began to rifle through the plastic sleeves. Finding the one he was looking for, he turned on the car and pushed it into the slot of the after-market player in the dash. Dido started to sing 'Here With Me,' but that wasn't the song he needed. He pulled the car back onto the main road and then pressed the skip button until he reached track seven.

By the time Dido started into the first chorus of 'Honestly Okay,' he was pulling onto the interstate, heading south.

~*~

An hour and a half later he turned the car off the twisting county road and onto Alice and John's long driveway. Alice must have heard the sound of the tires grinding against the gravel from in the house, because by the time he pulled up, she was standing in the doorway, waving. He turned off the car and climbed out.

"Hi, honey!" she said. There was an exuberance to her voice and her movements as she strode toward him. With open arms, she pulled him into a tight embrace. "Oh, I'm so glad you could make it down. It's awfully nice to see you."

"Yeah, so am I. Thank you for having me, it's nice to see you too." He held her tightly, enjoying the comforting scent of tea tree oil from her voluminous hair. When she let go and stepped backward Ryan was struck by the sight of her. Perhaps in the nine months that had passed he'd forgotten the finer details of Darren's face, but now he found them again in hers, and he felt his heart threaten to break open.

She frowned. "Aw, honey, there's some darkness in you yet, isn't there?"

He did his best to smile. "Isn't there in you?"

"Well, of course there is!" She laughed, and it was surprisingly warm. "I expect there always will be. Come on; we'll talk about it later. John is waiting inside."

He pulled his backpack from the back seat, locked the car, and followed her into the house.

After he settled in, they sat in the living room and talked. He told them about school and work and Thanksgiving with his family. Then they had a light lunch and headed into town to do a little shopping. Alice wasn't interested in door-busting, but she liked to shop the sales later in the day. They wandered around downtown Denver until the early evening, and then had dinner at a nice sushi restaurant before returning home.

Alice opened a bottle of wine and John put on an old Mel Brooks movie. They laughed and talked about everything and nothing. When the first bottle was empty, Alice produced a second and filled their glasses. When the movie was over, John rose sleepily and announced he was headed to bed. He urged them not to stay up too late—he was going to make sourdough pancakes for breakfast in the morning.

A few minutes after John retired, Alice turned off the television and filled her wine glass again. Ryan's was still half full, but she topped it off anyways.

"So," she said. "What's eating you, honey?"

He took a sip of his wine and exhaled, long and slow. "I'm not sure I can describe it."

She looked at him sternly and laughed. "Well, of course you can. I have a feeling if you try you've got a lot of words for it. I can *feel* it coming off you. When you first got here, I thought maybe it was about Darren. Now I'm not so sure."

"Well, it's sort of about Darren. I don't know. He's part of it. I think, you know, it's not something I'll ever probably *get over*—not entirely. But I've moved on. I really think I've moved on. I still see him sometimes in my dreams but it's—it's not what I'd have expected when I dream of him."

"Oh? What happens in these dreams?"

"Well, nothing. We just talk. They seem to happen after some emotionally charged event. We talk through it, I guess."

"Sounds like maybe he's your guardian angel."

Ryan pressed his lips tightly together. He didn't want to hear about guardian angels or visitors from the great beyond. He didn't believe in any of that. He focused for a moment on his breathing, light and shallow. "You know I loved him, don't you?"

She nodded her head, slowly. "Yes, I know that. He loved you too, I'm sure—in his own way."

"It wasn't the way I needed." He took another sip of his wine, shocked and a little ashamed of the bitterness in his voice.

"I don't know if that's entirely true. You're talking about romantically, right?"

He bristled in his chair. "Well, yeah." It seemed to him that this was an utterly inappropriate conversation to be having with Alice.

"You're uncomfortable," she said, astute as ever. "Don't be. Let's suppose it had gone differently. Let's change just one thing. Suppose that you and my son were in fact romantically involved. I'm sure that would have made you very happy, right?"

"Well, yes, of course."

"But then let's say he died anyways."

"Okay—"

"Would anything be different now about the way you're feeling?"

He considered the question deeply. "I feel very—alone. I'm lonely. I guess if I think about before—when he was still with us—I always wanted something more, but I wasn't—"

"But you weren't lonely, really. You were unfulfilled."

"Right."

"And if he had loved you in the way you say you needed him to, you might have been fulfilled for a while." She paused. "But he left us. And, honey, it doesn't matter what he was to you—to anyone really. The fact is, he left us, and he took with him whatever it was he brought to our lives. And now we just have to do without."

It was a dismal statement. "But how? How do we just *do without*? I've been looking. I've been searching for—I don't know. I want to say *a replacement* but that's not really the right word. I can't replace him, but I want—I *need*—something else."

"And how's that been going for you?"

"Not well." There was a quaver in his voice and a wetness at the edges of his eyes. "It's not going well at all."

"It's because you're looking in the wrong places."

"Huh?"

"Did you know that John is my second husband?"

He wiped his eyes lightly and took another sip of wine. "No."

"Oh, yes. I got married when I was nineteen. Oh, what a *loser* he was. He was mean and a drunk. Gosh, he was only twenty-three, but I knew even before we tied the knot he'd probably be in jail, or worse—dead—by the time he was forty."

"Well, why did you marry him?"

"Because he liked me. I was very insecure when I was young—I couldn't really tell you why. But I was shy, and I suffered from this incredible lack of confidence in anything I did." It was hard for Ryan to swallow. He couldn't imagine graceful, eccentric, *confident* Alice as ever being anything other than the woman she was today. Seeming to hear his thoughts, she continued. "Oh, you'd never have seen me with the big hair and the bright clothes I wear now. I was drab and plain. He was the son of my father's friend, and he liked me. So, I went out with him, and I overlooked all his flaws even though there were so many. I thought he was the best I could get—he was my security."

"So, what happened?" he asked.

"Well, we made it through two miserable years. Then one night he came home absolutely sauced, and he hit me. I'll tell you what Ryan, it hurt like hell, but that beating was the best thing that ever happened to me. It awoke something in me—a fire I didn't know was there, burning down deep. I picked myself up, and I left. I swore I'd never be treated that way again. I filed for divorce the next day, and that was that."

"Wow. And then you met John?"

"Not at first. Not for a while. You know, it was very hard. I made a resolution to never settle for less than what I deserved. That was kind of rich, looking back on it, because I was still insecure and really didn't *know* what I deserved. I started over from nothing. See, let me put it this way. It's all about—cake."

"Okay?" He laughed.

"I love cake more than about anything. If I wouldn't be three hundred pounds and malnourished, I'd eat cake three meals a day every day of my life. Well, for a while my ex-husband *was* my cake. He was the whole thing, and after I left him—"

"No cake?" He laughed lightly at the absurdity of it.

"That's right! No cake! Well, by the time I met John I'd learned to be my own cake. I found love and comfort and security in myself. I didn't *need* John. I wanted him, but I didn't need him. Now, twenty-five years later I have a tough time imagining life without him, but he's still not my cake. He's a part of it, sure. The frosting—the best part. He holds it all together. But if something—God forbid—was to happen? Oh, I'd be sad. I'd be angry. I'd mourn the loss of him for years. But in the end?"

"You'd be fine," he said.

"Right, honey. Because I'm still the cake. I think that's what you need for yourself—to love yourself first. When you can do that, you can be alone and never be *lonely*."

He finished the last of his wine. "Thanks, Alice."

"Anytime, honey."

~*~

Despite Ryan's slight hangover from the previous night's wine, John's sourdough pancakes were worth waking up for. John piled them high on a plate, and then they sat at the little kitchen table and ate them with orange juice and coffee. By the time breakfast was done, he felt a little better.

Shortly before ten he gathered his things and carried them out to the car. Alice said she wished he could stay another day, and truthfully he did too. It was Saturday morning, and Meredith's flight arrived on Sunday evening. From the Henderson's house, it was only a twenty-minute drive to the airport. It made a lot of sense, but he had a shift at the pool that afternoon that he couldn't afford to give up. He hugged them both tightly, got into the car, and started his journey back north.

A few minutes after he merged onto the interstate he looked down at the gas gauge for the first time. The light wasn't on yet, but the needle looked dangerously low. Even if the tank had enough gas to get him home today, he'd still need to fill up in order to collect Meredith from the airport. He decided he might as well take care of it now. Also, he'd been fighting a strong craving for a cigarette since the night before. A quick stop could kill two birds with one stone, so he pulled off at the next exit, drove into a small gas station just off the frontage road, and parked beside a pump.

After he had turned off the engine, he twisted his body toward the back seat and rifled in his backpack for his wallet. He stepped out of the car, put the nozzle of the pump into the gas tank, pressed 'Regular' on the pump and squeezed the trigger handle.

Nothing happened, so he tried again.

After squeezing the handle a third time with no result, he noticed a blinking sign on the console's yellow screen asking him to please pre-pay.

He groaned and pulled his debit card from his wallet. After dipping it into the machine's card reader, he quickly entered his PIN and waited. The yellow screen flashed the word *authorizing* repeatedly, then after ten seconds, the message changed to *please see attendant* and the machine spat out a short receipt. Ryan took it cautiously.

Declined.

He broke out into a cold sweat. His finances had been tight, sure, but it was difficult to believe he was out of money. The rent was due again in a couple days, and payday was an entire week away. He walked slowly toward the store hoping there was some sort of error with the machine.

As he pushed open the door to the gas station, an electronic bell announced his arrival and startled the attendant—a young man of about his age—who sat behind the counter. "Can I help you?" the attendant asked, scowling at the apparent interruption.

"Yeah, I tried to authorize pump number four. It told me to see attendant."

The other young man rolled his eyes. "Cash or credit?"

"Um, debit." Ryan handed over his card.

The attendant pressed a button. "How much do you want to put in?"

He thought maybe he shouldn't push it. "Twenty dollars. Oh, and a pack of those cigarettes in the green box, please."

The attendant turned on his stool and retrieved the cigarettes from a large display behind him. He swiped Ryan's card and waited. Then he shook his head. "Sorry, it says it's declined."

"That's impossible." He knew it wasn't.

"Maybe." The attendant shrugged his shoulders. "But that's what it says. D'you have another card?"

He bit his lip. "No—"

There was the envelope though—in the glove compartment. It still had nearly two-hundred dollars in it. He cringed inwardly at the thought of using it. The money wasn't his, and he had no right to it, but hadn't Meredith said it was there for emergencies? Sure, it was there for *her* emergencies, but he reasoned that if he ran out of gas on the way home that was going to be as much her problem as his.

The attendant returned the debit card. Ryan nodded and said, "I'll be right back."

On the short walk to the car, he considered risking it. He thought he had a little cash in his bedroom—maybe he could fill the tank just enough to collect Meredith from the airport, at least. Then he could tell her with some embarrassment that he was out of money and she could fill the tank again for the return trip. She'd probably be annoyed, but at least he'd keep his hands clean.

He opened the car door and sat in the driver's seat. For a full minute, he sat, breathing slowly in and out—considering. His craving for a cigarette was now almost unbearable, having been stoked be the stress of the situation. He leaned over, opened the glove compartment, and removed the envelope. Really it wasn't such a big deal—he'd pay her back. In fact, payday was only six days away, and the likelihood that she'd have an emergency and *need* this cash between now and then was slim.

As he walked back toward the store the only thing that gave him pause was Andrew. Meredith had made it clear that money was a sensitive subject for her, and that Andrew's actions involving money had been a big part of why their relationship had failed. He wondered as he stepped through the glass door again how she would perceive this. He wished he had a cell phone—that he could call her and simply ask. But then he was at the counter again, and he shook off his reservations. Meredith wasn't going to mind. He wasn't Andrew, and the situation was completely different. This wasn't rent money that was going to force her to work more. It was a small sum of cash—nothing really.

He removed a twenty and a five from the envelope and handed them to the attendant. "I'll take that pack of cigarettes, then put the rest on pump four?"

The attendant took the cash and shrugged. "Have a nice day."

Back in the parking lot he opened the pack of cigarettes and lit one, nervously. *Shit*, he thought as he inhaled. He could feel the envelope in his pocket—one-hundred sixty dollars left. He wondered what kind of food he had in the house, or if this pack of cigarettes would last him the week. While he was already taking a loan, of sorts, maybe he ought to just take the whole amount. He'd pay Meredith back on Friday. He'd pay back every cent of it, maybe even with a little interest.

He extinguished the butt and climbed back into the driver's seat, removing the envelope from his pocket. Maybe it was best to just ask her tomorrow night if he could borrow the money. He opened the glove compartment ready to put the cash back where it belonged.

Then he stopped. He might need something between now and then. Turning toward the back seat, he unzipped his pack and placed the envelope inside. When he picked her up from the airport tomorrow, he'd formally ask permission to keep whatever was left. If she said no—if she was adverse to the idea—he'd just give it back right then and there. Simple. Easy.

He didn't think she'd mind. He wasn't Andrew, after all.

~*~

Ryan made it home with enough time to take a quick shower before he hopped on his bike and headed in to work. The shift went smoothly, and he was back at home just after eight thirty.

When he walked in the door his nose perked up to the warming scents of cinnamon and pine. He stepped into the kitchen and smiled. Christmas music was playing. Beyond the little dining table in the space between the kitchen and the living room, Steven and Shelly were struggling to connect wiry branches to a tawdry artificial tree.

Shelly turned her head toward him with a look of concentrated frustration. "Welcome home," she said. Then her face melted into a truly genuine smile. "Are you any good at this stuff? It's supposed to be easy but like, I can't get *any* of these in."

Ryan laughed as he dropped his backpack to the floor and sprang forward to assist her. "When did you guys get a Christmas tree?"

Steven shook his head. "Oh, this afternoon. Shelly begged. I think it's more work than it's worth."

"It isn't!" she said. "I just need to celebrate. You know, like, make the season last. This is a special one."

Ryan smiled at her delight. "Why?"

"Because I'm going home! Home for Christmas for the first time since high school."

"To LA? With your dad?"

She looked at him with a warning in her eyes. "Nah," she said. "Christmas in LA is depressing. Ever hear that Joni Mitchell song where it doesn't snow and everything is green?" Her expression lightened again, and when she spoke, it was filled with her former exuberance. "I talked to my mom. I'm Chicago bound!"

He blinked with surprise. "Well, that's great! You're reconciling?"

She nodded. "It's a first step."

"So, I guess I'll have the house to myself." He took the branch she was struggling with and angled it slightly against the tree's center pole. He felt it lock into the groove and then he lifted it into place. "See? It *is* easy. The angle is just more extreme than you think it should be." He looked at Steven. "When are you going home?"

"The moment my last final is done—on that Friday."

Shelly clapped suddenly. "Hey! You could go the next day, right Steven?"

"Yes, I could—"

"Ooh! I'm not leaving until that Saturday. Guys, what if like, what if we had one last *awesome* party before the year is over? We could do it the night finals are done before everyone skips town."

Steven considered. "Well, I'm just driving so I guess that could work. Most of our friends are *from* Colorado, so it's probably not like anyone has flights to catch. What do you think, Ryan?"

"I think it's a great idea! Let's get everyone here."

Shelly nodded. "Yeah, like everyone. We'll celebrate the semester ending and the year ending."

"Yes!" Ryan said. "This has been a hell of year. I'm not going to be the slightest bit sad when it's finally over. It's a deal then?"

Shelly clapped again. "It's a deal. Now, are either of you any good at stringing lights?"

The following evening Meredith walked out of the airport looking visibly exhausted. She flung her luggage haphazardly into the backseat, then walked around and slumped into the passenger side.

"You look like you need some sleep!" Ryan said.

"Too much fucking family," she groaned. "It was a long trip."

He started to drive away from the terminal. "Do you want to talk about it? Did something go wrong?"

She looked at him, sleepily. He could smell liquor on her breath. "No, everything was fine. It's just a long time to be on point. You know—no swearing, don't drink too much, that kind of bullshit."

"It smells like you had a few on the plane."

"Oh yeah, three?"

He laughed. "You had a layover in Chicago, right? Three on the second plane? The one from there to here?"

"Oh, yep. And the layover was so long in Chicago, I had a few in the airport as well."

"Must've made for a nice trip."

"Yeah," she said, her eyes only half open. "How was *your* holiday?"

"Fine. Good, even. My aunt and uncle were in from Wisconsin. And I had a nice visit with Alice and John the next day."

"Oh! Did you get the oil changed?"

"I did." He paused. Now was the time to tell her about the money he'd borrowed. He wasn't sure why he was so nervous—it wasn't even two-hundred dollars, and a chunk of it had gone to gas. He took a deep breath and then started. "Oh, and I—"

She waved her hand dismissively. "That's nice. Thanks."

"Meredith, I wanted to tell you—"

"Sorry Ryan," she said. "I know I probably sound like a bitch, but can we just be quiet for a little while?"

"You're not a bitch," he replied.

"Thanks. I appreciate it."

"It's just, I wanted to tell you that I—"

He was interrupted again by the soft sound of her snoring. He thought about waking her long enough to get it out, but stopped. The nerve went out of him. He'd tell her when they got home, or maybe tomorrow. He'd tell her though, for sure. He turned the car onto the road leading back to the interstate. In the rearview mirror, the glowing red eyes of the giant blue horse stared at him accusingly. "I'll tell her," he said to the air as he drove on into the night.

CHAPTER 17

The holiday season on campus began the first day of December. Christmas trees and giant menorahs appeared in the centers of many of the school's broad, grassy lawns; wreaths with red bows and electric candles were hung on light poles, and a giant ice sculpture of a dreidel was placed in the courtyard in front of the student center.

A certain levity of spirit hung in the air, despite the stress of the semester's end.

Ryan felt none of it. As the last weeks of the fall term marched ahead at a merciless pace, he felt himself drowning. His grades had slipped dangerously low, and his upcoming final exams literally meant success or failure. To make matters worse, his December rent check bounced. Though the bank paid it, he was charged a twenty-five dollar fee, leaving him further in a hole he wasn't sure he could climb out of. Any intention he had of repaying Meredith the money he'd borrowed—and still neglected to tell her about—was dismissed. It simply wasn't feasible.

The holidays had always been his favorite time of year, but in spite of the decorations, the Christmas music, and even the tawdry tree they kept in the apartment, he felt none of it. He was bitter, lonely and broke—hardly in a position to feel holiday cheer. He kept his head down and did his best to study, but found it increasingly difficult to maintain his focus, choosing instead to succumb to the comforts of self-pity.

When finals week finally arrived, he greeted it resolutely. He did-n't feel the least bit prepared, but he consoled himself with the knowledge that after it was over—regardless of the outcome—he'd get a rest.

His first final was Tuesday morning—music history. He muddled his way through and then sulked home to nap, utterly disappointed in his performance. He laid down and was just about to nod off when the phone rang.

Plucking the receiver from its base he answered half-heartedly. "Hello?"

"Hey!" It was Meredith. "How'd it go? Your first final?"

"Oh, it went. I don't know. What's up?"

"Nothing. That's the problem. I'm climbing the goddamned walls. I've got my biggest exam tomorrow, but I really need a break from studying. Want to meet me at the Back Alley? We could hang out for an hour or so—I definitely need it."

He bit his lip softly and touched the thumb ring hanging around his neck. There were so many reasons to say no. Sadly, he couldn't really afford a three-dollar coffee at the moment. Also, he'd been ac-tively avoiding the Back Alley Café since the middle of November—it was Caleb and Tom's place, after all. Seeing one of them was the last thing he needed right now, and he supposed there was a pretty good chance one or the other might be there at any given time. Tom had surprised him there before. It could happen again.

Still, there was the faintest note of desperation in Meredith's voice. He thought maybe they could settle on a compromise. "Well," he said, "What if you stopped by here? I can make us some coffee, and we can put on some Christmas tunes, or whatever."

"No, no." Her words were short and clipped. "Come on, Ryan. We spend enough time in that shit hole you call a home. I'm asking for one hour out somewhere."

"One hour?"

"Yes. One goddamned hour. Jesus Christ!"

He laughed. "Alright. Alright. When do you want to go? Now?"

"Yeah, that sounds good."

"Are you walking? Do you want to call when you're about here, and we'll walk the rest of the way together?"

"No. You're closer, obviously. Go get us a table or something. I won't be far behind you."

"Alright. See you soon." He hung up the phone and exhaled deeply, letting his shoulders sag. As he walked slowly toward the door, he wished he'd let the call go to voicemail. Defeated, he grabbed his wallet and a jacket and headed out of the apartment.

A block later he started up the wooden steps to the Back Alley's upper deck. He stopped for a moment at the top, remembering his first visit at the height of summer. All the beautiful houseplants that formerly lined the deck were removed to the warmth and shelter of the interior, replaced instead by small spruce and holly bushes in large terra-cotta pots. The paper lanterns overhead had been switched out for endless strings of colored Christmas lights. The wrought-iron furniture remained, however, and Ryan was only a little surprised to see one of the outdoor tables occupied by a trio of students, bundled tightly and sipping hot beverages that steamed profusely into the frigid December air.

He smiled in spite of himself. That was the table where he'd sat with Brandon that first night—the night he met Caleb. It felt like ages ago already, even though only a few months had passed. That night had started with disappointment over Max and ended with so much potential. Looking through the distorted lens of nostalgia, he thought for a moment he'd been much happier then. A cold wind picked up suddenly and tore at his face. He laughed quietly at the absurdity of the notion, then opened the door and stepped inside.

He was accosted first by a wave of heat. Then the noise of the room built quickly in his ears until all he heard was a dull roar. The place was packed with students. Everyone seemed to have the same idea as Meredith—the same need to escape for a little while. He moved to the counter and ordered a large dark roast.

As the barista handed Ryan an oversized mug, a couple girls got up from a small table by the windows that looked out toward the alley below. Seizing both the mug and the opportunity, he zipped over to the open table and reached it uncontested. He set his cup down and smiled, then removed his jacket and hung it over the back of his chair.

After taking his seat, he took a small sip of the rich black liquid and sighed, actually content for the first time in a while. He *did* love it here, and was ultimately grateful Meredith had asked him to meet. He closed his eyes to breathe for a moment. Everything was alright. This first semester might not have been his best, but the next one could be better. And the rest of his problems—the loneliness and emptiness? They'd take care of themselves in time. It was just a matter of patience.

When he opened his eyes, his fears came to fruition. Across the room, a patch of blue caught his eye. Caleb was standing in his blue work scrubs by the cashier. Their eyes locked, and Caleb's mouth turned down into an expression of mute horror. Ryan bristled. He wanted to stand up and run away—to suddenly be anywhere else. He began to push back from the table, but his legs were frozen. His body twisted ineffectually, and after a moment he relaxed in resignation and forced his eyes down to his coffee cup.

The inky surface of the coffee reflected the ceiling above, where a poster of the Sistine Chapel ceiling had been plastered to the tile. It was the part of the scene where God and Adam touch fingers and God gives the spark of life. Ryan focused on Adam's curious, almost pained expression as it moved in the ripples within the cup. His heart was racing, and he tried to slow his breathing. Surely Caleb would just go away. Surely he'd just—

"Ryan?"

He looked up as Caleb sat cautiously in the chair opposite. "Caleb. You, um—you never called."

"I know." His voice cracked. There were tears at the corners of his eyes and he wiped at them lightly. "It's—well. I couldn't. I—um. I'm sorry. I'm just really sorry because I know I hurt you. And Tom, he—"

"Caleb, it's alright. I understand, I think. I—"

"It was so *shitty* of me. I don't know why I did it—why *we* did it. It's my fault completely but—Tom? Tom would *never* do that to me. He'd never—"

Ryan reached his hand across the table to rest it on top of Caleb's. The moment their fingers touched Caleb recoiled. Ryan spoke. "Caleb. Really, it's alright. I—I forgive you."

Caleb shook his head. "Thanks, but it doesn't matter. I can't forgive myself." He stood brusquely. "I'm sorry, Ryan. Sorry again. Bye."

Ryan was about to protest as Caleb turned away, but he was interrupted before he could begin by a startled cry. Caleb staggered back, having collided with someone in his distraction. Ryan was surprised when a moment later Meredith appeared beside him.

"Caleb," Meredith said, flatly.

"Oh, uh—Meredith. Sorry. I didn't see you."

"Yeah," she said. "I get that. Off so soon?"

"Yeah, I uh—gotta go."

"See ya." She sat coldly and looked at Ryan with an uncomfortable, silent intensity.

The gaze went on, and Ryan turned his shoulders slightly inward—withdrawing. Finally, he asked, "Aren't you going to have anything to drink?"

Her lips quivered slightly. "I don't think I'm going to stay."

"What? What do you mean? This was your idea to come here. You
said you needed to get out of the house. Do you want to go somewhere else?"

"Not with you, I don't."

"Oh—what's going on?"

"That's what I'd like to know. What the *fuck* is going on?"

"Meredith—"

She exhaled audibly. "So, I was getting ready to come over here,
and I couldn't find my wallet. I figured I must've left it in the car. I
went out, and I looked everywhere, and I still didn't find it. I knew it
was somewhere—I couldn't have lost it. It turns out it was in my
jacket pocket the whole time. Well, I didn't know that yet. All I knew
is that you were here already waiting. So, I went into my glove compartment to get some cash—"

"Oh—"

"Oh?" Her voice was rising. "Oh? So, you're not even going to deny it? You're not going to try to convince me that you got a two-
hundred-and-twenty-dollar oil change? Where the *fuck* is my money,
Ryan?"

"Meredith—I tried to tell you. I tried when I picked you up at the
airport, but then you fell asleep. I—I needed gas, and my debit card
got declined. I just needed something to tide me over, and I thought
you wouldn't mind the loan. I didn't want to, and I was going to pay
you back, but then my rent check bounced and—oh God. It's only a
couple hundred dollars! I'm sorry. I screwed up, but please! You
know I'm good for it!"

She rolled her eyes and mumbled to herself. "Only a couple hundred dollars? Yeah, that's where it begins. And exactly *when* did you plan to pay me back? Exactly *when* did you plan to tell me? You could've told me the day after. You could have said something the next week. Ryan, it's been almost a month! And do you know the worst part? You knew—you *knew* how I feel about this stuff. I don't get it. Is this some kind of self-sabotage or are you just that fucking stupid?"

"Meredith—" he was crying now.

"I was sure I was going to get here, and you would have some totally plausible explanation."

"It *is* plausible. It's not like I went on a shopping spree with your money."

"But then I got here and who is sitting at the table with you? Good old Caleb. Good old Caleb talking about how shitty it was, and how Tom would *never* do that to him. What was he referring to, I wonder?"

"Meredith—"

"Do you still want me to believe that *nothing happened*? Ryan, you are a liar and a thief. And me? I'm just a plain old fucking idiot."

He was angry now. "You're being unreasonable."

She slammed her fists heavily onto the table, causing Ryan's coffee cup to jump and spill over the sides. "Unreasonable? You have just proven yourself to be *everything* I've tried to cut out of my life! You are Andrew all over again. The difference is, at least he was fucking me. With you, all I'm getting is—*fucked*."

"I'm sorry," he said quietly. "I really am."

She shook her head slowly, and now she was crying as well. "I believe you, I do. But I don't trust you—not anymore. You were my best friend, Ryan."

"Not—anymore?"

"I'm sorry, but sometimes life doesn't come with second chances."

"So, that's it? Over *this*?"

"You don't get it. I'll admit I'm damaged. I'm all fucked up from my relationship with Andrew—even still. But do you have any *idea* how much more fucked you are? You need help, Ryan. You really need help."

"Meredith, come on."

"So, I'll see you at work, and we'll be civil. After all, if I stop doing the things I want to do because of you, then you win."

"It doesn't need to come to this."

"—But we won't be friends. And you'll pay back that two-hundred dollars." She wiped her eyes and stood to leave.

"Please, Meredith. I can't lose you. I can't—"

"Bye, Ryan. I wish you the best. I really do." Then she turned and walked away.

He looked down again at his coffee and lifted the cup absently to his lips. Tipping it clumsily he took too much of the hot liquid into his mouth at once, but found he was only vaguely aware of the pain as it scorched his tongue. He swallowed hard, barely tasting it. The noise and commotion of the café around him faded away, leaving him with a feeling of hollow isolation. He set the cup back down and wiped his eyes.

He needed to go—to get out of there. In one fell swoop, he'd lost Caleb and Meredith for good. Standing slowly, he pulled on his jacket and looked around the room. He expected this would be his last time in the Back Alley Café. What could these walls offer him now except the memory of bridges burning in a mighty conflagration? Leaving the mostly full cup of coffee on the table, he left the café and walked slowly, somberly home.

~*~

He found the rest of finals week to be a welcome distraction. Cramming last minute for his remaining exams allowed him a perfect opportunity to avoid processing both his encounter with Caleb and the fallout with Meredith. He spoke about it to no one and kept his head down. On the rare occasion that his mind came around to the subject, he assured himself he'd have plenty of time to react once the week was over.

Finally, Friday afternoon came. Shelly and Steven threw themselves into party preparations, and for once Ryan chose not to participate. Guests were supposed to start arriving at seven, so when Steven and Shelly made a run to the liquor store around five-thirty Ryan stepped out onto the deck for a cigarette.

The night was cold and dark, but there was little wind. As he slowly exhaled breath upon breath, the cloud of used smoke drifted aimlessly upward, spreading into a voluminous cloud before ultimately dissipating under a canopy of bright, winter stars. More than the nicotine, he supposed it was the sight of this dissolution into the ether that brought him peace. He wished suddenly he could dissolve himself so easily—melt effortlessly into eternity. After extinguishing the first butt, he immediately lit another.

He heard footsteps on the stairs from the parking lot below.

Peter appeared, bundled tightly in a down jacket and a floppy stocking cap. "Good evening. Mind if I join you?"

Ryan exhaled sharply. "No, of course not. You're quite early, aren't you?"

"Oh yeah, well, I didn't wanna wait. Everyone is on their way out of the dorms tonight. It's depressing. Steven said I could come whenever so—" He lit a cigarette of his own. "—Here I am!"

"Well, welcome! How did your finals go?"

"Oh, pretty good I think. Yours?"

"Meh, we'll see."

Peter laughed. "So, anyone else here yet?"

"No, it's just me. Steven and Shelly ran to the liquor store."

"Oh, okay. Not even Meredith?"

Ryan stiffened a bit. "Oh no, she—won't be coming."

"Really?" Peter's eyes grew wide. "Why not?"

Ryan waved his hand dismissively. "We had a little bit of a falling out. I'm hoping maybe we'll be able to smooth it over, but for now—"

"Aw, well, I'm sorry to hear that." He was quiet for a moment. "Hey, Brandon is gonna come tonight, isn't he?"

"Oh, yeah, I think so. I was sort of surprised. You asked Steven to invite him, didn't you? I'm glad you're feeling alright with that."

Peter shrugged. "Well, it's been almost two months since all that happened. Like Meredith said, there's no reason we can't be friends, right?"

Ryan nodded sadly. "Right." How many times had he tried to convince himself of the same thing regarding Darren? From the very beginning he'd felt a certain kinship with Peter over this subject, and now an overwhelming need to care for and protect him welled up inside. He decided he was going to act as Peter's guardian tonight. Perhaps he could do a little good to balance all the poor decisions and hurt he'd caused lately. "Well," he said, "when he gets here, if it starts to get to you even a little bit, just come find me, alright?"

Peter nodded. "Alright." He extinguished his cigarette. "It's really friggin' cold out here. Do you wanna go inside?"

"Yeah, sure. Let's go."

Two hours later Ryan stood in the kitchen with Peter as Shelly slowly stirred a stockpot full of mulled cider. He watched as she leaned over the pot and made a circular motion with her hand to waft the aroma up into her nose. She smiled. "This was always my favorite. My mom made it every year when I was growing up. She and the other adults would like, doctor it up though, like we're going to. But right out of the pot it was always booze-free, so I could have as much of it as I wanted."

Peter nodded. "It smells great!"

"Thank you! Just wait until you taste it. It's like—like the whole season in a cup. It's everything."

Steven appeared from the living room. "Alright," he said. "I've got the 'Holiday Hits' station blaring on the TV. Now we just need some damned guests. Where is everybody?"

Ryan nudged him lightly. "They'll all be here. Nobody misses our parties, right?"

"Right," Steven said. "Except—and not that I'm complaining but—where is Meredith?"

Peter's eyes widened, and he was about to speak, but Ryan shot him a warning glance and said, "Oh, she couldn't make it, if you'll believe that."

Steven scowled. "Hardly. That girl has been growing on you like a cancer."

"Well, with the break and all I guess you won't see her again for a while."

In-between the kitchen and living room Mars had been sleeping quietly underneath the Christmas Tree. Suddenly he jumped up and started barking. The sound of the front door opening echoed down the hallway, and Max's voice trilled, "Hello—"

Ryan smiled. "Max! Hello—"

"Merry Christmas! Happy end of semester!" Max replied as he stepped out of the hall. He was wearing a pair of dark jeans and the ugliest knit sweater Ryan had ever seen. "What do you think of my duds?"

Everyone laughed. "Oh," Ryan said. "That is an *ugly* sweater!"

"I know! Isn't it marvelous?"

"Oh, it's something. Hey, where is Jake?"

Max pressed his lips tightly together. "Oh, I don't know. He'll be along, but he said he had something to do first. Between you, me and the rest of the room, I don't think we're going to make it much past New Year's."

Shelly clucked. "That's awful!"

"Nah," Max replied. "It's alright. I've been thinking about ending it for a while; I just thought it would be nasty to dump the poor guy right before Christmas. He's alright. He's fine; there's just no—spark anymore."

Everyone nodded gravely. Ryan spoke. "Seems like you've got it all figured out then."

"Sure do, Mister. Let's just say that quitting Jake might be my New Year's resolution. Out with the old and in with the new." He winked, and Ryan felt himself instantly blush. "But hey, enough about that." He produced a paper bag Ryan hadn't noticed before. "Feel like a G and T for old time's sake? Tastes like a Christmas tree, after all."

"Oh, yeah, that sounds awesome!"

"Anyone else?"

"I'll take one," Peter said.

"I'll wait for Shelly's cider," Steven replied.

Max nodded. "Alright. Shelly? You're waiting for cider?" She nodded. "Three it is then."

By eight o'clock several more guests had arrived. Ryan, Max and Peter were on their second drink, and Shelly began passing around mugs of mulled cider with rum. Jake arrived, looking as pleasant, harmless, and boring as ever. Ryan felt a little pang of guilt as he shook his hand and then gave him a light embrace. If Max really planned to end things in the new year, Ryan was pretty sure Jake wouldn't see it coming.

A few minutes later, while Jake and Max were engrossed in a conversation with Steven, Peter came up and gently grabbed Ryan's elbow. "Come outside with me?" he asked.

"Alright."

As they stood on the deck, Peter shivered. "So, I'm a little nervous all of a sudden," he said.

"About seeing Brandon?"

"Yeah. I thought I was gonna be fine—I'd get a little liquid courage in me, and it would all be alright."

"But it's—not working?"

"Nope."

Peter shuffled toward him, turned sideways, and pressed his shoulder against Ryan's chest. "We should probably huddle together for warmth."

Ryan laughed in surprise. "Oh, okay." He put his arm lightly around Peter's other shoulder. "I don't think this is really doing very much."

"No." He took a drag off his cigarette. "But it's making me feel better."

"Hmm. I'd bet Steven would really appreciate it if you asked *him* to keep you warm."

Peter shook his head. "I know why people keep asking me about Steven. I like him a lot, but not like that."

"Well—you should probably tell him then. Wouldn't you have liked it better if Brandon had been more straightforward with you?"

"Well, yeah. I'm gonna tell him. I guess it's like Max said—right before Christmas isn't the time."

"I guess not." Ryan stepped away.

Back inside, the party continued. Ryan had a cup of Shelly's delicious cider and then Max poured him a third gin and tonic. By nine o'clock he was already a little drunk, so when a pair of strong arms encircled him from behind, he jolted in surprise and the breath went out of him. The arms released, and he turned, catching his breath again.

Brandon stood in front of him, smiling. "Hey there, stranger! I feel like I haven't seen you all semester!"

"Brandon!" He cried, perhaps too exuberantly.

Steven—who'd been chatting with Ryan before this interruption— nodded curtly. "Brandon. I'll let you two catch up. I need a fresh drink."

Brandon nodded in return, then turned his attention to Ryan. "So, what's going on?"

"Oh—" he began. He had a sudden urge to tell Brandon all of it— about Caleb and Meredith and school and money. He was certain Brandon would listen patiently, nodding at just the right moments, and in the end, have something really profound to say that would make all of Ryan's troubles seem a lot less troubling. This wasn't the moment though; there were too many other people around. "A lot," he continued. "Too much to tell you right now. It's been—"

Brandon nodded slowly. "I think I know some of it."

"You do?"

He laughed. "Don't look so scared. If you're referring to your situation with Caleb—come on. They were my friends first, of course I know. But we'll talk about that later. You're right, it's too much for tonight." He shook his head, slowly. "My what a long way you've come."

"What do you mean?"

"Since that night we drove up the canyon. Remember? You didn't think you were very *fun*. You weren't interested in taking risks. You were—"

"I was boring; I get it. This probably isn't the time to have *this* conversation either."

"Probably not. Let's just enjoy the party. Come on. I need a drink."

As they walked back toward the kitchen, Peter spotted them and came over slowly, intercepting them by the dining table. "Brandon," he said. "Hello."

Brandon smiled—a real, warm, honest smile. "Hey Peter. How's it going."

"It's alright. And you?"

"I'm good. Are you—enjoying the party?"

Peter swayed slightly on his feet and then giggled loudly in his deep baritone. "Yeah, I am. I'm a little—getting kinda drunk. I deserve it though. We all do, right? After the semester?"

Brandon laid his hand on Peter's shoulder. "You sure do, buddy. Hey. Do you want to clear the air?"

Peter looked confused for a moment. "Do I wanna clear the air?" Then his brain—a little sluggish from the alcohol—caught up. "Oh, about that morning after Halloween? Oh yeah, whatever."

"No, it's not whatever. I wasn't honest with you and for that I'm very sorry. I just wanted to, you know, let you down easy. I was hoping maybe you'd just move on without us having to discuss—"

Peter scowled. "You don't have to rub my nose in it, Brandon. I said it's whatever. I'm good." The expression on his face didn't agree, however.

Ryan took Peter's arm. "Excuse us, will you?"

"Sure," Brandon replied.

He led Peter across the room. "Hey, what's going on? Don't let him get to you."

Steven appeared beside them. "Yeah, what's going on?" he asked.

Peter rolled his eyes and leaned against a wall. "I'm fine. Sorry. I really am." Steven tried to wrap his arms around him, but Peter squirmed clumsily away. Instead, he placed his hands on Ryan's shoulders and, looking him directly in the eye he said, "I'm fine."

"Ouch," Steven said, quietly.

Ryan grasped Peter's wrists and lifted them off, letting his hands fall to his side. He looked at Steven, pleading with his eyes. "I need to run to the bathroom," he said. "Steven, stay here with him, won't you?"

"I guess—" Steven responded.

Ryan slowed his drinking slightly and did his best to mingle. He tried on numerous occasions to engage Max in conversation, but Jake was extremely demanding of his soon-to-be-ex boyfriend's attention, and it was difficult for Ryan to get a word in edgewise. Max kept flashing him apologetic looks as if to say he'd get away as soon as he could. Shelly remained in high spirits—a number of girls from the LGBT office gathered around her as she held court. Even Peter mellowed a bit and warmed up to Steven, who seemed relieved.

Sometime after eleven, Brandon asked Ryan to step out for a cigarette. After lighting up, Brandon smiled and said, "We'll have to do a better job of seeing each other in the new year."

Ryan nodded his agreement. "Yeah. I mean, I'm surprised actually. Isn't it going to be hard for you—being friends with Caleb and all? He's probably not going to like you spending time with me."

Brandon shrugged. "I've sort of moved on from Caleb and Tom, if I'm being perfectly honest."

"Oh? Why is that?"

"You know, people drift."

The front door opened and Peter stepped out onto the deck. "Oh," he said, frowning. "Sorry." He turned to walk back inside.

"Hey!" Brandon called.

"Hey, what?"

Brandon scowled. "You *can* come out here you know. If we're going to be friends you're going to have to occupy the same space as me at some point. And also, you're going to have to stop acting like a child."

"Oh," Peter laughed. "Oh, okay. I was gonna—never mind." He turned and walked inside.

Ryan frowned and extinguished his cigarette. "That was a little harsh, don't you think?"

"What? Now you're against me too?"

"I didn't say that. I just think—he's drunk, you know?"

"We're *all* drunk, Ryan."

"I'd better go check on him."

"Ryan—"

He didn't wait though. He walked back into the house. First, he saw Max and Jake, standing close and talking softly outside the bathroom door. Jake was touching Max's arm, caressing it lightly up and down. Ryan shuddered a little. He looked around for Peter. A cluster of partygoers huddled on the other side of the peninsula, but Peter wasn't with them. He looked to the right and found him standing alone in the kitchen. Ryan walked forward and rested a hand on his shoulder before asking, "Hey, are you alright? I think Brandon being here was a bad idea after all."

"I'm fine," Peter said, laying his forehead against Ryan's chest. "I told you I'm fine."

"Aw, Peter, it really *is* going to be alright. You're going to find someone else—someone better. I know it doesn't seem like it right now but—"

The front door opened and Brandon came back inside. "Hey guys—" he began.

At the sound of Brandon's voice, Peter lifted his head off of Ryan's chest. He looked Ryan directly in the eye, and his gaze held a glint of danger. By the time Ryan understood what was about to happen, it was too late.

Suddenly, Peter was kissing him with an energy that was at once clumsy and savage. Ryan pushed away, shocked. This wasn't right. "What are you—" he began to say.

Then he looked over Peter's shoulder. He saw Max and Jake, still standing close. Max leaned in and kissed him softly, inviting more. Jake responded, tilting his head and welcoming him in.

Something snapped in him then. Enough was enough. Didn't he deserve happiness? Hadn't he earned it? The year was ending—the most turbulent, horrible year of his life. He'd survived a car crash, an eviction, and the death of his best friend. He'd suffered heartbreak on top of heartbreak and more humiliation than anyone should ever be asked to endure. Now there was this boy standing in front of him, hurting, pleading for love. Who was he to withhold it? Weren't they the same? In that moment, he didn't care at all about burning bridges. He couldn't even begin to consider the consequences of the choice he was getting ready to make. Though he hadn't expected it to come in the form of Peter, the boy standing in front of him was offering everything he'd been wanting for so long.

It's what he deserved.

He looked at Peter, seeing him differently. He forgot the acned face and the thin hair. He saw only a kindred spirit offering him the validation and love he wanted more than anything on earth. He leaned in and initiated a second kiss. He took it slowly—inviting Peter in as Max had just invited Jake. Peter's body relaxed and he responded. They melted together for what could only have been seconds but felt like hours.

He lost himself in the twisting, turning of tongues.

A clatter from beyond the peninsula brought him back to reality. He stepped away and looked toward the sound. Everyone was staring, even Jake and Max. Steven stood in the middle of the crowd, shaking softly. His hands were open, and a formerly full cup of cider sat overturned at his feet, its contents soaking into the dirty, cream-colored carpet.

Ryan pushed away from Peter and swallowed hard. "Steven—" he said softly into the now silent room.

Steven responded with an unintelligible, guttural sound, and fled for the front door. Ryan looked toward Max, who was regarding him with an unexpected expression of contempt.

"Max—" Ryan said, his voice quavering.

Max shook his head slowly. "No, Mister. No. You don't get to be the victim. Not this time." He retrieved his coat and disappeared down the hallway after Steven.

Peter looked at Ryan. "Wow," he said. "That was—"

Ryan cut him off, turning his eyes down to the floor. "I think it's time for you to go home now, Peter."

"But I—"

Brandon stepped forward. "Come on, Peter. I'll walk you."

"I'm not going *anywhere* with you!"

"Yes you are. Come on." Brandon's voice was calm. He grabbed Peter's arm lightly and Peter twisted violently in protest. Brandon held him firmly and in a few seconds he became far more pliable. A moment later, they were gone.

Much of the room still stared as Ryan walked slowly out of the kitchen to his bedroom door. He slipped quickly inside and closed it behind him. Then he collapsed onto the bed as a deluge of tears burst from his eyes.

Later, when the sounds of the party died down beyond the bedroom door, Ryan decided it was safe to emerge. He pulled on a jacket and crept quietly through the empty apartment, down the hall past the kitchen to the front door. Passing by Steven's room he paused for a minute. There was a soft yellow glow spilling out beneath the door and he could hear muffled voices on the other side. He thought about knocking—about apologizing. Instead, he turned away and stepped out onto the deck. He sat down hard and lit a cigarette.

A few minutes later the front door opened, and Max stepped into the night. He appraised Ryan for a moment and then said, "You're smoking, too?"

Ryan was numb to the disappointment in his friend's voice. He shrugged absently. "Wouldn't you, if you were me?"

"I don't know, because I'm beginning to think I don't really know who you are."

He laughed. "Sure you do. I'm the same me I've always been. The same, pathetic, unloveable, worthless—"

"No, Mister. You weren't pathetic, unloveable, *or* worthless. You were great. You were special, unique and talented. But now look at you. I don't know why you changed. I can't believe you did that tonight."

"Okay, Max. I don't need the lecture."

"Apparently you do. Has it been that long since Valentine's Day? Have you forgotten how you felt when you saw Brandon laying on top of Darren—how humiliated you were? How could you do that to Steven?"

"Peter isn't interested in Steven—"

"And *Darren* wasn't interested in *you*! Steven is probably the best friend you ever had. He's been with you through thick and thin. God! He'd probably *die* for you. You know how insecure he is about this kind of stuff. What you did in there tonight? You'll be lucky if he *ever* forgives you."

Ryan stood, suddenly angry. "Oh yeah? And what about me? Hmm? I fucked up, I'll admit it. But you're not exactly blameless in this yourself, Max."

"What the hell are you talking about?"

"Oh, you know very well. What was that tonight, then—dangling that carrot? Oh, you're going to break up with Jake in the new year. Oh, winking and telling me it's time to make room for something new. You know very well how I feel about you, and then I had to look over and see you kissing him. It sure didn't look like the kind of kiss you give someone you're about to break up with."

"Okay, well, I haven't completely decided, alright?"

"So how am I supposed to feel? Steven's not the only one who is insecure. Do you know how long I've been hurting—suffering? I can't remember the last time I was really happy for more than about five minutes! So, don't you dare make me out to be some horrible monster when really you're not far behind."

Max shook his head. "Okay. I'm going to let you have that. I'm also going to go now. Sounds like it's best if we don't see each other for a while."

"Great. Join the list."

Max walked slowly forward and wrapped his arms carefully around Ryan and pulled him into a tight, lingering embrace. When he let go there were tears in his eyes. "I really hope you find yourself, Mister. You don't have to be this—ugly thing. I'll see you." He turned and walked down the stairs to the parking lot below.

Ryan walked back into the apartment. The light in Steven's room had been extinguished, but he paused anyways. After a couple deep breaths, he knocked. Seconds went by without a response, so he knocked again and called, softly. "Steven? Steven, I know you were just awake." Still, there was no answer. He knocked one last time and then counted slowly to thirty in his head.

Finally, he gave up and went to bed.

~*~

The following morning Steven was already gone by the time Ryan got out of bed. After three unanswered phone calls, Ryan settled down to the idea that things were likely going to remain unresolved until after Steven returned from the holidays. He sat at the dining table and worked his way through half a pot of coffee by the time Shelly joined him.

"Good morning," she said. "I think I had too much cider last night."

He sighed. "I don't feel so great myself. I'm surprised you're talking to me. It seems like no one else is."

She grabbed a mug from the pantry and filled it before sitting across from him. "I mean, that was like, pretty shitty of you. I'd be pissed if someone pulled that on me."

"I just wasn't thinking. I got caught up in myself, and I reacted. Steven won't answer my phone calls though, so I can't even apologize."

"Well, did you leave a message?"

"No, I think he needs to hear me say it when we can talk about it."

She nodded. "Yeah, okay. Well, it'll probably blow over, right?"

"Maybe. So, when are you leaving? When is your flight?"

"I'm flying out Friday—Christmas Eve."

"Oh?"

"Yeah, but early. Like, nine in the morning. I'll be back the twenty-ninth. I guess I didn't even ask you, can you take care of Mars while I'm gone?"

"Of course. I guess you're pretty excited?"

"Aw, man, Ryan! I've come a long way with my mom. This is like, a really big deal. I haven't been home for Christmas in Chicago since—God it's been a long time."

"Well, I'm happy for you." He was quiet for a moment. "Hey, Shelly?"

"Yeah?"

"Thanks for being nice to me this morning. I, uh—it's been a rough week."

"We all fuck up, Ryan. We all fuck up."

Throughout the following week, Ryan distracted himself from his sudden and devastating loss of friends by working extra shifts. So many people were traveling for the holidays he was able to nearly double his hours for the week. He tried Steven on Monday, Tuesday, and Wednesday, but still didn't get an answer. He comforted himself with the knowledge that eventually Steven would have to come home, and they'd sort it out then.

Friday morning—Christmas Eve—Ryan opened the pool. As he rushed, half asleep out of the house at 4:45 he checked for the eighth or ninth time to make sure he'd put clothes for the evening in his messenger bag. He wasn't planning on returning home until after dinner with his family. The jeans and sweater were there, just as they'd been the previous times he'd looked, so he walked out the door hoping the morning would go by quickly.

It did. In fact, the place was dead even through the normal lunch hour rush. With the holiday at hand, the city's swimmers had better things to do. Just after one-thirty he wished everyone a Merry Christmas and headed to his parents' house.

Once he settled in, he found that for the first time all season it really *felt* like Christmas. His brother and sister buzzed around the house in excited anticipation as his parents prepared a traditional feast of roast beef, au jus, and scalloped potatoes. Bing Crosby, Ella Fitzgerald and Amy Grant all took turns singing their renditions of Christmas classics through the CD changer in the living room, while the giant tree in the corner glittered and glistened with white lights and all of Ryan's favorite ornaments. For the briefest time, all of his troubles were absent from his mind—washed away by the magic of the day.

After dinner Ryan sat in the living room with his parents, sipping coffee. His eyes closed for a minute and he felt himself nodding off. He jolted his head up, surprised he didn't spill anything from the nearly full mug he held in his hand.

His mother was watching him, intently. "You're looking pretty tired," she said.

"I am pretty tired. This coffee isn't doing it. I *did* get up before five this morning."

"Maybe you should stay here tonight."

He laughed. "Mom, I only live seven blocks away. I'll be back in the morning."

"No, I know that. I just thought—it would be nice to have all of my kids under the same roof again. Even if it was just for a night."

He smiled sadly. The idea was awfully enticing. After everything that happened the idea of moving back home was more alluring than ever. He was sure all he'd have to do was suggest it, and his parents would welcome him back with open arms. He was about to tell her that he'd stay the night—that he'd stay forever.

Then he remembered Mars.

"I can't. I have to go home and take care of the dog." Guiltily he realized he should have stopped home after work. "Actually, shoot. I probably need to go now! The poor thing has been inside all day. I completely forgot no one else was home."

"Oh! Yeah, you'd better. Alright." She stood and embraced him as he headed toward the door. "Merry Christmas. Love you."

"Love you too. Merry Christmas." He said goodbye to his father, sister and brother, and then hurried out the door and back home.

When he reached the top of the steps he could hear Mars barking through the door. He groaned inwardly—how could he have been so stupid? The poor thing was probably dying to relieve himself.

He opened the door and called "Mars! Come here, boy! Mars! Let's go out!" But Mars kept barking. He walked slowly into the apartment, confused. "Mars? Come here, boy." Still, the dog didn't come.

The moment he stepped from the hallway into the kitchen he knew something was wrong. The Christmas tree was turned on and his nose filled with the sharp scent of fresh vomit. He caught his breath for a moment as the dog continued to yap and bark.

When he stepped around the peninsula, he saw her—laying on her side, curled into a fetal position in front of the tree. The dog stood beside her, still yapping and yelling. Mars turned his face up toward Ryan—eyes pleading for him to do something. He looked at her again, laying there. Her eyes were closed, but her mouth was open, and a large pool of vomit spread out in front of her. He felt a painful shot of adrenaline sear its way through his veins as he bounded forward.

"Shelly!" he cried, shaking her to check for consciousness. She didn't respond so he rolled her quickly onto her back and placed his face close to her nose and mouth, listening—pleading to feel her breath against his cheek. It was all he could do to keep from recoiling at the smell of the vomit. Her skin was cold and pale, and he thought immediately of Darren. This couldn't be happening to him again. Not again! Once in a lifetime was enough—he couldn't handle it twice in a year. He began to cry hot tears that burned as they rolled down his cheeks.

Then he saw her chest rise ever so slightly, and he let out the longest exhale of his life. Another shot of adrenaline scorched its way through him, and he turned her back over onto her side. Leaping up onto his feet he sprinted into the bedroom for his phone. He pulled it from the base, nearly ripping the entire unit off the desk, and dialed 9-1-1.

Half an hour later the paramedics had come and gone. On the way out the door, they told him they were hopeful—he'd gotten home just in time. He could call the hospital later or even come by to see her in the morning. Some kind of pills, they said, judging by the white fragments they observed in the vomit. The doctors would know more later.

He sat on the floor then, scrubbing at the stain she'd left and sobbing the whole time. Mars whimpered and laid down next to him. This was the last straw. If she didn't make it—hell, even if she did—he'd officially lost everyone. Merry Christmas and a Happy New Year.

His metamorphosis was complete, and it left him completely alone.

PART THREE:

LOVE

Ryan was nervous about Shelly coming home; he wasn't sure what to say to her. He'd visited twice at the hospital during her mandatory seventy-two-hour observation, but those visits had been brief. He couldn't stand the sight of the IV in her arm or the horrible, sterile smell of the place. Also, her presence left him quick to anger. Although he felt a measure of compassion, he also suffered from a low-simmering rage born of righteous indignation. How could she have put him in that position—finding her? After only a few minutes of her company, he could feel the fury working its way into his facial expressions and the tone of his voice when he spoke.

At one point during his second visit, he worked up the courage to ask her why she'd done it. She explained through an eruption of tears that at the last minute her mother rescinded the Christmas invitation. He understood the impulse, and it dampened his fury, but only slightly. Objectively, he was able to imagine her state of mind; surely the plan to kill herself had been an impulse, not something she'd been plotting.

Certainly, she hadn't been thinking of *him* when she swallowed an entire bottle of pills. In her desperation, the consequences of her actions were of no importance.

When he stopped to think about it, he realized her suicide attempt wasn't very different from sleeping with Caleb or kissing Peter. All three actions shared a common thread.

They were reckless and stupid.

Even understanding all of this, his anger remained. When she called the Monday after Christmas to tell him she was going into a two-week program at the mental health center, he had to fight to keep the excitement out of his voice. As calmly as he could, he told her that he thought it was a great idea and he hoped she'd learn a lot. He hoped she would find some peace with her mother and begin to heal.

He didn't say it out loud, but he hoped she'd stay there forever.

The two weeks passed quickly, however. Now it was January tenth, and the weather was unusually warm. As he drove Shelly's SUV slowly toward the south end of town, the dash displayed the temperature at sixty-two. He rolled down the windows a bit to enjoy the warm air. In another four hours, it would be dark, and the temperature would drop again. Tomorrow winter would return and the day's little vernal gift would be all but forgotten. Fresh air filled the cab and lifted his spirits.

He needed the lift. He was almost there.

A few minutes later when he pulled up to the front doors of the mental health center, she was already waiting with her small bag and a bright smile. She pulled open the passenger door and lifted herself in. "Hey," she said. "Thanks for coming to get me."

He pressed his lips tightly together and started the drive back to The Garden. "Yeah, anytime."

She laughed. "Better not be anytime. That was like—oh man, that was an experience!" She waited for a response that didn't come. "Hey, um, Ryan?"

"Yeah?"

"Look I—I'm really sorry. I don't know if I said that before. I don't really think I wanted to die. I don't think—"

He cut her off. "Shelly. It's alright. You're still here, and every-thing is fine. It's water under the bridge, right?" He wished he meant it.

"Yeah okay. Hey, speaking of—"

"Yeah?"

"Have you heard from Steven?"

He shook his head slowly. "No. Have you?"

"He called once about a week ago. I guess you left him a message saying what happened."

"I did. Well, it's good to know he's getting my messages. I figure he's going to have to come back at some point. Classes start again two weeks from today so—"

"Right. I mean, he can't still be mad at you, can he?"

"I don't know, Shelly. I don't know."

~*~

Twenty minutes later Ryan's heart leaped as he pulled the SUV in-to the parking lot behind The Garden. Steven's sedan was parked in its usual spot. As he turned off the engine, he looked at Shelly with nervous excitement. "He's here!" he said.

"Oh, wow. Okay, well I can like, take Mars for a walk or some-thing if you think you need some time alone."

"No, no. That won't be necessary. We can talk in my room if we need to, or on the porch. I doubt he's got anything to say that you can't hear."

She nodded and opened the passenger door. "Alright then, let's go." She grabbed her bag and started walking swiftly across the park-ing lot to the stairs. Ryan locked the SUV and followed behind.

When they reached the base of the stairs, they heard a clattering of feet from up above. A tall, slender girl with stick-straight black hair appeared at the top, smiled, and skipped down the steps. Ryan and Shelly stepped aside to give her room.

At the bottom, she paused and clasped her hands excitedly in front of her chest. In a high, shrill voice she said, "Hi, I'm *Ella*." She appraised them for a moment then continued, in a sing-song, lilting tone. "You two must be Ryan and *Shelly*! I'm so excited to meet you, but actually, I have to run." She winked. "It's alright though. I'll be seeing a *lot* more of you. I think I'm *the one*!" She hopped twice and then danced off before they had a chance to respond.

Ryan looked at Shelly. "Who the hell is that?"

She laughed. "Ella, didn't you hear? Come on. Maybe the holidays turned Steven straight!"

Once inside the apartment, Shelly marched straight through to the kitchen calling excitedly for the dog, but Ryan froze outside Steven's closed bedroom door. A bundle of flat-packed moving boxes rested against the wall of the hallway. He knocked and said, "Steven? Are you in there?"

From the other side, he heard footsteps. The door opened slowly, and then Steven was standing in front of him. Their eyes met for a moment, and Steven frowned before casting his gaze down toward his feet. "Hey," he said.

"Hey—what's going on? You haven't returned any of my calls. I was getting worried—"

"Were you? Sorry to have worried you."

"Of course I was! Steven, I wanted to say I'm sorry—to tell you in person. I—do you want to talk about this somewhere other than in your doorway?"

"No, not really. To be honest, I don't want to talk about it at all. I have a lot to do right now."

"A lot to do? Like what? Why do you have moving boxes? And who was that girl?"

Steven looked up at Ryan again. His eyes were wet and slightly red. "Oh, Ella? She's your new roommate."

Ryan's blood turned to ice, and he shivered. He must have misheard. For one short instant when he first saw the boxes he thought maybe that was the case, but he dismissed the idea for its absurdity. Steven couldn't possibly leave. They were like brothers. Like Max said, they'd been through so much together. The weight of Steven's gaze was crushing him now, so he did the only thing he *could* do. He laughed. "That's a funny joke."

"I'm not joking."

"But—you can't go. We have a *lease*."

"Yes, and I am exercising my right to sublet."

"Well, where are you—where will you live?"

"I found a one bedroom. The former tenant is studying abroad this semester, so I'm subletting from him."

"Is this all because of that stupid kiss? Steven! I was drunk, and I was hurting and he—Peter started that whole thing. I think he was trying to get back at Brandon and—"

"Enough!" Steven shouted. He took a few moments to breathe before continuing more calmly. "Enough Ryan. If you must know, yeah. That's a part of it—not all, but a part."

"Steven, I love you! You're like—like family to me. You can't leave me. I've lost everyone. Max is gone. Meredith is gone—I didn't even tell you about that yet. No more Caleb or Tom. I definitely can't see Peter anymore—"

Steven shook his head. "I love you too, Ryan. I might even go so far as to say it's unconditional. That's the really shitty part, you know? That's the part that makes this so hard. Whether Peter started it or not, you finished it. You did *the worst* thing you could do to me. Why? Because you were in pain? The Ryan Gregori I know wouldn't act that way—he'd bear it. He wouldn't bring everyone else down with him. But that's not what you did. Instead, you ruined our friend-ship, and I bet it's not even for the reason you think."

"Steven—"

"I don't really care about Peter that much. I'd figured out he was-n't interested in me. But it's the concept. It's the fact that you knew how I felt and you still did what you did. It's that you didn't care how your actions would affect me."

"I wasn't thinking about *any* of that at the time."

"Right! People make mistakes, Ryan! But that's not an excuse. If you didn't care this time, why should I believe you'll make a better choice the next time? This is my last semester of college. I need to start applying for jobs. I need to make sure I excel in my courses. I can't be—bogged down in all this *shit*! And Shelly trying to kill her-self like that was the final straw. Between the two of you, this house is too volatile."

"Oh, come on, Steven. Nothing like this is ever going to happen again."

Steven shook his head firmly. He was weeping now—openly. "And on top of it all, when I look at you—I'm just so fucking sad. I've already forgiven you. I forgave you right away but I just—I love you, Ryan, but I can't stand the sight of you. I can't stand what you've be-come. That love and that hate all mixed up together? That's got to be the most toxic thing on earth."

"Steven, please. I'm *begging* you! Don't go! We don't know that girl—that *Ella*. And besides, I *need* you. I won't bog you down. I promise. Please—"

"Don't beg, Ryan. Please don't beg. I need this for me, alright? Lis-ten, if you care about me at all please just let it go. Let me go."

Ryan looked down at his hands. They were shaking violently, and he clenched them into fists in an effort to still them. Exhaling, he re-leased and was relieved when they hung motionless at his sides. Steven was right—he knew that. This apartment was volatile. *He* was volatile. In his grand metamorphosis something went wrong. He'd expected to emerge from his chrysalis a Monarch, but instead, he'd come out of the cocoon a hideous moth. But that was all last year. Now it was 2005. A new year meant a new beginning. His friends were gone, Steven being the last and most important of them all. If this is what Steven needed, giving it to him was the least Ryan could do. Perhaps one good deed couldn't counteract all the hurt he'd caused, but it was a start.

"Alright," he said. "Alright."

"Thank you."

"When are you going?"

"The apartment is ready. Hopefully tomorrow."

"Do you need help moving? Can I help you pack?"

"No, I don't think so. I think it's best if I do this on my own."

"Alright." He stepped forward and wrapped Steven in a light embrace, and his heart sank as he felt Steven's body stiffen and slightly recoil at his touch. He released him and put on his brightest smile. "Good luck, Steven. Bye for now."

"Goodbye, Ryan."

~*~

Later that night Ryan sat out on the deck and lit a cigarette. As he'd suspected, a sharp chill was returning to the air. He inhaled and exhaled, blowing the smoke out slowly through the tiniest opening in his lips. He supposed it was about time to be done with cigarettes. They'd lost their appeal now that Caleb and Meredith were gone. As he shivered lightly in the breeze, he marveled at the memory of the day's warmth. He wondered if it had ever been so warm in January.

Suddenly he remembered the date. Last year—a year ago today. He and Darren had needed a bottle of vanilla vodka to take to that stupid party in Greeley. He remembered driving down Elizabeth Street—not too far from home—and then a flash of white in the intersection and the terrifying jolt of impact. That's when everything started. That was the beginning of what Meredith had liked to call *the education of Ryan Gregori*. He laughed to himself. Wasn't it more like, the *ruination* of Ryan Gregori?

It all seemed like a lifetime ago. Where was that meek, naïve kid now—the one who wrote songs in his little red bedroom when he was lonely? Where was the boy who scarcely touched alcohol and thought that smoking was a disgusting, senseless blight on society? Where had the Ryan Gregori gone that loved Darren Henderson—that was willing to wait until the ends of the earth for him to wake up and love him back? He used to think of love as something holy and pure—something to be earned. He supposed he hadn't done anything to earn it in a while because recently he'd been too busy simply trying to take it.

His mind drifted back to his conversation with Alice after Thanksgiving. She was right, he knew—he needed to learn to love himself before he could ever hope to find any sort of lasting relationship. But that in and of itself was a sort of cruel joke right now, wasn't it? How was he supposed to love this careless, disgusting thing he'd become when he hadn't even loved the pure, innocent kid he'd formerly been?

He had an overwhelming urge to be in the company of others, even though he knew it was absolutely the wrong thing to do right now. How could he learn to be alone if he wouldn't allow himself to be—*alone*? Ultimately, the craving for human contact and an escape from his own dismal thoughts was too strong.

His cigarette had burned down to the filter, so he extinguished it and headed back inside. He paused by Steven's room, where the pile of flat packed boxes in the hallway had dwindled as they'd been con-

structed and filled. He raised his hand to knock on the closed bedroom door, but thought better of it in the end. With time, he was
confident their relationship could be repaired. There was no sense in
pushing it now, so he continued on to his own bedroom.

Brandon seemed like the answer to his current problem. He'd
have preferred to see Max, but that was another relationship that was
going to require time to mend. He picked up the phone and dialed,
hoping Brandon was in town.

On the third ring, Brandon picked up. "Hello?"

"Hey, it's Ryan."

Brandon laughed softly. "Or should we call you Hurricane Ryan?"

"That's not very funny."

"I think it's funny. So—what's up?"

"Are you busy? I um—I don't feel like being alone right now."

"Hmm, well—I'd say we could hang out, but I wouldn't want to
make the television jealous. We've been spending a lot of time together over the last week."

Ryan laughed. "You're an ass."

"I won't deny it. Do you want me to come get you?"

"Yes, please. God, you're a life saver."

"Don't thank me yet. I haven't even showered today. You might as
well throw on some sweats—it's going to be that kind of night."

"Ha! Alright. How soon do you think you'll be here?"

"Fifteen minutes."

"Alright, see you then!"

"Bye, Ryan."

True to his word, Brandon arrived about fifteen minutes later.
Ryan was glad he'd taken the suggestion to wear sweat pants seriously, because when he climbed into the passenger seat of the SUV,

Brandon was dressed in grey fleece bottoms and a tight, white under-shirt under a winter jacket.

Seeming to read his mind, Brandon nodded approval. "Good. I half expected you to come down in jeans and a sweater. I'd have made you go back up to change. We're going to sit on the couch with a bottle of rum, a bag of chips and the remote control."

"That's fine with me. God, I just needed to get out of here."

"Alright then," Brandon said. "Let's go." He guided the car out of the parking lot behind The Garden and headed west. "So," he asked. "Why don't you feel like being alone?"

"Oh, too many reasons to get into, I guess. Shelly is home from the hospital today, and I've got this sort of low-simmering anger about the whole thing. And then Steven, he's—"

Brandon waited for Ryan to continue. The pause stretched on, so finally, he said, "Uh oh. What happened?"

"He's moving out."

"Wow, you really torched your village the night of that party, didn't you?"

"And then I realized just a little while ago that today is the anniversary of the day my car got totaled and I lost my apartment—"

"Alright, alright. You sound like you might start crying and that's not exactly the kind of night I was planning on having." He laughed to lighten the mood. "So, let's forget about all that for now."

"Okay, I'll try. I'm just really glad you answered the phone. I wasn't sure if you—well, it seems like I've lost everyone else lately."

Brandon waved his hand dismissively. "Nah. I'm still here. What kind of movie do you think you want to watch?"

A few minutes later Brandon pulled into a small development of newly constructed townhouses—three stories each with a garage as the first floor. For every two units, a wide stoop rose from street level to adjoining front doors. "I'm this green one, up here," he said, reaching over his head to press a garage-door opener.

Ryan's eyes widened. "You live *here*?" he asked. "All by yourself? This rent must be exorbitant!"

Brandon chuckled as he guided the SUV into the garage, then pressed the button to close the door again. "Yeah, all by my lonesome. My parents bought the place my sophomore year. They figure after I'm done they'll rent it or maybe even sell it for a small return." He turned off the engine and climbed out.

At the back of the garage, Brandon led Ryan through a door and up a rear stairwell. At the top, they entered into a beautiful kitchen full of polished stone countertops and modern appliances.

"Wow," Ryan said, looking around in awe. "I'm embarrassed to have *ever* had you over at The Garden. My apartment has always felt a little slummy, but compared to this—"

"Nah, don't worry about it. I'm definitely a little spoiled living here, but it's not like it's actually mine. If I want to stay after I graduate—which I don't—they'll start charging me rent. My parents are intolerant of what they call *non-performing assets*. The only reason I live here for free right now is because I'm still in school. They figure the mortgage is better than paying my rent somewhere they're not going to get anything out of it."

Ryan nodded. "Still."

"So, the living room is straight ahead. Go have a seat; I'll bring in some stuff."

"Alright." Ryan walked through the kitchen, past a small open dining area, and into the living room. In the corner, a gas fireplace burned, ensconced in sandstone. The walls were painted a calming tan. The television sat in the middle of the front wall, flanked by two large paned windows looking out toward the street. He took a seat on the large, overstuffed couch and exhaled luxuriantly as he sank in.

Brandon reappeared a minute later with two pint glasses filled with dark liquid. "Rum and coke?" he asked, handing one to Ryan.

"Oh, sure. Thank you."

He disappeared again and returned with a bowl of chips, then sat heavily on the other side of the sofa. "So, I guess you like the place?"

"It's beautiful."

Brandon took a sip of his drink as he plucked the remote control off the coffee table. "Mmm. Delicious. Hey, you don't mind staying here tonight, do you? I think I might want a few of these."

"Oh, um. No. I have to work tomorrow afternoon. But if you could drop me off when you get up—"

"Of course. Now, how about a comedy? I think that new Sandra Bullock movie is on HBO."

It was easy at first for Ryan to put his present troubles out of his mind. The movie was a romantic comedy, and despite his inherent loneliness, he laughed and smiled and teared up a little at the end. Meanwhile, Brandon proved to be an attentive and courteous host—refilling his glass several times over. It was only when the credits started to roll—when the movie's happy ending stood out in stark contrast to his own dismal situation—that he felt the weight of his now-familiar depression begin to bear down on him with a vengeance.

"Feel like a cigarette?" Brandon asked. "I've got a balcony off the kitchen."

Ryan smiled sadly. "Yeah, sure." He stood and followed Brandon back through the kitchen and then out a little door he hadn't noticed before. The night had become extraordinarily cold given the warmth earlier. The wind had picked up, and he struggled to light his cigarette.

"Here," Brandon said. He cupped his hands to better block the wind and Ryan was able to keep the flame lit on the lighter long enough for the tobacco to take.

"Thanks," Ryan said.

"I'm a little drunk. Fuck it's cold."

"Yeah. I knew the weather was going to change, but I didn't expect this."

"Are you feeling any better?"

"Not really. I was for a minute but—"

"Alright. So, what's the core of it?"

"I've alienated everyone—all the important people in my life. Meredith isn't ever going to talk to me again. I kind of, well—it was about money, and about Caleb. I wasn't honest with her, and she doesn't do second chances. And then that stupid incident with Peter at the party. I can't forgive myself for that. I hurt Steven—really badly. It was probably even worse than that time last Valentine's Day when you and Darren—" he stopped. "I'm sorry, I shouldn't bring that up right now. I shouldn't bring *him* up. It's the last thing I need."

Brandon laughed as he exhaled. The wind gusted and tore the pale blue smoke from his lips, spinning it upward into the night. "So, why did you do it? Why'd you kiss Peter that night?"

Ryan bristled. "I didn't. He kissed me."

"Ha! Oh, come on Ryan, do you want to talk about it, or do you want to make excuses? We can go inside and put on another movie if you'd like. But if you want to get it out you're going to have to be honest. I *know* he started it—I was right there. But that second kiss? The one that mattered? That was all you, buddy."

"Ugh. I don't know, Brandon. At the time, I convinced myself that I deserved it. But I suppose I did it for the same reason Peter did. He was just trying to, I don't know—make you jealous? Over his shoulder I saw Max kissing Jake—like, really kissing him. Just a little while before that Max had been telling me they were going to split up. He led me to believe that maybe we'd finally have our chance. And when I saw him—it wasn't an empty kiss they were sharing. I guess I just snapped. I wanted him to see, and I wanted him to—"

"To hurt?" Brandon extinguished his cigarette in a small bucket of sand. "Are you finished with that?"

"Oh, yeah." Ryan handed him the cigarette and Brandon pushed it down into the sand next to his own.

"Let's go inside."

"Okay."

Ryan took his seat back on the couch while Brandon picked up their empty glasses. "Hold that thought, okay? I'm going to fill these one more time."

His head felt heavy, and he already knew he was going to be at least a little hung over in the morning. "Alright. Last one."

"Last one," Brandon assured him.

Ryan closed his eyes for a moment. He heard a soft click, and then music started playing—an atmospheric, instrumental track with plenty of ambient pops and beats. He opened his eyes again just as Brandon was taking his seat next to him.

"I hope you don't mind." Brandon said. "I thought we'd leave the TV off now. This is a radio program called 'Echoes.' Sometimes Darren and I would listen to it at night. When you mentioned him, I started to feel a little—nostalgic."

Ryan was powerless to stop a short burst of tears from escaping the corners of his eyes. He threw his hands in the air and looked up at the ceiling while he laughed in exasperation. "Twist the *fucking* knife, why don't you?"

"Ryan?" Brandon asked, startled. "What is it? Do you want me to turn it off? I thought we'd moved past—"

"No, no. It's fine. Leave it. This probably won't be hard for you to believe, but Darren and I *also* used to listen to this program at night. I always thought it was sort of our thing, but clearly—"

"Ah." Brandon frowned. "That's what I thought too. He was full of surprises, wasn't he?"

"He sure was."

After a short, contemplative silence, Brandon spoke. He seemed to choose his words carefully. "So, while we're being honest, I have something to tell you."

"Oh great." Ryan laughed again.

"Well, I never wanted to before—not after we became friends. But now I think in a lot of ways you and I are more similar than we've ever been. It's about that Valentine's party."

"No, you don't have to explain. I said I shouldn't have brought it up."

"No, I *do* need to explain. See, everything I did that night?" He stopped for a moment to breathe, then took a long sip of his drink. "I did all of that on purpose. I knew exactly how you felt about Darren and I was worried that he felt the same way. I was so tired of feeling like I was just a hookup—tired of only seeing him late at night. Part of it was that I wanted to hurt you. I wanted to claim him publicly so that maybe you'd just, I don't know—go away."

Ryan wasn't surprised. He'd suspected as much at the time. Numbly he said, "I see."

"But more than that I just wanted *something* to happen. I figured I didn't really have anything to lose. Either I was going to get my way, or I wasn't. But I knew that no matter what, after that night everything was going to be different."

"And it almost worked out for you."

Brandon laughed. "Yeah, almost. I'm sorry, Ryan. I didn't know you then. Clearly, I was acting selfishly. Don't get me wrong, I live my life by the mantra that you've always got to look out for number one, but there *are* boundaries, and in this case, I crossed one."

"It's alright. Given my last few weeks, it would be pretty hypocritical of me to tell you to fuck off and storm out into the cold. That's why you're telling me, right?"

"You don't have to phrase it exactly like that, but yeah. I figure maybe now that you've been on the other side of it—maybe you understand?"

"Yeah, unfortunately, I think I do."

"So, still friends then?"

The question was ludicrous. Brandon was the only real friend that Ryan had left. The revelation hurt him, sure, but if it was a question of having Brandon or having no one at all, of course he was going to choose Brandon. Anyways, he assured himself, that was a long time ago. It was before they knew each other. Brandon would never do something like that to him now. He looked across the couch and saw him waiting, entirely emotionally exposed.

He really was a beautiful man, and he was being so kind. Ryan felt the sudden heat of attraction—the kind that usually made him feel guilty. He chose not to suppress it. Instead, he smiled as brightly as he could manage and said. "Of course."

Brandon sighed audibly, turning his thin, beautiful lips into an enormous grin. "Thanks. Maybe we shouldn't have had these last drinks."

"No." Ryan agreed. He was admiring the line of Brandon's jaw now, and considering the tight, compact shape of his muscled chest underneath his white shirt. The heat from the fire reached across the room, warming him. He felt safe here with Brandon. He wondered suddenly why he'd wasted all that time on Caleb when Brandon had been right in front of him the whole time. After all, they were probably a perfect match. Darren had loved them both, so why shouldn't they love each other?

After they had finished the drinks, Brandon disappeared up to the third floor. He returned a minute later with a heavy blanket and a pillow. "Will the couch be alright?"

"Oh, yes," Ryan said. He thought—without the least bit of shame—he'd prefer the bed, but he kept quiet. He'd bide his time and wait for a signal. Brandon *had* suggested they spend more time together in the new year. Tonight wasn't the night to try anything anyways—too much rum and too many tears might spoil it.

He thought suddenly of Peter and was aware of his own hypocrisy. Biding his time? Waiting? These were exactly the things he'd tried to convince Peter not to do. Tonight definitely wasn't the night though—he needed to think about this a little more, but he promised himself he wouldn't wait too long. He couldn't waste another year like he'd done with Darren.

Brandon looked at him oddly. "What are you thinking about?"

"Oh," he laughed. "Nothing. Just a little drunk and a little tired."

"Alright," Brandon said. "Well, if you need anything, I'll be right upstairs."

"Okay."

"Seriously—anything."

"Okay." He stretched out on the sofa and pulled the blanket up to his neck. "Goodnight."

Brandon lingered a moment as if he had something else to say. Perhaps thinking better of it he simply smiled and said, "Goodnight."

CHAPTER 19

By the time Ryan got home the following morning, Steven was already gone. Walking down the hall from the front door to the kitchen, he paused to look into the vacant bedroom. A patch of watery light filtered in through the window and illuminated a swath of empty, carpeted floor. After lingering a moment longer, he sighed—exhaling the too-familiar pain of loss—and wandered into the kitchen.

Shelly was sitting at the dining table, and she greeted him with a sad smile. "Hard to believe he's gone, right?"

He returned the smile but knew his eyes were cold. "Yeah, I don't know what I'm going to do without him."

"Maybe you should've thought about that before you kissed Peter." She laughed to lighten the mood. "It's alright. We'll look out for each other, won't we?"

He laughed as well—laughed to keep himself from screaming. Didn't she know this was her fault too? If she hadn't swallowed all those pills, maybe Steven would still be here. He wanted to yell—to make her understand how much damage she'd done. Couldn't she at least have had the decency to try to kill herself somewhere else? He shuddered to think about what might have happened if he'd come home later and found her dead. That would have been his final straw—his ultimate undoing.

But he had to get to work. This wasn't the time for that conversation. He swallowed his anger and said, "Yeah, we'll look out for each other. Any idea when Ella is moving in?"

"Um, Steven said this weekend, I think."

"Alright. I have to get in the shower."

The weekend came and so did Ella, with more boxes than Ryan thought she could possibly fit into the vacant bedroom. She annoyed him immediately—flitting up and down the stairs, in and out of the apartment with unbridled joy. She was thrilled beyond belief. Since her sophomore year in high school, she'd been militantly vegetarian with a few forays into becoming all-out vegan. "This is just so *serendipitous!*" she told them, at least seventeen times. "The Garden is totally my favorite restaurant *ever!*"

Sometime after unloading her car for the third time, she was joined by her boyfriend, Brett. A lean, heavily muscled varsity Lacrosse player, Brett communicated in short monotone bursts of three to five words at a time. He seemed to be Ella's foil in every way, and Ryan wondered how the relationship worked. He was tall while she was short. He was strong while she was frail. She could spend all day talking about nothing and he just plain had nothing to talk about. At one point Ryan tried to make conversation—small talk—asking if Brett was ready for the upcoming semester. The only response he received was a blank stare, as if Brett didn't understand the question.

In the end, however, Ella turned out to be a fairly innocuous roommate. Once the semester started, she kept mostly to herself. She cleaned her dishes and took out the trash. She spent at least three nights a week at Brett's, and the evenings she was at home she stayed mostly in her bedroom studying. She was no Steven, but she would do for now, Ryan supposed.

~*~

On the last Thursday in January Ryan returned home from work to find Peter waiting in his bedroom. He was dressed nicely in a striped blue button up and dark jeans. His hair was a bit longer, and he'd used some type of product to spike it lightly in the middle.

"Sorry," Peter said with an apologetic smile. "I didn't mean to surprise you. Shelly let me in."

"Oh. How long have you been here?" Ryan asked. "You could've waited in the living room where it's more comfortable."

"Just a few minutes. I was gonna call, but I thought maybe it'd be better to see you in person."

Ryan pressed his lips tightly together and reached with his left hand to grasp the thumb ring hanging from his neck. Peter moved over slightly to make more room on the bed, but Ryan took a seat in his computer chair. He looked at Peter for a long moment and then said, "So, what's up?"

"Well, I dunno. You tell me."

"I guess I don't know either. I've just been keeping my head down. I'm trying to make a little more of a commitment to my classwork this semester."

"Ah, I was kinda wondering why I hadn't heard from you."

Ryan smiled sadly. "Yeah—sorry. I guess you probably know about Steven."

"Yeah." Peter nodded. "I was gonna call him too; I just don't know what to say."

"Just start with the word *sorry*." His voice was gentle. "That's what I did."

"Did it work?"

He laughed. "Well, he still left, but yeah. I think it worked."

"And I was sorry to hear about Shelly, too. That must've been terrible for you—coming home and finding that."

"I'm trying not to think about it too much."

Peter was quiet for almost a full minute. When he spoke again, he seemed to pick his words cautiously. "So, the real reason I wanted to come by is because I was wondering why you didn't call or anything after that party. I was hoping maybe I'd hear from you during the break or—something."

Ryan shook his head. "I'm sorry—I just didn't even think of it. Between Shelly's situation and Steven moving out and getting ready for the semester—"

"I understand. It's only—I dunno. That kiss was real, wasn't it? Not the first one—I know why I did that. I was drunk, and I was trying to get Brandon to—"

"Yeah." Ryan cut him off. "I know." He wasn't sure how to proceed now. He turned his thoughts back to the moment of the kiss. Ultimately, his motivation had been the same as Peter's—he wanted to get a reaction out of Max. But in that instant, he'd justified it differently. He'd seen Peter as another version of himself—a lonely boy dying of a thirst that only love and validation could quench. And he'd be lying to himself if he said he didn't feel anything. For all the damage it had done, it was a *very* good kiss.

So he wondered why, in the aftermath, he'd forgotten how it felt. Why hadn't he considered Peter as a potential partner for real and not just a prop to prove a point? He looked at him—really appraising him as he sat nervously at the edge of the bed. Sure, Peter was no Brandon. He wasn't Darren or Max, but he was kind and intelligent. More than all the rest, he was available—right now.

The only problem was Steven. Of course, it was clear that Peter and Steven were never going to be anything more than friends, and probably not even that anymore. Still—

Finally, Ryan spoke again. "Yes," he said. "The kiss was real."

Peter exhaled audibly, smiling. "Oh thank God. I thought you were going to say—"

"But it should never have happened."

"What do you mean?"

"Oh Peter, you and I are too much the same. We don't like each other like that—not really. I could convince myself that I do, and I'm sure you could do the same. But if we were really supposed to be together—if the attraction was real—don't you think we'd have felt it a long time before that stupid kiss?"

"I dunno—I feel it now though."

"You don't, though! Not the way you should. Think about—Brandon."

"I don't wanna think about Brandon."

"No, really, just indulge me for a minute. Think about how giddy he always made you feel. You couldn't talk about *anything* else. You couldn't *think* about anything else. You deserve to be with someone who makes you feel like that. And so do I. Everything you're feeling for me right now and vice versa? That's all just a product of circumstance. We used each other to try to get the attention of the ones we both really wanted, and in doing so, we shared this wonderful, horrible, cataclysmic moment. If I kissed you again right now—it wouldn't feel like that this time."

Peter furrowed his eyebrows in frustration. "Well, so what? Maybe it wouldn't be a perfect relationship, but I *do* feel something. I know you do too. Couldn't we just give it a try? If it doesn't work, what do we have to lose?"

Ryan smiled sadly. "I've got a lot to lose, actually. I don't have many friends left, Peter. If we did this I'd probably lose you in the end, along with everyone else."

"Are you really telling me we can't be together because *our friendship is too important to you?*"

Ryan laughed at the absurdity of it. How many times had he been fed that exact line? Of all the excuses not to be with someone, this was by far his least favorite. "Yeah, and believe me, I've heard that one a million times. I can't believe I just used it, but please, Peter, it's true. And there is something else."

"Oh, what?"

"Steven. He isn't just my friend. He's like—he's like family to me. I think if I ever hope to reconcile with him, really, then you and I being together—"

Peter nodded. His eyes were wet, but he smiled. "Well, that's a lot better reason than the first one. I just wish—"

Ryan stood up from the computer chair and took a seat next to him on the bed. He put an arm around his shoulder and pulled him in, tight. "Don't be upset, Peter. Please, can we stay friends?"

Peter nodded against his chest. "Alright, Ryan."

~*~

Monday the thirty-first of January marked the start of a new session of afternoon swimming lessons. It also marked the first time Ryan would see Meredith since their falling out at the Back Alley Café. The prospect of the reunion was so terrifying he was barely able to maintain his focus during his morning classes. He moved through the day in nervous anticipation, imagining the worst. What if Meredith couldn't control her anger? What if she exploded on the pool deck—losing her cool in front of a group of four-year-olds and their parents, and calling him a liar and a thief again?

At least he could remedy the thief part. Over the past six weeks, he'd been carefully putting a little money aside each check to repay what he'd taken. He had it in his wallet now—all of it. Perhaps she'd take it graciously and be willing to make amends.

He got to work early to prepare. As he was printing rosters, he felt a light tap on his shoulder, causing him to jump and turn. "Cara!" he cried. "You scared the hell out of me!"

She laughed half-heartedly. "Sorry, Ryan. I just wanted to ask if you were okay. I noticed you're looking a little pale—"

It didn't surprise him. He was also sweating profusely. "Yeah, I'm alright—maybe a little under the weather."

She raised her eyebrows. "You look like death warmed over. Are you going to be okay for the session start?"

He swallowed hard and hoped she didn't notice. "Yeah. I'll be okay I think. I'll feel better once everything is set up.

"Okay, well, let me know if you need anything."

"Alright, I will."

By the time Meredith walked into the guard office at three forty-five, he was feeling slightly calmer. He looked up from his desk, and she smiled weakly. "Good afternoon," she said. "Do you have my rosters ready?"

He choked a little as he nodded. "Um, yeah." He rifled through the six packets of rosters he'd assembled until he found the one with her name on it, then handed it to her cautiously. "Here you go."

She plucked it from his grasp and began perusing the classes and names. "Thanks."

"Did you, um—did you have a good break?"

"Yeah, it was fine."

"Did you go anywhere or—do anything fun?"

She gave him a hard look. "A little of this, a little of that. You know."

"Yeah." He frowned. "Oh!" He reached for his wallet and pulled out the two-hundred twenty dollars he'd saved. "This is for you."

"Thanks." She took the cash, registering no emotion.

He wanted desperately to talk about what had happened between them. Her frigid demeanor terrified him. He'd hoped with a little distance she'd have come around. "Meredith, do you think we could—"

She held up her hand. "Whatever you're going to say, please don't say it. I told you we're going to have a civil, working relationship. I'm a swimming instructor, and you're my manager. That's all we are to one another. But if you push it—"

"Meredith, I've lost everyone. There has to be a way—"

"I'm sorry to hear that, Ryan. Hopefully you'll do better the next time around. Excuse me, I've got to change."

He was about to argue the point and further plead his case, but then Cara walked into the office. She smiled and said, "Meredith! Welcome back!"

"Very pleased to be here!" Meredith said.

"I'm glad to hear that. It's just not the same around here without you, right Ryan?"

He smiled as widely as he could. "Yeah. She's one in a million." The saddest part, he realized, was that he meant it.

~*~

February proved to be a calm month. As the days marched slowly forward, Ryan grew more accustomed to his solitude. In many ways, it was a blessing. Without the distractions of his formerly over-booked social calendar, he was free to focus on school and felt himself pulling ahead for the first time in his collegiate career. He was making financial headway as well. In the absence of lavish parties, he was free to not only take the occasional extra shift, but also to save a little money out of each paycheck.

Brandon made a habit of calling once or twice a week. They cooked dinner together at each other's apartments and watched movies. As time went on, Ryan's attraction continued to grow, but his resolve to make his intentions known dwindled away. With each passing interaction, he felt he had more to lose in the case of rejection. Instead, with mounting guilt, he continued to wait, searching desperately for any sign that his feelings were reciprocal. He realized, with the slow horror of a passenger on a sinking ship, that he was falling into a familiar pattern of behavior with no lifeboat to offer salvation.

Action was required—he knew it with unshakeable certainty. Fear of rejection or not, something needed to happen soon. Brandon was starting to look like Darren all over again.

On an otherwise unremarkable Saturday at the end of the month, Brandon called early in the day. It was snowing, and he had a craving for beef stew. He picked Ryan up just after noon and then they stopped at the grocery store for ingredients before heading back to Brandon's house. After working together in the kitchen and letting the stew simmer all afternoon, they sat down with full bowls and glasses of wine.

"You know," Brandon said, "We make a damned good team." He pushed his fork into his bowl and pulled it out with a tender, steaming chunk of beef. "This is the best stew I've ever had."

Ryan laughed. "I doubt it's the *best* you've ever had. It's pretty good though—better because we made it together."

"Ha! Right. It's got a little more love than the shit you get in the can."

"Love?" Ryan asked, his heart suddenly racing.

"Yeah. I mean, actually, that stuff in the can is pretty good for what it is. I just imagine it being thrown together by a bunch of grumpy old women in hairnets. Know what I mean?"

"Oh." He frowned. "Yeah, I suppose. I don't know; I've only ever had it homemade."

"Lucky you."

He took a sip of his wine. Now was the moment. "You surprised me for a minute there when you said *love*. I thought you meant—us." Suddenly his underarms were wet with sweat. He'd said it now—insinuated that there might be something between them—and Brandon was free to react however he pleased.

"I *did* mean us. We put time and care into the preparation."

Ryan exhaled with a mixture of disappointment and relief. "Oh, yeah. I guess this wine is going right to my head."

"I hope not. I was planning to have more tonight. You should probably stay over again. It's still snowing and the roads will probably be bad."

"Alright." He finished the glass. "Let's have another then."

Two hours and three glasses later, they sat on the couch together watching the fire. Brandon looked over and smiled. "Feel like listening to Echoes?"

"Yeah," Ryan said. His eyelids felt heavy. "Let's."

"Alright." Brandon switched on the radio. "I'm glad we did this today."

"Me too. You have no idea."

"Oh?"

Ryan turned his head toward Brandon, searching his eyes for even a hint of the warmth and affection he felt. It was there, wasn't it? He decided to try again. "Well, yes. I think I'm a lot happier when we're together."

Brandon laughed softly. "I'm glad to hear that. I'm happy we've been seeing so much of each other."

Ryan reached for the thumb ring around his neck and squeezed it tightly. After letting go, he asked, "Have you ever thought about—being together?"

"Oh I—" his eyes widened, and he laughed. "What? Have *you*?"

"Maybe a little." It was a lie of course. Ryan scarcely thought of anything else lately.

"Ah. Well—yes, I'll admit I've thought of it. I suppose I wish I'd met you maybe four or five years from now."

Ryan blinked. He wasn't sure what kind of response he'd expected, but this certainly wasn't it. "Huh? What do you mean?"

"I just mean, the timing is all wrong. Remember what I told you that first night we hung out together last spring—the night we drove up the canyon? The moment I'm done with school I'm out of here. I'm going west. It's like modern day manifest destiny—I need to spread my arms to the coast. I've got just over two months. Hell, I might not even stick around for graduation—they mail the diplomas anyways."

"But, do you have a job lined up already?"

"No, but I'm sure I'll get one. I don't care what I have to do. I know I'll land on my feet. The world is so big, and there is so much of it I want to see. And this place? I've outgrown it."

"Why are you telling me all of this?"

Brandon shook his head slowly. "Don't you see? I'm trying to have fewer connections—less ties. Starting a relationship right now—the kind you're talking about? That would be terrible. We'd just barely get going, and then I'd leave. That wouldn't be fair to either of us, would it?"

"But what if this could be it for us? What if we're the ones for each other?" He sighed. "Oh, I should've seen it last summer. Instead, I got all wrapped up in goddamned Caleb. I should've—"

Brandon reached his arm across the couch and rested his hand lightly on Ryan's leg to quiet him. "Don't, Ryan. We're not soulmates, if that's what you're thinking. You're just all caught up in the wine and the music and the fire." He was quiet for a moment, considering his thoughts. "This is how it was with Darren too, wasn't it?"

Ryan sighed. "Yeah, I think it was."

"Maybe it's time for you to get out of here."

He bristled. "What do you mean? We've had too much wine. I can't walk home in the snow and—"

Brandon laughed. "No! Not tonight! I meant in life. Maybe after this semester you should transfer somewhere—get a fresh perspective."

"What, like, come with you to California?"

"Ha! Tempting, but no. Could you imagine if you moved across the country with me and then things went south, even as friends?"

"That wouldn't happen."

Brandon shook his head. "Maybe, maybe not. It doesn't matter. When I go, I need to go alone."

Ryan fell backwards into the overstuffed couch cushion, letting the fabric and filling embrace him—swallowing his back and shoulders. He sighed as he reached for the thumb ring again and gently rolled it through his fingers.

Brandon watched him curiously as the music played on. "You still miss him?" he asked.

"I do," Ryan said. "I think I do. I don't think about him every day like I did in the beginning. I don't cry about it like I did. And right after it happened I felt so hollow. God, it's like I was just this empty shell of a man. I suppose the part I don't know is—did that get better? Did it get better or did I just get used to it? I don't know. How about you?"

"Every once in a while," Brandon replied. "Not too often, I guess. It makes me feel kind of shitty if I think about it too much—like I should be carrying this torch and I'm just not."

"I know what you mean. When I found him that night, I thought my life was over—that I'd never be the same. I guess the second part is true. I'm not the same—I'm a friggin' train wreck. But the first part—life does go on, doesn't it? It goes on, and you forget."

Brandon nodded and took a large gulp of wine. "The anniversary is coming up. Are you planning to do anything?"

"I don't know. At first I thought maybe I'd spend it with Alice and John, but they're going to be out of the country on a dive trip. They didn't want to be in town when the date rolled around."

"That's understandable. Well, it's what, next Saturday?"

"Yes."

"I can come over, if you want. We'll light a candle and— remember."

Ryan's eyes were wet. "Thank you. That'd be really nice."

"And you and I—we're okay, right? I'm sorry if you were hoping for something more."

He considered the question. He was disappointed, there was no doubt about that. For weeks now he'd been constructing a fantasy life with Brandon at the center. For equally as long he'd avoided raising the subject because he was certain a rejection would crush him. Yet here he was, rejection in hand, and it wasn't really as bad as he'd expected. Brandon was still sitting here next to him, smiling compassionately. Nothing had changed.

Finally, he said "Yes. We're okay."

"Great. Want to talk about something else?"

He laughed. "Anything else."

~*~

When Ryan awoke on the morning of Saturday, March 5th, he was surprised he hadn't dreamt of Darren. He'd been building up the date as some sort of macabre holiday all week, and each night Darren had appeared in his dreams. He supposed Darren's presence was his way of assuaging the guilt of letting go. His words to Brandon had been true—he thought of Darren less and less as time marched forward. Now, on the morning of the anniversary, he felt further removed from the entire situation than he'd ever felt before. The whole ordeal could've been a story he heard—something that happened to someone else living some other life.

The part he hated the most was that he felt nothing—not even the familiar hollowness that had been his companion for so many months. This was the event that had derailed his entire life; how could he approach its anniversary with such apathy? It was an odd thing to wish he could feel the raw pain of the moment again. He was ashamed by his numbness, even as the numbness dulled his shame.

As he climbed calmly out of bed, he decided to do whatever he could to elicit some sort of response from within. If only for a day, he wanted desperately to feel the way he had a year ago. Darren deserved that much, didn't he?

He left his bedroom to make a pot of coffee. He put a generous amount of ground cinnamon in the bottom of the pot before he set it to brew, hoping the aroma would trigger his emotions. Sitting at the dining table, he closed his eyes and inhaled deeply as the hot, dark French roast began to drip. He could smell it a little, and the aroma warmed him. There were flashes then—flashes of Darren at Asbury Drive, and here in the kitchen at The Garden. He was becoming slightly more tangible, and then—

"Good morning!" trilled Ella's voice as she came bounding out of the hallway from her bedroom. "That smells *delicious*!"

Ryan opened his eyes and frowned, then forced a smile as he turned in her direction. "Oh, thanks, good morning. I just put some cinnamon in the bottom—easiest thing in the world."

"Well, I'm *really* impressed! I'd never have thought of that! Do you think I can have some when it's done?"

He shrugged. "I don't know why not. I made a whole pot, and I'll never drink it all."

"Oh my God! Thank you!" She looked at him for a minute. "Are you—okay? You look a little—"

"Oh, yes. Sorry. Today is the anniversary of when my friend died. I told you about him—Darren."

"I totally forgot! You poor thing! Are you sure you're alright?"

He stood up. The coffee was done so he pulled a mug out of the pantry and filled it. "Yeah," he said. "I'm totally fine. That's actually part of the problem."

She looked at him, confused. "Okay? Well, if you need *anything*—"

"Thanks, Ella. Enjoy the coffee." He smiled at her—a real, genuine smile—then turned and headed back into his bedroom.

Sitting at his computer desk he sipped the coffee, trying to transport his mind back to the place it had been before Ella's unfortunate interruption. The moment had passed, however, and when the coffee fell flat, he sighed in exasperation.

Then he looked at his faithful Yamaha keyboard.

He rose very slowly, surprised he hadn't thought of it before. Taking a seat in front of the keys, he looked out the window into the bleak morning light. He switched it on and set the patch to *slow strings*. Then, with his eyes closed, he very carefully depressed the three keys with his left hand that formed the first chord of his 'Elegy.'

A jolt of something ran through his veins like ice water, and he shivered. With his right hand, he played the opening phrase of the melody. He moved his left hand to the next chord and continued on with his right. Then suddenly he was in it. He was there again in the reception hall as the string quartet played. He could feel the vibrations of the strings blending together and moving the air like a sonic earthquake. The music was seizing him—rattling him to the core. His heart was collapsing beneath the weight of the sound and then exploding outward again, full of so much love and joy and loss and pain. Here now was the last recapitulation of the theme—the part where the cello played such an intricate counterpoint with the violin. They were moving at once together and then in opposition of one another, causing the music to expand and contract like a living, breathing lung. The whole thing was tearing him apart, and he relished the release. The harmony fell away, and his right hand played the final hopeful notes.

Then there was silence. He felt shredded—eviscerated. He was breathless, and he hurt, but the pain was *so* good. He closed his eyes and smiled. "There you are, my friend," he said to the air. "There you are."

In a brief moment of clarity, he realized that the love and pain and all the rest of it had never really gone away. It was all there in the song and waiting within him, just under the surface. The love he'd felt for Darren wasn't some mythic thing. It wasn't a story that happened to someone else. It was as real today as it had ever been.

He thought about Steven. Nearly two months had passed since they'd seen or spoken to one another. Perhaps today was the time to attempt a reconciliation. *If not today*, he thought, *then when?* He moved back to the computer desk and plucked the phone off its base, then dialed the number and waited.

After five rings voicemail picked up. Ryan cleared his throat. "Hi Steven, it's Ryan. I don't know if you're ready to hear from me yet but—well, it's the fifth of March and you're obviously on my mind. I don't know if you planned anything for today but—well, I'm here at home. Brandon is stopping by later, but if you'd like to visit, or to talk, you know where to find me. I love you, and I'm sorry. I hope you're well. Goodbye."

He hung up the phone and closed his eyes.

In the early afternoon, there was a knock on his bedroom door. For the past several hours he'd been working on some lyrics for a new song about Darren—one with words this time. He'd been chewing over a particular turn of phrase for about ten minutes, and the gentle rapping of knuckles against wood startled him back to reality.

"Come in!" he called.

When the door opened, he expected to see Steven standing there, finally ready to reconcile. Instead, his eyes grew wide when Max stepped into his bedroom.

"Hi, Mister."

Ryan leaped out of his chair. "Max! What are you doing here?" He rushed forward and threw his arms around him, pulling him close. Max returned the embrace for several seconds and then pushed gently away.

"Well, I know what today is, and I wanted to make sure you were alright."

Ryan smiled brightly and gestured toward the bed. "Come," he said. "Sit."

"Alright."

After they were seated, Ryan continued. "I'm doing—surprisingly well. When I woke up this morning, I was just sort of numb about the whole thing. But then I sat down at the keyboard and—now I feel it all again."

"Is that a good thing?" Max asked.

"Oh, yes. I mean, I'm sad. I really am. But I'm just so glad to *feel something* about it all. Thank you for coming I—I wasn't sure if I was going to see you again."

Max shook his head slowly. "Neither was I, Mister. But you know, we all make mistakes. I just hope you're learning from yours."

"So do I. Do you talk to Steven?"

"Yeah, I've seen him a few times."

"How is he doing?"

"Really well, actually. He's keeping his head down, and he's sworn off boys for now, or so he says."

"That's good. I called him today but—he didn't answer. Do you think—does he ever talk about me?"

Max sighed, sadly. "No, not really. Not to me, at least. I know he misses you though. I think the sooner you two can bury the hatchet, the better."

"I'm trying, Max. He said he needed time."

"Well then, I guess you'll just have to wait."

"I guess so. Hey, how'd everything work out with Jake?"

Max laughed. "You'll never believe it. While we were on break, he called me up and told me he didn't think we should see each other anymore!"

"Seriously? He dumped you before you could dump *him*?"

"Isn't it hilarious? I had to pretend to be really upset! I made a whole huge scene just for the fun of it. How could he do this to me? He didn't even have the balls to do it person—that kind of thing."

"Oh, you're wicked."

Max winked. "I have my moments. But hey, I have some things to do later. Have you had lunch yet? I know it's kind of late, but if you haven't I thought—"

"No," Ryan replied. "And suddenly I realize I'm starving."

"Alright, let's go. And oh, Ryan?"

"Yes?"

"I know that I implied that maybe after Jake was over, we might finally give it a try. Do you think maybe I could take a rain check? I'm trying to be by myself for a while."

Ryan smiled warmly. "Max, I was pretty sure I'd lost you for good. I'll take you however I can get you. Friends is fine."

"Really?"

"Really."

Later that evening Ryan stood on the deck with Brandon and slowly exhaled a cloud of blue smoke. "I think it's about time I gave these up," he said. "Tonight is the night. I didn't make any New Year's resolutions, but I think for me tomorrow is the real beginning of my new year."

Brandon nodded slowly. "That's not a bad idea. Maybe I'll give it a try too." He shivered. "I wasn't expecting this snow."

"Neither was I." Ryan smiled. Sometime in the afternoon, the clouds had rolled in out of nowhere. Now, medium sized flakes were falling gently all around them. The ground was covered, and the snow was piling up quickly on the deck's railings. He looked up toward the sky. "That's one of my favorite colors."

"What color?" Brandon asked.

"The sky. I like to think of it as a stale orange—the way the snow clouds reflect the light from the city at night."

"Don't you mean *pale* orange?"

"No. I mean, it *is* a pale orange, but stale is the word I prefer—like it's faded and old and it's hung around too long."

"If you say so."

"It always makes me think of him."

"Of Darren?"

"Yeah. It seems like all our best and worst moments? They all took place under a sky just like this one. I'm glad I knew him, Brandon. I really am."

"So am I, Ryan. So am I."

CHAPTER 20

It was difficult to say at what point the idea of leaving Colorado changed from being a possibility in Ryan's mind to an inevitability. Since the moment Brandon breathed it into life, it had been lingering in Ryan's subconscious. Of course, he'd dismissed it at first—the idea was ludicrous. Apart from a short period during his infancy, he'd never lived anywhere else. His entire life was here—why should he move away? Where would he even go?

Nevertheless, as the winter lingered and stubbornly gave up its grip, he found himself wondering in quiet moments—why not? Most of the few friends he had left were graduating and would be gone by the start of summer. He had work, sure, but there were swimming pools everywhere. Even if he couldn't find another job in aquatics, that might be alright. He'd never done anything else—wouldn't it be nice to work in a bookstore, or at a café?

The only thing that really held him in place was his family, and he acknowledged guiltily that family wasn't much of an obstacle. Even though he lived a short seven blocks from his parents, he hardly ever saw them. It wasn't for lack of love. He'd simply learned growing up that when it came to family, there was a certain respected acceptability of distance. When he was no more than a baby, his parents made the courageous decision to leave rural northern Wisconsin for brighter pastures, even though doing so meant leaving everyone behind. For Ryan's entire life, grandparents, aunts, uncles and cousins were people he saw once or twice a year. Certainly, the few days he shared with these people were meaningful, but after separating again, normal life resumed with the knowledge that the family was still there if you needed it.

Besides, the idea of moving away wasn't entirely without its merits. Colorado had become a wasteland filled with constant reminders of his failures; he relished the idea of a fresh start—somewhere that all the tumult of the past year could whither into a distant memory. After all, the Back Alley Café was off-limits, haunted by the ghost of Caleb. Work provided near-continuous exposure to Meredith, who remained as icily aloof as she'd promised. Even his home at The Garden was poisoned with bittersweet memories of Darren, his near-romance with Max, and the falling out with Steven.

The crocuses climbed out of the ground, and then the tulips. Slowly the weeks passed, and the earth began to come back to life. There was something budding in Ryan too—waiting to bloom. Perhaps it really was time to be elsewhere.

On a sunny afternoon in early May, Ryan sat with Brandon at a small table outside a coffee shop in the Old Town district. He sipped the iced coffee he'd purchased inside and fanned his face ineffectually with his hand. The sun was beating down upon him fiercely, and he could feel sweat beading around his temples.

"That sun is ungodly!" he said.

Brandon laughed. "Oh, it's not that bad. It's just because this is the first really hot day of the year. Buck up! This is just the beginning. It'll probably cool off again after today anyways."

"Did you have to pick the only table without any shade?"

"Oh yes! I'm pretending I'm in sunny southern California already."

Ryan groaned. "You'll be there soon enough. Right now I'd like to pretend I was in cloudy northern Oregon or something. Do you know when you're leaving, yet?"

"I booked my plane for the day after graduation. I wanted to get out of here the moment my last final was done, but my folks weren't having it. My mother told me that after paying for four years of school and that damned townhouse, the least I could do was stick around so they could watch me walk."

"Any job prospects?"

"Yeah, I have a phone interview with a company in LA early next week. I floated my resume out to a few others. Someone is bound to pick me up."

"Good." Ryan took another sip of his coffee. "So, I haven't told anyone yet but—"

"But—"

"I think I'm going to leave. Colorado, I mean."

Brandon's eyes grew wide, and he smiled excitedly. "Really? You're actually going to do it?"

Ryan shrugged. "Well, kind of. I don't know. My aunt and uncle live in Wisconsin, and they're going on this trip to Alaska. At least, I think they're still planning to go. I need to call them. Anyways, they asked me way back at Thanksgiving if I wanted to watch their house while they're away."

Brandon rolled his eyes. "So, you're moving to—Wisconsin?"

"If they'll still have me, yeah. At least for the summer. I don't know; it seems like a great opportunity to clear my head and figure out what I really want to do. I don't think I'll *stay* there. It's a small town, and I mean *really* small. But I'll go and try to write some music, maybe get a part time job. I'll figure it out. Then at the end of the summer? I guess I'll either come back here or head somewhere else. Either way, I think I deserve the break, don't you?"

"Well, yeah. You know I've been encouraging you to go, but—what about school? Wouldn't it be better to just transfer some-where?"

He shrugged. "Yeah, I suppose. I just don't know where it is I want to end up yet. I can always do a semester at a community college wherever I land. It won't be the end of the world."

"I guess not. Well—I'm excited for you. It's a big move, literally."

"Thanks," Ryan said. "To be honest, I'm scared to death." Most of the ice in his coffee had melted, so he finished it in two large swal-lows. "Are you about done with that?" Brandon's glass was still half full. "Come on, I need to get out of this sun."

~*~

When Ryan returned home later that afternoon, he found a square, silver envelope addressed to him in the mailbox. As he walked up the stairs to the deck, he carefully slit it open with a fin-ger. Inside was a single piece of heavy card stock with words in a cel-ebratory font printed in green and gold.

Graduation Party:

Please join us for an afternoon barbecue to celebrate
Steven's graduation!
When: Sunday, May 28, 2005 from 1pm - 5pm
Where: 1124 Highlawn Court, Thornton

Please RSVP to Lisa (Mom) no later than May 21

Ryan perused the invitation again, holding it as though it was very fragile and might disintegrate in his hands. This was certainly a turn of events he hadn't expected. After Steven had failed to return his phone call on the anniversary of Darren's death, Ryan had given up. Max said he needed more time, so Ryan conceded. Perhaps that time had now passed, because here in his hand he held a glimmer of hope—an idea that maybe their friendship could be salvaged.

As he walked through the hallway into the kitchen, his initial excitement dwindled. Was there really any point? Later in the evening he was planning to call Aunt Carol, and assuming she still wanted his help, he was going to be leaving. Anyway, who knew where Steven would end up? If he stayed in the area, he'd settle down in Denver at least. Even if Ryan returned to Colorado at the end of the summer, the chances he'd see Steven on a regular basis were pretty slim. He dropped the invitation on the peninsula and walked into his room.

Suddenly he was angry. Why would Steven have waited all this time to try to reconcile? Why save it until the very end? He should've just let it go—allowed their history to dissolve into the atmosphere. And at a party no less? A celebration like that was no place to have a heartfelt conversation about how sorry Ryan was and how royally he'd fucked things up.

He decided he didn't want to wait until the evening to call Carol. It needed to be done now. It was time to set the plans and buy the plane ticket because Steven's untimely little peace offering was just that much more salt in his wounds. He plucked the phone up from its base and dialed the number.

After the third ring, Carol answered. "Hello?"

"Hi, Aunt Carol. It's Ryan."

"Oh my God! Ryan! How are you, my dear?"

"I'm doing pretty well. Are you and Charlie excited about Alaska? You're still going, aren't you?"

"Oh, we're going alright! Just about a month from now. Well—six weeks maybe. I don't suppose you're asking because you want to take me up on my offer? Julie's husband is still being a real stick in the mud about it."

He laughed. "Well, actually—"

After he had hung up the phone, he breathed a long sigh of relief. Now that the decision had been made he felt every muscle in his body relax. Carol was going to book him a flight to Green Bay for Thursday, June 23rd. Then he'd spend a couple days with her and Charlie—learning the ropes—before they left town the following Monday morning. He had about six weeks to put his affairs in order.

As he looked around his bedroom, he felt just the slightest twinge of sorrow. Though he'd suffered at The Garden, he'd had some pretty great times too. He walked to the paned windows on the outer wall and swung them open and outward, letting the warm spring air rush in and embrace him. His time at The Garden was nearly done. Now, finally, there was a tangible end to this miserable chapter of his life—everything was about to change.

He walked back to the bed and let himself collapse. He closed his eyes and allowed his mind to wander back to the problem of Steven and his damned graduation party. Perhaps his initial anger had been a bit extreme. He didn't really want their friendship to dissolve into the atmosphere. How could he? Steven was practically a brother, and he'd been hoping for this reconciliation for a long time.

He sat up again. Maybe he should just call him. Perhaps they could even get together once before the party to clear the air. Even if the time they had left with one another could be counted in weeks—even days—Ryan supposed that was better than never seeing him again at all.

Retrieving the phone, he dialed Steven's number.

The answer was almost immediate. "Hi Ryan."

He froze for a minute, surprised. "Steven?"

"Yeah, can you hear me?"

"I—I *can* hear you. How are you?"

"I'm alright. You?"

"I'm good!" He exhaled. "I didn't expect you to pick up. I—got the invitation to your graduation party today."

Steven laughed. "Oh, you did?"

"What's funny?"

"Nothing. Everything. I don't know. I told my mom not to send you one, but I guess she didn't listen."

"Oh." Ryan winced. "Sorry. Well—I don't have to come. I mean, I probably can't get down to Thornton anyways. Sorry, I'll let you go—"

"Ryan! No! Wait."

He sighed loudly. "What?"

"I didn't want her to send you an invitation because I wanted to invite you myself. I thought after everything—I thought that just getting a card in the mail would've been too impersonal."

"Oh! So—you actually *want* me to come?"

"Of course I do! Look, I'm sorry I left. I'm sorry I reacted so poorly. If I'd just grown a set of balls and told Peter—"

Ryan was smiling so widely the corners of his mouth hurt. He was surprised to feel hot tears, burning as they streamed down his cheeks. "Steven!" he said. "Don't you *dare* start apologizing to me. You didn't do anything wrong. This whole mess—it's all me."

"No, it's not all you. I could've let go sooner. I should have called you back on the anniversary. I shouldn't have waited so long."

"Forget about all of that. It doesn't matter. So, can I—can I see you before the party? I still might not be able to go. I don't know how I'd get down there without a car."

"Well, Max is going. I'm sure you could ride with him. But as far as getting together, probably not. I'm closing myself off from everything until after finals."

"Okay. Well, I'll talk to Max."

"Alright Ryan. I really miss you."

"Bye Steven. I miss you too."

~*~

The three weeks before Steven's party passed by at breakneck speed. Classes ended, and Ryan breezed through finals week. He was pleased that even if he didn't return to the University after the summer, he'd ended this chapter of his higher education on a good note.

His spirit surged with an unexpected levity as the anticipation of his imminent departure gripped him; he was ready for something fresh and new. The summer stretched out before him, offering nothing but endless potential. Sequestered away in the quiet, beautiful north woods, he was certain he'd write amazing music. He was also hopeful that maybe through the process he'd find a way back to himself—to a somewhat improved version of the Ryan Gregori he'd been before all the difficulty started.

Max picked Ryan up at noon the day of Steven's graduation party. As he guided the car down onto the interstate, he turned his gaze momentarily toward Ryan, and then back to the road. "Are you ready for this?" he asked.

Ryan scrunched his shoulders and then relaxed them again as he sighed. "As ready as I'll ever be, I suppose. I'd have liked to see him once before I get tossed in with the family and friends."

"Well, you know how this stuff goes, Mister. The end of the semester is rough."

He laughed. "Not compared to the end of the last one."

"No," Max agreed. "I guess not for you. I'm glad you came through it alright. Are you getting all geared up for your crazy summer at work?"

Ryan chuckled. "Well, actually—" he hadn't told him yet. So far the only people that knew about his grand plan were Brandon, his parents, and Aunt Carol. He was going to have to sit down with Cara tomorrow at work. He also planned to tell Steven today, if they had a quiet moment.

"Actually what?" Max asked.

"Actually, I'm leaving—headed to Wisconsin for the summer, at least."

"You're going *where*?"

Ryan laughed quietly. "It's just northern Wisconsin. It's not like it's Saturn. And like I said, it's probably just for the summer. After that I'll be—well, I don't know where yet."

Max was quiet for a full minute. When he finally spoke, he said "I don't know, Mister. This sounds awfully impulsive."

"I don't disagree with you. It *is* awfully impulsive. I also think it's exactly what I need. This last year and a half flipped my whole world upside down. I think I need a new, fresh start."

"Well, sure but—you don't sound like you want to come back."

He considered the statement carefully. Did he? Didn't he? When he responded, it was the truth. "I don't know, Max. I guess that's a part of it. I need the summer to figure it out."

"But why now?" There was an edge to his voice that teetered between anger and desperation. "You've just started mending all your fences. I thought things were really looking up for you."

"They are but—look. Could there really be a more perfect time? You and Steven and Brandon—all three of you are done with school now. Brandon is leaving for California tomorrow. I know you're sticking around for a while, but you won't stay forever. And who knows where Steven is going to end up. Then you've got the living situation. I can't even entertain the idea of living with Shelly for another year. The Garden really lost its luster after Steven left—I was going to need to move anyways."

"Sure, but maybe just across town. What about school? You finally started again, you can't just stop now."

Ryan frowned. "I'm surprised at how opposed to all of this you sound."

"I'm sorry," Max replied. His tone softened. "I guess I figured you'd always be right here. As school was ending, I came to terms with saying goodbye to a lot of people. I wasn't expecting you to be one of them."

"I think I have this idea. I'd be lying if I said I believed it all the time but—I'm starting to think that we are responsible for our own happiness."

Max laughed heartily. "Well, of course we are, Mister. How else is it supposed to work?"

"I don't know! I've just spent so much time being *unhappy* over the last year and a half. I kept waiting for some shining knight to come along and take all of the pain away. You know what I mean, don't you?"

"I do. But, Ryan? You don't have to run away to find happiness in yourself."

"I'm not running away."

"Aren't you?"

"No," he said, and he was very certain. "I'm not running away. I'm running *toward*. I'm going to find something there—my great epiphany. I'm going to find—myself."

~*~

Just after one-thirty, Max pulled into the quaint suburban cul-de-sac where Steven had grown up. The little circle was lined with clean, modern ranch houses set back behind wide, immaculate front lawns. Without looking at the address, it was immediately apparent which house belonged to Steven's parents. A cluster of green and gold balloons was tied to the mailbox, floating lazily in the air—a universal signal that a party was taking place beyond.

"It looks like there are a lot of people here already," Max said as he parked the car along an empty stretch of curb several houses away. He switched off the engine and swung open his door.

Ryan followed and then stretched as he stood on the sunny sidewalk. "I'm a little nervous," he said.

"Don't be. It's just Steven, after all. It'll be like the two of you never missed a beat."

Ryan laughed. "It's not Steven I'm nervous about! It's everyone else. I hate walking into a room full of people I don't know in a setting like this."

"Don't sweat it. Come on."

Max started forward, and Ryan followed reluctantly behind. They reached the mailbox and then turned up the long paved walkway to the front door. A sudden breeze passed through a pair of blooming crab apples on either side of the path, causing the blossoms to shimmer as they perfumed the air. Ryan breathed in deeply and felt himself relax as Max rang the doorbell.

A moment later the door opened, and a middle-aged woman with shoulder-length, straight salt and pepper hair stood beaming before them. "Hello!" she said, with great enthusiasm. "Welcome, I'm Steven's mom, Lisa. And you two must be—"

"I'm Max." He extended his hand. She shook it gently. "And this is Ryan."

She took Ryan's hand then and held it. "Oh, I'm so glad to finally meet both of you. Come on through. Everyone is in the back." She led them into the house, through a formal living room at the front door, past a family room, and then into the kitchen where a set of French doors opened onto a deck that overlooked an enormous back yard. They stepped through, and once outside again Ryan's nose filled with the aroma of grilling meat. A cluster of older people stood in a corner laughing and drinking beer—family friends he supposed—while others of various ages stood in the grass beyond. A small group of children yelled in excitement as they kicked a worn old soccer ball around the far end of the yard. There were perhaps thirty guests in all, and it warmed Ryan to think of so many people here to celebrate his friend.

Lisa smiled at them. "Let's see," she said. "Where is Steven?" She scanned the grass. "Oh—there! Steven!" she called.

Then Ryan saw him too—toward the back of the yard near to where the children were playing. He turned at the sound of his mother's voice, already smiling. He locked eyes with Ryan, and his smile grew even larger as he walked happily toward them. After climbing the few short steps up onto the deck, he stood, beaming. "Hi guys," he said. "Thanks for coming."

Ryan couldn't speak just yet. Instead, he opened his arms and wrapped Steven in a firm, tight embrace. He held it and whispered. "I'm so glad to see you."

After he let go, Steven gave a little smile. "I'm glad to see you too." There was something different about him—an almost palpable sense of self-confidence that hadn't existed before. He turned and hugged Max as well. "Come on, do you guys want a beer? I know we're usually more of the wine and mixed drinks crowd but—"

Ryan chuckled. "Please tell me it's Miller Light." Now everyone laughed. "A beer would be great."

Three hours later, as the party was winding down, Steven and Ryan sat in lawn chairs in a shady patch of grass. Closing his eyes, Steven tilted his head back and took a sip from his bottle of beer. "So, when are you leaving?"

Ryan sighed. Steven had taken the news of his imminent departure much better than Max. "About three weeks?"

He opened his eyes again and turned to look at Ryan. "It's going to come quick, isn't it?"

"Yeah. I suppose it is. I have a lot to do. I haven't even told work yet."

"I guess you'd better do that."

"Yeah. Where do you think you're going to go now?"

"I've mostly been applying to places in Denver, but I'm keeping my options open. I'll move back here with my parents until I find a job. Hopefully it won't be too long."

"Steven—"

"Yes?"

"I'm sorry. I really am."

"I know, Ryan."

"Thanks for giving me another chance—even if we don't have very long."

Steven laughed. "You talk about this like you're dying. Ryan, you could decide the day you get there that you're coming back at the end of the summer. Jesus, even if you moved to Timbuktu, I'm sure you'd still be back to visit from time to time." He took another sip from his beer. "I have an idea. Instead of thinking of all this as goodbye—as the end? Why don't we think of it as *to be continued*?"

Ryan smiled sadly. What a nice idea, even if he didn't really believe it. "Alright," he said. "To be continued."

~*~

Later that night Ryan knocked on Shelly's door. Though it was late, he could see the light was on so he was confident she was awake. From the other side he heard Mars yip, lightly, and then the shuffling of feet. The knob turned and then she was standing in front of him, blinking. "Ryan," she said. "What's up?"

"Can I talk to you for a minute?" he asked.

"Yeah, I guess so." She stepped out of the bedroom and took a seat on the futon in the living room.

He sat beside her and took a few breaths before beginning. "So, I wanted to tell you that—I'm leaving."

Her eyes widened. "Where are you going?"

"Wisconsin first—my aunt and uncle's place. Then, I don't know. Maybe back here. Probably not."

She frowned. "I wish you wouldn't."

"Excuse me?"

"It's just, like—I know things have been different this semester. And I guess—we were never really that close. I know I kinda fucked things up at Christmas and then when I came back we didn't really talk about it. But—"

"But you want to talk about it *now*?"

"No, no. I guess, remember when we said we had to look out for each other? That we needed to take care of each other? I really took that to heart. And I guess it's like, I've just felt a lot better that you're around. I know I didn't ever say—thank you."

"Thank you?"

"Yeah, like, thank you for saving me. Thanks for coming home on Christmas Eve. Thanks for sticking around when you didn't have to. You could've left like Steven left."

He shook his head. "You don't have to thank me for that. Where would I have gone?"

"It doesn't matter. But I mean, I guess you're going now."

He frowned in surprise. "I didn't know it meant that much to you that I was here."

"I guess I could have told you. When are you leaving?"

"Three weeks." He thought for a minute. "How are you—I know we didn't talk about it but—how are you doing?"

She laughed and shrugged. "I'm doing okay. Like, I have good days and bad days, the same as always. Mostly good days. I'd have told you if it was getting bad again. My thing is, I just can't talk to my mom, you know? If I do, it all starts to spiral. I can't trust her. Even when she gives me a glimmer of hope that we could reconcile? Well, that's what Christmas was, wasn't it? Then she pulled the rug right out from under me at the last minute."

He put a hand on her shoulder. "I'm sorry too. I'm sorry we waited so long to talk. And thank you also. Even when I was at my worst this last fall and winter, you didn't judge me."

"Nah." She smiled. "We all fuck up."

"We can still watch out for each other, you know."

"Yeah. I guess we can. I wish you luck, Ryan, I really do."

"Thanks, Shelly. You too."

~*~

As Ryan's mother turned off the toll road, he looked out the window to take in the splendor of the Colorado front range one last time. The day had finally arrived. Everything he was taking with him was packed into two suitcases in the back seat while everything he wasn't was boxed and resting in his parents' basement. He craned his head for a final look at the perfectly formed prominence of Longs Peak to the north. In spite of Steven's assurances a few weeks previous that he *could* come back at the end of the summer, something about this moment felt final.

Perhaps he was due for another metamorphosis—a better one this time. Whatever was ahead, no matter if he was gone for months or years, he was certain the next time he laid his eyes on the Rockies, he would be a very different man.

The car seemed to turn forever, slowly taking the exit 270 degrees before accelerating back onto the airport road, heading directly east. The mountains were behind him now, and he exhaled.

His mother spoke. "Can I be honest and tell you that I still don't completely understand this?"

He laughed nervously. "Can I be honest and tell you that I don't either?"

"Well, I wish you wouldn't," she said. "I have this sense that you're very—lost right now."

"I'm not lost. I'm fine, mom. I just need this to clear my head."

"Well that's fine, it's only—I wish you already had a return flight. It's the open-ended part that bothers me. All this talk of, well, *maybe I'll come back or maybe I won't*. That's hard on me."

"I'm sorry. What can I do to make you feel better?"

She shook her head and laughed. "You could stay. But since I know that won't happen, you could promise that you'll be happy."

He was quiet for a moment. "I think that's what all this is actually about. I think I'm trying to—find my happiness."

"And you think you'll find it by yourself at Carol and Charlie's house?"

"No," he said. "Probably not. But it's a place to start—somewhere to make a plan."

"Okay, Ryan. Well, you know you can always come home, don't you?"

He smiled with tears in his eyes. "Yeah, I do. I love you, Mom. I'm sorry we didn't see more of each other these last couple years. But I love you."

She looked at him with eyes as wet as his own. "I love you too." Then she laughed as she turned her gaze back to the road. The giant blue horse with its blazing red eyes was just ahead. "Ugh!" she said. "I wonder if *anyone* likes that thing."

He wiped his eyes and laughed as well. "I know I don't—not usually. Today it served an unexpected purpose though."

"Oh?"

"Yeah, I doubt this was the artist's intention, but it sure lightened
the mood, didn't it?"

She laughed again. "I guess it did. Do you—want me to park? I can
go in with you and stay until you're through security."

"Yes, that's what I want, but—just drop me off if that's alright?
This goodbye is already hard enough. Maybe it's best we don't let it
linger."

She nodded and turned the car toward the terminal. "Alright. Be
happy, Ryan. Be happy."

After a quick but tearful goodbye at the departure doors, Ryan
dropped his bags and headed through security. He boarded an auto-
mated tram that played a jaunty melody as the doors opened and
closed, and then held tightly to a bar as the little train moved through
the tunnel to Terminal A. He exited and found his gate. Within the
hour his plane boarded. The cabin door closed and it was done.

He stared out the oval window as the plane pulled away and started rolling slowly toward the runway. A sudden, unwelcome wave of
uncertainty washed over him. Hadn't this been a rash decision in the
end? He began to weep, heavily—each inhalation of air becoming
more of a sob than a breath.

The kind-looking middle-aged woman sitting next to him looked
in his direction. "Oh, it's alright, sweetheart. Flying is safer than driving, you know. Just hold on for about one more minute, and we'll be
in the air—you'll see."

He thought about telling her he wasn't scared of flying—that was-
n't it at all. Instead, he just nodded and did his best to quell the tears.
Why did this departure seem so final? The flight was only two hours,

after all. If everything started to fall apart, he could leave Carol and Charlie's mid-morning, buy a return ticket, and be home again in time for a late lunch with his parents.

Somewhere over Nebraska, he calmed himself enough to realize it wasn't going to work out that way. The summer ahead was going to be fruitful.

After a short layover in Chicago, Ryan boarded another smaller plane. He sat on the left-hand side and watched the great patchwork of land pass beneath him—emerald green, sage, and mahogany squares stitched together by tan and silver roads, and embroidered with trees. The great expanse of Lake Winnebago shimmered in the afternoon sun, and before he knew it, the plane was descending again. As it circled downward, Lake Michigan came into view. At first, he could see the other side, but as the plane continued to give up its altitude, the Michigan shore disappeared, and the lake could've been an endless ocean.

After he got off the plane, he walked from the gate down a short hallway to the baggage claim. Carol and Charlie were waiting. Seeing him from a distance, Carol began to waive frantically. "Ryan! Hello!"

He smiled at both her exuberance and her accent. The way she said the world *hello* was so warm and round. With a renewed sense that this decision had been the right one, he rushed forward to meet her.

Charlie got to him first, pulling him into a brief hug with a mighty clap on the back. "Good to see you, Ryan. Glad you could make it, kiddo."

"Thanks, Charlie," Ryan replied. He stepped away and turned toward Carol.

"Aw, come here," she said, arms outstretched.

He embraced her. "Thanks for letting me come."

"Letting you come?" she said, pushing away in mock exasperation. "You don't ever need permission to come home."

He laughed lightly. He thought about reminding her, again, that this hadn't been home since he was a baby. It wasn't worth it. Instead, he said, "Thanks, Carol. Really. You have no idea how much I needed this."

"Anytime, dear boy. I hope you're gonna find what you've been missing."

So did he.

CHAPTER 21

Ryan's responsibilities in Carol and Charlie's absence were simple. He was to water the outdoor plants as needed—at least three times a week—and mow the grass on Fridays. The day after he arrived, Charlie took him out to the shed and showed him how to work the riding mower.

"Now," Charlie said, "Don't give her too much at once or the damned thing'll give out on you. If you want to go a little faster, push this toward the rabbit. Slower, pull back toward the turtle. Got it?" Ryan nodded. "Now, be careful around the trees. You don't want to ring them. You know what I mean by that?"

"Yeah," he replied. "That's when you damage the bark around the base, right?"

"Yep. Get as close as you can, but don't ring them. They'll dry right up and die on you."

"Alright. Why Fridays?" Ryan asked. "Why not Tuesdays, or Saturdays, or any other day?"

"Oh," Charlie shrugged. "It doesn't matter that much. I get into a habit of mowing on Fridays because then if we have people over on a Saturday or Sunday it's all fresh. I think once a week is good enough, but just keep your eye on the weather. If it's gonna rain on Friday, it's best to cut the grass on Thursday instead. If it's been raining all week, maybe you wait until Saturday for things to dry out. You get the idea, don't you?"

"Yes," Ryan said.

"Alright then, let's head in."

They left the shed, and Ryan looked out over the property. The area was more expansive than what Ryan would call a lawn—two acres of lovingly manicured grass on a hillside that sloped gradually downward to a slow-moving, chocolate-colored river. The edges of the lawn were lined with ornamental shrubs and fruit trees that gave way to a wild expanse of woods on both sides. At the top of the hill sat the house—a two story Victorian, painted yellow with a wide veranda circling the first floor.

"How long does it usually take you?" Ryan asked.

"Oh," Charlie said. "I don't know. Maybe an hour?"

"That's not bad."

"No, not bad at all. My advice though? Do it first thing in the morning. If you wait too long that sun gets so goddamned hot. And if there's any humidity you'll feel like you're suffocating. Also, don't forget the bug spray. These damned mosquitos can get to be the size of birds."

Ryan laughed. "Alright, I've been warned."

Later that evening, when they sat down to dinner, Carol smiled. "So, what are you going to do with yourself?"

Ryan had just taken a large bite of his cheeseburger—Charlie had grilled—and he held up one finger, guiltily.

Carol laughed. "Take your time." She lifted a fork full of pale yellow potato salad to her own mouth and chewed it happily.

Ryan swallowed. "That burger is excellent, Charlie. Um, I guess I'm going to look for a job—just part time."

"The gas station in town is hiring," Charlie said, "If you just want something close by."

"Oh, thanks! Look! There's my first lead." Truthfully the gas station was the last place he wanted to work. He preferred the idea of working in an ice cream shop, or waiting tables at a restaurant. Really, he was hoping maybe he could get a job at the tiny bookstore in the next town over. Carol was leaving him with her car. He didn't want to travel too far every day, but a twenty-minute drive wouldn't be terrible, he supposed. He looked at Carol. "But other than that, I'm going to try to write some music—maybe keep a journal. I'm just going to *think* a lot. I need to decide where I'm heading from here."

Carol clucked. "Well look! You just got here, don't start thinking about rushing off already!"

"No, no! Not like that. I don't know if I'll stay past the summer, but I meant, where I'm heading *in life.*"

"Ah." She nodded, knowingly. "I get it now. Well, I'd like to say that you could probably have a mighty fine life right here. Maybe not *right* here in the country—you seem a little more the city type to me. But why not look at Green Bay or Appleton?"

"I will," he assured her. "Nothing is off limits."

Charlie laughed, suddenly. "Did you ever see that Jack Nicholson movie?"

"Oh! Oh!" Carol cried. "Which one?"

"Not *you*, Carol. I know you've seen it."

"Which one?" Ryan asked.

"The one in the hotel. Remember Carol? That goddamned ugly hotel? Wasn't it like, a bunch of pink triangles stuck together on the side of a mountain or something? You know the one I'm talking about—"

Ryan laughed. "Are you thinking of *The Shining*?"

Charlie slammed his fist onto the table in excitement. "That's the one! Right? Where he's taking care of the hotel all winter with his family, and he goes crazy?"

"Yes," Ryan smiled. "I've seen that one."

"Well, don't you pull any of that shit here this summer!" He laughed again. "I guess maybe it could get pretty lonely here for a young guy like you. Carol, can't you just see it? Writing music all day and climbing the walls? I probably oughta lock up the guns!" He nearly collapsed onto the table under the weight of his own laughter.

She scowled at him then. "That's not even funny, Charlie. Anyways, it's not like we live on the moon!" She looked at Ryan. "You've got family around. If you start to get lonely just give your cousin Julie a call. She's not that far away."

Ryan laughed again. "Oh, don't worry. I think I'm going to be just fine."

"Alright, well, if you're not, just call Julie."

Later, they sat in the living room. Carol made bourbon manhattans and they watched television as Charlie thumbed through an atlas. "Hey, Carol," Charlie asked. "What do you think about stopping in Banff?"

She looked over, absently. "Banff? Yeah, sure. How much time will that add on?"

"Well, depends. If we just do the British Columbia route one way instead of going through both times—well, I guess it'd be a wash."

"Yeah, alright. Sounds good." She took a sip of her drink and looked at Ryan, who was slowly nursing his own. "I guess I probably shouldn't have made that for you, eh?"

His eyes widened. "What do you mean? I'm not drinking it too fast, am I? It's strong."

"Ha! Oh god no! Charlie, what's that thing you like to say when people are drinking too slow?"

"Oh!" He guffawed. "D'you need a nipple for that?"

Carol laughed uproariously. "Yeah! Right! No, I was just thinking, you're not *quite* twenty-one yet, are you?"

Ryan blushed. "Oh, no. A couple weeks though."

"You look like a deer caught in the goddamned headlights!" Carol winked. "I'm just giving you a hard time. Drink up. No, I was just thinking—Charlie, I guess we oughta give him his birthday present now."

Setting down the atlas, Charlie nodded. "Yeah, I guess he could probably use it." He stood and left the room, reappearing a minute later with a card in a pale blue envelope. "Here you go!"

Ryan looked at the envelope warily. "I can wait, you know. My birthday isn't until the eighth."

"Nope," Charlie replied. "Open it now. We'd like to see you open it."

"Okay—" He gently tore open the top of the envelope. The card inside was tastefully plain, illustrated with a layer cake topped with a single candle and the words *Happy Birthday* embossed across the top. When he opened the card, his eyes widened. Inside was a check for $2100. "Oh! Wow, this is—this is too much, you guys. Thank you but—"

Carol scowled. "But nothing. You're goddamned welcome. We know it took a lot for you to come out here. This way you don't have to worry if you can't get a job right away."

"I don't know what to say."

"Y'already said it," Charlie replied. "Twenty-one hundred for twenty-one years. Now don't go spending it all in one place!"

He laughed. "Hardly. Thanks guys. Really."

Carol smiled. "You're very welcome, my dear. You're very welcome."

~*~

In Ryan's first week of solitude, he established a comfortable routine. After getting out of bed around ten each morning, he showered, made a small breakfast, and sat down with a notebook of staff paper. Midway through the week his keyboard arrived from Colorado—his mother shipped it—and he was delighted. He set it up in front of a window overlooking the lawn, and he wrote and played until late afternoon when it was time to start thinking about dinner. After eating, he moved to the veranda with a glass of coffee—on ice—and watched the sun sink slowly in the sky. It was the height of summer, and at this latitude, the daylight lingered in the atmosphere until well past nine. The nights typically ended with television and a mixed drink or two, and then it was off to bed sometime after one.

He watered the plants dutifully, and then on his first Friday he climbed onto the riding mower and cut the grass. It was eleven by the time he started, and Charlie was right—he should've done it earlier. The hot sun was almost unbearable, and the situation was compounded by the heat coming off the mower's engine. Still, it took just about an hour, as Charlie suggested.

It was an idyllic week, but by the time Ryan reached his second Monday, he began to feel the walls closing in, ever so slightly. He thought about Charlie laughing as he referenced *The Shining*. It was time to start looking for a part time job, even though the generous birthday gift he'd received was more than enough to carry him to the end of summer.

He wrapped up his writing for the afternoon and walked into the kitchen for a glass of water. Noticing the calendar on the wall, he was surprised to see that it was Independence Day. The surprise came less from the fact it was a holiday, than from the realization that he was already out of touch with the real world. Typically, the fourth of

July was a day he looked forward to—fireworks and barbecues and time spent with friends. This year, however, it had completely snuck up on him. Indeed, today could've been any day. Already they were melting together and he'd only been in Wisconsin a week and a half.

He probably ought to call Julie, he thought. She was about seven years his senior, but still close enough in age that they had things in common. Maybe she and her husband were having a barbecue. He picked up the phone and then looked at the time on the oven clock. It was already after five. Even if Julie was entertaining—even if she invited him over—it was almost an hour's drive. He'd still need to clean himself up a bit, and it would probably be seven by the time he got there—hardly worth it unless he wanted to stay over.

He didn't really want to stay over.

It was an odd sensation; he felt isolated, and even a little lonely, but the effort required to see his cousin seemed to outweigh his malaise. The apathy terrified him. He put the phone back down, poured himself a whiskey and diet cola, and sat heavily in a chair in the living room.

Still, he thought, he ought to do *something* to celebrate the day. He remembered one particular summer—he'd been nine years old, and his family was in Wisconsin for a two-week visit—Carol and Charlie brought him to the fireworks in town. There was a tiny lake at the end of Main Street, and everyone gathered at the narrow beach to watch the show—three guys in boats launching the colorful bombs into the night sky. The show was simple and quick—ten minutes—but it was beautiful to watch as the fireworks above reflected themselves in the inky water below. They lit his nine-year-old imagination on fire.

He sipped his drink and smiled. He could go down there tonight, he thought. Why not? Then he looked at the alcohol in his hand and decided he'd better save it for when he returned. Getting up again, he put the drink in the refrigerator and started preparing dinner.

Main Street was densely parked all the way down to the water, so Ryan had to park on a side street several blocks from the little town beach. He walked quickly, observing how fast the last cobalt light of the day was dissipating from the sky. As he approached the beach, he felt his senses engage and he remembered a little of the magic from that night so many years ago. A light, warm breeze caressed his arms and face. The scent of grilling meat and sweet, fried dough filled his nose. Every step forward brought laughter and conversation to his ears. The happiness was infectious, and he was grateful he'd chosen to come.

He stopped when he reached the crowd at the water's edge. Perhaps three hundred people were assembled in a mass on the beach. At the edges, there was still room, but Ryan didn't feel like wading through the crowd just to claim a spot of sand for the ten-minute show. Instead, he looked to his left where a grassy hill sloped down to the water. A handful of families laid on blankets near the bottom, while at the higher reaches couples—mostly teenagers—dotted the grass in thinly spread pairs. He thought the top of the hill was as good a place as any, so he wove his way up and through, finding a secluded spot above them all.

He sat down in the cool grass with his back against a tree and looked down on the people below. Ten feet away a young couple—he guessed they were his age—sat close to one another, talking and laughing. The boy pushed the girl, and she shoved back in playful protest. Although he was alone, both literally and figuratively, as Ryan watched them interact, he smiled. Love existed. He closed his eyes for a moment, inhaling the sweet perfumes of the summer night.

A high, warbling whistle brought him back. Then there was a crack like thunder. He opened his eyes again just in time to see the first explosion above the water—a cascade of glowing red light, leaving a trail of sparkling dust behind as it descended to the lake below. The crowd let out a collective gasp and fell silent. A second whistle accompanied a second rocket, which exploded into a large ball of purple and gold.

The whistles and booms and explosions came with greater frequency, creating a blanket of white smoke across the otherwise clear night sky. As the scent of saltpeter and sulfur filled his nose, the rockets continued to burst, and his spirits rose higher. This was beautiful—magical even! He was nine years old again, and life was simple. There was no need to worry about car accidents or evictions, dead friends, or constant failure at love. In the moment, there was no one to betray him and no one to betray. Past and future did not exist. It was only the present—the now.

He wanted to stand up—to dance and sing. The happiness swelled up within him, creating a phantom pressure in his chest and around his temples. He was ready to burst with it. He wanted to tell someone—to share it. This feeling was too intense to keep to himself. He looked down at the young couple in front of him.

She was laying with her head on his shoulder, and he'd placed an arm around her. They weren't moving. How could they, wrapped up in the moment and in each other? Ryan watched as she lifted her head slightly. Then the boy turned and kissed her—the kind of long, lingering kiss that said he meant it. Another huge boom startled them both, and they looked up at the sky, laughing.

Something was very wrong—Ryan's mood was suddenly listing, and he felt powerless to stop it. Soon he'd be swamped—sinking. His initial pleasure at seeing the young couple—at being reminded that love existed—was souring now. He tried to remind himself that this magical chemistry he observed between them was something attainable. It happened to lots of people. It could happen to him. It *would* happen—

The fireworks came now at their greatest intensity, popping and bursting at a ferocious tempo. Here was the finale already. The sky lit up so brightly that Ryan needed to shield his eyes for a second.

Then there was only darkness and silence. The show was done. The crowd below him started to lift their voices in a triumphant roar.

This should've been it—the moment to join his voice with theirs and shout his happiness out into the night. He could've been a part of it, but he couldn't bring himself to utter a sound. Instead, he kept his eyes on the young couple in front of him as they clapped enthusiastically. The boy whistled, the girl yelled, and Ryan cringed. All the joy had gone out of him.

He hated it.

As he stood to begin the slow walk back to the car, he hung his head in disappointment. Was this whole experiment—this summer of solitude—just a terrible mistake? Was it failed already? He was supposed to be learning to love himself, and yet even the slightest reminder that others had found this thing he yearned for and hadn't attained sent him reeling—careening off course toward a daunting precipice. Didn't he deserve what that young couple had? What had they done to earn it that he hadn't? His mind filled with images of Steven, Meredith and Caleb. He thought of Peter, offering himself again in January and how easily he'd dismissed him. Maybe that could've grown into something if he'd let it.

Perhaps he didn't deserve love after all. He thought maybe he should get a ticket home tomorrow. The sudden hollowness that gripped him was suffocating. How was he supposed to learn to love himself when he couldn't even stand his own company?

Back on Main Street, he merged with the crowd exiting the beach. As they pressed in around him, talking and laughing, he picked up his pace. He needed to be away—to be alone. He couldn't stand the idea of being party to other peoples' revelry at the moment. He took the turn off Main Street into the blessed quiet of the night, got into Carol's car, and drove home.

Later he sat back down in the armchair with his now-flat and watery whiskey and diet. He sipped it, dissatisfied, and placed it on a coaster. A few lines of lyric were forming in his head that needed to be written down, so he got up and retrieved a pad of paper and a pen. After he was seated again, he closed his eyes and hummed out loud. He smiled sadly and began to write.

Feels like I'm standing on the outside looking in
So much to say, but where to begin?
Feels like I failed again
Victim of my own deception—

Putting the few words on paper made him feel a little better. No, he wouldn't run home—not just yet. Perhaps this initial disappointment in his progress was just a part of the process. Perhaps in this solitude, he could find a way to be happy with himself, even if he had to hurt a little to get there. He stood up again and freshened his drink. It was time for a chorus. He hummed for a while, then continued.

I'm just a boy
Just a little boy—
Blindly following a dream that doesn't mean anything
To anyone but me—

He stood again and moved to the piano to lay down a few chords and play the melody he'd been humming with his right hand. There was something here. Maybe if he could get it out—write the pain into a song—maybe it would dissipate into the sky just as the light had done before the fireworks started. Maybe this was the first step toward discovering the fantastic light-show that waited within.

He returned to the armchair and finished his drink. It was time for bed. Tomorrow would be better than today.

~*~

Julie called the next morning around ten. Ryan didn't recognize the number on the caller ID, so he hesitated before answering, but ultimately picked up the phone.

"Hello?" he said.

"Hi, Ryan? It's Julie."

"Oh!" He was surprised. "Hey, how's it going?"

"Not bad, not bad. How are you? Are you settling in alright over there?"

He laughed. "Yeah, I'm doing fine."

"Did you do anything for the fourth? I'm sorry, I meant to call and invite you over, but things just got away from me."

"Oh, don't worry about that. Actually, I thought about calling you yesterday also. I didn't even realize what day it was until late afternoon. I swear I've lost touch with reality already."

She chuckled, and it reminded him of Carol. "Well, that's alright. Anyways, I'm calling because I was on the phone with mom. She reminded me that you have a *bigger* holiday coming up, don't you?"

"Oh, my birthday?"

"*Yeah—*" there was her mother's signature exuberance again, "Your twenty-first birthday is on Friday! Do you have plans already?"

"Nope. I was probably just going to let it pass, honestly."

"Ryan! You only turn twenty-one once, you know."

He conceded the point. "Well, what do you have in mind?"

"Let me take you out! I'll leave Jack home with the kids. We can go somewhere in Green Bay. I know this guy at work who raves about this club. You know, maybe you could—meet someone?"

"Oh, I don't know, Julie. I don't think your mom would like the idea of me driving all the way to Green Bay, getting liquored up, and then driving home at two in the morning."

"Oh please! Come *here* first and I'll drive us in. You can go wild! Then I'll bring us back, and you can sleep it off here." There was a sound of commotion through the phone. Then, muffled, Julie exclaimed "Emma! Don't you wipe that snot on your shirt! You go in the bathroom and get some tissue!" There was a pause and then she spoke again, more clearly. "Sorry, Ryan. Emma has come down with one of those nasty summer colds. Don't you think they're always worse in the summer? You're not supposed to get sick when it's warm out. Anyways, she's been a goddamned snot factory for the last three days, and she *hates* tissues."

He laughed. "Yuck. Sorry to hear that, I hope she feels better."

"Me too, she's putting mommy over the edge. So anyways. Friday is the day, right?

"Yeah."

"Alright. Why don't you plan to get here around seven? We'll have some dinner and hang out for a while before we go. Deal?"

He smiled thinking maybe he didn't really have a choice in the matter. "Alright. See you Friday then."

By the end of the day, Ryan had abandoned his plans to look for a job—at least this week. The song he'd started the night before was beginning to take shape, and he thought his time might be better spent expanding the lyrics and fleshing it out. Tuesday gave way to a productive Wednesday and Thursday, and before he knew it Friday morning arrived.

He forced himself out of bed at seven-thirty, made a plate of scrambled eggs and got ready to mow the lawn. He looked longingly at the empty coffee pot on the counter as he slowly chewed. Coffee would be his reward for getting the yard work done, he decided. He finished the eggs, rinsed his plate and headed outside. It was already getting warm, and the air was thick. If he'd waited any longer, the chore might have been unbearable. He climbed onto the mower and started working his way around the yard.

As he guided the mower up and down the grass between the river and the house, he thought about the evening to come. It was nice of Julie to offer to take him out. Having a song to work on had definitely helped stymie his feelings of isolation, but he recognized that he was going to have to socialize at some point. Carol and Charlie had been gone for nearly two weeks, and apart from his telephone conversation with Julie, he hadn't had any actual human interaction. He wondered how the evening would go. The last time he'd been dancing was Halloween, and he feared that all the progress he'd made toward being comfortable in that environment was probably lost by this point.

So maybe he had to start again. It wouldn't be the end of the world. And he'd have Julie with him. He finished the lawn and headed inside, excited about the evening for the first time since she'd mentioned it.

When Julie called at three, the excitement went out of him. "Ryan?" she said after he picked up the phone. Her voice was hoarse.

"Hey," he replied. "Are you—okay?"

"Ugh! I caught whatever it is Emma had. I was hoping I'd feel better as the day went on but—"

"It doesn't sound like it's working out that way."

"That's because—" she sneezed, "It isn't. I don't think I'm going to be able to take you out tonight. I'm so sorry. We can do it next week—"

"Oh." He tried hard to hide the disappointment in his voice. "That's alright. Sure, next week is fine."

"It doesn't *sound* fine. I'm sorry. I could send Jack with you instead."

Ryan laughed. "No, keep your husband at home. Someone has to take care of *you*."

"Alright, what about—hey, my friend from work is still going out tonight. You could probably just leave mom's car there overnight and stay with him. His name is Tim. Do you want his number? I'll call him too."

"Okay—"

"I'm so sorry, Ryan."

"It's really fine. We can just go next week."

"No, no." She rattled off the number. "Did you get that?"

"Yeah." He wrote the number on a piece of paper next to the phone. "Thanks Julie, feel better. I still don't know if I'll go but—what's the name of the place anyways?"

"It's called Axis."

He laughed. "Axis?"

"Yeah, what's so funny?"

"I just don't know why clubs have to have such stupid names."

She laughed too. "Alright. Give Tim a call, okay? I'll talk to you soon."

"Alright Julie. Bye." He hung up the phone, defeated.

Did he dare to go by himself? He wondered if he'd even be able to find the place. *You only turn twenty-one once.* What a stupid notion—he was no stranger to alcohol. Why should the idea of drinking it in public be so holy? Besides, he'd done that already too—when Caleb used to bring him drinks at Paradox. There was absolutely no point in spending his night alone at some club he'd never been to, surrounded by people he was never going to know. He picked up the piece of paper with Tim's name on it and began to crumple it in his hand.

Then he stopped.

Actually, he thought, the idea was beautiful. If he wanted to learn to love himself, he needed to learn to be by himself—even in a crowd. He could walk in, anonymous, and focus on the beats. It didn't matter if his dancing was poor—who would know him enough to judge him? Even if he made a complete fool out of himself, what did it matter? The opinions of strangers he'd never see again didn't hold any weight. Also, he supposed there was a certain strength in going alone. No one *ever* went alone to Paradox.

It was decided, then. He finished crumpling the paper with Tim's number on it and threw it away. If she asked, he could tell Julie he'd written it down wrong and didn't want to bother her again by calling back.

He climbed the stairs to the second floor and stepped into what doubled as Carol's office and Charlie's gun room. As he switched on Carol's ancient computer, he looked around and shook his head. Two glass corner cabinets held three rifles each and a collection of pistols, as well as boxes of ammunition. He walked over and started to examine them more closely through the glass, wondering why anyone needed so many guns. Then the computer beeped, and the Windows theme announced the desktop was up and running.

He returned to the computer and took a seat. After struggling to get it to connect to the internet—they had a spotty dial-up connection—he did a quick search for the club's address. Looking at a map, it seemed easy enough to get to. He wrote down the details and smiled. This was going to be an adventure.

He managed to maintain his excitement—and his confidence—throughout the afternoon and evening. It wasn't until he drove across the bridge into downtown Green Bay that he began having doubts. As the dark waters of the Fox River flowed longingly toward their terminus in the bay just beyond, he found himself fighting an urge to turn around and drive back to Carol and Charlie's. The idea of going out alone in a strange city was noble, sure, but in practice, it was downright terrifying. He came to a stop light at the other side of the river and closed his eyes for a moment.

He could do this.

The light changed to green, and he turned the car left. Up a couple more blocks he turned right onto Main Street and drove slowly, looking for the address. Two minutes later he saw it—an old three-story brick building, unmarked except for the large stainless steel street numbers on the facade. He turned the car once more and came around to a parking lot behind the building. After shutting off the engine, he exhaled. This would be a great time for a cigarette, he thought—if he still smoked.

He climbed out of the car and looked across the parking lot. A green awning over the back entrance had the word *AXIS* written upon it in stylized white letters. A small group of people stood near the entrance laughing and smoking. Ryan stood up straight, tensed every muscle in his body, and then relaxed again. He stepped forward nervously, surprised at how heavy his feet felt. This was no way to start the night. He closed his eyes one last time and willed his fears to disappear. Then he walked forward again, feeling lighter.

A bouncer waited beneath the awning. He smiled as Ryan came to a stop in front of him. "ID, please?" He asked. Ryan fumbled in his wallet and produced his license. The bouncer scrutinized it for a moment, and then smiled again. "Happy birthday," he said. "Enjoy!"

"Thank you," Ryan replied. He placed his license back into his wallet and stepped inside.

Beyond the door a stairwell led upward, emerging into a large, dark room with exposed brick walls and a worn wooden floor. A long bar ran the length of one wall, and groups of young men clustered in teams around pool tables. At the far side of the room, floor to ceiling paned windows looked out onto Main Street. A second exposed staircase opposite the bar led to another floor where a delicious, pulsing *thump, thump* beckoned Ryan forward. He crossed the room and climbed the stairs to the third floor.

His eyes widened. Paradox had nothing on this place. Against the backdrop of a Kylie Minogue video projected onto the wall above a stage, a few early partygoers spaced themselves evenly on a dance floor that took up half the room. Beyond the dance floor, a beautiful circular bar was ringed by tall, red stools. Another set of floor to ceiling windows completed the back wall. He looked around for the DJ and found him in a booth to the left of the stage, nodding his head to the music, ears encased in giant studio headphones.

He made his way across the dance floor to the bar. When the bartender approached, he took a seat and said, "Jack and diet, please?"

"You got it!"

The bartender returned a moment later with a glass and handed it forward. "Thanks," Ryan said. "So, what time does it pick up around here?"

The bartender considered a minute. "Let's see. It's about, ten? I'd say in an hour this place'll be hopping. First time? I haven't seen you in here before."

"Yeah, first time."

"Well, welcome to Axis! Enjoy!"

Ryan nodded and took a sip of his drink. His fears were gone now. With the addition of this liquid courage, he was certain the night was going to be a success. He laughed a little inwardly, glad he'd decided to come.

By the time he finished his second drink, the dance floor was starting to fill up. He was about to order another, but then he heard a familiar voice start to whisper through the speakers. Being in the first, mild stages of inebriation, he leaped off the bar stool with excitement as the remix of Gwen Stefani's 'What You Waiting For?' started to layer beats.

He moved fluidly to the dance floor, weaving through the crowd until he found himself in the middle. His hips began to sway, and his feet found the beats perfectly. He closed his eyes and turned his face upward. Could there be a more perfect song at a more perfect moment? Gwen Stefani began to sing about taking chances and conquering fears—about *growing*. This was it. It was everything he wanted and hoped to accomplish here.

The song continued, and suddenly the blood was hot in his veins. He opened his eyes again and looked around the room. It was filled with beautiful people and he was one of them. It didn't matter that he was alone, or that just like at Paradox, the others were clustered in two and threes. They were here with him; he was here with them. It was a shared experience despite his solitude.

The track ended, and he continued dancing through the next, and then the next. He became gradually aware of another body close to him. Then there were hands resting lightly on his hips from behind— gentle, testing. Ryan leaned backwards slightly, pressing his shoulder blades into the other dancer's firm chest as an invitation. The hands pulled him closer, and they pressed together sharing an electric, anonymous heat. It continued for a minute, then the hands began to twist, turning him around. He resisted—he wasn't ready to see the mystery man's face yet. Instead, he pressed backwards, moving and bending in an attempt to prolong the moment.

Finally, his curiosity and the persistent attempts of his partner were too much to resist. He turned and gazed happily into the face of the mystery man—tall and tan, with dark brown hair and chocolate eyes. His gaze was intense—hungry. The mystery man asked the question without speaking, and Ryan opened his mouth slowly, inviting him forward. Tongues touched first and lips locked. Their bodies stiffened in unison and then relaxed as they melted into the kiss, still moving in time with the beats. It continued on—there was no reason to stop—and Ryan felt himself begin to quiver. He pulled away reluctantly and smiled.

The mystery man smiled as well, but didn't speak. Instead, he simply placed his hands on Ryan's hips again and continued to dance. Another two tracks came and went before he stepped away. "I'll be back," he said, over the music.

Ryan nodded.

He didn't come back though. Around twelve thirty Ryan left the dance floor to get one last drink. He scanned the room hoping to catch a glimpse of his unexpected dance partner but couldn't find him. Perhaps he'd gone down to the lower level. Maybe he'd left. Ryan smiled to himself as he sipped on his Jack and diet and walked back out to the floor. It didn't matter, he realized. He was alone, and he was fine.

When the DJ announced last call, Ryan took it as his cue to leave. He was getting tired now anyways, and he felt alright to drive. He descended the two flights of stairs, stepped out into the warm night and began heading to the car.

"Hey!" a voice shouted behind him. Ryan turned. There he was— the mystery man—leaning against the side of the building by himself, smoking a cigarette. "Leaving already?"

"Oh. Hey. Yeah, it's last call and I'm driving. I think I'm ready."

"Well, I'm glad I caught you. I said I'd be back, didn't I? Weren't you going to wait for me?" He winked.

"Sorry, I assumed you'd left."

"Nah, I had some friends here—felt like I shouldn't ignore them. They're gone now. Are you sure you don't want to come back in with me?"

Ryan turned his lips up into a small smile. "Thanks, but I have a long way to go, and I'm getting pretty tired. Have a good night." He turned and started to walk again.

"Wait!" the mystery man called after him. "Wait up!" Ryan turned again, and he was standing just a few feet away. "If you're tired, why not stay at my place? I live in De Pere—we could be there in ten minutes."

Ryan looked at him, considering. He shivered under the intense weight of the mystery man's gaze. He *could* go home with him, he supposed. What did it matter? They'd probably never see each other again, and he'd been awfully lonely. He thought of the couple on the hill during the fireworks—how he'd envied their closeness. Now this beautiful man stood before him, propositioning him, and while he was certain it wasn't going to lead to anything lasting, it was a little glimmer of hope that love could happen to him after all.

"Alright," he said. "Are you—ready to go?"

The mystery man nodded. "Yeah, just follow me in my car." He dropped his cigarette and ground it with his heel. "Let's go."

He climbed into Carol's car and followed the mystery man's sedan back toward the river. They drove south and west through the mostly empty streets, then over a bridge. A couple turns later the mystery man pulled into a cul-de-sac and parked. They climbed out of their vehicles, and Ryan followed him into a modern split level.

The mystery man took off his shoes by the door. "You can just leave yours right here," he said. Ryan followed suit, then the mystery man led him up a short flight of stairs, down a hallway and into the bedroom.

The floor was covered with soft, luxurious wall-to-wall carpeting, and an enormous king-sized bed flanked by side tables beckoned from the center of the room. The side tables each held a lamp, along with several standing photographs in frames. The mystery man switched one of these on, then turned off the overhead light and said, "Would you like anything to drink?"

Ryan swallowed nervously. "Oh, no. I'm fine thanks."

"Alright. Well, why don't you get comfortable then." He pulled off his shirt, revealing an impressively flat stomach that was just as tan as the rest of him.

"Okay—"

"Unless you don't want to. We can just sleep if you want, but I thought—"

"No. It's alright. I didn't come here just to sleep." He slowly undressed and then laid down, naked on the bed.

The mystery man smiled again, pulled off his jeans and underwear and climbed on top of him. "Well, if you didn't come here to sleep, what *did* you come here to do?"

When it was over, Ryan laid on his back, exhaling softly in the afterglow as the mystery man rested beside him. "Thank you," he said, quietly.

The mystery man laughed. "Not sure I've ever been thanked for sex before."

"Well, there's a first time for everything." Ryan turned happily onto his side and looked at the photographs on the side table for the first time. There were three. The largest showed the mystery man in board shorts and a tank top with his arm around someone else—a muscled blond in similar attire. Ryan's heart skipped, and he swallowed hard as a burst of nervous sweat wet his underarms and dampened his forehead. "Who—who is this in this photo?" he asked.

He felt the mystery man stiffen beside him. "That's—my boyfriend."

"Your—you're in a relationship?"

"Hey man, I'm not into drama, so I hope you aren't either. That's got nothing to do with tonight."

Ryan turned, angrily. "The hell it doesn't! Where is he?"

"Away. It doesn't matter."

"Un-fucking-believable." He stood and started to dress.

"Where are you going? It's almost four in the morning."

"I'm going home. I'm out of here."

"Hey, man. Relax. You don't know anything about our relationship or our dynamics. What's the big deal, anyways? You didn't think this was going to turn into something, did you?"

Ryan laughed. "No. I knew this was a one-time thing. For God's sake, I don't even know your name."

"Right. So, I don't get why you're freaking out."

"Because I'm worth more than second fiddle. It might have been one thing if you were single, but I'm not willing to just be your stand-in for the night."

"Excuse me?"

"Never mind." He started walking toward the door. "I'll see myself out."

He made it to the car before he started crying. Why hadn't he just walked away in the parking lot? The night had been perfect—*perfect*! He could've driven home on a high, rejuvenated and ready to continue his self-discovery with a renewed vigor.

Instead, he'd given in to temptation. Now, once again he was just the throwaway toy boy. The sky was already beginning to lighten in the east as he guided the car back toward Green Bay. This was going to be a setback—there was no doubt about it.

As he pulled into Carol and Charlie's driveway the sun was just peeking over the horizon—the first sunrise on the first full day of his twenty-second year. *Happy birthday*, he thought. This year was off to a hell of a start.

CHAPTER 22

"Don't you think it would be nice to just—stay here forever?" Darren asked as he crouched by the pond. He pulled his arm back and then let it spring forward again. The flat, round stone he'd been holding flew from his hand and skipped across the glassy surface of the water. "One—two, three, four five—six! Damn, that's the best I've done so far!" He turned and looked at Ryan, golden hair shining in the sun. "So—what do you think?"

Ryan laughed lightly as he watched the willows across the water swaying in the breeze. "Yeah, of course it would be nice. It never seems to work out that way though, does it?"

"No, I guess not. It could though, you know."

He shook his head. "We'll just have to settle for these dreams. I *know* I'm dreaming right now."

Darren regarded him with a grave look. "You do? You *know* you're dreaming?"

"Yes, of course. We've been here before—this pond. It was springtime last year. I'd just screwed things up with Max. Don't you remember? You told me you never really liked him."

"Oh yes, I remember. It's just—don't you know that lucid dreaming is dangerous? It might be better to maintain your ignorance."

Ryan frowned. "What do you mean? How can dreaming be dangerous?"

Darren walked from the water's edge to take a seat on the bench beside him. He seemed to chew his words for a while. "I didn't say *dreaming* is dangerous. I said that *lucid* dreaming is. Come on, creeper. You can figure this out. If this is a dream and you know that to be absolutely true—then all of this is manifested by your own mind, isn't it?"

"I guess so."

"Even me." Darren laughed. "Don't look so uncomfortable. I guess you don't like that idea. What, did you really think I was visiting you in your sleep from beyond the grave?"

"Darren—"

"Or maybe I'm just screwing with you. Maybe I *am* the real deal and not just some figment of your imagination."

Ryan crossed his arms. "I'm not really interested in this line of conversation right now. Let's just enjoy the warmth and the breeze."

"Okay." Darren shrugged. "It's your dream." He stood again and started to search the ground for another stone to skip. "See, that's where it gets dangerous. If you're dreaming and you're aware of it, you should be able to control it. And of course, if I'm just this idea your brain is manifesting, then it stands to reason that everything I say—especially the things you don't really want to hear—"

"Can we stop, please?"

"The things you don't want to hear are actually things you believe, deep down. See? I told you ignorance is bliss. Before, you might have been able to deny the legitimacy of anything I say. But now—now that you *know you're dreaming*, what's your excuse? I guess I'm just the mouthpiece. The mouthpiece of the *real you*."

As they'd done once before, dark storm clouds materialized in the sky, quickly obscuring the sun. The breeze took on a chill. Ryan didn't like where this was going. Silently he stood and started to walk away from the pond, down the path lined with apple trees. A moment later he could hear Darren's footsteps close behind. Turning, he scowled. "Stop following me. Why are you being so cruel? I told you I didn't want to talk about this. Why couldn't we just sit in the sun and watch the pond?"

"I told you that we could. Isn't that how I started the whole conversation, Ryan? Didn't I say I wished we could stay there forever?"

"That's impossible, Darren. What am I supposed to do? Not wake up?"

Darren grinned broadly, and it made Ryan shudder. "It *is* possible, you know. Eventually, we all sleep forever, don't we?"

"This is unbelievable. Are you suggesting I *kill myself*?" He laughed. "Whether you're some spirit from beyond the grave or just a figment of my imagination, it doesn't matter. You're stupid. Suicide is the option of last resort—it's something people do when they have absolutely no hope left. And it's *never* the answer. It doesn't solve *anything*."

Darren rolled his eyes. "Oh, how very textbook of you. I'd argue that it solves a lot of problems. It takes the pain away, doesn't it? I mean, consider an old man who has had cancer three times. It comes back again. He's lived a full life, why shouldn't he pull the plug, rather than suffer through another round of painful, humiliating treatment? And then, think about animals—our pets can be our dearest, closest friends. Yet, at the first sign that they're suffering, we're quick to euthanize them because, well—it's the *humane* thing to do."

"Okay, there's just one problem. I'm not an old man *or* someone's beloved pet. I'm not in pain. I *have* hope."

Darren scowled, suddenly furious. "You have hope? Why the *fuck* do you have hope? Hope for what? Should we go down the list?"

Ryan turned away again. "Go away, Darren."

"It's *your* dream. Make me go away! No? I'm still here."

"Darren—" he started walking faster now. The wind was picking up, and in the distance, he heard the first, low rumble of thunder.

"First of all," Darren called, still walking close behind, "You're utterly unlovable. Let's just get that out there right now. I didn't want you—not one bit. Max said he did, but every time he had the chance he just let it go. Then there's Caleb. Oh, I *liked* Caleb. He really made you believe for a little while, didn't he? Well, he ended up picking Mark Twain in the end—twice!" Darren laughed. "Peter thought he cared about you, but you were just convenient. Then in the end with Brandon—I was really rooting for you there. Obviously, you and I share a similar taste in men. It's too bad he wouldn't touch you with a ten-foot pole. Oh, and it *is* a ten-foot pole!"

"Stop it!" Ryan shouted. "Why are you being so cruel?"

Darren caught up to him now. Placing a hand on Ryan's shoulder, he spun him around and looked him dead in the eye. "Because someone has to. You need to *wake up*! Look at your life! Aren't you ready to just press reset? We could sit by that pond *forever*! Hell, we could live at Elizabeth Street together. Anything is possible."

"Go away!"

"No, not while you still think there is *hope*. I won't! Let's see, what's next? Oh, how about the way you ruin lives, and I'm not just talking about your own. Should we talk about Steven?"

Ryan shoved him forcefully, but Darren didn't budge. "Don't you dare talk about Steven!" It was starting to rain now. The drops were enormous and cold, greedily stealing his heat as they began to run down his arms and forehead.

"You know," Darren said, "The only reason he forgave you is because he was certain he'd never have to see you again. And Meredith? Aw, I liked her too. Who knows how much you damaged her. Did you know?—"

"Please," Ryan sobbed. "Please stop now."

"Did you know you were the first person she really connected with after her big, messy breakup? Didn't you notice that you were really her *only* friend?"

"I want to wake up now. God, I'm begging you, Darren. Just *go away*!"

"Alright, alright." He laughed. "Just relax. We can talk about something else." He thought for a minute. "Oh! I know! How about instead of the past we talk about your *future*? Hmm? That's a nice, bright, shiny topic, isn't it?"

Ryan nodded, slowly. "Yes. Everything is going to be better from here on out. I learned my lessons."

Darren nodded as well. "I believe you. So yeah. The future. Let's see. You're twenty-one, with only one year of college, and you're currently living in the middle of nowhere. You've got a little money, but that'll run out eventually. You've got three options. Option one! At the end of the summer, you can go back home. That doesn't sound very good, does it? There isn't a whole lot left for you there. Whatever bridges you managed not to burn will surely have up and washed away by the time you return—pretty grim prospects I'd say."

"I'm not going back there."

"No," Darren agreed. "I wouldn't. Option number two? Stay in Wisconsin with Carol and Charlie. Man, you can live a really rewarding life working at that gas station in town. I mean, you'll have to fill out an application first, but I hear six dollars an hour can buy a lot out here in East Bumblefuck. Plus, if you really save up your money, you can go back to Axis with Julie on the weekends. Maybe mystery man will be there with his boyfriend next time. You could introduce yourself! So that brings us to—"

"Option three," Ryan said, sadly.

"Oh! Why so *glum*? Is it because option three is totally unrealistic? I think you should do it. With no job, no apartment, and very little money, why don't you pick up and move to New York or San Francisco or Chicago? Hell, aim higher. Go to London, or Paris. I'm sure you can rent a little flat, write some kick-ass music you won't even play for other people, and make a zillion dollars. Definitely go with that option, okay?"

Ryan hit him again, hard in the chest. Then he hit him again, and again. "I *hate* you! I *hate* you!"

Darren stepped backwards and lifted his hands in surrender. "Whoah, now. Harsh words. Remember who you're talking to."

As quickly as the rain had begun, it stopped. The sun emerged again, and in the distance, birds began to sing. Ryan wiped his eyes. "Are you happy now, Darren?"

He shrugged. "Are you happy, Ryan? Do you still have *hope*? Listen, whatever you decide to do—it's your choice. I'll just be waiting here by the pond, or at Elizabeth Street." The singing of the birds was different now. It sounded more like a telephone. Darren's eyes widened. "Uh-oh. I wouldn't answer that if I were you—"

~*~

He woke in a cold sweat. He must have cast off most of the bedding as he struggled in his dream, because he lay naked and shivering as a ceiling fan overhead blew cool air down onto his skin. Downstairs in the kitchen, he could hear the telephone ringing loudly. Thank god, he thought. What a nightmare!

Even though he knew he wasn't going to make it in time to answer before the machine, he swung his legs over the side of the bed and stood up. Then he pulled on a pair of shorts and a shirt and started down the hallway to the stairs. Halfway down the machine picked up.

"Hello," the recorded message began in Carol's perpetually enthusiastic voice. "You've reached Carol and Charlie—and *Ryan for the summer*! We can't get to the phone right now because we're in *chilly Alaska*! Get us on our cell, or leave a message for Ryan. Talk to ya later!"

The machine beeped, and a familiar voice began to speak, heavy and strained. "Hey, Mister?" It was Max! Ryan reached the bottom of the stairs and began to rush forward into the kitchen to answer, but a somber note in Max's voice gave him pause. "I guess by the message I have the right number. I um—I'm sorry to leave this on the machine, but I wanted you to know as soon as possible. Shelly. This morning she—" a long pause ensued. When Max continued, there was a soft crack in his voice. "She passed away. Um, Ella found her and called the ambulance, but it was too late. We're all thinking this is the same thing that happened at Christmas but—no one found a note yet that I know of. I guess there'll be more details later. If um—if you want to call, I'll have my phone on. Alright. Uh—sorry. Bye." The machine clicked.

Ryan felt cold tile against his skin. He was sitting on the kitchen floor, suddenly unaware of when or how he'd sat down. Surely he was still dreaming. Any moment now Darren was going to appear, laughing. He closed his eyes and opened them again several times expecting the scene to change. It didn't. He was still on the kitchen floor with Max's voice ringing in his ears. He lifted his left hand to his chest and fiddled with Darren's thumb ring, absently. Outside, birds were chirping happily, and warm, beautiful light streamed through the windows. It looked like a really nice day.

Slowly, carefully, he stood and pressed play on the answering machine. Max's message repeated. He pressed play a second time, trying to wrap his head around it. After the recording ended a third time, he turned away, deciding it must be true. He walked over to the coffee pot and filled it from the sink, vaguely aware of his utter lack of emotion. After loading a filter full of grounds, he set the coffee to brew and walked into the living room.

He switched on his Yamaha keyboard and sat in front of the window. Looking out across the wide, sunny lawn toward the river below, he placed his fingers and began to play. Though his voice was hoarse and his mouth tasted sour and sticky from the drinks at Axis the night before, he began to sing in *oohs* and *aahs*.

He reached the second verse—this was the song he'd been working on all week—and sang the words out loud.

—It's dull here in this watery light
Colorless and bitter as December nights
Not sure I deserve the right
To keep on breathing

I'm just a boy
Just a little boy—
Blindly following a dream that doesn't mean anything—

He stopped and laughed out loud to himself. She'd finally done it! As the old adage went, *if at first you don't succeed, try, try again.* He stood up from the keyboard, realizing that he was oddly happy for her. What was it that Darren had said in his dream? Sometimes it was the *humane* thing? Clearly, this is what she'd wanted. Life had dealt Shelly some pretty cruel cards, and ultimately it was her choice whether to play them or fold her hand.

Hadn't he helped her in the end by moving away? That Sunday after Steven's graduation party she'd told him she didn't want him to go. They weren't close—they'd never *been* close, and there wasn't much of a chance that they ever would've been. Still, for some odd reason he'd been important to her. She'd said so—told him that night. Of course, it was too late by then. The ticket was already purchased.

So he went to Wisconsin and got out of her way. He told her they could still look out for each other and left her with Carol and Charlie's number. Had she even considered calling him?

The coffee was done—he could smell it. Walking back into the kitchen he pulled a mug out of a cabinet and filled it all the way. Then he walked slowly out onto the veranda and took a seat in a rocking chair. The day was sweltering, but he sipped his hot coffee anyways and smiled. What a beautiful fucking day. Gently, he pushed with his feet, and the chair began to tip back and forth. He started to sweat just as a light breeze picked up, causing the leaves of the woods beyond the lawn to shimmer softly in the summer sun. Birds continued to sing while large, fluffy clouds drifted lazily by overhead—a beautiful fucking day, indeed.

He sat there long after his mug was empty, thinking—content at the moment simply to exist. Below him, the river flowed on, the breeze continued to blow, and the birds kept up their relentless singing. Truly, today was no different from yesterday. Tomorrow would be no different than today. Shelly was gone, sure, but what did the river care? It had cut through this land since before man walked the earth, and likely it would continue long after. Shelly and her passing? It meant nothing to the river. He looked toward the woods. The trees didn't care either. The clouds overhead? They were made of water vapor trapped in an endless cycle—evaporation, condensation, precipitation—that had gone on since the beginning of time and would continue on to the end. What did Shelly matter to the clouds? What did *he* or *anyone* matter, really?

He thought about his own idea of eternity—about Darren's energy after his last breath dissipating up into the atmosphere and ultimately becoming a part of everything. Perhaps by now, nearly a year and a half later, a little bit of Darren's heat might have made its way into one of these very clouds. It was a nice idea, but it still didn't matter. Darren meant nothing to the universe. No one did.

Finally, he stood again and walked inside. Though it was only early afternoon, he traded the coffee mug for a glass of whiskey on the rocks, then sat in the armchair and sipped it slowly.

Maybe if no one really meant anything to the grand scheme—maybe Shelly's actions were right. Why should she suffer every day against the pain of unbalanced brain chemistry? Why endure the constant emotional trauma of a fractured relationship with the woman who'd brought her into the world? Why tolerate any of it when ultimately, it didn't matter? He supposed her act of suicide was far more righteous than he'd once have believed. Taking her life must have required equal measures of courage and cowardice. How could he or anyone begrudge her that?

He finished the first glass of whiskey and poured himself another. What did it feel like, he wondered? When she swallowed that whole bottle of pills—he assumed it was pills again this time, but it didn't really matter—did she feel at peace? Was there a sense of relief after she'd committed herself wholeheartedly to the act? Was there regret? The question tantalized him, and he felt a sudden compulsion to know.

He stood then, leaving his glass of whiskey and ice to sweat on a coaster, and began to climb the stairs. When he reached the landing, he walked slowly forward and paused in the door to the office—the gun room. It was difficult to say how long he stood there. He wasn't hesitating; that wasn't it. He was just—existing again. A dull ache in his feet suggested that quite some time had passed by the time he finally stepped into the room. He walked slowly forward until he reached one of the corner gun cabinets.

Inside, amongst the rifles, a shiny silver revolver sat on a glass shelf. It was beautiful and clean, like some kind of precious jewel glittering in the light. He tried once to turn his eyes away from it, but found he was powerless to do so. The gun had him now—under its trancelike influence. It called to him, begging him to open the case and to hold it.

With a childish excitement, almost gleefully he opened the case and picked it up off the shelf. The feeling that washed over him was nothing short of euphoric! He turned it over and over in his hands, surprised and delighted at its weight. Was it loaded, he wondered? Carefully, he slid open the chamber—six bullets. He closed it again. Then, holding it by the barrel, he turned and walked out of the room and back down the stairs.

He placed the revolver on the end table next to his glass of whiskey and sat down again in his chair. Then he picked up the glass and took a long sip. He wasn't going to use the gun—not really. He just wanted to look at it a while longer. All his life he'd never really understood the allure of firearms, at least not until today. It was simply the most beautiful thing he'd ever seen. And powerful! He could feel that too. Why had Shelly bothered with pills when she could've used a gun? It was so much more beautiful. So much more *efficient*. If she'd have gotten her hands on a gun the first time, she might have saved herself six months of torment.

He thought about her final moments again—the glorious gloaming of her consciousness. She must have felt ecstatic! What courage! What *resolve*! Had she embraced the inevitability of her own death in those final moments when it was too late to turn back?

The gun called to him again, and he turned his gaze, looking upon it lovingly. He set down the whiskey and picked it up again. What did it taste like, he wondered? How would it feel in his mouth? He lifted it carefully toward his face and opened his lips. When he pressed them down upon the barrel the steel was cold and smooth—slightly oily.

His hand found the trigger, and he bit down, slightly, feeling the metal against his teeth. What a feeling of peace! Is this how it had been for her? He was on the precipice now of life and death, and it was exhilarating! Nothing in his entire life had felt this exciting. It was ironic in a way, that as he stood at the edge of eternity, he felt more *alive* now than he ever had before. One little movement—the twitch of a nerve—and he could be there beside the pond skipping stones or sitting in the living room of Elizabeth Street again.

Suddenly nothing mattered. It was just him and the gun. All the failure and all the hurt was evaporating out of him. The river didn't care that he'd never found true love. The trees didn't mind that he'd hurt those closest to him. The birds outside were still singing. The sun was still shining.

The earth continued to turn beneath his feet.

He closed his eyes and felt the trigger. This was it! This was the moment—

~*~

The phone began to ring.

Ryan opened his eyes. He could taste metal and gun oil. With a guttural cry, he pulled the barrel from his mouth and fought to keep from throwing the revolver across the room. With his hand shaking, he lowered it carefully to the table and stood as he began to sob.

What was wrong with him? What had he been thinking? The phone continued to ring as he shook violently and collapsed to his knees. A great wave of nausea was overtaking him now, and he reached clumsily for a small waste bin beside the chair. He grabbed it just in time to catch the first spray of vomit that leaped from his mouth. He heaved two more times before collapsing onto his back, sobbing and gasping for air.

The phone continued to ring as he propped himself onto his elbows. Grabbing the arm of the chair he pulled himself to a sitting position and then slowly, carefully, he stood, willing his legs to hold him.

The answering machine picked up. "Hello, you've reached Carol and Charlie—and *Ryan for the summer*! We can't get to the phone right now because we're in *chilly Alaska*! Get us on our cell, or leave a message for Ryan. Talk to ya later!"

He was stumbling toward the kitchen when the beep sounded.

"Hey, Ryan." It was Steven's voice this time. "I was hoping I'd catch you—"

He rushed forward, nearly falling again and picked up the phone. "Steven!" he screamed into the phone. Then calmer, "Steven!"

"Ryan? Are you alright? What's wrong?"

"Oh, God—" he sobbed. "Oh, Steven, it's so good to hear your voice."

There was silence for a moment. Then, "Are you—oh, you must've heard about Shelly. Did someone call you?"

"M—Max," he said.

"I'm sorry. It's—it's terrible. Do you want to talk about it?"

Ryan shook his head vehemently even though he knew Steven couldn't see. "No. No, I don't. I—uh. I'll be fine." His voice was much calmer now. He walked to a cabinet and filled a glass of water to rinse his mouth. "Excuse me one second?"

"Sure—"

He swished the water between his teeth and then spit it into the sink. After repeating once more, he said, "Alright. That's better. Did um—did *you* want to talk about it? Is that why you called?"

"Partially. Are you sure there's nothing wrong?"

Ryan considered a moment. When he answered, it was the truth. "No. Nothing is wrong."

"Okay, well—I have some news."

"Oh?"

"I got a job offer."

Ryan smiled. "Congratulations! That was pretty fast, huh?"

"Yeah, I can't believe it!"

"So, where is it?"

"It's in Boston."

Ryan's eyes widened. "Wow! That's going to be—a change."

"Yeah, to be honest, I'm terrified."

"You're going to take it though, right?"

"Oh, yeah. I can't turn it down. What they offered is amazing."

"Well, congratulations again."

Steven was quiet for a moment. "So, the reason I'm telling you all of this is—did you decide what you're doing after the summer is over?"

Ryan laughed and shuddered simultaneously. "To be honest, I haven't really given much consideration to anything past today."

"Okay, well I was thinking maybe—I've been looking at apartment rentals all afternoon. It's hard because I don't know the city at all. I don't know where the good parts are or the bad parts. All I know is I'll be able to *afford* a place by myself, but it will be pretty tight. And I could probably just get a room somewhere with strangers while I figure things out but—"

"Oh, Steven. You're going to be fine. Don't worry about it. You're going to meet amazing people and make awesome new friends."

"Well, I don't doubt that but—remember at my party? We said *to be continued*?"

"Yeah?"

"Well, what if we—*continued*?"

Ryan felt his eyes begin to water again. When he spoke, his voice was unsteady. "Steven, are you asking me to move to Boston with you?"

"Well—yes. That's what I'm asking. You were saying you wanted to go somewhere new and get a fresh start. There are a million schools there, and I know they have swimming pools if that's what you wanted to do for work."

His voice cracked. "But *why*? Why would you ask *me* of all people to go with you? I was horrible, Steven. How could you want to be saddled with me in a strange city?"

"Because—"

"Because *what*?"

"Because I love you, Ryan. I mean, not like *that*—like my brother. You know that. Even when things were so shitty this last spring—I don't know. You were there for me, and I was there for you long before that brief period of discontent. We can't let one mistake define our entire friendship. People like you and me? We want the love of others so badly and seem to keep coming up short. The least we can do is care for each other—unconditionally."

"I—don't know what to say."

Steven laughed. "Just say yes, goddamn it!"

Ryan laughed as well. "Do you have a start date?"

"Sometime around August first."

"Can I sleep on it?"

"If you have to."

"Alright, I—uh, I have to go. I'll call you tomorrow, okay?"

Steven clucked. "You *are* acting awfully weird. Alright, Ryan, talk to you tomorrow."

"Bye." He hung up the phone and slid down onto the kitchen floor. With closed eyes he shook his head, uncertain whether to laugh or cry.

~*~

"Here I am," Darren said. "Just like I promised." Indeed, as Ryan laid down to sleep that night, this was exactly what he feared. Darren smiled warmly as he stretched out on Cara's sofa. They were in the living room at Elizabeth Street again, and everything was exactly as it had been. "And look! All the stuff is here again." He sat up to make room. "Would you like to sit down?"

Ryan shook his head. "I'd like you to leave. I have nothing to say to you."

"Don't you?" Darren looked hurt. "I knew you weren't going to do it, you know."

"Then why did you push me so hard? Why did you put the idea in my head?"

Darren rolled his eyes. "Didn't we go over this already? I *am* your head, remember? Whatever is in there, you put there yourself. Now please, come sit down. I—I don't think I have very long."

Reluctantly Ryan did as he was asked. After seating himself, he turned to Darren and said, "Why are you here? Why do you keep haunting me?"

"Well—that's the thing. I don't think we're going to see each other for a while, and I wanted to say goodbye."

"Where are you going?"

"I don't know. Elsewhere. You don't sound too upset about it."

Ryan considered. "I'm not. Good riddance to you."

"Ouch!" Darren laughed. "That's alright; I'll take it. Can I ask you *why* you're so happy to be rid of me though? I thought this is what you always wanted—you and me together in this cozy little house. What's changed?"

Now it was Ryan who laughed. "*Everything* has changed! When I look at you, all I see is—all I see is failure. I see failure and misery and pain. You remind me of everything I've done wrong, literally and figuratively. You were there after I missed my chance with Max, ready to rub it in. After I slept with Caleb? I didn't even get a single night's rest before you were there again telling me all about how I was taking what wasn't really mine. And then last night? Let's not even get started on last night. You are toxic, Darren. You're toxic and I don't want anything to do with you."

Darren stood up, smiling more brightly than he'd ever done in life. He walked slowly around the room, touching the walls and pictures. Gently, almost lovingly, he rubbed his fingers against the leaves of the large rubber tree in the corner. "This really is a beautiful home. I suppose my only criticism is—you should fill it with things that are yours."

"What do you mean?"

"Well, everything here belongs to Cara, doesn't it?"

"Yes but—I know I'm dreaming again. Why does it matter how it's furnished?"

Darren looked at him sternly. "Sometimes I think you suffer from a serious failure of imagination. Do I really have to spell it out for you?"

"Apparently so."

"This place is where you were happiest, isn't it?"

"Oh, yes. Definitely."

"And then in a cruel twist of fate, it was taken away."

"Right, you know this."

"Wrong!" Darren clapped his hands. "There is your *biggest* mistake! Of all the lessons you've learned this past year and a half I can't believe you still haven't wrapped your head around this one."

"Darren, I'm not wrong. I had to leave, remember? That's why I ended up at The Garden."

"Then why are we here?"

"I don't—"

"Come on! This is it! It's the *big epiphany* you've been waiting for! Come on! If you lost it—really lost Elizabeth Street—then *why are we here?* How *could* we be here? How can we be in a *place* that you've *lost?*"

"Because it isn't real!" He was getting angry now. "What do you want me to say? Anything is possible in a dream."

"Oh, come *on,* Ryan! It may be a dream, but it's still real. You're so close! Can't you feel that couch beneath you? Isn't the ground solid beneath your feet? Don't you *smell* it—that sweet scent that only an old house like this can give off? If you lost Elizabeth Street, how can we be here?" He let the question linger for a moment before he continued. "And regardless of how you feel about me right now—I know I'm presently the vessel you've put all your fears and doubts into—if you lost me? If you lost the *real* me, how can *I* be here either?"

Ryan's eyes widened. "Because—"

Darren's opened wider. "Because—"

"Because all of it is inside of me."

"Hallelujah!" Darren hopped up and down excitedly. "He's finally got it! Jesus Christ! You had me worried there for a while, creeper!"

"It's always been inside me," he said, quietly.

Darren sat back down beside him. "Exactly. I think you've glimpsed this idea a time or two, but you haven't really understood before, have you? This house? It's your happiness. And me?"

"You're love."

Darren placed a hand on Ryan's knee. "That's right. I'm love. You see it now, don't you? You thought you lost us both, but we've been right here, just waiting for you to wake the fuck up!" He laughed. "Don't get me wrong, Ryan—it's alright to be lonely sometimes. It's okay to be sad. You *should* yearn for the love and companionship of others. Desire for something more is what motivates us to keep moving forward—to become better versions of ourselves. Don't ever stop yearning, but—"

Ryan laughed. "But I can't forget that everything I really need, I already have. It's inside of me."

"It always has been."

"Be the cake. Be your own goddamned cake."

"Excuse me?"

"Oh, it's just something your mother said. I heard her, but I guess I wasn't listening."

Darren stood up and stretched. "Well, I think I'm going to get out of here. You should stay a while though."

Ryan frowned. "Wait. Don't leave now. It's just getting good."

Darren shook his head. "We'll see each other again, just not for a while."

"But, if you're *love* and I've only just found you—"

He shoved him lightly. "Do you have to take everything so goddamned literally? I'll be around. You know where to find me now."

Ryan stood and embraced him tightly. In life, Darren might have pulled away after a moment or two, but now he let the embrace linger. Ryan whispered, "I miss you."

"I know." He stepped away and walked to the front door, twisted the knob and swung it open. Then he turned around and smiled in a way Ryan had seen him do so many times before. It was enigmatic—Mona Lisa in a beautiful twenty-one-year-old boy. "Be happy, Ryan." He turned again and raised one hand in a parting gesture.

Without hesitation he stepped out the door and into the night.

When Ryan woke, it was mid-morning. He climbed out of bed and pulled on a pair of shorts and a shirt. Outside he could hear the birds singing, and he smiled at the sun streaming through the bedroom windows. It was going to be another beautiful day. As he walked to the bathroom, his feet felt light.

His heart felt lighter.

He appraised himself in the mirror for a moment and smiled. It was all inside of him. There was just one thing left to do. He reached behind his neck and felt for the clasp of the little silver chain that held Darren's thumb ring. After fumbling for a moment he engaged it, and the chain came away. He held it in his hand and laughed. How could something so small and light weigh so much?

He left the ring and its chain on the edge of the sink, turned, and walked downstairs. He filled the coffee pot and set it to brew, and then looked across the kitchen to the telephone.

He needed to call Steven.

CHAPTER 23

As the wind picked up, Ryan watched the world's largest seagull hover in place before landing deftly on a pylon just off the end of the wharf. Out on the harbor white caps were forming, turning the surface of the water into a vast mountain range of short, snow-capped peaks. He pulled the collar of his jacket higher around his neck and closed his eyes. The cold air that whipped past his face was causing his skin to tingle.

He felt Daniel's hand on his shoulder, so he turned and smiled. "Isn't this beautiful?" he asked.

Daniel raised his eyebrows and scrunched his nose. He was bundled tightly in a thick down jacket, scarf, and knit hat. With a gloved hand, he pushed his glasses higher onto the bridge of his petite nose. "If you say so. Are you all set? You know I'm just skin and bones—I can't stand out here forever. There's a reason we're the only ones here, Ryan. It's January tenth, not the middle of July."

"I know, I know. Yeah, I'm ready. I just can't get enough of the ocean. It's weird to think I won't see it for ten days."

"*This*," Daniel gestured with both arms outstretched, "is *not* the ocean."

"Yeah, so you've said. It's the *harbor*. Blah, blah." Ryan shoved him lightly. "I don't make that distinction. It's salt water, and if I jumped off the edge and landed in a little boat, I could theoretically row all the way to France—or India or Australia."

Daniel offered him a small smile. "You're an odd duck, Ryan. Remind me again why I like you so much?"

"I don't think you have a choice in the matter. Come on, let's get you some coffee or something before you turn into an actual icicle."

Ryan looked out at the harbor one last time, then turned and began to walk beside Daniel up the length of the wharf. The wind died down the moment they reached the street, leaving the air feeling the slightest bit warmer. Boston rose up in front of them, silhouetted against the tangerine and violet sky. The sun was descending quickly. After crossing the street, they turned right, and then a block later to the left. Smooth concrete slabs gave way to cobblestones underfoot. The three long stone buildings that comprised Quincy Market beckoned them forward, offering warmth and light.

Daniel tilted his head. "Let's get coffee here? At this hour we can probably get a seat somewhere under the dome. It's as good a place as any to wait."

Ryan nodded his agreement. "Alright, let's go."

They walked quickly across the cobblestones and up the steps into the central market building. Once through the heavy doors, a great wave of heat crashed into him, bringing with it the scents of every major world cuisine. Garlic and curry mingled with fried potatoes, freshly baked cookies and clam chowder. He could smell sesame oil and barbecue sauce, and onions—onions cut through everything. It was both intoxicating and overwhelming.

"Come on," Daniel said. "I think this ice cream place up here on the right sells coffee."

Together they walked slowly down the wide hall as food vendors offered them tantalizing samples of this and that. Ryan declined each in turn, focused on the promise of the strong black coffee that waited ahead. Daniel stopped at the ice cream stand and ordered two cups. He paid, handed one to Ryan, and then they continued on.

In the center of the market building, the hall gave way to a wide square room filled with tables beneath an impressive frescoed dome. A set of stairs against the wall led to an upper level, and Ryan followed as Daniel mounted these two at a time. At the top, they found an empty table next to the enormous windows that looked down onto the cobblestone court below.

Daniel took a sip of his coffee appreciatively. "Mmm," he said. "I really needed this!"

Ryan took a sip of his own. "Yeah, so did I. Hey, thanks for spending the day with me."

"It's no problem—one of the perks of having a variable schedule. What else was I going to do with a Tuesday off? I probably would've just sat at home watching TV in bed."

"Well, yeah. I hope this was more interesting."

"Oh, definitely! By the way, I wanted to say again what an amazing job you did last night at the open mic. You'll do it again, right?"

Ryan laughed. For the last couple of months both Daniel and Steven had been pressuring him to perform his music in public. Daniel knew a guy who ran an open mic night in Cambridge, and slowly but surely, they'd worn down his resistance to the idea. He'd been nervous, sure—he nearly forgot to turn on the keyboard before he started playing. The lights above the little stage had been so hot, and he was able to feel the eyes of everyone in the room waiting expectantly.

But the moment he struck the first chords and leaned into the microphone, all that fell away. His voice came out clear and strong, and he lost himself in the music. He played four songs in total, and when it was done the applause was genuine. He ordered a whiskey and diet and sucked it down thirstily, feeling both exposed and exhilarated.

Later, the host congratulated him and told him he should come back again.

Ryan took another sip of his coffee and looked at Daniel, smiling. "Thank you. I'm really glad I did it. And yeah, I think I'll do it again when I get back."

"You'd better! You have way more talent than most of the people there last night. It was nice to hear you sing outside of your living room."

He blushed. "I'll get there. Maybe one day I'll even figure out a way to sell something and get paid."

Daniel shrugged. "Even if you don't, you'll always be able to say that at least you put yourself out there. There's no rush anyways. It's not like your swimming pools are going to dry up."

"No," Ryan agreed. "They'll still be there." He sighed inwardly. When Steven arrived at Carol and Charlie's to pick him up in the little U-Haul, he'd sworn up and down that the last thing he'd do when they got to Boston was work in a pool. Of course, it became quickly apparent that the need for money outweighed his desires to branch out into other fields of work. He landed a nice position in the aquatics department at one of the universities, convincing himself he was going to keep looking for other jobs.

He didn't though, and that was alright. He loved his new pools, and his flexible schedule offered him ample time to write. For now, it was good—great even. He was able to help Steven with the rent, and he wasn't going hungry.

Daniel's phone started ringing. "Oh!" he said, fumbling in his jacket pocket. Locating it, he looked at the little screen, flipped it open and held it to his ear. "Hey babe," he said. "No, we're at Quincy Market. Why don't you stay there, we'll just walk over. It'll be fast. Okay. See you in about ten minutes? Alright—" he hesitated for a moment. "Bye."

Ryan smiled. "Steven?"

"Yeah. He's done with work. I said we'd meet him there if that's alright." There was an odd look on his face.

"What's going on?"

"What do you mean?"

"You had this expression on your face—what was that pause?"

"Oh—it was that obvious?"

"Yes."

Daniel looked down at the table. "Well, I was about to say—I love you."

Ryan's eyes widened, and he clapped. "Why didn't you?"

"I don't know—I'm worried he'll think it's too soon. It's only been three months. I don't want to freak him out."

Ryan laughed. "Oh, he'll freak out alright."

"See?"

"No, no. In a good way! Do you really mean it, Daniel? You think you love him?"

He shrugged and looked up at the ceiling. "I don't *think* I love him. I know I do. I haven't ever met anyone like Steven. I'm so glad you made him come out that night—I know he didn't want to."

"Well, you're welcome! I definitely think you should tell him."

"Does he feel the same way?"

Ryan raised his hands in the air. "Oh no. I'm not playing this game. Just tell him. Hell, you guys are going to have the apartment to yourselves for the next ten days. Why don't you make dinner or something some night, pour a little wine and—"

"Yeah okay. I'll figure it out. We'd better go though, or you could miss your plane."

"I'm not worried about that. I've got, what, three hours still?"

"Something like that. But Steven is waiting for us." They stood up to go. "Hey, when are you going to let me repay the favor?"

"What do you mean?"

Daniel scowled. "You know exactly what I mean. I've been trying to set you up with my friend Josh *forever*. When you get back will you at least go out with him once? We could do a double date—totally casual at a bar or something."

Ryan smiled coyly. "I'll think about it. I'm sure I'd really like him, but I'm in a good place right now. You know, I feel like I know myself better than I ever have before, and I'm so focused on the music—"

"Ugh! You're impossible!"

"I'll get there, Daniel. But right now, I'm fine being alone." He smiled because he meant it.

~*~

From the back seat, Ryan saw Steven's brow furrow in the rearview mirror. They were headed down into the tunnel beneath the harbor en route to the airport, and the traffic wasn't moving.

"Did you guys ever play that game when you were kids?" Steven asked. "The one where you hold your breath through the tunnel? Well, I don't recommend you play it now—you'll suffocate."

Daniel laughed. "See, Ryan? Never underestimate the power of rush hour traffic. That three hours you had is being eaten up quickly."

Ryan looked at the clock on the dash—5:10pm. His flight wasn't until 7:30 and the airport was just on the other side of the tunnel. "Nah," he said, "I'll be fine. We'll be out of this mess in ten minutes."

As if agreeing with him, the traffic began to lurch slowly forward, and then the car was in the tunnel. Steven sighed again. "Alright. Finally. Let's hope this continues. So, Ryan—are you excited yet?"

He considered the question carefully. "Yes and—no. I'm conflicted."

"Why?" Steven asked. "I'm jealous, actually. I wish I were going home for ten days."

"I don't know. I mean, there is a lot to look forward to. I can't wait to see my family, and I'm pretty sure I'm going to meet up with Max. Then at the end of the trip I'm going to spend a night with Alice and John. But at the same time? My life here is so good, and I'm so happy. I think part of me is just nervous to leave this place—like I won't be able to get back, or something. I know it's stupid."

From the front seat, Daniel laughed. "Ryan, you're coming back. You've got the return flight. And if something happened and you missed it—if every plane in the world was grounded—"

Steven cut in. "We'd find a way to get you back. I'd be pretty peeved about it, but I'd drive all the way home and pick you up if I had to."

Ryan blushed happily. "That's a really sweet sentiment. I don't know—it's going to be fine. It's going to feel different though. All our friends are gone for the most part. And it'll be weird being so close to The Garden and not living there. It'll be weird to think—Shelly's not there."

"I think maybe you should look at it differently," Steven said. "All the bad things are gone—all the stuff that made you want to leave in the first place. Right? And you said it yourself. Life is really good right now." The traffic was breaking up and Steven began to accelerate slightly.

"You're right," Ryan said.

"I know."

Ten minutes later Steven guided the car into the busy departures bay of Terminal C. He flipped on his hazards and popped the trunk as Ryan climbed out of the back seat. Then Steven followed and met him behind the car as he pulled his single suitcase from the trunk.

Steven smiled and wrapped him in a tight embrace. "It's going to be fine."

"I know," Ryan replied.

"I mean it. And in ten days you're going to be back here wishing the vacation wasn't over already."

"You're absolutely right."

Steven placed a hand on Ryan's shoulder. "I also wanted to say—and I'll have to say it quickly because there is already a state trooper walking over here to tell me to move along—I wanted to say thank you."

"For what?" Ryan blinked.

"For everything. For our friendship. For our highs and lows. I'd never have been able to do this move without you. I'd definitely never have met Daniel. I think I'm actually in love with him."

Ryan chuckled quietly. "You're welcome."

"What was that little laugh for?"

"Nothing. Thank you too, Steven. Thanks for second chances. Thanks for loving me unconditionally."

Steven scowled. "I know I started it, but enough of this sappy shit!" He shoved Ryan playfully. "Alright, get out of here before this officer yells at me."

Ryan gave him another quick hug. "Alright. See you in ten days?"

"See you in ten days." Steven closed the trunk and climbed back into the car. Then he waved and began to drive away.

~*~

Over the hum of the engines Ryan heard the ding, and then a voice started over the intercom. "Alright folks, the in-flight crew is going to come through the cabin to collect any remaining items of trash as we begin our descent into Denver. I've turned on the fasten seatbelt sign, so please remain seated for the remainder of the flight.

It's cool on the ground, about twenty degrees, and it looks like it could snow tonight. Anyways, we'll have you down shortly—at about 10:15 pm local time. Thank you again for flying with us."

Ryan looked out the window and felt the pressure beginning to build in his ears as the plane dipped lower. This was it—he was nearly home.

When he'd left in June, he hadn't been sure when he would return. All he knew for certain is that when that day arrived, he was going to be different—a better version of himself than the one who had left. As he regarded the lights of the front range to the north, twinkling softly on the ground, he smiled to himself.

He *was* different. The great epiphany he'd been searching for in Wisconsin had come crashing down upon him, and he hadn't looked back. There were no more dreams of Darren taunting him or criticizing his decisions. There was only love—love for himself and those around him. In the months that followed he never put the thumb ring back around his neck. It was tucked away now, in a desk drawer in his room back in Boston—all but forgotten.

He didn't miss it.

He thought about Steven and Daniel—on the brink of confessing to one another that after three months of dating it was the real thing. It was love. Even a few months ago the situation would've crippled him with feelings of jealousy and personal failure. Instead, he realized—to his delight—he was truly happy for them. Steven deserved this more than anyone he knew—more even than himself. And if it could happen to Steven—

He figured he ought to give Daniel's friend Josh a try. He was in a good place after all. Why not give someone the chance to be the icing on his cake—the best part, that held it all together? He'd think about it a bit more. He was fine, after all. Actually, he was more than fine. He was thriving.

Two years ago today he wouldn't have been able to say that—when he was on his way to Greeley with Darren, having lost his truck and Elizabeth Street in one fell swoop. Indeed, he'd picked this date to return home for a reason. That was the beginning of the worst year of his life. He hoped today was the beginning of the best.

The ground was very close now. He could see the runway. He closed his eyes for a minute and felt the bump and hop of the plane's wheels making contact with the earth. He lurched slightly forward as the plane suddenly slowed, and then sat back as the cabin lights came on.

He was home.

The plane pulled up to its gate, and there was a clicking as the jet bridge was engaged. Then the cabin door was opened and passengers began to stand in the aisles and retrieve their things from the overhead bins. Ryan waited patiently for his turn, then stood and walked down the aisle.

As he turned to step off the plane, a pretty brunette flight attendant smiled and said, "Enjoy your stay!"

"Thank you," he said, and then started up the jet bridge to the terminal.

His mother was waiting at baggage claim. She embraced him tightly, and he buried his head in her shoulder. When they finally stepped away from one another both their eyes were wet.

She smiled. "Sorry. I guess I didn't realize how much I missed you. I mean, I missed you, but then seeing you—"

He hugged her again. "No, I understand. I guess I didn't realize how much I missed you either."

"Was it a good flight?"

He nodded. "Not too bad. It's nice to stretch my legs though."

"How many bags do you have?"

"Just the one."

Twenty minutes later his mother turned the car out of the airport and headed west toward the toll road. Across the median, the giant blue horse stood on its hind legs, and Ryan could see its beady red eyes reflected in the rear-view mirror. He laughed. "God that thing is ugly."

"Yes, it is," his mother replied.

Ryan looked at the sky and sighed. The lights of the city in the distance reflected against the thick, low clouds—the color a stale orange that meant snow.

She looked at him briefly. "What was that for? That sigh?"

"I'm happy."

Reaching her hand across the center console, she squeezed his knee lightly. "You are?"

He *was* happy. Everything he'd been—everything that happened in this place. It had formed him. Darren and Max, Caleb and Brandon, Meredith, Peter and Steven. Shelly. He was indebted to them all. All that loneliness, longing and pain were simply the pressure it took to turn coal into diamonds—to make mountains rise from the sea.

The first dry, tiny flakes began to fall, barely touching the windshield before flying off once more into the night.

He smiled at her again.

"I am," he said.

ACKNOWLEDGEMENTS

While the act of putting down the words of a manuscript is a solitary endeavor, no writer exists in a vacuum. It took a great deal of support over the course of many years to bring this novel to completion, and even more to take the courageous step to self-publish.

First and foremost, I must thank my husband, Brian. Without his encouragement to take the indie author route, this novel might still be languishing in the depths of my hard drive. Thank you for your unwavering love and support, and for sharing your life with me. I love you more today than yesterday, and will tomorrow more than today. Through the rain and clear skies. . .

Thanks as well to my extraordinary family. I'm blessed to have parents, aunts, uncles, grandparents, siblings, cousins, and in-laws who love and support me just as I am. It is on the foundation of your unconditional love that I am building my dream of writing.

Add to this a host of passionate, encouraging friends, and I'm truly a lucky man.

Erin Kress, as perhaps my earliest reader, I'm forever grateful for your insights at the beginning of this project and throughout. LeeMarie Kennedy, thanks for being my writing buddy and encouraging me to jump back into the pool after I'd been dry a while.

Ken Mallon, Annie Hamilton, Grace Bachman, Sam and Mel Yazejian, and Amanda Corbyn, thank you for coming along on the journey as I was serializing my first draft online. Your feedback was truly invaluable. Also, thanks to the many others who followed along. Your weekly readership helped propel this project to its completion.

Linda Greene, Zack Stadtmueller, Chris Lancaster, and Morgan Anderson—coworkers and friends—thanks for reading through my drafts at their various stages and giving your thoughts and support.

Special thanks goes as well to a trio of indie authors who offered guidance and encouragement once I decided to take the plunge into self publishing. Luke Harris, Marcus Lopés, and Ramona Flightner—and Bill Paine for putting us in touch—thank you! You helped show me this process is not only possible, but fun!

Thanks to Paul Martin from Dominion Editorial for helping to make this novel shine, and the amazing people at Damonza.com for the stunning cover art.

Ann and Gerry. Thank you for bringing your extraordinary son into this world. Though he left us too soon, his impact upon my life cannot be measured. I am honored to have known him, and further honored to consider the two of you a part of my family. My love to you, always.

And there are many, many others, though they are too numerous to name here, but finally. . .

Thanks to you, too, dear reader. Writers cannot exist inside vacuums, and neither can their novels. Thanks for spending your time with me and my words. I'm hoping this novel is just the beginning of a long and happy friendship between us.

Gregory

ABOUT THE AUTHOR

Gregory Josephs is an author of LGBT fiction who spends a lot of time indulging his insatiable curiosity—about everything. He believes in self-love, authentic food, and that procrastination is the product of an intensely creative mind.

Gregory was born in Wisconsin in the middle of an unusually long, humid heatwave in July of 1984. Though he and his parents moved to northern Colorado a short two years later, he spent many of his childhood summers happily swimming and biking around the lakes and rivers of the Northwoods with his cousins. During these formative stays he learned to enjoy warm, humid nights, hate the sweltering days, and fall in love with the idea of everything *North*.

Growing up in the southwest, at some point there was more hot sauce than blood running through his veins. Early on, his foodie parents instilled a love of Mexican cuisine and anything with peppers. That love continues to this day, and even though he currently lives about as far from Mexico as one can get in the lower 48, it's a rare day that he doesn't down a jalapeño.

He's a foodie too, now, with an unslakeable curiosity about how food is made and where it comes from. When he isn't writing he's likely in the kitchen fermenting something—bread dough, cheese, sauerkraut, and most recently mead. He has an addiction to cooking magazines, though mostly he skips recipes and cooks off the cuff.

During his teenage years, Gregory discovered his loves of swimming, language, and music. Competing year-round in the pool taught him the discipline he now applies to writing, while his passion for language (especially French) ignited an enduring love-affair with the written and spoken word. Coupled with years of playing flute and piccolo, he started studying music theory, and by the age of fifteen was a prolific songwriter, enjoying a modest amount of fame in his living room.

After high school, Gregory worked full time as an aquatics manger while double-majoring in music composition and French. The sudden, dramatic loss of his best friend triggered an initially unsuccessful metamorphosis of self (and inspired this book, which is absolutely a work of fiction) that saw him abandon school and flee to Wisconsin to pick up the pieces. Alone in the Northwoods, he discovered that self-love was the true key to happiness. When a friend invited him to move to Boston, he was unable to resist the allure of the North, and has called Massachusetts home for over a decade.

Gregory continues to swim and write music, but now the written word has emerged as his true passion

Alongside his photographer husband, Gregory regularly collects fiestaware and sips whiskey while entertaining his rambunctious cats. He can't imagine a better life.

This is his first novel.

CONNECT WITH GREGORY

Twitter: @gjosephs
Facebook: /gjosephsauthor
Web: www.gregoryjosephs.com

Did you love this book?

Please consider leaving a review at
Amazon.com and
Goodreads.com

www.ingramcontent.com/pod-product-compliance
Lightning Source LLC
Chambersburg PA
CBHW051203120726
47905CB00004B/972